To the Bloody End

DFZ Changeling Book 3

Rachel Aaron

For Linda, the Mortal Spirit of Copy Editing, whose divine intervention saved this manuscript's bacon.

Series Information

By a Silver Thread

With a Golden Sword

To the Bloody End

Other Series set in this World

The Heartstrikers

The DFZ

See the back for more details!

Copyright and Publishing Info
To the Bloody End

Aaron Bach
"Writing to Entertain and Inform."
Copyright © 2024 Rachel Aaron

ISBN Paperback: 978-1-952367-23-6

Cover Illustration by Luisa Preissler
Cover Design by Rachel Aaron
Editing provided by Red Adept Editing

Prologue

The DFZ cowered in the dark. It was an inglorious position for the Spirit of the Living City, hiding under a pile of trash deep below the ever-moving roads and buildings that were her trademark, but it was the only place left where she felt safe. The monster had taken over her streets, and her citizens loved him for it. They called his name and prayed to him to keep them safe when they used to pray to her.

The loss of worship wasn't what bothered her. People in her city were always free to think or do or prostrate themselves before whatever they liked, but without their belief, the DFZ couldn't move like she used to. Piece by piece, the Hero had taken her over, forcing her deeper and deeper into the darkness she'd risen from: the hole beneath the frenetic, ever-moving Sea of Magic that was her birthplace.

Twenty-five years ago, she'd been dragged screaming into life from this very spot. When she'd fought Algonquin—the terrifying Lady of the Great Lakes herself—for control of her city, this was where she'd planted her feet. It was the deepest part of her vessel, the bedrock of the divine nook humanity's hopes and fears had carved out just for the DFZ. And it was falling apart.

The DFZ had done her best to patch the cracks. She was the Living City, after all. There was nothing she couldn't rebuild. But while Fenrir had destroyed her buildings and smashed her roads, the damage the Hero and his faithful had done was much, *much* worse. They'd attacked her foundations, the dream of the DFZ itself. They'd turned her beautiful city of magic and freedom into a platform for the Hero to spew his hate, and the higher he rose, the farther she got pushed down.

She was so deep now that she could barely move her
streets, or talk to her priests. The world was forgetting about her
in their rush to worship the Hero, leaving her behind like trash in
the gutter. But the DFZ had never been a city for quitters. Even
here at her lowest, she kept lifting her buildings, sending up her
superscrapers and highways to show her citizens that she was still
here, still alive. She was determined to stay that way until it killed
her—an irony the Living City was not in the mood to appreciate—
when she caught the smell of blood.

The DFZ whirled away from her work, her beady eyes
flashing orange in the dark. She'd been pushed so far down now
that the only shape she could take was the rat she'd been born as.
But DFZ rats were famous for their size and ferocity, and the city
spirit did hers proud, baring her sharp yellow teeth like daggers at
the handsome man with the golden sword who was suddenly
standing on top of her trash heap.

"So this is where you've been hiding."

The DFZ responded by throwing a trash can at him, and
the Hero rolled his eyes. "Don't waste my time," he said in a
mocking, hateful voice. "You couldn't hurt me even before I
became a god. Surely you realize there's absolutely nothing you can
do against me now."

Of course she'd realized. No one had felt the Hero's boot
harder than the DFZ, but that didn't explain what he was doing
here. He might have seduced the hearts of her citizens, but this
was *her* vessel, the magic that made her herself. She might have to
follow his orders up top, but down here, nothing, not even him,
could stop her from being herself. But when she shot an I-beam
out of the ground to punt his smug face back into the city and out
of the sacred place he never should have been able to weasel into,
the Hero didn't even wobble.

"That doesn't work on me," he said, standing firm on her
undulating trash. "You cower in this pit as if its walls can keep you

safe, but you didn't make this place. This hole, like every spirit vessel, was dug by human hands, and as the greatest of all humans, I have come to claim what is mine."

It will never be yours! the city hissed, her orange eyes shining stronger than her brightest streetlights. *You're no god, not one of us. You're a murderer and a charlatan whose only talent is looking good on TV! You tricked your followers into giving you power, but I see you when the cameras are off. You were never the Hero you claimed to be!*

"So what?" the Hero said placidly, stabbing his golden sword into her trash so he could lean on the hilt. "All of godhood is trickery, even yours. You're supposed to protect your citizens, but you've known what I was for years, and you never stopped me."

Because you were always in your stupid barrow! the rat hissed.

"So many excuses," he tsked. "But your time is coming to a close, DFZ. I'm the brightest star in the sky right now. Everybody in the world is wishing on me, which means I'm not in your city anymore." His already cruel smile grew crueler. "You're in mine."

NEVER! she roared, throwing her mountain of trash at him. *I am the Detroit Free Zone! No one owns me!*

"You don't get a choice anymore," the Hero said, flicking her attack away with his hand. "Do you not understand what's happened? I'm a human soul who's gained the power of a god. When I move magic now, I push with the belief of *billions,* which is a lot more people than you've got."

The DFZ was about to tell him to try it when his magic clamped down on her neck. The Hero's power had always been bloody, but even when he'd forced her to build his stupid tower, it'd never been as strong as this. He slammed into her harder than Algonquin's wave, pinning her squealing rat form in place as thick, iron-scented red liquid began welling up through the trash beneath her.

No! the city screamed, thrashing against his hold as the blood rose over her paws. *You can't do this! This is my vessel, my city! I was born to be this! You can't take it from—*

A flood of crimson drowned the rest of her screams. Victor watched her vanish with a triumphant Hero's smile, his dry feet planted on the blood's rippling surface as the rising tide carried him back to his city.

Chapter 1

Three months after the Ascendence of the Hero

Despite living in the city for thirteen years, Valente hadn't seen much of the DFZ. He'd gone all over it as Victor's knight, from the highest Skyway penthouses to the darkest parts of the Underground, but none of that counted in his mind since he hadn't been wearing his head. Feelers and fairy vision were great for spotting lies and threats, but they were terrible at actually seeing. For that, you needed eyeballs, a luxury Valente hadn't had for a long, long time.

He had it now. Despite the troubles that came with having a cursed face he couldn't allow anyone to see, Valente had worn his head every single day since he'd been freed. He'd wanted to see the city for real, to finally experience it with all his human senses.

Too bad there wasn't much left these days that was worth looking at.

It was all Victor's fault. He ruined everything he touched, and the Living City was no exception. What had once been a vibrant, vertical metropolis of soaring superscrapers and neon-lit urban canyons was now a monument to the Hero's vanity. Fenrir's damage was mostly repaired, but all the elevated bridges, moving buildings, and rampant capitalism—the things that made the DFZ the DFZ—had been replaced by an orderly sunburst grid of dull, flat streets full of dull, flat buildings radiating out from the shining monstrosity that was Hero's Hall.

The building was a literal temple to Victor's ego. He'd made the DFZ dig up all of Detroit's old cathedrals and Frankenstein them together into a televangelist's fever dream. The result was so huge, it took up the entire square where the Black Rider had fought Orlando. It wasn't as tall as Victor's private skyscraper next door, the Hero's Tower, but Hero's Hall was obviously meant to be the new DFZ's centerpiece. Every building in town had been rebuilt to face it, and every major road ran straight to it. Even the grand hotels by the lake had been moved downtown so they could offer rooms with views of the Hero, the only thing anyone was allowed to look at anymore.

"I hate it too."

Valente glanced down in surprise to see Lola standing right beside him. She was dressed as a middle-aged male tourist with a potbelly and a T-shirt with Victor's face emblazoned on the front. The disguise was flawless, right down to the puffiness beneath the man's eyes from the grateful weeping the Hero's faithful were prone to. She even sounded like a man, but Valente still knew it was her. No matter what she wore, the light that was Lola always shone through.

"It's almost over," she assured him in the stranger's voice, placing a hairy but confident hand on his arm. "We've got him for sure this time."

Valente nodded silently, lifting his hand to tug at the collar of his own disguise.

Since Victor still thought the Rider was dead by his own hand, Lola had used her gossamer to turn Valente into a traffic cop for today's operation. His double vision made it hard to see the result, since the fairy's sight still pierced illusions, but if he squinted just right, he could see the red coat and protective helmet of the Hero's Public Security Forces. She'd even made him a motorcycle, an obnoxiously loud one covered in garish red and gold paint.

It was a ridiculously good job. Lola's illusions had always been top-notch, but her skills had jumped even higher since she'd eaten Alberich and taken over his kingdom. Victor himself could have walked right past them and never known, but Valente felt like he was suffocating, which was all wrong. He used to love being covered in Lola's warm magic. Now, though, all he could think about was what that magic told her about him. Did she feel the truth? See that he was—

"Are you okay?"

"Good enough," Valente said, dancing around his head's inability to lie. "How much time have we got left?"

Lola looked at the old-style smartwatch on her disguise's pudgy wrist. "Thirty-one minutes and twenty-four seconds." Her blotchy face screwed into a smirk. "The 'Hero' is never late."

"He always was punctual," Valente agreed, looking down the wide, freshly paved road toward the glaring lights shining out from the hideous ball of cathedrals. "I've got this angle covered. Everyone looking for tickets has been directed to Lamb's labyrinth, and Tristan's turned the security office into an endless party."

Lola chuckled. "That should keep them busy for days. Dee's got eyes on the cathedral's media control room, so—"

"Dee?" he asked.

"My double," Lola explained. "She told me this morning that 'doppelganger' was too long and ugly to be a name, so now she wants to be called 'Dee.'"

"I thought she wanted to be called Angelica?"

"That was yesterday," Lola said in an exasperated voice. Then she gave him another serious look. "Are you *sure* you're okay? Your voice sounds odd."

"I'm good at the moment," Valente insisted, forcing his numb lips to speak each word perfectly so they wouldn't become a lie and choke him. "Just tired."

"It has been a crazy start to the year," Lola agreed, looking up at the clear winter sky. "But this time is the last. I *know* it."

Valente nodded, but even that gesture was hard to get past his head's magical ban against lying. He trusted and believed in Lola with all that was left of his heart, but she'd said the same thing seventeen times now. He'd never stop fighting at her side, but it was getting harder and harder to believe.

That was a critical weakness. Fairy magic depended on belief. If he let his faith in Lola waver, it would undermine everything they were trying to do. He *had* to believe it would work, and he was focusing on doing just that when Lola's hand landed on his shoulder.

"I have to get going," she said, looking at him with a soft expression that didn't match her current face. "But I was wondering, when this is over, do you want to get dinner?"

He tilted his head in confusion, and her tourist's face began to turn red. "I know you don't eat actual food," she said in a rush. "And the only restaurants left in Victor's dystopia are corporate chains, but I still thought it might be nice to get out for a while. You know, just the two of us."

Her hopeful look at the end nearly killed him. At any other point in Valente's life, the invitation would have been a dream come true. Lola was seeking him out, *asking* for his company. It was what he'd wanted from the first moment he'd seen her shining through the darkness of their life under Victor, but...

"I don't think that's a good idea."

Watching her face fall as he spoke hurt worse than anything Orlando had done to him. Valente would have taken the words back right then if he could have, but his voice refused to work, because any denial would have been a lie. It *wasn't* a good idea for them to be alone. If it was just him and Lola, all the caution in the world wouldn't be enough, and she'd be the one to pay.

"Let's just focus on the mission," he said, praying she didn't notice the desperation in his voice.

"Yeah, sure," she replied flatly, making him wince under his disguised helmet. "You keep this road on lockdown. The more idiots we can redirect away from Victor's stupid multi-cathedral, the better our chances."

"You can count on me," he said, which was the absolute truth. Even if his only role in this plan was to sit on his bike and direct tourists into a fairy's maze, he would do it to the best of his ability. It was the only thing he could give her now, but it still stabbed when she walked away, her frumpy tourist body slumping like a deflated balloon.

He almost got off his bike to chase her before he caught himself. His hand still shot out, reaching after her as if he could snatch it all back. It was a stupid, pointless gesture, but at least the sight of his hand was a good reminder of what was at stake. Even with Lola's beautiful magic all over him, his fairy eyes saw the truth. Under the bright yellow of his costume's fake glove was another: his own hideous, blood-stained gossamer, falling apart.

Only his fingers at the moment, thanks to Simon, but the sight was still enough to make Valente drop his arm at once, clutching his numb hand against the handlebars of his fake bike as the ringing in his ears got worse and worse. He smacked his helmet a few times to make it stop, locking his eyes back on the empty road he was *supposed* to be watching but was suddenly shaking too hard to focus on.

There was no point in getting upset, he reminded himself. Dwelling on problems only made them worse, and it wasn't as if he hadn't known this was coming. Everyone had told him a knight couldn't survive without his king. He'd thought he'd dodged that bullet when Simon brought him back from the dead, but Valente should have known he'd never get that lucky. He wasn't a true fairy. He wasn't even a beautiful blend like Lola. He was a hack job, a headless man stapled to a dead monster, and now that the knighthood oaths were no longer forcing it to function, Valente's head was doing what all dead things did. It was rotting. Rotting like roadkill right off his shoulders, and he was rotting with it.

His black gossamer, which had once been so cold, was tepid and numb. He didn't feel pain or temperature, didn't get hungry, didn't sleep. He was more like a ghost now than he'd ever been as the Black Rider, but as uncomfortable as it was to feel death creeping over him, that wasn't actually what Valente feared. Rotting alive was still better than being Victor's slave, but he was terrified of Lola finding out.

She'd been *so* happy when she'd woken up and discovered they were all alive, though not as happy as Valente. He'd had his freedom, had his life. The only part of his paradise that was missing was Lola, and then, like a miracle, she'd come back. He hadn't even cared that Victor wasn't dead. The day she woke up, there was *nothing* Valente believed they couldn't do. Then he'd taken off his gloves to touch her and noticed that his hands were falling apart.

It'd been all downhill from there. He'd gone straight back to Simon to see what could be done, but the problem was with Valente's head, not his human soul. The best the blood mage could do was patch him back together, but there was no stopping the rot.

He'd almost told Lola then. Part of him, the cowardly part that was afraid to die, felt that she should know, if only so he could say goodbye. But the rest of Valente, the better half, refused to put that burden on her. As her copy had told him in the mailroom, all Lola had ever wanted was for everyone to be alive and safe. If he told her what was happening to him, he'd ruin that. He was going to die whether she knew or not, so until he actually keeled over, Valente was determined not to let her down.

Not that he was doing a good job so far considering how she'd just left, but there was no way Valente could keep his secret if he let himself be alone with her. He only had to hold out a little longer. If Lola was right about her plan, today might be the day the Hero died, and then he could fall apart in peace knowing he'd helped give her a world without Victor. Valente was telling himself to be satisfied with that when he felt something slide between his numb fingers.

He jumped a foot off his bike. His first thought was that the decay must have been even worse than he'd realized if someone had been able to get that close without him noticing, but the street was empty when he whirled around. Even the few businesses that had survived Victor's purge were pulling in their signs and closing their doors in preparation for the Hero's daily miracle. Valente was searching the emptiness with what was left of his feelers for the culprit when he realized the thing was still in his hand.

Dread spread through what was left of his body, bringing back a bit of the Rider's cold as Valente looked down to see a memo pad clutched in his yellow-gloved hand. It was the same kind he used to write on when he wasn't wearing his head, a rectangle of soft gray recycled paper held together with a flimsy wire spiral. The tiny notebook was so cheap, it didn't even have a cover, which was how he saw the word written at the top of the first page in shaky pencil.

HELP.

Valente dropped the thing like he'd been bitten. He hadn't touched a notepad since Lola had dropped a piano on him, but it was clearly real wood pulp, not gossamer. Since pads of paper didn't just appear out of thin air, someone must have slipped it into his hand. It was the only plausible explanation, and yet…

Valente bent over, snatched the notepad off the pavement, and held it right up against his disguise's face so his glowing eyes could see it through the visor of the motorcycle helmet that was hidden underneath. He stared as hard as he could, but there was no mistake. That was his handwriting.

He searched his pockets, feeling for the golf pencil he used to carry that had clearly been used to write the message, but he didn't find it. Valente hadn't thought he would. Just like the paper, he hadn't carried a pencil since he'd gotten free, but if both the pad and the pencil weren't his, where had the message come from?

He spent the next half hour trying to figure it out, but he was still as confused as ever when the Hero's Hall lit up behind him, its stained-glass windows shaking with the roar of the crowd inside.

~~~

Lola stood in her assigned place at the foot of Hero's Hall's massive stadium-style bleachers, the only spot of silence in a crowd that was losing its collective minds. All around her, people from every corner of the planet were screaming at the tops of their lungs, their faces shiny with tears in the harsh TV lights as the announcer breathlessly informed them that the Hero was on his way.

This whipped the crowd into an even greater frenzy, forcing Lola to shift her grip on the enormous amount of gossamer she was supporting. Considering what would happen if she dropped it, the magic should have been the sole focus of her attention, but the only thing going through Lola's mind right now was that she was an *idiot*.

What had she been thinking, putting Valente on the spot like that right before a mission? They were *supposed* to be bringing down Victor, not indulging in stupid crushes. It was absolutely a crush too. The one night they'd spent together hadn't been romantic for either of them. It'd been a rebellion, an act of defiance against the man who'd stomped on them their entire lives. That had been all she'd wanted at the time, but Valente had been so sweet afterward. Always been sweet, really, which was why she'd started thinking…
~~~

Lola gave herself a hard shake and focused back on the screaming crowd. All this gossamer would be for nothing if Victor walked in and spotted one of his adoring worshipers looking like a sad sack. She could blow the whole operation, waste everyone's work. She owed them more than that, especially since she'd so obviously been wrong. The only thing Valente wanted from her was to get the job done, so Lola shoved her bruised heart down to the bottom of her gossamer and tapped a finger against her disguise's hairy ear to get Dee's attention.

"How's it looking up there?"

It's great! her copy replied cheerfully through the magic that formed them both. *You should have seen me go! I got control of the whole media booth before the stupid A/V guy even knew what was up. Changeling power!*

Lola rolled her eyes.

But that's not what's important right now, Dee said, proving once again why Lola still didn't entirely trust her judgment. *Tell me how it went with Valente!*

Lola winced. She hadn't told her double what she was planning—hadn't even known she would do it herself until the stupid question had popped out of her mouth—but she wasn't surprised that Dee knew. It used to be her doppelganger only had access to Lola's memories from before the moment Lola spun her off. Now that she was out and about all the time, though, she used the fact that they were still technically two pieces of the same magic to constantly stick her nose into Lola's thoughts. Dee was especially quick to hone in on the emotional stuff, but while that usually made her the best person to talk to, Lola wasn't up for a rehash of being turned down.

"Let's stay focused on the mission," she said sternly, stomping every feeling that wasn't hate for Victor down into the parts of herself where even Dee didn't go. "You've got control of the cameras?"

I've got control of everything, her double reported smugly. *This is the control room, after all. Jamie actually just came through to make sure we were good for the live broadcast.*

Lola froze. "Jamie was there?"

Yeah, but it wasn't bad. Her narrow mind is still as intolerant of gossamer as ever, but she wasn't around long enough to do any actual damage. She just blazed through her checks and skedaddled to do one of the other billion things on Victor's list. I actually felt kind of sorry for her. She looks really stressed out.

"Don't waste your sympathy on Jamie," Lola said bitterly. "She knows exactly how bad Victor is, and she's *still* licking his boots. She deserves whatever she gets."

Yeah, but I still feel bad for her. Lola felt her doppelganger's lips pull into a worried frown. *She looks really scared.*

She had every reason to be. Her boss had spent the last three months turning the DFZ into a fascist police state and taunting the rest of the world to do something about it. The US government currently had the largest domestic military force ever assembled sitting just across the border in Ohio. The Heartstriker dragons were also putting together a strike team, and if the earthquakes that occasionally shook the area were any indication, the Merlin Council was building up for something as well. If Jamie wasn't scared to face all of that, she was even more delusional than Lola thought.

"Jamie can take care of Jamie. We're here for the real monster. How long until he comes out?"

According to the big glowing timer thingy, we're live in two, Dee replied. *You ready for this?*

"As ready as I'm gonna be," Lola said, placing a hand on her disguise's potbelly. "Just make sure the cameras stay on Victor. We need the whole world to see the Hero die, or they won't believe it."

Dee's laugh floated through their shared magic like a shiver. *Don't worry about that! All the main stage cameras are bolted to the ground. I couldn't film anything other than Victor even if I wanted to, and no one misses the Daily Miracle. Jamie was just saying we're up to two hundred and twenty million viewers worldwide. That should be enough proof for anyone.*

"Then the only thing left is to do it," Lola said with a bracing breath. "Thank you, Dee. I couldn't have pulled this off without you."

Thank yourself, Dee insisted. *You're the one who put everything together.*

"I just hope it works this time."

She could already feel Dee revving up her usual pep talk when Lola dropped her finger, cutting the mental connection. Although she'd become very good at controlling the enormous sea of gossamer that came with Alberich's head, these next few minutes would need her total concentration. All the more reason she should've waited before saying something to Valente, but she couldn't be too mad. She'd been obsessing over how to ask him out practically since she'd woken up. Now that it was over and the worst had happened, she could stop worrying about it.

It was a good thing Lola wasn't a true fairy, because that was a whopper of a lie. In classic human style, though, she forced herself to swallow it, throwing everything she had into the massive tapestry of gossamer she'd been weaving for the last five days. This wasn't going to work unless everything was perfect, but while he was a very tough sell, Lola had been performing for Victor her entire life. Despite everything he'd changed, he was still the same awful person, which meant she knew him better than anyone.

That was the weapon Lola had chosen for this fight, and she grabbed it with all she had, screaming as loud as the rest of the crowd as the lights dimmed and the announcer—or, rather, Dee posing as the announcer—came on to proclaim that the Hero had arrived!

As always during these events, Victor entered like a sunrise. His armor, a new addition made just for media appearances, reflected the glaring television lights like a suit of molten gold. His sword shone even brighter, shooting a beam of yellow light across the darkened stands as he crossed the stage to the raised podium positioned like an altar at its center. As he climbed into position, the building's exterior lights flashed on, illuminating the cathedral's stained-glass windows until they glowed like rainbow fire. The sudden burst of colored light bounced off the Hero's armor like a disco ball, filling the darkened hall with millions of reflected sparkles, a dazzling effect Jamie had dubbed "the world's only light."

The display was cheesy and ridiculous, so, naturally, everybody loved it. Through her human side, Lola could feel the tide of magic pouring into him as the whole watching world threw their hopes at Victor's feet like roses. He accepted the adoration as his due, his handsome new face set in a dazzling smile that, for once, actually looked sincere, but why wouldn't it? Victor had always loved being idolized. He looked like he was having the time of his life as he climbed the final step to the podium and took his place in front of the world he'd taught to worship him.

What happened next was standing practice. Just like every other day since he'd become the Hero, Victor began his media appearance with a ten-minute rant about how fairies, dragons, and spirits were the root of all of humanity's problems. Lola didn't know how his followers could swallow that bilge given that Victor had *made himself a spirit* in front of their eyes three months ago when he'd beaten the Wild Hunt, but she supposed the whole point of blind devotion was the ability to ignore that kind of hypocrisy.

Even the fact that Victor's army of magically superior blood mages had, according to him, died from a single rear assault not even dramatic enough to be caught on camera didn't seem to faze them. The crowd ate up every word that dropped from his lips, which explained why he looked so happy. Bastard was living the dream up there.

If Lola hadn't known what was coming, she couldn't have stood to watch him being so smug. It was only the knowledge that she was about to wipe the smile off his face that allowed her to keep her cool, cheering on cue along with the rest of the crowd as Victor finally finished his hate speech and moved on to the part everyone had actually tuned in for: the Daily Miracle.

The Daily Miracle was why so many people still worshiped the Hero despite the red flags he threw up every time he opened his mouth. Each day at noon sharp, Victor chose one of his followers to receive a miracle. The media had dismissed the act as a publicity stunt at first, but they changed their tune when the people Victor chose started going on TV to prove that the Hero really had cured their cancer or whatever. He fixed magical problems, too, even turning people who'd been born without the mage gene into magic users capable of passing the standard exams.

It probably did look miraculous to anyone who didn't understand blood magic. But while Simon could have done all of that and more, to the normal public, whose only knowledge came from anti-blood-mage propaganda and movies, the miracles were just more proof of Victor's divinity. An ironic twist since those were the exact same miracles he used to sell illegally before becoming the Hero.

No one even seemed to care that the people Victor healed had to take pills to keep their "miracles" from going away. That was all brushed under the rug of the Hero's cult, which was rapidly reaching major-religion status. But all that attention was going to turn against him today.

Lola stopped cheering long enough to shoot a smug glance over her shoulder at the darkened window of the control room where Dee was waiting. She hadn't actually expected her double would be able to take over the whole thing. Dee's only job had been to make sure the name of the man Lola was impersonating got inserted into Victor's teleprompter. Sure enough, when the time came for the big event, the right name flashed up on all the screens next to the picture Lola had used to craft her disguise. The actual Henry Wallace from Colorado Springs was enthralled in a fairy sleep inside Tristan's barrow, leaving no one to call out Lola's ruse as the spotlights found her in the shouting crowd.

As always, the sudden attention landed on her like a hammer. Even with a monarch's gossamer at her fingertips, that much direct scrutiny hit *hard.* The only reason Lola didn't melt on the spot was because she'd made sure no one had any reason to doubt. She'd even called Henry's mom this morning to talk about how nervous "he" was feeling, laying the groundwork for dismissing any odd behavior as stage fright.

Even so, the walk up to the podium was the longest Lola could remember. If Alberich's power hadn't been so strong, the weight of all that jealousy would have ripped her apart. She didn't dare look at anything but Henry's leather shoes as she climbed the stairs and crossed the red-carpeted stage to the kneeling cushion that always sat in front of the Hero's podium. Victor himself was already there, his expression making it clear how very greatly he'd condescended to come down and heal whatever it was that Henry had wrong with him.

The next part was actually the hardest. She'd thought she was past the worst after she'd survived the initial hit of attention, but Lola hadn't accounted for her own rage when she heard Victor say, "Kneel."

It was just a stage command. Victor always instructed his supplicants to kneel, even though most people threw themselves at his feet the second they made it up the stairs. From the expression on the Hero's dazzling face, he clearly expected Lola to do the same, but by the time she made it to the pillow, her knees were locked like two steel bars.

If this hadn't been the moment everything was for, she would have left them like that. Lola had sworn she'd never—*never*—kneel to Victor again, but he wouldn't heal someone who was standing, and the longer she waited, the more suspicious he'd become. He was already giving her an odd look, his blue eyes digging into her in the way that still made her feel one inch tall.

Why, oh, *why* hadn't she impersonated someone with knee problems? But it was way too late to change course. She was already off the deep end, so Lola forced her legs to bend, bowing her head as low as she could so the cameras wouldn't see her snarl.

"Henry Wallace," Victor said in a voice that probably sounded patient to his fans but that Lola recognized as bored. "You have been chosen from among millions to receive..."

Lola squeezed her eyes shut. Just the sound of him so close made her magic pulse with rage and fear. She'd thought she was ready for this, but she'd clearly underestimated how raw her wounds still were. If she let his voice get to her, she'd blow it, so Lola cut off the outside world, focusing instead on the lump hidden inside her, the only part of her body that wasn't gossamer.

As usual for Victor, he talked forever. It was probably no more than a few minutes, but Lola felt years older by the time his cool hands landed on Henry's bald head. She'd taken great pains to make sure that part of her costume was flawless. She actually felt Victor flinch as his fingers made contact with the sheen of realistic sweat covering the hard, scaly skin of Henry's scalp. There was no way he'd know she was gossamer until he actually touched her magic, by which point it'd be too late.

Lola knew the second it happened. All at once, Victor went from an actor going through a familiar role to the deadly, furious monster she remembered. His hands clenched down on Henry's sweaty skull the same way he used to grab her head as a child, forcing Lola's neck back until she was staring into his burning, furious eyes.

"You."

The whisper was shockingly intimate. He must have cut his mic, because even though they were still on stage, it felt like he and Lola were the only two people in the world. She couldn't even hear the crowd through the pressure of his anger as Victor's fingers dug into her skull.

"When will you learn this won't work?" he hissed, dragging Lola up until their faces were inches apart. "I *won*. There are no takebacks, no do-overs. This power is mine forever. When will you realize that nothing can change that?"

"Never," Lola whispered back, letting the illusion of her T-shirt dissipate so he could see the explosive vest hidden under Henry's potbelly.

The Hero's blue eyes narrowed. "You already tried explosives."

"Not like this."

For one beautiful moment, Victor's confident sneer wavered. Then he threw her to the ground and whirled to face the crowd, which was no longer cheering. All the tear-streaked faces of his faithful vanished a second later as the whole arena dropped their masks, revealing the truth.

In the space of one breath, everyone in the building—the cheering crowd, the security guards keeping order in the aisles, even the camera operators—showed their true colors. They were gossamer—*Lola's* gossamer—and every single one was wearing the same explosive vest that was strapped around Lola's chest.

That was all she gave Victor time to see before she threw herself at the stunned man who'd hurt them all so much. The man she hated more than any other as she hit the button taped to her palm.

Every copy of Lola in the building did the same, mirroring her final action as the grand cathedral of the Hero's Hall was engulfed in an explosion big enough to be seen from space.

Chapter 2

Lola woke up with a gasp. For a horrible moment, she was sure she was dead. There was no other reason everything would be so dark and heavy and *wet*. Her chest felt like it was being crushed under a boulder, and her head seemed stuffed full of wool. She was really starting to panic when a pair of giant hands grabbed her face and began gently wiping the gunk from her eyes, cleaning the crust away in delicate little strokes until Lola was finally able to pry her lids open.

"Thanks," she breathed, rubbing her hands over her eye sockets to clear the rest of the disgusting crusties that were apparently part of being human. When she could see again, she tilted her still-cotton-stuffed head up to grin at the wall of teeth looming above her. "You're a lifesaver, Toothy."

Her creature beamed and shuffled away, making room for Dee, who poofed back into existence a few seconds later.

"Man, talk about going out with a *bang*!" her double cried, leaping into the air to give the much taller Toothy a high five. "Do you think we got him this time?!"

"No way to know until we see the news reports," Lola said, turning her painfully creaking neck to see where they'd woken up.

It was always different. The first time Lola had come to inside her new barrow, she'd thought the weird version of her old apartment with its oh-so-convenient door was all there was. Over the next few days, though, she'd learned that was very, *very* not true. The room she'd woken up in after defeating Alberich had been nothing but an emergency raft, a thrown-together pocket meant only to protect her while she slept. The moment she'd started moving around, the rest of Alberich's kingdom had rushed over to meet her, burying Lola in its magic until she was up to her eyeballs.

Not that it should have been surprising given how far his Wild Hunt had roamed, but the previous Underground King had had barrows hidden all over the world. Once Lola ate his head and he'd stopped doing whatever he was doing to keep them separated, all those magical spaces had started pulling back together, merging and mixing into a super barrow of constantly changing caverns and passages that Lola had no idea how to navigate or control.

It wasn't entirely random. Certain things were always true, like how her human body was always at the barrow's lowest level. Lola suspected this was because that was the point where her human death and the fairy king's barrow met, but even she couldn't say for sure. All she knew was that now, instead of dying when the gossamer chunk holding her soul got destroyed, she woke up in her human body, which on this particular day lay on a bed of flowers inside what appeared to be a cavern full of glowing waterfalls.

"Oh, this is niiiiiice," Dee said, running over to splash her hands through the nearest glowing pool, which turned out to be full of scuttling bioluminescent crabs. "You gotta hand it to Alberich. Dude knew how to Magical King."

"Or he was just bored," Lola grumbled, leaning hard on Toothy's furry paw as her creature half escorted, half carried Lola's feeble, fleshy body over to the biggest pool so she could wash herself off.

Washing was something she did every time she woke up. No matter how big a hurry she was in, Lola always took time to clean her human shell. She didn't know if it was strictly necessary—her body had slept in Alberich's barrow for twenty-eight years and never needed a bath—but not washing up made her feel super gross.

Weirdly, the barrow seemed to have picked up on this. The first two times she'd woken up, she'd been in an apartment with no bathroom and a desert respectively. She'd pitched a royal fit over that last one, which must have done something, because every time since, she'd always woken up somewhere with water. The barrow had even started providing cleaning supplies. Usually in the form of weird soap fish and sponges that were actually snails, but Lola appreciated the effort. It was nice to know that the barrow was trying, too, even if she wasn't much of a monarch yet.

"Okay," she said when she'd cleaned all the gross biological gunk off her flesh. "Put me back, and let's get this over with."

As delicately as she'd pick a flower, Toothy tweezed the body they all shared between her claws and carried it back to the bed of flowers. Once her human bits were safely stowed, Lola closed her eyes and spun herself a new body. As always since she'd taken over Alberich's gossamer, it came together in a snap. One second, she was naked and dripping on a bed of grassy-smelling plants, the next, she was on her feet and dressed for spelunking in a waterproof jumpsuit, knee-high rubber boots, and a hard hat with a super-bright LED flashlight built right into the top.

"Isn't that overkill?" asked Dee, who'd dressed herself in a bright blue tank top, yellow shorts, and flip-flops made from glittery pink plastic. "This is *your* kingdom."

"Which is exactly why I'm taking precautions," Lola replied as she spun herself a three-foot-long electrified baton made for shocking bison. "Fairy courts are top-down affairs. All anything out there has to do is eat me, and they become the next Underground King."

Dee gave her usual shrug, but Toothy at least looked suitably serious as she rolled aside the boulder that blocked the exit to the glowing cavern where their real body was stashed. Lola gave her monster-self a thankful smile and took point, striding out prod-first with Toothy on her left and Dee trailing sullenly behind.

Ninety-nine percent of the time, Lola had zero regrets about eating Alberich's head. Being semi-immortal was super useful, and the insane amount of gossamer that came with being a fairy monarch was the only reason she could do things like fill an entire stadium-cathedral with suicide bomber copies of herself. She didn't even feel the loss of the gossamer she'd incinerated making Victor's pyre, a far cry from the days when cutting off a car was a major setback. But while being king was great most of the time, there were still parts she hated.

This next bit was definitely on that list. Since Lola's human body was always stowed at the very bottom, she had to climb through hundreds of levels of wild barrow to get back to the upper, shallower floors that she actually controlled. This trip *always* included the troll pits, which Lola now understood why Tristan had had such a hard time with. They were absolutely horrible, stinking black holes full of nightmare creatures that broke her brain to see.

The only good thing she could say about the pits was that at least the monsters inside gave her a wide berth. Lola assumed this was out of respect for the cruel king she'd been before. She didn't know how long that ploy would keep working, though, which was why Lola always made sure Toothy was with her whenever she passed through.

"You could just change it, you know," Dee pointed out as they skirted the edge of the bubbling pits of molten gold that filled the next cavern. "You're the king now, not Alberich. All this stuff is just furniture left over from the previous tenant. Clear it out, and you're good!"

"Easy for you to say," Lola grumbled. "You're not the one who has to do it."

"You redecorated the upstairs just fine," Dee reminded her, taking off her plastic flip-flops, which were rapidly melting in the heat. "Why can't you do the same down here? At the very least, you could put in an elevator."

"You think I haven't tried that?" Lola snapped, crossing her arms tight over her chest. "I hate this walk as much as you do, but this place isn't the same as upstairs. Alberich was the Underground King for uncountable eons. Even Morgan isn't sure how long he ruled. That kind of control doesn't just go away overnight, and the deeper we are, the older and more entrenched his stuff gets. There's a reason my part of the barrow only goes down three layers. Scraping the surface was easy, but this stuff is the bedrock. It doesn't roll over just because I say so."

"I bet it would if you put in more effort," her doppelganger insisted. "You've been throwing all your gossamer at Victor since you woke up. Of course your barrow is running wild! You haven't given it any attention."

Lola stomped her boots down. "If all you're going to do is criticize me, you can wait upstairs."

"It's not criticism," Dee said, blithely ignoring Lola's scowl as she skipped ahead. "As your creation, it's my job to help you become your best self, and you can't do that if you're always focusing on Victor."

"Only because he won't *die!*" Lola cried, sticking the bison prod under her arm to count off on her fingers. "I've shot him in the neck, heart, and straight through the eye. I've cut off his head, drowned him in the Detroit River, crushed him under a tour bus, and dropped him thirty stories off a balcony. He should be dead thirty times over, but he *isn't.*"

"What else did you expect?" Dee asked with a shrug. "He turned himself into a spirit. So long as people believe in the concept that created him, he'll always rise again."

"That's why we went so big this time," Lola reminded her pointedly. "Victor might be a spirit magically, but he's still acting like a man, and no *man* can survive a hug from a cathedral full of suicide bombers." She clenched her fists in anticipation. "If we can just get enough people believing that the Hero's dead, it won't matter what he's made himself into. Why do you think I told you to keep the cameras on him?"

"There were a *lot* of cameras," Dee admitted, then she scowled. "But even if we did get him for real this time, that's no reason to keep ignoring everything else. You've got a whole kingdom you haven't even explored yet! You're the one who always says we're not giving Victor anything else, so why are you giving up being a king?"

"I'm not giving up," Lola said stubbornly, striding ahead. "It's a matter of priorities. I've got all of eternity to be the Underground King, but if we don't stop Victor soon, he's going to get bigger than we can handle."

He nearly was already. Just as she'd predicted back at Tristan's, Victor had taken his victory over the Wild Hunt and rolled it straight into his next project, which seemed to be putting every spirit he could reach under his boot. The Merlin Council hadn't said anything official yet, but it was obvious to Lola that the DFZ was now completely under Victor's control. Even Algonquin, the famous Lady of the Lakes who'd trashed Detroit during the original return of magic, hadn't risen to challenge him. She'd pulled her waters back instead, leaving a good hundred feet of new shoreline between her lakes and the Hero's city.

Lola wasn't surprised by that. Victor always made things worse, but she was done being a bystander. She was going to take him out *now*, before he could finish laying the groundwork for whatever he was planning to conquer next. None of their efforts had succeeded so far, but this had been their biggest attack yet. Surely, *surely* blowing up an entire cathedral had done *something*.

Unfortunately, Lola had no way of confirming that until she got back to the parts of the barrow she controlled. Even the magical gossamer phones she whipped up for herself on the regular now couldn't get a signal down here, so she gripped her bison prod and picked up the pace. Toothy matched her easily, but

Dee complained the whole way, huffing at Lola to wait up as they pushed out of the molten gold cavern into the jungle of dense black foliage that filled the next layer of Alberich's underground world.

<center>~~~</center>

As always, the trip up from the bottom of the barrow took forever. Not quite as much forever as the first time, which had taken a full two days, but it was still hours before Lola felt the hard, jagged lines of Alberich's leftover gossamer give way to the soft, welcoming feel of her own. At least they spotted the troll pits *before* they walked into them this time. The leftover fear of Alberich must still have been working, because none of the denizens tried to eat her, but they did get uncomfortably close, prompting Lola to zap a few with her bison prod to make sure they didn't get any ideas.

As always, defending herself kicked Dee off into a diatribe. From the way her double carried on, you'd think Lola had forgotten her own origins, but she remembered *exactly* how violent her monster could get under Alberich's influence. That was why she zapped them, because if the old king was still kicking around anywhere, it'd be down here. He wasn't haunting her or anything like that, but Lola knew some part of him must be lurking in the barrow's depths, because the depths were still there.

That was one aspect of her new kingdom that Lola had taken the time to worry about. As she knew from Alberich's gloating during their battle, barrows took a *lot* of magic to maintain. Magic that she, as a changeling-human hybrid, couldn't provide. Unlike an actual fairy monarch, she couldn't eat human emotions to fuel the magic that kept everything going. She wasn't sure what was fueling this place, but it had to be coming from

Alberich, because it certainly wasn't her. Lola didn't even know how to replenish the magic she so freely took out.

Her best guess was that the barrow was still coasting on the glut of power Alberich had built up before Victor cut him down. That was convenient when she needed to pull out huge globs of magic for her campaign against Victor, but knowing her kingdom was powered by human fear of the Wild Hunt definitely didn't make her want to get to know the place better. She might have sympathy for the hideous trolls that watched them from the shadows, but she still zapped them without hesitation, keeping Dee and Toothy safe as they bashed their way through vaults of cursed treasure and stinking underground swamps until she finally spotted the metal ladder that led back to her part of the barrow.

Lola broke into a sprint the moment she saw it, scrambling over a pile of skulls—*human* skulls, some of which still had flesh and bits of hair clinging to them—toward the exit. She changed her clothes as she climbed the ladder, dissolving the disgusting cave-mud-covered boots right off her feet. She did her jumpsuit next, then her hard hat and finally her electrified prod. By the time she stuck her fingers through the holes of the perfectly normal-looking DFZ manhole cover set in the stone above her head, Lola was wearing the same bright-blue tank top and yellow shorts as Dee. When she was certain she looked normal and not like a terrifying sewer creature, she put both her hands on the bottom of the manhole cover and pushed up, flooding the old, bloody caves with afternoon sunlight.

The sight made her weak with relief. Too weak, apparently, because the manhole cover immediately started to sink back down. Lola was struggling not to get knocked back into the skull pit when Toothy's paws appeared beside her human hands, tossing the manhole cover away like a dead leaf to reveal the cozy interior of Lola's new house.

Sticking with the apartment would have been simpler. But even if she couldn't eat fear to replace it, Alberich's barrow was still stuffed with more gossamer than Lola knew what to do with. With so much power at her fingertips, she'd seen no reason not to go big, especially given how many people she had to house these days. Case in point, Simon grabbed her hands the moment they came into view, hauling Lola out of the hole to join him in the sun-dappled living room.

She gasped like a diver coming up for air. Even if it was made from the same gossamer as everything else, it was always *such* a relief to be back in the light and open air after being so deep underground. A relief and a delight, because unlike the rest of Alberich's hole, this part of the barrow belonged entirely to Lola.

She'd modeled it after her favorite part of University Heights, the only neighborhood in the pre-Victor DFZ where you could still get a house on the ground that wasn't under a bridge. She'd taken some liberties with the landscape, adding a tall hill right on the edge where the sidewalks ended and the city gave way to the wild forest that had been Reclamation Land. Her house was smack on the hill's crest: a sprawling old-Detroit-style two-story with gothic brickwork, a spacious yard, and a fantastic view of the double-layered DFZ in the distance, which, since this was Lola's fantasy world, still looked the way it used to before Victor ruined it.

"Welcome back," Simon said, offering his hands to Dee next, who took them with a beaming smile. "You're getting faster. It only took you five hours to get back this time."

"New record," Lola agreed, looking excitedly at Simon's smile. "So, did we get him?"

The happy expression slipped off Simon's face, and Lola flopped onto the couch with a groan. "How did he live through that?" she wailed, startling Toothy, who was still trying to wiggle her gigantic furry body through the manhole. "I packed that place with enough explosives to launch him into orbit! How is he not dead?"

"If it makes you feel better, you definitely scared him," Simon said, walking over to switch on the old-style TV from Morgan's prison, which had appeared in the house for reasons Lola wasn't willing to pry into. He had to bang on the top a few times to get the old set to stop jumping, but eventually the picture stabilized into a twenty-four-hour news channel, which was running nonstop coverage of the Hero's breathtaking escape from the terror attack at Hero's Hall.

"See?" Simon said, pointing at the small picture-in-picture screen showing an infuriatingly still-alive Victor giving an interview from his tacky penthouse office. "He was on TV not ten minutes after it happened. Didn't even take the time to put his armor back on, which means he was more concerned with showing people he was still alive than he was with his image. I think that proves our theory about belief being key to his resurrections."

"It doesn't matter how right we are if we can't make it work," Lola grumbled, getting up to replace the manhole cover now that Toothy was through. "That was our best try yet, and he still came back like it was nothing."

"You came back, too," Simon reminded her, rolling the carpet over the closed manhole with his foot. "We haven't lost any pieces in this match, but Victor's going to be rebuilding Hero's Hall for months. That's not nothing."

"But still not enough," Lola said bleakly, sinking back onto the couch. "And it won't take him months. The DFZ is entirely his now. He can rebuild anything we knock down, and he comes back from the dead even faster than I do."

"But it costs him more," Simon insisted, taking a seat in the worn wingback chair on the other side of the coffee table. "The only price you pay for dying is a caving expedition, but Victor has to put on a full media blitz. Even if the major networks are falling over themselves to have the Hero on, showing the world he's not dead still costs him time and resources. It may not be the blow we wanted to land, but it still counts."

Crummy as she was feeling right now, Lola couldn't help flashing Simon a weak smile. "Since when did you become the optimist?"

"I've always been an optimist," Simon said. "And so have you. It's the only way we survived growing up with Victor."

"He's right," Dee said, entering the room with a cookie in her mouth. Lola hadn't even seen her leave, but her double was suddenly coming through the kitchen door with a family-sized pack of chocolate sandwich cookies in one hand and bowl of pretzels in the other.

Lola pushed herself up at once. "Where did you get those?"

"Your barrow!" Dee replied excitedly.

Lola blinked at her. "The Underground Kingdom stocks Oreos?"

"It's a treasure trove of untold delights," her double assured her, peeling the plastic panel off the cookie pack like she was lifting the silver cover off a royal feast. "Which wouldn't be a surprise to you if you took my advice and spent some time actually getting to know your new kingdom."

Lola rolled her eyes and helped herself to a cookie. When Simon leaned in to do the same, though, she grabbed his wrist. "What are you doing?" she hissed. "That's fairy food!"

"I'm not worried about getting trapped in your barrow," he told her confidently, wiggling out of her grasp. "I trust you completely, and it's not as if I've got anywhere else to be."

That was sweet of him to say, but Lola was still sweating bullets as Simon pried the two halves of his cookie apart and began eating them piece by piece. Trust or no trust, fairy food was dangerous. Lola had never touched the stuff herself until she started making her own, though she still didn't know how she did it. Dee claimed the food just appeared in the pantry, which Lola supposed wasn't too far off from Tristan's always-stocked banquet table, but it still gave her the jeebies. She'd never had her magic make stuff without her knowledge before.

"Don't look so stressed," Dee scolded, walking over to offer the bowl of pretzels to Toothy, who was already curled up in her favorite sunbeam under the bay window. "It's not like you're making monsters in your sleep. It's a cookie. Life's never bad with a cookie."

"Tastes normal enough to me," Simon said, popping the rest of his dissected Oreo into his mouth as he glanced over his shoulder at the front door.

Lola looked, too, biting her lip as she realized they were one person short.

"Where's the Rider?"

"Out scouting," Simon said, his voice oddly tense. "He said he was going to take advantage of the chaos and the costume you gave him to check the border again."

Lola lowered her face so Simon wouldn't notice her disappointed look. Valente had always been here when she'd woken up before. She wasn't sure if that was because he really was worried about the border situation or if she'd made things even more awkward than she'd feared with that incredibly badly timed dinner request. She was reliving the whole embarrassing sequence in her head when she remembered Simon was still looking at her.

"I just hope he sees some movement this time," she said, striving for maximum nonchalance to cover her lapse. "Killing Victor wouldn't be nearly so hard if we weren't doing it alone. Every major power in the world is currently sitting in Ohio, and they haven't done squat. I would've thought the dragons would be in Victor's hair by now at least. Aren't they supposed to be territorial?"

"It's no small thing to invade a sovereign city-state," Simon said patiently. Then his lips quirked. "And the Dragon of Detroit *is* called 'the Peacemaker.' Surprise, surprise, but he's not exactly a warmonger."

"He's not going to be the dragon of anything if he waits much longer," Lola said grumpily. "What about the United States? They have the largest military in the world, *and* this is happening in their backyard. Why aren't they invading yet?"

"Oh, they want to," Simon said, grabbing another cookie from the plastic pack. "That's actually part of the holdup. President David Heartstriker has made it clear that if the US military enters the DFZ, they're changing the name back to Detroit and keeping it. It's become the center of his reelection campaign, which naturally sets the Peacemaker and other DFZ allies against him."

"So you're saying they're worthless."

"I'm saying there's a lot of political friction, which I'm sure is part of Victor's plan." Simon's brows pulled into a scowl above his creepy new blue eyes. "He knows he can't hold out if the US starts bombing, which is why he planted the idea of taking back Detroit in the president's head."

Lola blinked in surprise. "You think that was Victor?"

"If it wasn't, he certainly hasn't done anything to change the president's mind," Simon said with a shrug. "Getting your enemies to fight amongst themselves while you get stronger is a classic Conrath move."

"*Ugh,*" Lola groaned, cramming a cookie into her mouth in pure frustration. "How is he *always* one step ahead? We're stronger than we've ever been, and it still feels like nothing's changed!"

"Things *have* changed," Simon insisted. "Not as much as we'd like, but think about what you just did. You filled Victor's cathedral with an entire gossamer crowd without him realizing and then blew the whole place up. If Victor hadn't been the Hero, he would have been dead twenty times over."

"But he *is* the Hero," Lola said, shaking her head. "It's not enough, Simon. We have to do more. I don't know how, but—"

She stopped with a shiver. Even after three months, she still hadn't gotten used to the feeling of someone knocking on her magic. The offering that came next felt even weirder, but at least this time it was a pleasant sort of weirdness.

As the master of a proper fairy barrow, Lola got to set the terms by which people found her. Even known allies had to approach with the right key for her home to reveal itself. Tristan's had been a dirty fantasy, while Alva had demanded blood. Lola being Lola, her key was food, and the figure rapping his knuckles on her door had definitely delivered. She could already smell the fresh fried dough and sugar as she peeled back her magic to allow Tristan to waltz through her front door.

"Hello!" the fairy said cheerfully, holding up a stack of doughnut boxes. "I brought 'damn, he's still alive' commiseration presents."

"You are welcome in my kingdom," Lola said, shoving Dee's pack of gossamer cookies aside to make way for the actual carbs.

Toothy perked up, too, her flat nose quivering as she caught the smell of sugar. Dee had already snatched the top box out of Tristan's hands and was ripping the lid open to locate the doughnut with the most sprinkles.

"Truly, you are three sprouts from the same acorn," Tristan said, handing a box to Toothy, who immediately dumped the entire dozen into her mouth. "Though I don't understand why you haven't added more to your cause." He turned to give Lola a pointed look. "A monarch needs a court. You can't hope to beat Victor by yourself, even if there are three of you."

"I'm not interested in adding more fairies," Lola said as she grabbed a box of doughnuts for herself. "This place is crazy enough as is, and I've got you."

"I am quite the asset," Tristan agreed, holding open the lone remaining box to offer Simon a doughnut, which the mage politely declined. "But one knight does not an army make, especially if he's not even *your* knight."

"Then you should be saying this to Morgan," Lola said, pausing to nibble the frosting off her strawberry-sprinkled cake cruller. "Where is she, anyway?"

"Still indisposed," the knight said sadly, dropping his lanky body into the chair next to Simon's. "My queen is a great and terrifying power, but twenty years locked inside Victor's head would take a toll on anyone, and Alva left her barrow in shambles. Add in the fact that most of our court has been reduced to their heads, and my lady had no choice but to bow out for a spell. She'll reemerge stronger than ever when the time is right, but until she does, I'm afraid Lamb and I are all you've got."

"Where is Lamb?" Simon asked.

"Still working," Tristan replied with a wave of his long-fingered hands. "She's an artist at heart, and you asked her to make a labyrinth big enough to keep all the actual ticket holders for Victor's miracle show busy. Naturally, then, it's taking forever."

Lola frowned. "Taking forever to do what? She was done with the labyrinth this morning."

"Building is only the first step," the knight informed her solemnly. "You can't expect a fairy to make a spectacle like that and *not* put on a show. She's got each one wandering through a maze of their own inadequacies where the only exit is to admit to their deepest, most hidden desire. It's a classic of our court."

"Oh, well, I guess that's fine," Lola said, putting her nibbled doughnut back in the box before grabbing a fresh one to start the icing-stripping process all over again. "So long as she doesn't keep them like that for a hundred years or anything."

Tristan made a non-committal sound, but Lola had bigger worries than the existential status of a few thousand of the Hero's most faithful.

"I think it's time we tried a new approach," she said, setting down her new doughnut solemnly. "We've gotten really good at killing Victor, but that clearly isn't working. We need a different angle, so what else have we got?"

"He's too big to trap in an illusion," Tristan said grimly. "And enthrallment doesn't work on spirits."

"He's never been susceptible to enthrallment," Simon pointed out. "Blood magic's total control over the self makes us highly resistant to those sorts of tricks."

"Resistant doesn't mean immune," the knight told him with a teasing smile. "Would you like me to demonstrate the difference on you?"

"There's no point listing all the things that *won't* work," Lola said before Simon could snap back. "We need to figure out what *will*."

"He can't be immune to everything," Simon said confidently. "If the Hero was a normal spirit, I could just banish him. I actually think that's what the Merlin Council has been trying to do for the past three months. Obviously, it's not working, but I think I've figured out why."

He scooted to the edge of his chair, fixing Lola with a determined expression that his new blue eyes made look so much like Victor's, she shivered. "I can't say for certain since I've only seen him do it on TV, but after reviewing all of his Daily Miracle broadcasts for the past two months, I'm positive that Victor is still using blood magic."

"I thought that was obvious," Lola said, dropping her gaze so she wouldn't have to look at what their old master had done to

Simon. "Even now that he's the Hero, he still won't shut up about blood magic."

"That doesn't necessarily mean he's using it himself," Simon reminded her. "Victor's a born liar. Nothing he says can be taken at face value. That's why I spent so much time watching his footage. Again, it's impossible to say without being there myself since you can't feel magic through a recording, but I know Victor's style better than anyone, and it really looks to me like he's still using the same tricks as always."

"So?" Lola said.

"*So,*" Simon said, his smile getting wider, "that means he's still casting human magic, and you can't cast human magic without a human soul."

He said this as if it were the answer to all their problems, but Lola still wasn't following. "If his soul is still human, why doesn't he die when we kill him?"

"Because he's the same as you," Simon explained. "You're both human souls mashed into something bigger. In Victor's case, he's wrapped himself up in the Spirit of the Hero. I don't know how much of him is which, but if he's still casting magic, *especially* blood magic, then some part of him must still be human. And if we can isolate that part—"

"We can kill him," Lola finished, getting the idea at last. "Fantastic! How do we do it?"

Simon scowled. "That's the bit I haven't figured out yet. Just because a weakness exists doesn't mean we can exploit it. Also, if he really has made himself into a mage with a spirit's capacity for holding magic, that's *really* bad."

"How bad?"

His scowl grew grimmer. "Let's just say I understand why the Merlin Council is being so cautious. Loath as I am to agree with Victor on anything, human magic is the most powerful force on this plane. We're the power that shapes the magical landscape.

Without our beliefs to dig their vessels, spirits like the DFZ wouldn't exist. The only reason we're not the unquestioned masters of the universe is because our souls are so small compared to everything else, but—"

"Victor fixed that," Lola finished, remembering the huge red expanse of his death. But while Victor becoming an unkillable super-mage sounded like the bingo of worst-case scenarios, Simon was smiling again.

"Why do you look like that?"

"Because, as bad as this is, it could also be the solution we've been waiting for," he said. "Being a mage with a spirit-sized vessel to draw from has made Victor incredibly, almost unbeatably powerful, but even he can't change the laws of magic. If he's human enough to cast spells, then he still has a death, and anything with a death can die."

"Could've fooled me," Lola muttered, rubbing her hands over her face. "I get where you're going now, but even if Victor does still have a death, how do we leverage that? The last time I went into his soul, it didn't go so well."

"We absolutely can't try that again," Simon agreed. "He was a god inside his death even before all this happened. I don't want to think about what he'll be like now."

"Then what do we *do*?" Lola demanded, banging her head against the sofa cushions. "We've already done everything!"

"That's exactly the point I was trying to make," Simon said, his eyes lighting up the way they always did when he had a plan. "*We've* already done everything we can think of, which means it's time to take this fight to someone else."

"Who?" Lola asked. "You just said Victor's got his enemies tied up in political drama."

Simon's lips curled in a smirk. "Not all of them. Victor's changed himself a lot, but if you cut away the trappings, he's still the same thing he's aways been. He's a blood mage, and who's the best at killing blood mages? Who's the one force Victor's *always* been afraid of?"

Lola's eyes went huge. "No."

"Yes," Simon said with a bloodthirsty grin. "We're calling in the Paladins."

Chapter 3

Simon spent the rest of the evening convincing Lola to go along with his plan. It was always the golden hour in her barrow, so he wasn't sure exactly how long they argued, but Tristan got bored and left halfway through, so it must have been a while. Eventually, though, he got her to agree with the general concept, which freed them to move on to the part of the plan Simon was less confident about: how they were actually going to convince the Paladins to attack.

He was baffled why they hadn't already. The Paladins were zealots backed by the authority of the United Nations. The only reason he and Victor hadn't been under constant attack before was because the DFZ refused to allow any foreign law enforcement over her borders.

Simon was sure that rule was being enforced even more strictly now that Victor had his boot on the city. What he didn't understand was why the Paladins still cared. This was no longer a matter of crossing an international border to summarily execute a private citizen. Victor had rebuilt the DFZ into a monument to the power of blood magic. *Nothing* should have been able to keep the Paladins from coming down on that, so where were they?

None of Simon's research over the past month had been able to answer that question, but he did have a good idea how to force their hand. A good idea that rapidly evolved into a *great* idea once Lola stopped balking and started helping, which was no surprise. They'd always been at their best when they were working together. Victor had known that, too, which was why he'd been so careful to keep them isolated, but the bastard couldn't stop the train this time. Simon knew *exactly* how scared the old man was of the Paladins' magic, a sorcery unique to their order created for a single purpose: to be blood magic's counter.

Even Simon didn't know how it worked, but he was sure the Paladins were the weapon they'd been looking for: the sword that would finally chop off Victor's head for good. The only reason he hadn't suggested bringing them in sooner was because the Paladins would kill him as fast as they killed Victor. At this point, though, Simon didn't care. Lola had already died a dozen times trying to bring Victor down. It was Simon's turn to take a hit, especially since this plan actually had a chance of working.

They were still hashing out the details when Lola fell asleep. As always, the sight filled Simon with protective tenderness. Victor used to insist she was just being lazy since real fairies didn't need sleep, but Lola had been quick to drift off for as long as Simon had known her. As a child, he'd considered it his duty to guard her, watching in awe as she'd shifted shape with her dreams. He still felt that way as he turned his back to Toothy and Dee, who'd passed out hours ago, so no one would see him brush Lola's dark hair away from her cheek with his fingers.

She always was your weakness.

Simon snatched his hand back like he'd been burned. He shoved the familiar voice back at the same time, but not far enough.

You always were so adroit at burying your feelings, Victor's poison whisper floated through his mind. *But where has that effort gotten you? You had her all to yourself for ten full years, and aside from one chaste kiss when you were literally the only boy she knew, she's never even glanced your direction. But she spends less than a week with the Black Rider, and he got to—*

Simon slammed his walls down, beating the hateful voice back with all his might until nothing was left but his own pounding heart. He was still struggling to reclaim control when he heard something moving behind him. He whirled in his chair, already braced to see Victor standing over him, but his old master wasn't there. Instead, Dee was getting up from where she'd been sleeping in the crook of Toothy's furry elbow.

"Sorry to startle you," the doppelganger whispered as she nudged Lola's monster awake. "But we need to get her to bed."

Simon nodded numbly, standing up to move his chair out of the way. Toothy trundled into the gap with a little nod of thanks, reaching down to gently pluck the sleeping Lola off the couch.

"We'll clean up," Dee said quietly as she started gathering the empty doughnut boxes. "You should get to bed, too, Simon. You look like you need the sleep."

That wasn't untrue, but Simon didn't want to sleep. He'd been stuck in this barrow doing nothing while Lola risked everything for months. Part of the reason he'd been so excited about this plan was because he'd get to actually help for once, not just stand here being useless while Toothy carried Lola up the stairs, cradling her beautiful, soft, ever-changing magic in the way Simon never had.

Pathetic.

Simon ignored the whisper and started helping Dee move the furniture back into place. He would have done more, but Lola's double insisted she had it, practically shoving Simon out of the room. He left with a stumble, shoving his hands into the pocket of the white doctor's coat he still wore despite having no more patients as he trudged through the kitchen toward the house's back door.

The sight waiting for him through the windows was almost enough to knock him out of his bad mood. Even after living here for three months, the view from Lola's backyard never failed to take his breath away. It still amazed him that the same Lola—who hadn't been able to keep a car together until she was seventeen—had made all of this. He could see the whole DFZ rising in front of him like a concrete mountain, its soaring buildings sparkling like jewels in the rose-gold light of the barrow's eternal sunset. The gracefully sloping Skyways were packed with cars from the evening rush, and every window in the giant buildings had little people moving behind it.

Even knowing he was looking at an illusion—the same frozen sunset he'd been living in for months—it felt so real. As real as the brick step beneath his feet, which was also gossamer. He could smell the grass in Lola's backyard, hear the roar of the distant traffic. It all felt as true and solid as his own body, but the very best part was the piece Lola had made just for him.

Occupying the entire right half of her massive backyard was a perfect replica of the Victorian revival mansion Simon had operated his clinic out of back when he was a doctor in the DFZ. Lola had given the place a new coat of paint so it wouldn't look dingy now that it was out from under the oppressive shadow of the Skyways, but otherwise it looked exactly as Simon remembered. Not that he needed all of that space now that he no longer had staff or patients, but he deeply appreciated the thought she'd put into it. It was nice to see something familiar in the otherwise nonsensical world of her fairy barrow, and having a house of his own made it easier to manage the shade of the blood mage that still lay inside his brain like a corpse.

Oh, are you acknowledging me now?

Absolutely not. Humans subconsciously moved magic toward whatever they paid attention to, and Simon wasn't giving Victor another drop of his.

Such an ungrateful apprentice.

The whisper hadn't even finished before Simon shoved it back in its hole. He refused to let what had happened in his death control him. He was no longer a terrified child with no choice but to listen. He was the master of his own soul, and he would not—

Who do you think taught you those powers? Victor's voice whispered, the soft words creeping through Simon's barriers like a stench. *You act all high and mighty, but I was there at your start. I've always known you're nothing but a—*

Simon hit the voice with a punch of magic. That shouldn't have been possible since barrows, being separate spaces completely cut off from the real world, had no ambient magic, but Simon was a blood mage. So long as he had his own soul, he needed no other magic. He crushed the corpse of Victor's voice in his fist, grinding his old master down until nothing remained of the whisper but a cruel chuckle.

He was drenched in sweat by the time he finished. The voice wasn't gone—it was never gone—but at least he wouldn't have to worry about the old man for a while. That was the best he was going to get, so Simon decided to take Dee's advice and get some sleep. Shaking his throbbing head, he walked across the grass and up his porch steps to open the jingly front door of his duplicated house. He was stumbling into what had been his clinic's waiting room when he realized he wasn't alone.

The house's front parlor was covered in mice. They froze when they saw him, clutching their little dustpans and brooms, which they'd been using to clean the illusion of his hardwood floor. Still more mice were standing on what had been his receptionist's desk, using her padded office chair as a ladder to reach the stained-glass shade of her parlor lamp, which they were polishing with tiny tufts of cotton. For one long second, Simon and the mice stared at each other, and then the little creatures resumed their cleaning as if he weren't there.

Simon relaxed as they got back to work, crouching down to watch the tiny, furry cleaning crew attack his reception area. Growing up in the DFZ, he used to hate vermin of any kind. The rats especially had been terrible, but these mice he loved. They were adorable with their soft gray coats and tiny scrub brushes, but Simon would have liked them even if they were ugly, because they were Lola's.

They'd never said a word that he could hear, but Simon was certain these mice were Lola's low creatures. With the exception of Victor's stolen home, every fairy barrow he'd been to had them, though Simon didn't think Lola knew about hers yet. She'd certainly never mentioned them in his presence, and the mice always vanished whenever she got close. They also disappeared at the sight of Dee, Toothy, and the Black Rider, but they didn't seem to mind Simon at all.

He theorized that was because he was human. Theorizing was all he could do, though, because the mice never talked to him. They looked up whenever he caught them cleaning, but otherwise it was like he didn't exist. Simon was fine with that. He liked being the only one who knew about them. It made him feel special, though it was hard to traverse the room when the tiny cleaners refused to move out of his way. He was picking a path around them to the staircase that led to his bedroom on the second floor when Simon heard a step on his porch.

The mice vanished before the sound finished, their bodies disappearing into the floor so fast, it was like they'd gone straight through the boards. Simon was still blinking at the now-empty room when he heard the bells jingle, and a familiar brooding figure stepped through his front door.

Simon shook his head with a sigh, crossing his arms as he turned to glower at the man whose grimy motorcycle boots were leaving a trail of dirt across his freshly cleaned floor.

"What happened to you?"

The Black Rider shook his cracked helmet and closed the door behind him with a *thump*. It wasn't a loud sound, but the fact that Simon had heard anything at all was a bad sign. Victor had made him work with the Black Rider on several occasions, and the man was normally as silent as a ghost. If he was dragging badly enough to slam doors, things must be even worse than Simon thought.

With one final, longing look at the stairs to his bedroom, Simon turned around and started down the hall toward the clinic's exam rooms.

"Come on, let's get you checked out."

The Rider followed without a word, shadowing Simon down the short hall to the small but cozy patient exam room at the far end.

"How did you get inside?" Simon asked as he pulled a fresh sheet of paper over the padded examination table. "Lola went to sleep thirty minutes ago. Unless you knocked hard enough to wake her up, the barrow should be sealed."

"I didn't wake her up," the Rider said, sounding both tired and insulted that Simon would even suggest such a thing. "Dee let me in."

Simon hadn't realized the double had the power to open the barrow without Lola's permission. The doppelganger had always done her own thing, though, so Simon accepted the explanation with a shrug. He had enough to worry about, because from the slow, pained way the Rider was hauling himself onto the exam table, they were both in for a very long night.

"What happened?" Simon asked again, nodding at the crack that ran down the center of the Rider's mirrored visor like a fault line. "That helmet was brand-new this morning. Did you get into a fight at the border?"

The Rider shook his head. "No one saw me. I just did my normal rounds and came back. I didn't even notice it was broken until I took off Lola's disguise."

Simon scowled deeper and tapped the crack with his fingers. The Rider flinched at the motion, his leather-clad shoulders hunching up as if Simon had poked an open wound.

"It's definitely getting worse," Simon announced, stepping back to look the Rider over. "Decay in the body is to be expected, but the increasing entropy of your physical objects is worrisome."

He didn't even have to mention that this new crack was in the same place as the old one, right where Victor's sword had cut when he'd sliced the Rider's head in half. "I think we should do another exam."

"There's no point," the Rider said, leaning back against the wall with a *thunk*. "I've got a fairy head that's slowly rotting off my body. You already told me it can't be fixed, so what's the point in more prodding?"

"Just because I can't put your head back exactly the way it was doesn't mean the case is hopeless," Simon said stubbornly. "That fairy's been dead since before Victor stapled your soul to it, but you were stable for a decade as the Black Rider."

"Because of the oaths," the Rider said. "Knighthood oaths are absolute. So long as Victor ordered me to stay together, the head *couldn't* collapse. Now that I'm free, though, nothing's left for it to hold onto. You healed my soul and my physical body, but human magic can't bind gossamer. That's why Victor had to get the oaths from Tristan in the first place."

"That doesn't mean they're your only option," Simon told him, crossing his arms over his chest. "I didn't bring you back from the dead just so you could fall apart on me. Your stability under the oaths proved it can be done. We just have to find another way to achieve that same result."

"I didn't come here looking for a cure," the Rider said with a resigned shake of his head. "I just need you to do the thing again."

Simon ground his teeth. "Reaching into your soul to re-knot it around a rapidly decaying lump of gossamer isn't a 'thing.' It's major surgery that takes a toll on both of us, and it's clearly losing effectiveness. I tied you back together just two days ago."

"It still helps," the Black Rider insisted, unzipping the front pocket of his jacket with his bloodstained gloves. "And I need to do something. Look at this."

He passed Simon one of the hand-sized memo pads he used to carry for communication when he'd worked for Victor. Simon didn't know the Rider still bothered with the things now that he had his head on all the time. When he tried to hand the pad back, though, the Rider said, "Turn it over."

Frowning, Simon did as he asked, flipping the pad over to reveal a page covered in writing.

"Whoa," he said, blue eyes widening as he stared at the wall of repeating words written in spidery pencil. "Did you write this?"

"Not that I know of," the Rider replied, tilting his head down until his cracked visor reflected the column of *HELP*s marching down the page. "But that's definitely my handwriting. There was just one at first, but the page was filled by the time I got back to the barrow. Since new words only appeared while I wasn't driving, I'm pretty sure I'm the one writing them, but I have no memory of it."

Simon's frown deepened.

"This isn't the first time my body's done stuff I'm not aware of," the Rider continued. "But it used to happen only when I fought the oaths. I know those are gone because I wouldn't be falling apart if I was still a knight, but I don't have any other way of explaining it." His breathing hitched inside his helmet. "I'm worried that—"

"If Victor was still able to control you, he wouldn't be using it to ask for help," Simon said confidently as he handed back the memo pad. "This has to be something else. Have there been other incidents like this?"

The Rider shook his head as he returned the pad to his pocket. "Just the writing."

Simon crossed his arms and began rapidly tapping his fingers against his coat sleeves. "And I don't suppose you'd be willing to talk to Lola about this?"

"Absolutely not."

"Then I don't know what to tell you," Simon said. "I've already been over every bit of your soul, and it looks fine. As fine as a soul that's been shattered by death and stitched back together with blood magic can be, anyway, but this isn't a problem my magic can fix. Whatever's wrong with you, it's gossamer related. That means you need a fairy, not another patch job."

"I've already talked to Tristan," the Rider said. "But he just told me to have Lola make me a knight again."

Simon arched an eyebrow. "Would that work?"

"Probably," the Rider said, gripping the exam table until the paper ripped. "But I won't. Even if it's Lola, I'll never go back to being a slave. I also don't want to put that kind of burden on her. Monarchs bind their knights for life. Now that Lola's a true fairy, that might be a *very* long time. I don't want her to get stuck with me for all eternity out of pity. She's suffered enough for my sake as it is."

"There, we agree," Simon said, thinking the problem over before shaking his head. "But there's nothing else I can suggest. Unless we stop the decay, anything I do will be temporary at best. Your head is going to keep degrading until it eventually falls apart. When that happens, you'll go from a magical headless Rider to a normal headless man, which means—"

"I'll die," the Rider finished. "I know."

"Then why won't you ask Lola to help?" Simon demanded. "I understand if you don't want to become her knight, but fairy magic is more than just oaths. Lola's pretty new at this, but she's still a fairy monarch *and* a human. If anyone can figure out a way to fix what's wrong with you, it's her."

"That's why I can't ask," the Rider said. "I can't keep running to her for help, especially since all of this is my fault. I'm the one who chose to become Victor's knight, and not just because that was his price for saving my family. I *asked* him to cut off my head and replace it with the fairy's because I wanted his power."

He tilted his helmet toward the floor in shame. "The knighthood oaths can't be spoken unless you mean them, and at the time, I meant every word. When I saw Victor kill the monster none of us could touch, I thought he was a hero. I wanted to be strong like him, to hurt everyone who'd hurt me. I regretted that later just like Tristan said, but I wasn't some innocent little kid like you and Lola. I was sixteen. I knew *exactly* what I was doing."

The Rider lifted his head to look at Simon again. "I don't mind paying for my stupid mistakes. This reckoning's been a long time coming, but I refuse to drag Lola into the mud with me. You know how she is. Even if I tell her I don't want to be her knight, if she knows she could have saved me, she'll blame herself when I die. I won't do that to her."

"Better than dying without telling her what's wrong and leaving her with the guilt that she could have done something."

The Rider turned away. "She'll get over—"

"No, she won't," Simon snapped, glaring him down. "I know Lola better than you ever will, so trust me when I say this is the worst thing you could possibly do to her. The whole time we were captive and she was fighting Victor, she wasn't doing it to bring him down. She was trying to save us, because that's what Lola does. She helps. She *cares*. You might not value that, but I do. If you want to throw your life away as penance for past mistakes, that's your choice, but don't hide it from her like a coward."

"I'm not throwing my life away!" the Rider yelled. "I'm *trying* not to be a burden. You brought me back to life. I'll always be grateful for that, but between you and Tristan, I know there's nothing that can be done. I'm not going to beg Lola for a miracle when she's already killing herself three times a week trying to beat Victor, especially since I know she'll just offer to make me her knight. It's the obvious solution, and like you said, Lola's kind. *Too* kind. She'd take my oaths in a second if she thought it would save me, but I can't give them. Even if it's her, I'm *never* swearing absolute obedience to someone else ever again."

The Rider's body was taut as a wire by the time he finished, and Simon rubbed a hand over his face.

"Let's try this from another angle," he said in the calmest, most measured voice that he could manage. "From the moment I collected your body off the ground, you became my patient. So long as you are in my care, I have an obligation to your well-being and privacy. It might not sound like much, but life with Victor didn't leave me a lot of moral ground to stand on, which means I take the few promises I could keep very seriously. That is why, as your doctor, I won't be telling anyone about your condition, but I also won't be patching you up again until you tell Lola the truth."

The Rider's helmet whipped back around. "Did you hear *nothing* I just—"

"I heard you loud and clear," Simon said. "But those are your feelings, not hers. We've already established that I can't fix what's wrong with you, and I see no reason to keep helping you limp along when you're doing nothing but perpetuating the problem."

"But—"

"Lola has fought tooth and nail for you," Simon snapped. "If you're determined to die and leave her alone, that's on you, but she deserves to know before it happens, and she deserves to hear it from your lips."

"You'd like that, wouldn't you?" the Rider said in the coldest, nastiest voice Simon had ever heard come out of his helmet. "You've always been in love with her. If I die, that just makes it easier for you to—"

He cut off with a choke as Simon grabbed the part of him that was still human and yanked him off the table. He'd entered the Rider's soul so many times now, it wasn't even a struggle to lift

him into the air. But while Simon was heartily ashamed of himself
for losing control, there was something he had to say before he put
this idiot down.

"Listen very carefully," he said through clenched teeth.
"Because I'm only going to say this once. I *do* love Lola. I love her
more than you can possibly understand. If I thought it would save
her pain, I would break your neck and throw your body to the
bottom of Algonquin's lake. The only reason I'm not doing that
right now is because it wouldn't."

He jerked the Rider closer. "During the decade I trained
under Victor, Lola was the only other soul I knew that wasn't him.
How could I not love her? Want her? She was beautiful and kind,
and I was a desperate teenage boy. If you'd come along during
those years, I would have killed you just for looking at her. But I'm
not a teenager anymore. I can think with more than my hormones
now, enough to understand that the only person who gets to say
what Lola wants is Lola."

He took a shuddering breath, easing his control as he
lowered the gasping Rider to the floor. Simon sank down next to
him, digging the heels of his palms into his eye sockets so he
wouldn't have to look at anything as he spoke the truth that hurt
more than any other.

"I know that isn't me. I've been trying to get her attention
for twenty years, but she's only ever seen me as a brother. I'd be
lying if I said that didn't hurt, but just because I can't have what I
want doesn't change what she is to me."

He pulled his hands away to look at his palms, staring at
the tough, creased skin crisscrossed with tiny, pale scars from all
the times he'd cut himself casting Victor's spells. There were a lot
more scars these days, but if Simon squinted, he could almost see
the colorful stick-on bandages Lola used to spin with her own
gossamer to patch him up. They'd looked awful with their badly
drawn cartoon characters, and they hadn't stopped a single drop of

blood, but she'd put them on with love, and Simon had never taken a single one off before it dissolved on its own.

"She's my most precious person," he whispered into his fingers. "The only reason I survived those horrible years with Victor was because she was next to me. I've always told myself I'd do anything, *anything* to make her happy, so if she's decided she likes you, I'm going to do everything in my power to make sure you live up to that. I'm definitely not going to let you die in secret and leave her crying. So if you want any more help from me, you'll go up there and tell her exactly what's going on, because I will let you die a thousand times before I help you break her heart."

He heard the creak of the Rider's leather jacket as the bigger man lowered his head. Sitting this close to him on the exam room floor, Simon could feel how wrong his magic felt. His normally frigid gossamer was warm and sticky, like a dead thing rotting in the sun. Thinking about what that might mean turned his stomach, but Simon stuck to his guns. He was about to offer to call Dee so she could wake Lola up for them when the Rider rose to his feet.

"Thank you for everything you've done for me, Simon," he said, his deep voice as soft as his dying gossamer.

"You're welcome," Simon replied, standing up as well. "Does this mean you're going to tell her what's going on?"

The Rider gave him a long look through his unreadable mirrored visor before leaving without a word, his boots clomping loudly down the wooden hall as he let himself out of Simon's house.

Chapter 4

If there was one part of becoming the Underground King that Lola hadn't been prepared for, it was the dreams.

Given Alberich's obsession with fear and nightmares, she'd braced for the worst, but all her dreams since eating his head had been the normal, nonsensical mishmash of random memories and childhood anxieties. The difference was the *intensity.*

Lola had never understood what Tristan meant when he'd said her dreams were vivid. Things could get pretty real when she was feeding someone, but the rest of the time, Lola felt that her dreams were actually the most normal things about her.

Not anymore. Now that she had her barrow, even something dumb like running late because she'd forgotten how to drive was a 4D cinematic experience. She could feel every bump on the steering wheel of the random wood-paneled station wagon her brain had decided to give her for some reason, taste the hot exhaust of the other cars racing by while she struggled to remember how to work a clutch. Even the soft ticking of the car's old-fashioned analogue clock rang like hammer strikes inside her skull, taunting her with how late she was going to be despite the fact that her sleeping mind couldn't actually tell time.

It was all the usual, stupid, brain-dumpy stuff turned up to a million. No wonder other fairies didn't sleep unless they had to. Dreaming in a barrow was *exhausting.* It reminded her of when she used to feed Tristan, but the knight had never made her go for so long. Lola felt like she'd been spinning a gossamer marathon when she finally pried her eyes open to see Dee sitting on the edge of her bed like an impatient puppy.

"*Finally,*" her copy groaned when she saw Lola blinking. "We were beginning to worry you'd be in there forever!"

Dee looked over her shoulder at Toothy, but Lola's sweet little monster just snuffled and cuddled deeper in the giant pile of pillows Lola had made for her. Seeing she was getting no support there, Dee turned back to the original with a glare.

"How long was I out?" Lola asked, starting to get nervous.

Her double's face grew stricken. "Almost eight hours."

"Dee," Lola said, struggling not to laugh. "You realize eight hours is normal for most people?"

"Not for me!" Dee cried. "I only rest two, three hours a day at *most*. Since I was made to be you, that makes this weird. Also, you normally only sleep six hours a night."

"Which is an unhealthy schedule that I've been trying to change," Lola said, shaking her head in an effort to clear the last of the barrow dreams. Damn crazy things stuck like glue. "Humans need rest, and the human half of me is holding up a lot these days."

That was the understatement of the century. Lola might have gotten Alberich's barrow through digestion, but her human death was the anchor that kept this place rooted. If she reached out to the edges of her barrow, she could feel the Sea of Magic bumping over Fenrir's pit, which was why Lola didn't do that anymore. Homes were supposed to be places of safety, and it was hard to feel safe when you were basically a magical flounder hiding in a hole at the bottom of a sea of chaos. Lola didn't even know where her death's porthole to the Sea of Magic was anymore, and she had no intention of finding out. Like all fairy magic, barrows worked best when you didn't scrutinize them, and since Lola had no idea how the majority of hers was still standing, she made sure to look at it as little as possible.

"Did Valente ever make it back?" she asked as she slid out of bed.

She'd wanted the actual information, but Lola felt like a genius when her double snapped out of her very un-Dee-like fretting.

"Sure did! He knocked about half an hour after you fell asleep, so I changelinged-up and opened the door. He brought you a fried pie!"

Lola smiled. She loved fried pies. She loved even more that Valente knew that and had thought to bring one as his barrow opener, even though it must have been murder finding a fry stand that was open so late. Or maybe it had been early? It was always five o'clock in her barrow, so Lola wasn't sure. She didn't even know what time it was now since gossamer cell phones didn't sync with regular clocks until you took them outside.

She worried about that for a moment before deciding it didn't matter. She needed her sleep, and the time was what it was. She was far more interested in breakfast. Barrow dreaming always left her ravenous, and fried pies tasted almost as good cold as they did hot. Grinning in anticipation, Lola threw her covers back onto her bed and stretched out her arms to get dressed.

At least this part of her life was easier than it used to be. Getting dressed in anything but the most basic basics used to mean reference photos and tons of double-checking, but Lola barely had to think about what she wanted to wear these days. There was no more obsessively tweaking her gossamer to make sure the rainbow jelly that formed her body moved like real fabric. All she had to do was picture what she wanted and her magic did the rest, covering her body in a hot-pink cardigan, a white turtleneck with a fun print of cheeky tropical birds sitting on polka dots, and a pair of broken-in jeans that hugged her like an old friend.

"Oh, that is *nice*," Lola said, rubbing the impossibly soft yarn of her new sleeves against her cheeks as she walked over to open the giant curtains on the floor-to-ceiling windows that formed the north-facing wall of her new bedroom.

When she'd first furnished her barrow so they could live in it, she'd been super-duper careful to make sure everything made sense. The last thing she needed was for the ever-observant Simon to notice her architectural planning was off and accidentally melt the house she'd built for him. She'd thought it'd be a nightmare having real people living inside her gossamer, but managing the barrow was actually easier than passing off a fake car because people expected barrows to be weird.

Once Lola realized her freedom, all the brakes had come off. Her bedroom was Exhibit A. It'd started as just a normal old room on the second floor of her cozy house, but as soon as Lola realized it wasn't going to melt, she'd gone a little extra. Her door still opened into the hallway at the top of the stairs, but the bedroom itself was a penthouse apartment at the top of what had been her favorite Skyways superscraper.

When Lola pulled back the curtain, she was treated to an unimpeded bird's-eye view of the DFZ as she'd loved it best. Everything from the Detroit River in the east to the forested Reclamation Land in the west was spread out before her in an ever-moving urban tapestry. To her left stood the towering Dragon Consulate, surrounded by the flashing wings of the dragons who constantly came and went, and beyond that was the elegant spire of Merlin Tower. There was no Fenrir destruction, no ugly monuments to Victor's ego. She *had* replaced the Canadian side of Lake St. Clair with a wall of enormous white-capped mountains, but otherwise the city looked just like Lola remembered it from the first time Victor had let her go out alone: a shining promise of unimpeded freedom where anything was possible.

Even though she'd done it all herself, it still awed her how much magic she could use now without thinking. An illusion like the window in front of her would have taken everything Lola had back when she was working for Victor, and it still would have only worked from one angle. Making a full gossamer environment that people could actually walk around in was the realm of true fairies, and while Lola still didn't see herself as one of those, she was continually amazed by what she could do. She could've sat up here all day, watching dragons and helicopters fly through the city. Had done so several times, in fact, which was why there was a recliner set up next to Buster's new cat tree in the corner where the giant windows met.

She was tempted to flop into it now. Buster was already snoozing on the seat. It'd be so easy to scoop her chonky boy into her lap and forget all about the stupid man she couldn't kill. That was always the danger of barrows, though, so Lola forced herself to give Buster only three pets before turning away. She was spinning herself a pair of comfy house slippers for the trip down to the kitchen when she felt something punch the wall of her bedroom.

There was no other way to describe it. The barrow was gossamer just like the rest of her, and that had definitely felt like a fist.

"Whoa," Dee said, grabbing onto Toothy, who'd rolled out of her pillow pile into a defensive crouch. "Are you seeing this?"

Lola couldn't unsee it. The floor-to-ceiling windows of her penthouse were bulging inward, stretching out the lovely view of the city like it was printed on the surface of a balloon. It reminded Lola of the time the Black Rider had broken Tristan's highway illusion in the parking lot before they'd gone to Alva's, but this wasn't Valente's doing. She could feel him downstairs in the living room, nowhere near this. But if he wasn't the one pushing…

"Do you think it's Alberich?" Dee whispered, clinging to Lola's arm while Toothy growled beside them.

"Alberich is dead," Lola said firmly, getting a grip on herself.

Holding fast to your truth was even more important inside a barrow than it was outside. Her illusionary bedroom might be bulging, but Lola's core was as strong as ever. Stronger, even, because she knew exactly what she was now, transforming her hand into a clawed fist very much like Toothy's as she ripped the memory of the city aside to reveal the pressure beneath.

Sure enough, it was a troll. Not a bumbling, moss-covered monster like the one she and Valente had faced at Victor's mansion. That troll had been sent by Alva, which meant it was actually one of Morgan's and thus shared the queen's nature-centered aesthetic. This troll had sprung from Alberich, so, naturally, it looked like a nightmare.

The troll towered over Lola's three selves like a mountain of wet, muscular shadows. Its mouth was round and ringed with teeth like a lamprey's, and its multiple eyes were white and blind. Its clawed hands, all five of them, were already curled into fists from where it had been pounding on the penthouse windows that now lay like a shredded movie projection screen at Lola's feet. When Lola raised her own fist in response, though, the creature immediately put up its hands in surrender.

Lola frowned. She was used to seeing trolls down in the lower levels, but this was her part of the barrow. She might only control the top three floors, but inside that space, her rule was absolute. This troll shouldn't even have been able to get here, much less wreck her bedroom.

It must have sneaked in while she was asleep, Lola decided. What better way to make yourself king than by gobbling up the previous ruler while she was dreaming? The troll didn't seem to want to mess with her now that she was awake, but with so many other people in her barrow, Lola wasn't taking any chances. She'd already grabbed the troll's gossamer in an iron fist and started shoving it back toward the depths, turning her head away from the spray of spittle when it roared at her.

"What?" she roared back. "You mad because I'm not on the menu anymore? Go get your breakfast somewhere else!"

The troll bellowed even louder, its claws peeling huge gouges in the flat black stone that had replaced her illusionary city, but it was out of its depth. She had to be wary climbing up from the depths, but they were in her territory now, which was a whole different ball game. Lola was rolling up her sleeves to give the troll a serious thwacking when Toothy tapped her on the back with a gentle claw.

She looked over her shoulder to see her creature and her double staring at her with equally worried looks. "Uh, Lola?" Dee said quietly, tilting her head at the bellowing troll. "I don't think it came here to attack."

Lola rolled her eyes. "Then why did it punch down my window?"

"I think it was trying to get your attention," Dee said, a smile breaking over her face. "Look! It's got something in its mouth."

"How?" Lola asked, squinting through the tangle of the troll's twisted limbs. "Its mouth is an open ring of teeth."

"Not *that* mouth," her doppelganger said, pointing at the top of the thing's hideous face. "There's another, smaller one between the fourth and fifth eyes. Or maybe that's a toothy nose?"

Lola didn't want to know. This was why she didn't go down into the barrow's lower levels unless she had to. She hated the stupid Nightmare King's freaky nightmare monsters. Not that she didn't recognize the unfairness of that given her own origins, but seriously, who had *teeth* in their *nose*?

"Just ease up on the pounding, would you?" Dee pleaded, pulling on Lola's sleeve. "Let's hear it out."

"Trolls can't talk," Lola reminded her, though she did relax the pressure enough that the troll no longer had to cling to the floor with all its claws to keep from being blown to the bottom of the Underground. She was certain it would use the freedom to attack again, but the troll didn't move any closer. It dropped to its knees instead, crouching in front of Lola as it reached up with the smallest of its five arms to dig the thing Dee had spotted out of its nose-mouth.

"What's it doing?" Dee whispered.

"Hopefully not throwing a spit-wad booger at us," Lola muttered, readying her gossamer just in case. "Trolls' fluids are caustic. The one Valente and I fought at Victor's could melt stone with its spit."

"I don't think it's trying to melt us," Dee said, her eyes as wide as they could go. "I think it brought you a gift."

Lola was opening her mouth to ask where in the world her featherbrained copy had gotten *that* idea when the troll finally dislodged the object from its toothed nostril and held it out. The thing was so covered in blackish-green slime, Lola couldn't even make out its shape until the troll used its claws—the same knifelike claws as her own monster, Lola realized with a twitch—to scrape off enough of the goop to reveal the item's true nature.

It was a crown. An enormous circlet the size of a Hula-Hoop made of slimy, yellowed teeth.

"Ew!" Lola said, jerking away.

"Don't be rude," Dee scolded. "You're its king. It's probably just trying to curry your favor."

"No thank you."

"Come on, it's not *that* bad."

Lola gave Dee a flat look, and her other self sighed. "Okay, okay, I admit it does have a bit of an odor, but it's the thought that counts! This is also the first act of goodwill you've gotten from Alberich's court. A slimy, stinky one covered in troll snot, but *still.*"

Lola ground her teeth. The troll was waving the hideous crown at her like a flag, clearly desperate for her to take it. Dee was motioning as well, but Lola's hands stayed glued to her sides. It wasn't that she didn't want to make peace. It'd be fantastic if she could move through the lower levels of the barrow without worrying about something taking a bite out of her. It was just…

"I don't want to touch it," she whispered.

"Why not?" Dee whispered back.

Lola's already clenched fists squeezed tighter. "It smells like him."

"Like who?"

Alberich. The fairy king's musk didn't make her panic like Victor's blood did, but after the desperate fight inside her death, that cloying mix of fear-sweat and predator-breath wasn't a scent Lola was ever going to forget. The same odor was rolling off the crown now, but the troll wasn't giving up. It clawed its way forward on its belly, pushing the crown at Lola like a life preserver.

"You're going to insult it," Dee hissed. "Just take the stupid thing!"

Insulting a troll strong enough to push all the way up here and punch down her window definitely sounded like a bad idea. So, though it went against every instinct she had, Lola forced herself to reach out, using the tips of her fingers to pinch the spiky crown between two massive incisors that still had meat clinging to their roots.

"Thanks."

The troll beamed at her with a hideous happiness and backed away, sliding its body along the ground in some kind of slither-bow. Lola nodded in acknowledgement, but most of her attention was focused on fighting not to throw up.

The moment she'd touched the slimy crown, Alberich's laughter had echoed in her head. She hadn't heard a peep from the dead king since she'd eaten him. His memories still bubbled up occasionally, especially if Morgan was around, but otherwise he'd seemed well and truly dead. Holding the crown, though, Lola suddenly felt like he was standing right behind her, watching her with that mocking smile on his hateful, boyish face.

The sensation was enough to cover her gossamer body in a very human cold sweat. Fortunately, Toothy's claw was still on her elbow, reminding her to keep it together until the troll had slithered back into the dark hole from whence it came.

The moment it was gone, Lola threw the crown away. Dee squawked when she hurled it, then squawked again as the giant circle hit the ground and shattered into hundreds of individual teeth. Lola was surprised that it broke so easily, but she wasn't mad in the slightest. She'd already swept the teeth away with her gossamer, bundling up the whole mess and shoving it down into the barrow's depths where she wouldn't have to hear Alberich laughing at her from beyond the grave.

"What'd you do that for?" Dee demanded, throwing out her hands after the vanished teeth. "Now we can't put it back together!"

"Good," Lola said, restoring her penthouse windows with another sweep of her hand. "I don't want to put it back together. Now, let's get moving. Victor still needs to die, and we've lost enough time as it is."

Grumbling about wasted gifts, Dee tromped out of the bedroom. Lola went next with Toothy bringing up the rear, the three of them sticking tight together as they made their way down to the living room where Simon and Valente were waiting in utter silence.

Very, very uncomfortable silence.

"Looks like I'm the last one up," Lola said, forgetting all about the troll as she struggled to push through the tension that filled the room. "Did I miss breakfast?"

The Rider shook his cracked helmet and pointed at the propped-open kitchen door, where Lola could see the bag of fried pies Dee had mentioned earlier sitting on the island.

She ran over at once, shoving one of the fried dough pouches straight into her mouth. The pastry was cold and slightly stale from sitting out all night, but Lola still rolled her eyes back in bliss. She ate two more in rapid succession, stuffing herself until the ravenous hunger from the barrow dream began to fade. Only when she had a solid cushion of carbs to fuel her through whatever drama was going on in the other room did Lola finally turn around.

"Okay," she said, looking back and forth between the silent men. "What happened?"

"Nothing important," Valente said, his unnaturally smooth voice tight with suppressed anger. "Simon and I had a disagreement, but that doesn't change what needs to be done. I was just asking him to explain the plan you two came up with last night again."

"What part didn't you understand?" Lola asked, reaching back to snag another pie.

"All of it," Valente said, turning his mirrored helmet toward her. "Hopefully you can explain it better, because what he just told me sounds like suicide."

"Not if we do it safely," Simon said in the flat tone of someone who'd already made this point many, *many* times.

"You want to kidnap a Paladin," the Rider snapped. "There is no safe way to do that."

He turned back to Lola, clearly expecting her to agree, which she kind of did. She'd had the exact same reaction yesterday before Simon talked her around.

"It's the only thing left that we haven't tried," she said, walking over to lean against Toothy, who'd plopped down in her usual spot under the window. "After the Hero's Hall failure, I think it's pretty clear that we can't beat Victor by ourselves. Whatever he's become, it can't be hurt by physical means. That's where the Paladins come in."

"The magic Victor uses to perform his miracles is the same blood magic he's been doing all his life," Simon picked up. "And blood mages are precisely what Paladin magic was developed to kill. They're the only other humans Victor fears."

"He *used* to fear them," Valente said, crossing his arms. "That doesn't necessarily mean anything now."

"I think it does," Simon argued, fixing the Rider with a cold stare made even worse by Victor's blue eyes. "Victor hated living in the DFZ. He always said it was filthy and unorganized, but he put up with it because the DFZ was the only city in the world that didn't allow Paladins. He's *still* there even now that he's the Hero, and I bet you it's for the same reason."

"If he's so scared, why haven't the Paladins gone after him yet?" Valente demanded. "You think any of this is news to me? I was the one Victor ordered to keep the Paladins off him. I've fought them plenty of times, enough to know they're not the sort who hold back. But the Hero's been living it up as the world's blood mage for almost four months, and they're still twiddling their thumbs, same as the rest of the world. If they were really the hard counter to blood magic you say they are, why haven't they taken him down?"

"I've been wondering the same thing," Simon said, taking his phone out of the pocket of his white jacket and setting it flat on the coffee table. He tapped the screen next, turning on the AR projector to throw a glowing, 3D map of the greater Detroit area into the air.

"The Paladins have a base right next to the American forces here," he said, pointing at the cluster of red dots on the highway just north of Toledo. "According to news reports, they've brought in their entire order, which is appropriate considering they'll be fighting the most powerful blood mage in human history. What I don't understand is why they're still sitting around in their camp."

His finger moved to a much larger circle marked with a red, white, and blue flag. "It makes sense that the Americans are dragging their feet. Even with the president salivating over a chance to bring Detroit back into the union, a ground invasion against a neighbor is a huge thing. There are all kinds of treaties and red tape in their way, not to mention the Dragon of Detroit's objections. Unlike the US, though, the Paladins aren't a country. They're a special branch of the United Nations whose only mission is the eradication of blood mages. Victor's rise is exactly the sort of thing they were founded to prevent. They should have been storming the DFZ from the moment he went public, so why aren't they moving?"

"I don't know," Valente said.

Simon shook his head. "Me neither, but *something* is clearly holding them back. Since they're still a government agency, I'm betting it's a legal matter. International treaties, justification for invasion, that sort of thing. But all of that goes out the window if the Hero attacks them first, so here's my plan."

He pointed at the Paladins' base again. "We're going to kidnap a member of their order and pin the blame on Victor. Once one of their own is at the blood mage's mercy, no law in the world will hold them back. All we have to do then is make sure they can get to him, and they'll take Victor down for us."

He finished with a confident smile, but the Rider's shoulders were hunched.

"You really think it'll be that easy?"

"Nothing about this is going to be easy," Simon assured him. "But unlike blowing up his PR events, cutting off his head, or any of our other assassination attempts, this is something we haven't tried before, which means it still has a chance of working."

Valente sighed inside his helmet. "I see your point," he said at last, turning toward Lola. "Who's doing the kidnapping?"

"You, me, and Toothy," Lola said. "Simon can't go for obvious reasons, but the three of us are mostly gossamer. That should make it easy to slip through security, and it's not as if we're actually going to kill anyone. We're just going to nab a Paladin and take them on a little trip. Once the rest of the order gets the wrong idea, we'll release our catch into Victor's tower and let them do their job."

Valente huffed again. But while he didn't seem happy with the plan, he must have given up on fighting it, because all he said was, "Do we have a specific target, or are we just grabbing the first Paladin we see?"

"Of *course* we have a target," Simon said, tapping his phone again to bring up a picture of an elderly man with an eye patch standing in front of a podium. "This is Stefan Hansen. He used to be one of their commanders, but age and injuries took him off the front lines, so now he works as the Paladins' public spokesman."

"I see," Valente said, reaching out to turn the picture floating above Simon's phone. "You're grabbing someone they can't hide."

"He won't be a soft target," Simon warned. "No Paladin is. But he should be easier to handle than their active members, and his public appearance schedule means he's easy to find."

"He's actually giving a press conference this evening," Lola picked up. "Our plan is to grab him on the way to the venue, which is just outside the US's defensive perimeter. There should be a gap between the time he leaves the militarized zone and the time he gets on stage when he'll only be guarded by a security detail. That's our window."

"Makes sense," Valente said. "When do we leave?"

Lola was about to say they had plenty of time when she noticed the clock at the bottom of Simon's AR projection. The one from his actual, real, non-gossamer smartphone that still told the actual time, which was a lot later than she'd realized.

"Looks like we go right now," she said, cramming the last of her pie into her mouth before turning to point her finger at Dee, who'd already changed into a spy-movie catsuit. "You're staying here."

"Awww," her double groaned. "But I want to go on the heist!"

Lola was unmoved. "It's a kidnapping, not a heist, and someone has to stay behind and make sure Simon…"

"What about me?" Simon asked as she trailed off.

Lola bit her lip. She'd been about to say *Make sure Simon doesn't get eaten by a troll,* but that joke was no longer funny after this morning. Seeing a troll on the upper levels, even if it was just trying to bring her a present, had shaken her confidence hard. If she put the idea in Simon's head that being eaten was a possibility, he'd start worrying about it, which—due to the belief-based nature of gossamer—meant it might actually happen. All the more reason to keep her big mouth shut, and to always leave a piece of herself behind to make sure the control she *did* have never slacked.

"All right, all right, I'll stay," Dee said, following Lola's logic through their shared magic. "But you'd better bring me back something good."

Lola had no idea what they could bring back from a camp of stoic blood-mage slayers that would count as "good," but she promised to bring back a present as she motioned for Toothy and Valente to follow her to the back door that led to her low roads.

Chapter 5

Lola's low road collection wasn't as numerous or wide-ranging as Tristan's, but it was *much* better organized.

Instead of a terrifying hallway full of unmarked doors, she'd turned the half of her backyard that wasn't being used for Simon's house into an outdoor transportation hub. As soon as she stepped out of the kitchen onto the thick grass, Lola had her choice of several neat flagstone paths, each leading to a different style of door. There were front doors and interior doors and patio doors and shopping center doors with posters for weekly specials covering the glass.

She'd done her best to make each one look as different—and as close to the matching door they led to—as possible. She'd also added signage. Each freestanding door had a National Park Service-style wooden sign hammered into the grass beside it detailing where the road went, when she'd made it, and why.

Tristan had rolled his eyes at the whole concept and accused her of being a micromanager, but Lola found the organization comforting. It made her feel more in control, and she liked the Alice in Wonderland vibe of all the different doors standing out in the sunshine like wickets. She just wished she had more.

Tristan hadn't been kidding when he'd said low roads were his specialty. He typically had multiple hallways going at the same time, any one of which could support up to a dozen doors going all over the planet, and those were just the ones he'd let her see. Lola suspected he had another secret set just for court business, which, now that she could make her own low roads, struck her as insane. He was just a knight. Lola was a *king*, and her high score so far was ten, all of which went to the DFZ.

At least that last part wasn't her magic's fault. For a low road to work, you had to believe in where you were going, and that was hard to pull off for places you hadn't personally been. As an ancient and eccentric fairy, Tristan had roved all over the world. Other than the occasional trip across the bridge to Canada and that one time Victor had taken her and Simon to the Grand Canyon, Lola had never left the DFZ, which severely limited her travel choices.

It wasn't all bad. Since both ends of her roads were local, there was no need for crazy hallways. Her low roads could be traveled in the few inches it took to form a believable doorframe. She could also open them on the fly so long as she was going back to her barrow and one of her ten slots was open.

She still wasn't as fast as Tristan, who could pull a perfect white-painted door out of a crack in the sidewalk with a snap of his fingers, but it worked well enough. Since she'd done nothing but try to kill Victor for the past three months, and he never left the city, the fact that she could only make local low roads hadn't been a problem yet. Now, though, Lola was seriously wishing she'd taken a trip through Ohio at least once, because the closest she could get them to their target was a 7-Eleven on Factory Row.

Victor's takeover of the DFZ had changed the city down to its foundations, but even he hadn't messed with the giant industrial park that spanned the DFZ's southwestern border. The massive automated factories had been there since Algonquin's time, pumping out hardware components for the mana-contact technology that had made the city so rich in the first place.

Ironically, given her hatred of all things human, the Spirit of the Great Lakes was the one who'd invented the mana-contact chips that allowed human magic to integrate with phones, cars, and everything else, kicking off the AR revolution that was still rolling nearly a century later. But while everything else from Algonquin's time had been purged from the city ages ago, the DFZ had never touched her factories. Lola wasn't sure if that was because shutting down the region's oldest economic engines went against the Living City's capitalist nature or if Algonquin had simply bribed her to let the factories stay, but she was happy about it now. Being surrounded by a massive industrial hellscape full of automated assembly lines meant there was no one to disbelieve when she walked up to the sliding door that served as her generic entrance to all things supermarket and planted her feet on the faded welcome mat.

The barrow leaped to meet her. Up here in the area she controlled, the magic was eager and obliging. It jumped as soon as she flicked her fingers, instantly disconnecting the previous low road from the vacant downtown corner market she'd used to get everyone in position for their failed cathedral raid. For a moment, Lola could feel the intense, terrifying nothingness the low roads ran through yawning beneath her. Then the connection snapped back into place, linking the barrow to a location Lola was much more comfortable with.

When the automatic door slid open with a welcoming *bing* a second later, she was staring at the familiar red tile floors, gray metal shelves, and wall-to-wall advertisement-covered windows of a freestanding convenience store. Like most businesses left over from the pre-Hero days, the shop was dark and dusty, though that wasn't entirely Victor's fault this time. This place hadn't done good business even before the Hero's takeover reduced the city's population, probably because it was in the worst location Lola had ever seen.

Despite their giant size, the factories of Factory Row only employed a dozen people at a time, most of whom worked remotely. That left little demand for snacks, soda, beer, toiletries, and other convenience-store staples. The only reason Lola knew about this place was because it had the only Slurpee machine in town that still carried the discontinued Kiwi Kooler flavor.

She'd loved that neon-green sludge back when she was Victor's monster. The machine was still over in the corner, its motionless tanks full of melted liquid so artificially colored that Lola could tell the flavors even in the dark. Seeing it hit her with a pang of nostalgia for her lost city, but she kept herself on target, creeping over to the tinted windows to check the empty parking lot that surrounded the shuttered convenience store like a black ocean.

"All clear."

Back in the sunny garden, Toothy ducked her huge head to squeeze her furry body through the low road's automated door. She couldn't straighten to her full height without knocking the panels out of the drop ceiling, so she fell onto all fours and wedged herself between the dusty metal shelves full of expired jars of cheese dip to make room for Valente.

As usual these days, he came through like he couldn't wait to get back out, his feet landing on the plastic welcome mat with a *thump.* The sound was hardly noticeable even in the empty store, but for the normally silent Rider, it was practically a stomp. It was definitely loud enough to make Lola wince as Valente joined her at the dusty window.

"How far are we from the border?"

"Half a mile," Lola answered apologetically. "Sorry it's a hike, but this was the closest location I had on tap. Technically, I could have made a door into the magical prison you rescued me from during our last incident with the Paladins, but coming out inside a jail cell didn't seem like a great idea."

"I don't mind a little walking," Valente said, stepping back from the windows. "Let's get this over with."

Lola turned away so he wouldn't see her disappointment. She knew he wasn't thrilled with their plan, but she hadn't expected him to be like this. Valente was normally super supportive. It was one of the reasons she'd liked him even back at the beginning when she'd still thought the Black Rider was a murderous urban legend. He'd been all-in on her other plans to kill Victor even when they'd gotten crazy, but he'd seemed so distant recently. It felt like they'd gone back to being mistrustful strangers, and Lola hated it.

"Listen," she said before she lost her nerve. "I'm really sorry about what I said yesterday. I never meant to put you on the spot like—"

"I'm not mad at you," he interrupted, his cracked visor turned determinedly toward the empty parking lot outside. "I just want to get this done."

And get away from you, Lola's brain added unhelpfully.

She quashed the thought. She and Simon had just bullied Valente into a plan he thought was reckless and stupid. Of *course* he wouldn't be peppy about it.

She should be happy he'd agreed to come at all, given that they were going up against the people who'd burned him to ash the last time they'd faced off. Valente hadn't been wearing his head that time, so Lola was sure it'd be a different story now, but there was no denying this was much riskier for him than it was for her and Toothy. If things went south, Lola and her creature would just wake up back in her barrow. Valente might *actually* die, which made this a much bigger ask for him. He'd still come along, though, so Lola told her insecurities to shove it and walked back over to Toothy, who was still crouching between the shelves.

"Why did you bring her again?" Valente asked as Lola helped her creature navigate the minefield of spilled chip bags so she could join them at the convenience store's front door. "I thought the whole point of kidnapping a desk-job Paladin was that we wouldn't have to deal with a serious fight."

"Yeah, but we still have to make them think it was Victor," Lola said, keeping a firm hold on Toothy's fur to make sure she knew she was also part of this conversation, even though she couldn't speak. "The Paladins we fought in the parking lot saw me turn into Toothy after you… you know. Point is, they think she's Victor's monster. If she's the one who gets seen grabbing their guy, they'll assume she's doing it on Victor's orders, and unlike you and Simon, she's not supposed to be dead."

The Rider's face was impossible to read behind his cracked helmet, but Lola got the feeling he didn't think much of that plan. He didn't say anything, though. He just hit the button to unlock the half of the shop's automatic doors that wasn't currently a low road and got to work on the security cage that protected the front of the shuttered store from looters. By the time he'd rolled the wall of metal netting back onto its spool, Lola had Toothy in position.

"Okie-dokie," she said when they were all standing in a knot by the now-functional door. "Costume time."

"How *will* we be sneaking over the border?" Valente asked. "Simon said you had a plan, but he was light on the details."

"Because I didn't tell him any," Lola said, grabbing a huge handful of gossamer from her now-infinite reserves. "I love Simon, but fairy magic works on belief, and he can get pretty overthink-y. I learned a long time ago not to tell him what I was planning when it came to stuff like this, because whenever I did, he'd start nitpicking every little inconsistency and melt my gossamer to soup. These days, we just trust each other to do our jobs and leave the details out."

"These seem like pretty important details to leave out," Valente said, nodding at the white glare of the security floodlights, which shone clearly over the tops of the factories despite the bright winter afternoon. "Ever since Victor came to power, the US has turned their border with the DFZ into the most militarized zone on the planet. The National Guard has blockades and checkpoints set up on every bit of pavement, and I'm sure they've got drones watching the rooftops as well. I know your magic's gotten sturdier since you became a monarch, but that's a lot of scrutiny."

"Not if we stay below their notice," Lola said smugly as she placed her hand on top of the crouching Toothy's head. "Observe."

Her creature grunted in surprise as magic exploded from Lola's fingertips, covering Toothy's huge furry body in a blanket of sparkling rainbow gossamer. Its raw form lasted only a second before the magic congealed, transforming Lola's twelve-foot-tall other self into a large bird with a long black neck, a round brown body, black webbed feet, and a white-marked head whose beady black eyes were level with Lola's waist.

"Ta-daaa!" she said, stepping back.

"Lola," Valente said, clearly trying his best to keep an open mind. "That's a goose."

"A Canadian goose," Lola said proudly, tightening her magic against his disbelief. "Very common around the lakes this time of year and protected by both the North American Migratory Bird Act and the Spirit of the Great Lakes as one of her precious native species."

"So?"

"*So?*" she cried indignantly. "Have you *met* a goose? They're aggressive, foul-tempered, vicious little monsters." She grinned at her creation with wicked delight. "Trust me, none of those soldiers are going to want to mess with us when we're dressed like this."

"I get it," Valente said, finally sounding impressed. "Even if they're checking everything that moves, no one pays attention to birds. We can just fly over the border."

Lola winced. "Not exactly," she said, placing her hand on the empty space high above the goose's head, the area that was actually Toothy's shoulder. "Since you two aren't changelings, I can't alter your physical shape. The goose is just a disguise, so unless you can already fly on your own, it won't give you wings. Honestly, though, that's a good thing. I've turned into birds before, and let me tell you, flying isn't nearly as easy as they make it look. Fortunately for us, geese can also walk, so we're going to *waddle* past the checkpoints!"

"Waddle?" the Rider repeated, sounding far less impressed.

Lola put her fists on her hips. "If you've got a better idea, I'm all ears."

Valente's black-clad shoulders slumped with a sigh. For a moment, he just looked exhausted. Then he spread his arms, inviting her to do her worst.

Lola did so with great care. As tough as she knew the Rider was, Valente's gossamer had been weird since he'd gotten free of Victor. He used to feel like an ice sculpture: hard, unyielding, and freezing cold. Recently, though, his magic had lost nearly all of its chill. He'd also stopped eating, or at least he wasn't eating *her* dreams. Both possibilities worried Lola greatly, but he snapped at her every time she asked about it, so she'd learned to keep her mouth shut. He felt almost warm this time, though, which was alarming enough for her to take a risk.

"Hey," she said as she gently wove the illusion around him. "Are you doing all right? Your magic feels—"

"It's nothing you need to worry about."

Lola winced. The weird warming must not have affected all of him, because his voice was as cold as a knife in snow. But while Lola knew he was telling the truth, since his fairy head couldn't lie, "It's nothing you need to worry about" was a long way from "I'm fine."

"I know this isn't a great time," she said, biting her lip. "But your magic feels *really* different. If it's because you're free of Victor, that's great and I'm super happy for you, but I wish you'd tell me. I'm not trying to be pushy. It's just..."

She paused, brain scrambling for a safe way to end that sentence. Now was absolutely *not* a good time, especially so close on the heels of yesterday's disaster, but the way his normally icy magic was practically melting under her fingers was really freaking her out. She'd been waiting three months for a good time to say this and never found one, which probably meant it didn't exist. Saying nothing felt even worse, though, so Lola sucked it up and went for it.

"You're important to me," she blurted. "I know what happened between us that night was a one-time thing, but…"

She trailed off, staring hard at the rainbow magic she was still working between her hands. "You're the only person ever who saw the real me and didn't flinch. When I was collapsing, you helped me hold together. When Victor ordered you to hunt me down, you did everything you could to undermine him. I know how hard that was, but you never turned on me, no matter what he did. I can't say how much that means, so if there's anything I can do to help you now, anything at all, all you have to do is say the word."

That was much more than she'd intended to confess, but when Lola glanced up to see how he'd taken it, the Rider was looking pointedly away.

"You don't owe me anything."

"It's not about owing," Lola snapped, angry that he didn't already know that. "Unlike Victor, I don't track debts. I want to help because you're *you*. Again, I'm super sorry I made things awkward yesterday by asking you out to dinner. It's fine that you said no, really. I don't hold it against you, and I *definitely* don't want it to be the reason you push me away."

She reached through her building magic to lay her hands on the leather of his chest. "*Please*, Valente. I know something's wrong. You don't even have to tell me what it is if you don't want, just let me help. Let me—"

"No."

The word came out of him like a bullet. It was so sudden, Lola actually flinched. Valente used the opportunity to step away, putting a foot of distance between himself and her drooping fingers.

"I'm not upset that you asked me to dinner," he said in a measured voice that told Lola he was picking his words very, very carefully. "I didn't mean to hurt your feelings—"

"This isn't about my feelings," Lola said, furious with herself that it kind of had been. She'd gotten so tied up in her own sense of rejection, she hadn't realized how dilapidated the Rider was looking, and not just his magic. His body was also in tatters. She could feel the rough edges through the gossamer she'd wrapped around him. Something was *definitely* wrong, but when Lola opened her mouth to say so, the Rider cut her off.

"I don't want your help."

"But—"

"I can't keep being your responsibility," he said in an icy voice. "I know you mean well. You always do, but this isn't something you can fix. Now let's get back to work. This plan doesn't have a big window."

There was so much Lola wanted to say to that. She wanted to yell at him that there was nothing wrong with asking for help when you needed it and he was being stupid for not telling her what was going on. He was the one who'd done the impossible and killed Orlando because she'd asked him not to die. Didn't he know that cut both ways? That she could also move the world for him if that was what it took? What was the point of having all this gossamer if he didn't let her use it for what mattered most?

But while she was screaming on the inside, Lola didn't say any of that. She didn't know what the right move was in this situation, but she was certain that pushing would only make things worse, and Valente had a point about the timing. Geese weren't exactly speed walkers, and they only had an hour to get into position before the Paladins left for the press conference. If they were going to make this risk pay off, they couldn't dawdle here having arguments that went nowhere.

It wasn't as if he wouldn't be coming back to her barrow later, so Lola forced herself to let it go, covering Valente in an extra-thick coating of gossamer until his goose was a perfect match for Toothy's. She did herself last, squishing her body down and lengthening her neck until they were three geese standing in a convenience store.

At least her frustration made it easy to stay in character. Lola was a feathery ball of pure cussedness as she led the way out the door, slamming her webbed feet down like mallets as she began the long waddle across the empty parking lot, completely beneath the notice of the flocks of US Army surveillance drones whizzing overhead.

~~~

Valente had never been happier that geese couldn't talk.

It took an agonizingly long time for the three of them to waddle across the heavily fortified border. Even though he still had his own legs beneath Lola's gossamer, Valente had to keep his walk slow enough that the goose's feet wouldn't scamper at an unbelievable pace and break the illusion. This kept them moving at a crawl, but other than taking forever, Lola's plan worked perfectly.

In the decades since the DFZ had become its own political entity, the US government had torn up all the surface streets that used to connect Detroit to the rest of America, in a desperate effort to force people to use the official immigration checkpoints. Since this flew in the face of everything Detroit Free Zone stood for, the Living City had always moved new roads in as fast as her neighbor could tear them down. That had stopped like everything else when Victor took over. But while all the vehicle routes were
~~~

locked down, that didn't matter to pedestrians, and it especially didn't matter to birds. Thanks to Lola's cleverness, they were able to walk right under the checkpoint booms, and the few soldiers who did try to get in their way jumped right back out of it when Lola hissed at them with her toothed beak.

It wasn't acting. Valente could feel her anger seething through her magic, and he didn't begrudge her a bit of it. He'd be mad, too, if she'd given him the brush-off he'd used on her, but his mind was made up. If anything, what Lola had said in the convenience store had only dug his heels in deeper. He was now certain that she wouldn't hesitate to make him her knight if she knew what was happening, which meant he'd have to turn her down. He'd have to look her in the face and tell her he'd rather die than bow his head to another king, even if it was her.

For all his convictions, Valente wasn't sure he could do that. He'd sworn up and down that he'd never sell his soul again, but this was Lola. Unless his oaths directly forbade it, he'd never been able to deny her anything. He'd barely been able to give her the brush-off just now without choking. If she said she wanted to save him, Valente knew he'd cave, and then they'd be stuck in the exact position he'd sworn never to put them in.

That was the crux of all his problems. He'd told Simon he didn't want Lola to blame herself for his death, and that was true, but not as true as his cowardice. Valente couldn't tell Lola the truth because he knew he wouldn't be strong enough to say no when Lola did what she always did.

Even now, despite everything, he was desperate to talk to her. He'd have given an arm to go out to dinner or breakfast or wherever else she wanted just so he could spend more time with her before the end. Even at the start when she'd treated him like a monster, there'd never been anyone's company he wanted more than hers. If she held out her hand, Valente wouldn't be able to stop himself from taking it, and since that would doom her as much as him, the best thing for everyone was for him to stay away.

It was a bitter, bitter pill to swallow, but at least the bitterness made it easy to play his part. Valente was a fantastically ornery goose, puffing out his chest and hissing at anything that got close as the three of them waddled their way across the dead grass to the US side of the border.

As soon as they stepped out of the DFZ, the city's famous hyper-dense urbanization collapsed into American suburban sprawl. The roads became enormous asphalt arteries that peeled off the highway into strips of fast-food chains and big-box retail surrounded by acres of parking packed with military hardware. Officially, the tanks were there to ensure the protection of American territory, but Valente knew an invasion when he saw one. The US was *definitely* looking to use this opportunity to retake Detroit, but despite the convoys that constantly rolled by, the militarized zone actually worked in their favor. All of the armored vehicles, cameras, and cannons were pointed at the DFZ, leaving no one to notice three angry geese waddling down the highway toward the spot Simon had selected for their ambush.

He'd made a good choice. The press area where their target was scheduled to appear was in a parking lot on the southern side of the militarized zone. To reach it, the Paladins would have to drive down I-75 through a dense retail area that included an outlet mall. To prevent a traffic nightmare, the highway had been slightly elevated at this point so that the mall traffic could flow beneath it, meaning that, to reach their destination, the Paladin convoy was going to have to cross a bridge.

Simon was clearly not the only person who'd recognized this strategic weak point. The mall bridge had a full Humvee of soldiers milling beneath it to make sure no one planted any bombs. Again, though, no one looked at the geese. Lola, Valente, and Toothy waddled right past the bored soldiers and up the graveled slope toward the narrow point where the bridge reconnected with the ground. Once they were deep in the shadows, it was easy for the Black Rider to wrap his magic around the soldiers' heads, suffocating the entire unit from behind without even getting out of costume.

"Good job," Lola said as she dropped their disguises. "Our target should be driving over our heads at some point in the next ten minutes. Simon reviewed all the news footage he could find, and he says the Paladins never leave their camp in anything less than a convoy. That means we'll be dealing with at least three armored SUVs. I thought about nabbing all of them to cover our bases, but our target's probably going to be in the middle car, so I'll just grab that one."

"You're planning to steal the *entire* SUV?" Valente asked as he grabbed the nearest unconscious soldier by his boots and started dragging him over to the drainage ditch.

"Toothy can do it," Lola said confidently. "Especially here." She pointed at the highway's cement underbelly running over their heads. "Lurking under bridges is a fairy classic. I'll get her good and big, and then she'll come up from the underside like a bridge troll. We'll put on a big show to make sure the Paladins realize it's the same monster from before. Once they've got the message, Toothy will grab the middle SUV and shove it down the low road I'm about to make."

Valente frowned. "How are you going to fit a car through a door?"

"Garage doors are still doors," Lola reminded him. "I actually already installed the exit in my garage last night while Simon and I were planning. All I've got to do is set up the entrance on this side, and we're good to go."

"You're still talking about shoving an entire SUV full of angry, armed Paladins into your barrow," Valente said as he tossed the last soldier into the ditch. "What's your plan after you get them in?"

She chuckled. "That's the easy part. Let's just say I have a lot more resources for dealing with murderous zealots in my own home than I do out here. All I need you to do is guard my back while I make the door. A patrol at the wrong time could still wreck this whole thing. Once I get the road open, though, your job is done. You can go right through the new door back to the barrow and leave the rest to Toothy and me."

Valente scowled behind his helmet. "You want me to leave you here?"

"It's the safest way," Lola said with a shrug. "If we mess this up, the worst thing that happens to us is a hike through my barrow. If the Paladins see you, though, they'll go for the kill, and since you're wearing your head, they might just get it."

Her voice grew quiet as she turned to focus on the gossamer garage door she was lifting out of the bridge's shadows. "I wouldn't have bothered you at all if I hadn't needed someone who could knock people out quietly and whose magic doesn't melt when folks look at you the wrong way, but we're almost done. As soon as I get this door open, you're free to go."

She nearly had it up already. The industrial metal garage door was already standing implausibly in the middle of the road. When Lola wrapped her hand around the handle at the bottom, the small rectangular windows lit up bright white as the door connected to the sprawling parking area beneath her barrow where she kept all her cars. He got a glimpse of her lovely smile when she saw her success, but when she started rolling the new low road open, Valente touched her shoulder.

"I think I should do it."

"It's fine," she said, throwing the garage door open with a bang. "It's not as heavy as it looks."

"I wasn't talking about the door," Valente said, craning his neck back to look at the brightly lit highway above their heads as the plan formed in his mind. "I think I should be the one to grab the Paladin."

She looked absolutely horrified. "Why would you want to do that?"

"Because it makes sense," he insisted. "The whole point of this plan is to force the Paladins to fight Victor, but I've faced lots of Paladins before the ones I fought with you. They attack anything associated with blood magic, and they hate Victor's guts in particular. If they haven't taken action against him yet, something huge must be holding them back, and I don't know if Toothy will be big enough to break that."

"Why not?" Lola demanded. "The Paladins saw me turn into her right before they arrested me for being one of Victor's blood mages. She's as good as a smoking gun."

Valente turned his cracked visor back toward her. "Not as good as me."

Lola stared at him in shock for a second, and then her lovely face screwed up in fury. "Are you out of your mind?" she yelled. "You can't let them see you! Have you forgotten you're supposed to be dead?"

"That's exactly why I'm perfect for this," he argued. "There's been a lot of confusion about fairies in the last few months, but even back before Fenrir wrecked the city, the Paladins knew I worked for Victor."

"But—"

"Whether they recognize her or not, Toothy is obviously a fairy creation," Valente reminded her. "If she's the one who makes the grab, it'll be easy for Victor to claim the fairies are setting him up. But if the Paladins see me up there, there's nothing he can say. He's been trying to claim I was in league with the fairies since he killed me, but the Paladins know better. They *know* I work for

Victor, because I'm the one he sent to stop them. If I come back from the dead and attack them now, there'll be no question in their minds that Victor's the one behind it."

"That doesn't make it a good idea," Lola argued, her voice shaking as she grabbed his arm. "This whole area is under military surveillance. We got this far because we were geese, but if you go up there and start punching cars, there's no way we can stop word from getting back to Victor that you're alive. He'll hunt you down!"

"Not if this works," Valente said. "You and Simon both believe that the Paladins are the only hope we have left of killing Victor. If that's really true, then I think it's worth the risk to make sure they do their job."

"Yeah, but..." Her voice faded as she looked at him with so much fear it broke his heart. "You could *die.* The Paladins turned you to ash last time, and that was only three of them. I know you're a lot more powerful with your head, but there's going to be an entire security convoy up there, and Victor will be even worse. He can't have you coming back from the dead after your public execution. If he finds out you're alive, he'll stop at nothing to—"

"I don't care," Valente said, pulling out of her grasp. "I *want* Victor to see me. I want him to look at the wave of Paladins crashing into his plans and know that I'm the one who sent them. I want him to know he failed."

"I get that," Lola said, biting her lip. "Believe me, I understand exactly how you feel, but this is *really* dangerous."

"Doesn't matter," Valente said, summoning his silent motorcycle for the first time in weeks. "I'm doing it."

Lola threw up her hands in frustration. Valente knew he was being unreasonable, but he couldn't explain his actual logic without telling her the truth.

He was out of time. Even if Simon had been willing to keep patching him up, Valente knew the end was near. He could feel the rot in every part of his body now. The only reason he'd objected to Simon's plan was because Paladins were insanely dangerous and he didn't want Lola anywhere near them, but his own life was a different story. Unlike her, he was already as good as dead. With this, though, he didn't have to be out.

Valente's gloved hands clenched around the familiar handles of his bike. If the Paladins were the weapon, then he was determined to be the one who swung them at Victor's face. It wouldn't be as satisfying as killing his former master himself, but if he could get his vengeance and give Lola a world without Victor, that was good enough. It also helped that, if he died fighting the Paladins, he'd be spared the impossible choice of letting Lola save him. He was sure she'd still feel guilty, but a clean death in battle was much less messy than turning down knighthood. Soldiers died in war all the time. It was simple, easy. It was also as good as he was going to get.

Decision made, Valente hopped onto his bike before Lola could stop him, yelling over his shoulder at her to have the low road ready. He was about to send her a Paladin.

She yelled something back, but Valente didn't wait to hear it. He didn't have the strength left to keep pushing her away. He was going to fall apart soon no matter what he did, so Valente threw the last of his magic into making sure his final hurrah counted, gunning his silent bike up the highway exit ramp to the top of the bridge.

He stopped in the middle, turning his motorcycle around until he was facing the line of white SUVs that was already making its way down the empty highway toward him. Through what was left of his weakened feelers, he could sense Lola's furious gossamer twisting below him. Their argument must have really upset her, because he could feel the road she'd just made jerking like an angry muscle. She must have still been determined to hold up her end of the plan, though, because a few moments later, the swell of magic solidified, and the low road locked back into place.

The Paladins were dangerously close by this point, but Valente still took one last chance to close his eyes, using his fairy sight to stare down through the bridge at Lola's glimmering sunlight magic. He looked as hard as he could, burning her beautiful light into his memory as the sound of cars got closer and closer. Only when the Paladins were nearly on top of him did he open his eyes again, forcing himself to turn and face the enemy coming up the bridge.

There was no way they hadn't seen him. His all-black getup was meant to be inconspicuous, but even on a winter day like this one, no one could miss the iconic Black Rider on his famous black motorcycle. Doing this at night would have made for an even better show. The Black Rider was always most terrifying in the dark, but Valente didn't want to scare them. He wanted to enrage them so they'd charge right into the trap.

So far so good, from the look of things. Despite having plenty of room to turn around, all three of the armored SUVs in the convoy gunned their engines and sped up, tightening their formation into an arrow that was clearly meant to run him down. Valente let them come, sitting on his bike at the center of the bridge until the enemy was only a few feet away. Then, when the first car was so close that he could see the reflection of his cracked visor in the tinted windshield, Valente shoved his coiled magic underneath its front tires.

His normally freezing gossamer was warm and sluggish, but it was still enough to send the racing SUV flying into the air. He whacked the car with a second slug of gossamer as it arced over his head, sending it careening into the wall of billboards that lined the highway. He pulled the same trick on the rear SUV, sliding his gossamer under its tires before curving the magic like a ramp so that the huge car shot off the road to the right. This left only the

SUV in the middle of the convoy, the one that was supposed to have their target.

Valente had specifically saved that one for last. He no longer had enough control over his decaying magic to handle more than one thing at a time. With both of its guards sent flying, though, the target vehicle seemed to have lost its nerve. Its tires squealed on the pavement as the driver hit the brakes and tried to turn around, but Valente got there first. Using all the magic he had left, he wrapped the car in an invisible hand and lifted it off the road.

He'd only raised it a few feet when a white-glowing sword cut through the armored passenger door into his magic. If he'd been at his usual strength, that wouldn't have bothered him. In his current sorry state, it felt like being stabbed through the chest. For a horrible second, Valente staggered, nearly losing his grip on the car. Then he pulled himself back together, twisting his magic tight as a steel cable as he lifted the SUV over the bridge railing and dropped the vehicle into Toothy's waiting claws.

The moment he felt Lola's monster catch it, Valente slumped onto his handlebars. He must have been in even worse shape than he'd realized, because his magic fell apart the instant he stopped pushing, and his body wasn't doing much better. That sword hadn't even touched his actual flesh, but he could still feel the hot blood running down the inside of his riding suit.

His silent motorcycle vanished next, dropping him onto his knees. Down beneath the bridge, he heard Lola shouting at him to come on—they had the target. He tried to yell back, but the magic that composed his head was too soft to form words anymore, so he pulled out his phone instead and texted her a message.

Go, he wrote. *I'm going to check on the ones I threw.*

That wasn't remotely true, but the nice part about not being a real fairy was that he could lie all he wanted so long as he didn't have to speak the words out loud. He wasn't sure if Lola believed him, but she had her hands full with the Paladins they'd just caught, and she was always quick to think the best. A bright soul like hers would absolutely believe the Black Rider was checking to make sure the people he'd thrown were okay, not making up an excuse to hide the fact that he couldn't move.

Sure enough, she texted back saying she'd leave the low road open and meet him back at the barrow. Her beautiful light vanished a second later, leaving him alone on the bridge.

He collapsed on the pavement the moment she was gone. It felt nice to be flat, but Valente knew the peace wouldn't last. He'd done a good job getting them out of the way, but being thrown off a bridge wouldn't do anything but slow a Paladin down. They'd be storming up here any minute to butcher the blood mage's monster, and this time there'd be no Simon to put him back together.

That was Valente's choice, though. As much as he hated lying to Lola, he hated the oaths even more. Lola was loved by so many. She'd move on, but Valente would only get the chance to be free once. Considering he'd technically been dead since the day Victor cut his head off, he'd already gotten much more time with her than he'd deserved. He was telling himself to be satisfied with that when a pair of black motorcycle boots stepped into his dimming vision. Very *familiar* motorcycle boots.

That was the last thing Valente saw before the gloved fist landed on his head, dropping him gently into oblivion.

Chapter 6

Lola barreled through the garage door like a shot. The low road shook violently as she crossed it, but given how fast she'd thrown the thing together—and how upset Valente had made her right after—she was happy it held at all. Tristan always made this part look so easy, throwing up doors wherever he wanted. But while the shaking would have been a problem if she'd followed the knight's example and moved her barrow to the other side of the planet, Lola had always been a DFZ girl. She had to put up with the instability for only two steps before she popped out of the dark underpass and into the fluorescent brightness of her garage. Toothy was already there, shoving the white SUV the Rider had tossed them into the cage Lola had built between her sedans and her trucks.

It would have been better to empty the garage entirely, but Lola had put so much effort into pre-making all these cars. After a lifetime of spinning everything on the fly, being able to instantly summon a fully stocked work van or detail-perfect sports car was an unheard-of luxury. Putting the target in the same room as all her rides was a risk—Lola hadn't forgotten what the Paladins did to her last car—but the garage was the most normal-looking of all the rooms in her barrow.

She'd much rather redo a few four-doors than deal with a mind as rigid and narrow as a Paladin's trying to wrap itself around her dream house upstairs. That was bound to be some nuclear-grade disbelief, as poor Toothy was already finding out. Lola's creature was already looking alarmingly melty as she closed the steel cage around the Paladin's SUV, so Lola quickly sent her back upstairs. She'd done her job perfectly, brave girl. Now it was Lola's turn to hold the line as she focused all of her gossamer on the cage.

She'd barely finished tightening her grip when a bright-white glowing sword slashed through the SUV's front passenger door. From the scorch marks on the paint, this wasn't the first time that had happened, but it was Lola's first experience facing a Paladin head-on. Valente had done all the work last time, and then, after he'd "died," Lola had been too busy turning into a monster to pay attention to anything else. She knew she was in for a rough ride since Paladins didn't seem to come in anything less than hardcore, but that was why she'd brought the car here. As a fairy monarch in her own barrow, there was nothing a human could do that Lola couldn't handle.

At least, that was how she felt until the Paladin's sword finished cutting through the car and slammed into her cage.

It felt like getting punched in the teeth. Lola had done her best to make the metal cage look as real and heavy as possible, but that didn't seem to matter. The moment the glowing sword touched her gossamer, the Paladin's absolute belief that this blade could cut anything hit Lola like a train. The cage could have been made of diamond or granite or fifteen feet of concrete, and the Paladin's ironclad faith wouldn't have changed.

In the end, it was only the fact that they were deep inside a barrow where Lola controlled everything from the light to the air to the gravity that kept the Paladin from cutting out of her prison. It still took everything Lola had to hold the sword in place, pushing against the Paladin's belief with all the power she'd stolen from Alberich plus the conviction of her own human soul that no sword swung by a person could cut through six inches of tungsten carbide. "Impossible" wasn't a word Lola normally used, but she dug into it now, pushing on the Paladin with a whole barrow's worth of magic until, after what felt like years, the Paladin's sword stopped moving.

Lola was drenched in sweat by the time it happened. The cage had held, but the SUV inside was destroyed, melted into slag by the armored figure standing on the other side of the tungsten bars.

There was only one. No driver or guards as Simon had told her to expect, but Lola wasn't sure that was good luck on their part when the woman in the gleaming spellworked armor holding the white-hot sword met her eyes with a glare of pure hate.

"Aw, crud," Lola wheezed, sinking to her knees as the Paladin kicked her with yet another wave of disbelief. "We got the wrong one."

"Not who you were expecting?" the woman said in a cold voice that, Lola realized with a jolt, she recognized. This wasn't just any crazy Paladin. It was the sword lady who'd fought Valente toe-to-toe in the parking lot, the one who'd been shouting orders at the others. Lola had seen her on the news, too, but she couldn't remember the woman's name until Simon burst through the door at the top of the garage stairs and said it for her.

"Grand Marshal Nadja."

He spat the name like a curse, and the Paladin's lips curled into a zealot's smile.

"Why did you grab *her*?" Simon demanded, running down the steps toward Lola, who was still panting on the polished concrete floor. "She's the worst one!"

"You told us to get the middle SUV!" Lola cried. "All the windows were tinted! How were we supposed to know the wrong Paladin was inside?"

"Everyone goes for the center of the convoy," the Paladin informed them casually. "That's why we always put the hardest target inside." She removed one hand from her sword to push up her ballistic-glass faceplate so she could look Simon over. "You're Victor Conrath's apprentice."

"Former apprentice," Simon corrected, keeping his distance behind Lola.

The Paladin shrugged her armored shoulders. "Doesn't matter. Your soul's still stained." She flipped her faceplate back down and raised her glowing sword. "Once a blood mage, always a blood mage."

She slammed her blade into the cage as she finished, clearly intending to slice right through the bars into Simon. There was no way she could have actually reached him from that distance, but the conviction behind the blow still made the metal bulge as Lola struggled to keep her in.

"I should have known Conrath was still in league with the fairies," the Paladin said calmly as she swung again. "The others believed his alliance with the Wild Hunt was over after the battle of Hero's Square, but I told them never to trust any show that liar puts on, and I was right." The cage rang like a gong as she hit it again. "Where is your master, monsters?"

"He's not our master!" Simon yelled as Lola dug her fingers into the concrete floor, which was bulging like putty from all the effort she was putting into keeping this lunatic caged. "We hate him just as much as you do! We brought you here because we want to help you kill him. If you'd just calm down and listen—"

"*I will never fight beside the traitors to humanity!*" the Paladin roared, knocking Lola to the ground. "You're all the same, predators and parasites feeding on the weak. You disgust me!" She slammed her sword into the bars hard enough to bow the garage's cement walls. "It's only a matter of time until I destroy this prison, and then you'll pay the price for selling your souls to Victor Conrath!"

"Would you *stop?*" Lola cried, shrinking the cage until the Paladin could barely move. "I know we don't exactly come off looking like the good guys here, but we don't work for Victor anymore!"

"Then why was his Black Rider waiting for us?" the Paladin asked, planting her metal boots on Lola's bars. "We've known for years that he's the blood mage's puppet. I thought he'd served his final purpose when Victor cut his head in half, but I should have known better. The blood mage never throws away a weapon."

"He did this time," Lola said, keeping her hands clasped tight in an effort to hold the Paladin still. "The three of us—Simon, the Black Rider, and me—we all used to be his weapons, and he threw us all away the moment it got him something better. He thinks we're dead, but we survived, and we're fighting him with everything we've got. You know the bomb that took out Hero's Hall? That was us. We're on the same side!"

The Paladin stopped pushing on the cage to give her an incredulous look. "You're the idiots who've been showing the entire world that the Hero really is immortal?" Her lips curled back in a sneer. "Are you sure you don't work for Conrath?"

"At least we've been trying," Lola snapped. "Your stupid 'order' hasn't done squat but sit on your butts!"

"There, we agree," the Paladin admitted, though she didn't stop trying to rip the bars apart. "We should have stopped Victor Conrath twenty years ago. He's been known to us for at least that long, but his presence in the DFZ made things difficult."

Lola glowered. "Didn't seem to stop you from attacking the Rider and me in the parking lot."

"We had special permission from the city at the time," the Paladin said dismissively. "Permission she immediately revoked when she sided with the blood mage who destroyed her."

"She didn't *side* with him!" Lola cried, shaking with fury. "Victor stomped on the DFZ the same way he stomps on everyone. The only reason the city's doing what he says is because his boot is on her neck!"

"Doesn't change the situation," the Paladin said, finally stopping her pushing to give Lola a hard look. "The Paladins are a highly respected international organization. We earned that respect by obeying the law. Even for a target as dangerous as

Conrath, trespassing into sovereign territory to arrest one of its citizens is a violation of trust. Trust we must maintain if we are to continue our mission. Believe me, if we hadn't been strictly forbidden to enter the DFZ before war is formally declared, my sword would already be in Victor Conrath's neck."

Lola was aghast. "*That's* why the Paladins have left Victor sitting pretty on his new throne for so long?" she cried. "You were waiting for *permission?*"

"We were waiting for the law," the Paladin replied with a superior sneer. "We are not criminals or vigilantes. We are justice, and justice must always be above reproach."

She hadn't seemed to care much about justice when her battle mage was burning Valente to a crisp, but before Lola could say anything, Simon cut in.

"If that's your problem, then we just handed you the perfect solution," he said. "None of us work for Victor anymore, but your people don't know that. They'll think the Hero kidnapped you, which means—"

"He attacked first, giving us just cause to hit back," the Paladin finished with a bloodthirsty smile. "I'm well aware of the situation. Why do you think I haven't made a serious effort at killing you yet?"

"Could've fooled me," Lola grumbled.

"You gave us exactly what we needed," the Paladin went on, ignoring her. "The moment I saw the Black Rider waiting on the bridge, I gave the order." She glanced down at the ballistic watch built into her spellworked gauntlet. "That was five minutes ago, which means my forces should be starting their assault on Hero's Tower as we speak."

"They're already attacking?" Simon said, his blue eyes widening. "As in right now?"

The Paladin gave him an unimpressed look. "Did you not listen to your own words? The only reason we didn't do this ages ago was because we weren't allowed, not because we weren't ready. My order has been prepared to assault the blood mage's stronghold for months. All we needed was a justification. A justification you just gave us, for which I am in your debt." She paused. "That doesn't mean I'm not going to kill you."

"Of course not," Simon said.

The woman nodded and tapped her finger in the empty air. Lola thought she was testing the bars again when she realized the Paladin was using the augmented reality interface that was still active inside her glowing helmet.

"I don't have signal in here, but my people don't need me to tell them what to do," the Paladin said proudly. "By this point, our public relations arm will have delivered footage of the Black Rider's attack on our convoy to every major media outlet. We already presented evidence that the Rider was under Victor's control to the international courts two years ago, so the legal groundwork is laid. I'm sure the Hero's supporters will still try to stop us, which is why we're moving fast. By the time they find a judge to hear their argument, the blood mage will be dead, and our mission will be complete."

That sounded like a headache to Lola, but she was relieved the Paladins were so prepared. She should've known they would be. Rooting out and killing blood mages and their accomplices was their reason for existing. She just couldn't believe this was happening so quickly. Valente wasn't even back yet.

"We have to get in there," Simon said, crouching down beside her.

"Why?" Lola whispered, covering her mouth with her clasped hands so the Paladin wouldn't overhear. "I want to watch Victor die as much as you do, but the whole point of this was to force the Paladins to do what we couldn't."

Simon shook his head. "The Paladins know how to kill blood mages, but *I* know Victor. I have to be there to make sure they finish the job."

"I don't think that's a good idea," Lola said, looking pointedly into Simon's blue eyes. "Victor's already invaded your mind once. There's no telling what he'll do when his back's really against the wall. What if he takes you over completely?"

"He can't do that."

Lola scowled. "I don't put a lot of stock in what Victor 'can't' do anymore."

"Neither do I," Simon said, his face determined. "But this is a totally different situation. The blood from his pills is long gone. That doesn't mean I'm safe. No one's ever safe from Victor, but..." His clenched fists squeezed tighter. "I *have* to do this, Lola. I have to see him die. It's the only way I can get him out of my head."

Lola bit her lip. She'd been avoiding asking Simon what Victor had done to him. He'd been through so much already, and she didn't want to poke the wound. She knew the connection couldn't be direct or Victor would've come for them ages ago, but she also knew better than anyone that Victor didn't need to be present to hurt you.

"If you're that determined to go, then I'm going with you," she said, pushing herself up. "But can we at least wait until the Rider gets back? He outed himself to Victor to set this up. I know he'd want to be there for the finish, and we're probably going to need his help."

"There's no time," Simon argued. "The attack's already rolling!"

"All the more reason to wait for backup," Lola said, tilting her head toward the Paladin, who was glaring at Simon like she was trying to explode his head with her mind. "I can keep her boxed while we're in my barrow, but once we leave, the Rider's the only one of us who can keep her from killing you."

Simon heaved an impatient sigh. Then he turned and walked toward the Paladin's cage.

Lola had to squeeze tight as the woman lunged at him. She was frantically putting together a fridge-sized blob of ballistic gel to catch the Paladin's sword in case she decided to lob it at Simon's face when the blood mage put up his hands.

"I'd like to propose a truce."

The Paladin spat on the concrete at his feet. "I don't make deals with filth."

"You'll want to consider this one," Simon promised, pulling his lanky body to its full height. "You already know who I am, so you should also know that I was Victor Conrath's protégé for twenty years. What you might not be aware of was that he acquired me as a child for the express purpose of molding me in his image. I was one of many children he abused, but while I had no choice but to learn his magic, I was never like him."

"The stain on your soul says otherwise," the Paladin said, giving him a piercing look. "You must have hurt a lot of people to earn a mark that deep."

"I have hurt people," Simon admitted. "But unlike Victor, I'm ready to pay for my sins, so here's my offer." He pointed behind him at the straining Lola. "As you saw when we brought you here, Lola can open doors to anywhere she's been. Since she's fought Victor inside his tower before, that means she can open a passage into his private penthouse, *behind* all his defenses. We can give you a straight shot into Victor's back line but only if you promise not to attack us."

"Impossible," the woman said flatly. "There can be no quarter for blood mages."

"Then do it after," Simon spat. "You can arrest me or kill me or do whatever you want *after* Victor is dead. But until that happens, I want to help."

The Paladin shook her head. "No deal. I won't give him another ally."

Simon looked incredulous. "We're offering to help you stab him in the back, and you *still* don't believe we're his enemies?"

"I believe the blood mage takes whatever he wants," the Paladin said crisply, looking Simon up and down. "And he's clearly an old hand at taking from you. Even if you're telling the truth and this isn't a plot to deliver me straight into Conrath's hands, you're too much of a liability to bring into battle."

Lola secretly agreed, but Simon didn't give up.

"I know I'm no match for him," he admitted. "But I'm also the only one who knows what he's actually capable of. You've killed a lot of blood mages, but I promise you've never faced anyone like him. He's a monster in the truest sense, but I worked under him for twenty years. No one knows his blind spots better than I do. If you want to win, you're going to need me."

The Paladin arched a graying eyebrow. "And if he puts you back under his control?"

"Then kill me," Simon said, spreading his arms in surrender. "I'm not afraid to die, but I am deathly afraid that he won't. I've seen him come back too many times to leave his life in someone else's hands. I'll stay out of your way during the actual fighting, but I need to confirm Victor's death with my own eyes. Once I'm certain he's gone, I'll turn myself in peacefully."

"*Simon!*" Lola hissed, but he waved her down, keeping his attention on the Paladin, who seemed to be giving his proposal serious consideration.

"I'll agree on two conditions," she said at last. "First, your girl needs to transport all my Paladins, not just me. Surprise attack or not, I'm not foolish enough to think I can take Victor Conrath by myself, especially if you might be in the mix as well. Second, if you use any blood magic of your own, you will instantly be considered an enemy and struck down. But if you are truly there only as an observer *and* you surrender yourself as soon as the blood mage is dead, you have my word that you will not be harmed for the duration of this operation."

"Done," Simon said, reaching out his hand.

The Paladin sneered at his offered palm. "I'm not touching that," she said, but she did sheathe her sword. "Now tell your fairy monster to let me out. The sooner we get to the battle, the sooner Conrath dies."

Simon nodded and looked over his shoulder at Lola, but she held her ground, jerking her head at him until he came back over.

"I don't like this," she whispered when he got close.

"I'm sorry. I should have asked you before I told her about the doors," he said quickly. "But I know you can do it. Victor's wards have never stopped you before, and you've gotten a lot better at—"

"I'm not talking about the doors," she snapped, giving him a pleading look. "Why did you tell her she could arrest you?"

"Because it was the only way to get her to agree."

"We don't need her to agree," Lola argued. "If you just want to make sure Victor's dead, I'll hide you, and we'll go to the tower by ourselves. We don't need murder lady!"

"I do," Simon said grimly, looking at the scowling Paladin. "This might be our last shot at actually killing Victor. We can't afford not to swing our hardest, and the Grand Marshal is their best."

"It's not worth it," Lola pleaded. "The whole point of killing Victor was to set us free. That can't happen if you're arrested!"

"It never was going to happen," Simon said with grim determination. "Victor won't be defeated until every part of his empire is demolished. That includes the apprentice he made in his image."

"Oh, Simon," Lola whispered, leaning her body against his, since she couldn't let go of the Paladin's cage long enough to hug him. "No, no, no, you can't think that way."

"Just because you don't like it doesn't mean it's not the truth," he said quietly, pressing his face into the crown of her head. "I have to do this, Lola."

"No, you don't," she argued, whipping back to glare at him. "Nothing Victor did is your responsibility! We're his victims, not his accomplices. The Paladin doesn't understand that because she's a cruel, narrow-minded person, but I *know* you, Simon. It doesn't matter how bloody your soul is. You don't deserve this!"

"I never said I did," Simon said with a sigh. "I'm doing this out of practicality, not guilt." He held out his scarred hands. "You heard what she said. The blood magic stain never goes away. The Paladins will be after me for the rest of my life no matter how victimized I was, and that's exactly how it should be. Blood magic *should* be intolerable. It's a horrible, abusive power that no one should wield."

"That doesn't mean you should give yourself up!"

"I can't hide in your barrow forever," he said with a shrug. "And you know perfectly well that Victor isn't responsible for all my crimes. He only took me in because my soul was already stained."

Lola glared daggers at him. "Stuff you did as a kid doesn't count."

"Blood always counts," Simon said, his face determined. "My mind's made up. If we're successful, Victor will be defeated and all his crimes will be exposed, including the ones against us. I've been ready to die to achieve that for years. Think about it that way, and getting arrested is actually a step up."

Lola didn't agree with any of that, but she already knew it was hopeless. As ever, Simon was going to do what Simon was going to do, though he would lose his window if they didn't get a move on. Lola cared about him too much to waste his resolve like that, so, with a final nervous look at the killer waiting on the other side, she released her death grip on the Paladin's cage.

It felt like letting go of a guillotine rope. The moment she stopped squeezing, the bars fell apart like so many sticks. The Paladin stepped over them without a glance, walking away from the smoking wreckage of her car to stand in front of Simon and Lola with a sneer on her proud face.

"You'd better be as good as he says," Lola snarled as she grabbed Simon's hand. "I'll open your damn doors, but if your people can't do this, we're out."

"If we can't kill Victor Conrath, nothing can," the Paladin said with absolute confidence as she nodded at Simon. "He already knows. That's why he's staking his life on us, and why Conrath cowers in the DFZ. All those with stained souls know we are not normal battle mages. We are Paladins of a higher purpose, and we will not fail."

Lola rolled her eyes and pulled out her phone to inform Valente of the new plan.

Going on the attack, she texted. *I'll leave the low roads open. Meet us at Victor's when you're ready.*

She was still waiting for his reply when the Paladin stomped in front of her, motioning impatiently for Lola to lead the way to Hero's Tower.

Chapter 7

Getting there proved to be much more of a challenge than Lola anticipated.

It shouldn't have been. Like Simon had said, Lola knew exactly where she was going. She should've been able to walk up the stairs, head out to her travel garden, and make a new low road straight to Victor's doorstep. Easy-peasy. As with everything since the Paladin had gotten involved, though, there was nothing easy about it.

The problems started the moment Lola tried to get them out of the garage. Since Simon had straight-up told the Paladin that Lola was a fairy who opened magical doors, she'd assumed the woman's mind would be more open to the seemingly impossible. After all, what were a few windows overlooking a lost version of the DFZ when you were about to take a fairy portal to a blood mage's stronghold? Any *normal* person would've dismissed Lola's charming living room as the least weird part of this situation, but she'd barely gotten the door open when the wave of disbelief hit her smack in the face.

She closed it again immediately, locking the three of them in the narrow garage staircase as the white-painted walls wobbled like jelly around them. "Okay," she said, wiping the stress-sweat off her face. "Not going that way."

"What's wrong?" the Paladin demanded right behind her.

Lola shot the armored lady a deadly look, which was unfair. Both Dee and Toothy had been waiting in the living room when she'd opened the door. That would have shocked anyone, but the Paladin hit like a damn train. If they were going to make it anywhere in the barrow, *especially* through something that required as much acceptance as a low road, Lola would need to do a little prep work.

"All right," she said, turning around to look at the Paladin, who was scowling harder than ever. "What was your name again?"

The leather-faced woman clamped her jaw, so Simon said it for her.

"Grand Marshal Nadja."

"Nice to meet you, Grand Marshal Nadja," Lola lied. "I'm Lola. I know we didn't get off to a great start, but if I'm going to be your taxi into Hero's Tower, there's a few things you're going to have to accept. The first is that I'm a fairy, and this is my barrow."

"What does that mean?" the Paladin asked suspiciously.

Hoo boy.

"It means we're not in normal space," Lola explained. "Think of it like being in a dream. Stuff here is… stretchy, let's say. It isn't going to match your usual expectations, but if you relax and go with the flow, I can use that stretchiness to get us into places we couldn't normally go, like the top of Victor's tower."

"I understood that part," Nadia said impatiently. "How does it work?"

Lola shook her head. "It won't if you ask questions like that. Fairy magic is based on belief. It only works if you *believe* it works. If you don't, the magic can collapse and dump you into the void between worlds."

The Paladin arched a graying eyebrow. "Shouldn't you have mentioned this earlier?"

"I probably shouldn't have mentioned it now," Lola said, gritting her teeth against the pulse of disbelief the Paladin had just put out. "I know being an uncompromising hardass is your whole schtick, but if I'm going to get you to where you need to go, you can't be judging every little thing."

"So you expect me to just blindly accept whatever you do?"

"That would be great," Lola said encouragingly. "You know those fairy tales where people get lost in the forest and end up at an enchanted castle? Think of it like that, except we're going downtown."

"That doesn't make any sense."

"It's not supposed to make sense," Lola said, striving for patience. "That's how fairy magic works. It's *magic.* It does things that seem impossible, but if you don't accept that it *can* happen, it won't work."

"That sounds ridiculous, but fine." The Paladin closed her eyes. "Tell me when we get there."

Lola heaved an enormous sigh. Revealing how the barrow worked had been a terrible move. She'd gotten so spoiled by Simon and Valente just accepting everything she did, she'd forgotten the first rule of fairy magic: never explain the trick. Why hadn't she just covered the stairway in psychedelic lights and told the woman they were walking through a wormhole? Now she had to deal with this steel-minded hardcase knowing it was all fake.

At least the Paladin's eyes were closed. Removing the visual element made things a little easier, but Lola still had to figure out how to give the woman a sense of movement she'd believe in long enough to actually move them.

"Why don't you use a boat?"

Lola jumped a foot in the air. She'd been so focused on the Paladin, she hadn't realized Dee had opened the door until the double stuck her head through.

"Who's that?" the Paladin demanded, eyes flying open.

"*No!*" Lola cried, but it was too late. The Paladin had already seen the two Lolas, and the blast of disbelief that came out of her was powerful enough to punt Dee across the living room.

"Would you quit it!" Lola yelled, running to her doppelganger's side. "Dee, are you all right?"

"Of course," Dee said cheerfully, popping herself out of the living room wall, which had stretched like taffy to catch her.

"You're okay, and we're part of you, so that means we're great. Right, Toothy?"

Lola's creature, who was hiding under the couch—not very effectively, since she was still so big from grabbing the Paladin's SUV that the couch looked more like a hat on her than a piece of furniture—whimpered pathetically.

"She hates conflict," Dee informed Lola.

"I know that," Lola snapped. "She's *my* other half! Now, what's this about a boat?"

"Boats are very dreamy," Dee said with an air of great mystery. "They take people long distances in seemingly no time at all, and you can always feel them moving even if you can't see where you're going."

"That's actually a pretty good idea," Lola said, leaning over to give Toothy a reassuring pat before heading back toward the door the quick-thinking Simon had closed to keep the Paladin from doing any more damage. "You two stay here and keep the roads open for the Rider. We're going to need all hands on deck for this one."

"Doesn't that mean we should go with you?" Dee asked. "Valente's probably going to head straight for Hero's Tower anyway."

Lola gave her a mental pinch for using Valente's real name where other people could hear it. "Stay put," she ordered, doing her best to sound like the monarch she was supposed to be. "If this thing goes bad, we'll need somewhere to run. Your job is to keep the doors open and make sure the barrow is ready to receive. Understand?"

Dee gave her a gallant salute, which Lola interpreted as a yes. Toothy, the more responsible one, was already extricating herself from the couch. When Lola was sure both her other selves understood the assignment, she opened the door to the garage just enough to slip her body through.

"Change in plans," she announced as she squeezed in next to Simon on the top step. "We're taking the boat."

Simon gave her an incredulous look. "The boat?"

"The. Boat," Lola said through clenched teeth.

"Right, the boat," he said, finally getting the hint. "That will get us there even faster."

"What boat?" the Paladin asked suspiciously.

"Victor's changed the DFZ a lot, but even he can't stop the weather," Lola said, weaving lies around the truth to form a believable story as she hurried back down the stairs. "Thanks to the lake effect, this area has always gotten a ton of precipitation. To channel all that water, the DFZ had to put in huge storm drains all over the city, including directly below Hero's Tower. That's our way in. We'll just sail up the drain."

"You have access to the storm water system from here?" the Paladin asked, the punches of her disbelief growing softer as she bought into the story. "Where is it?"

"This way," Lola said, hopping down the last few steps to land back on the smooth cement floor of her giant garage.

She spun her gossamer as she went. A big storm water system probably *did* run under the city, but Lola didn't know anything about it. The whole thing was just a cover story to explain the tunnel she was frantically weaving into existence behind the bus-sized RV she'd whipped up for herself just in case she ever got the chance to go on vacation.

It was a damn good show. By the time they got around the giant vehicle, a perfect copy of an old DFZ storm grate was waiting in the parking garage floor. The heavy black metal cut into Lola's hands just like the real thing when she stuck her fingers through the square-edge bars, and the access shaft below had slime on the walls and a rusty metal ladder that looked like it'd been there for fifty years.

"And this will give us underground access to the blood mage?" the Paladin asked, her disbelief fading now that Lola was giving her things she could understand.

"It'll take us straight to him," Lola promised, hurrying down the ladder, which felt believably rusty and unstable even to her.

The Paladin went next, followed by Simon. Lola adjusted her barrow as they went, stretching the climb a few extra feet to buy herself time to finish making what lay at the bottom.

When their feet finally hit the ground, they were standing on an underground dock built inside a gigantic drainage pipe filled with frothy, dirty runoff from the streets above. It even smelled like street water, filling the tunnel with a dankness Lola would have bragged about if it wouldn't have ruined the illusion.

"Where's the boat?" the Paladin asked.

Lola grinned and pointed upstream, where a green fishing boat with a brand-new outboard motor was tied to a pipe.

"Is it fast?"

"Super fast," Lola promised, setting expectations for the quick work she was about to make of this trip. "Hop in."

The Paladin did so at once. Simon followed more slowly, giving Lola a nervous look. She gave him a firm glare back and stabbed her finger at the plastic seat in the middle.

It wasn't really his fault. Simon had more experience with fairy weirdness than most, but he was still a logical person who expected the universe to follow rules. In his mind, a low road was a door, not a boat. Lola could tell him the truth was neither of those things until she was blue in the face, but he still wouldn't fully buy into the illusion until he experienced it for himself.

Fortunately for their timetable, Simon's innate trust in her meant his disbelief didn't hit nearly as hard as the Paladin's. Lola weathered it with barely a flinch as she hopped into the back of the boat and started the motor, sending them speeding down the dark tunnel with only the flashlight from her phone to light the way.

"How far is it?" the Paladin yelled over the roar of the outboard motor bouncing off the drain's curved, slimy walls.

"Not far!" Lola shouted back, keeping her eyes on the tunnel she was making up as they went. This was a lot freer and looser than she usually liked to play it, especially with such an unforgiving audience, but they didn't have to go far, and their target was somewhere she knew *very* well.

Lola had staked out Victor's place constantly over the last few months. Her spying hadn't turned up much information, but it had given her a local's understanding of the streets surrounding Hero's Tower. Case in point, the rusty ladder she pulled their boat up to a minute later led to a real drainage grate that was built into the actual sidewalk right outside the entrance to the Tower's underground parking deck.

Lola even let the Paladin go up first while she tied off the boat. Not that it mattered since all of this was going to poof the moment they left, but Lola had finally remembered what it was like to fool normal people. The little details were what made things feel real, so she focused on every one, even to the point of making the wet nylon rope believably slippery as she struggled to tie it into a functional knot.

By the time she'd secured the boat and joined the others at the top of the ladder, the Paladin's disbelief was totally gone. That foundation of trust would be critical when Lola had to make more shortcuts later, which she absolutely would, because the scene outside Hero's Tower was even crazier than she'd expected.

The Grand Marshal hadn't been kidding when she'd said they were prepared for this. Victor's tower was surrounded by a parking lot of armored vehicles. Lola counted twenty SWAT trucks like the one the Paladins had used to block her car the first time they'd fought, and the gray sky was thick with thumping police helicopters. As a child of the famously freewheeling DFZ, Lola had never seen anything like it, but Grand Marshal Nadja was grinning like a proud parent.

"Fifteen minutes from mobilization order to full enclosure," she said, checking her watch. "Not bad. Let's go see where the front line is."

"You mean just walk in?" Lola said, glancing at Simon, who suddenly looked very alone and exposed. "Won't they—"

"They won't do anything so long as you're with me," the Paladin said confidently. "We're a disciplined organization, and I'm a woman of my word. So long as you keep your end of the bargain and refrain from using blood magic, none of my people will touch you until Victor Conrath is dead."

That was what they'd agreed, but Lola still felt like she was walking into the mother of all traps as the Paladin led them down the ramp into the Tower's underground garage, where a bunch of cops in riot gear had set up a perimeter.

The police all jumped when they saw Nadja, which made sense given that she was supposed to be kidnapped by Victor. Lola was scrambling to think up a lie that would explain how they'd gotten here when the Paladin bellowed at the cops to stop gawking and give her a radio.

"Why does she need a radio?" Lola whispered to Simon. "Doesn't she have a com in her—"

"All of my communication equipment was deactivated remotely the moment I was compromised," the Paladin said as the cops scrambled to obey, handing her their own radios rather than taking the time to find new ones. "Standard procedure to prevent a leak. Fortunately, the old-fashioned ways still work."

She wiggled her new radio at them before hitting the button to bark into the receiver. "This is the Grand Marshal. I'm on-site. What's the situation?"

If the person on the other end was surprised to hear their missing leader suddenly talking over a police channel, he was too disciplined to let it show.

"This is Battle Mage Commander Zimmer. Happy to hear your voice, ma'am. We've secured the front entrance, but we've run into a bit of trouble."

"On my way," Nadja said, breaking into a run as she charged a set of fancy stairs that, according to the signage on the wall, connected the underground parking deck to the main lobby.

Lola and Simon ran nervously after her. It felt like a terrible idea, charging straight into Victor's tower to join a bunch of blood-mage killers with no strategy, no real allies, and no weapons, but there was nothing else they could do. Trusting the Paladins *was* the plan, so Lola rolled with it as best she could, spinning up some riot armor for herself and Simon behind Nadja's back as the woman ran up the marble stairs.

She finished their new outfits just in time. The stairs from the parking deck had been empty, but the Hero's fancy lobby was stuffed with Paladins wearing the same spellworked silver armor as Nadja. Theirs was less grand than the Grand Marshal's, but it was still huge and bulky, forming a wall across what should have been an airy atrium. The Paladins jumped out of the way when they realized who was behind them, shouting welcomes in relieved voices as the Grand Marshal pushed her way through.

Nadja accepted their greetings with a curt nod and marched straight to the front of the line. Lola made sure that she and Simon stayed on her heels. They both had gossamer riot armor covering their faces now, but Lola didn't think for a second that would stop the Paladins. Some of them were already reaching for their weapons when they spotted Simon, and Lola tensed to run. Before anything could happen, though, Nadja turned to speak over her shoulder.

"These are witnesses under amnesty," she said flatly, giving her men a hard look. Once every Paladin let go of their weapons, Nadja lifted the commandeered radio back to her lips. "This is the Grand Marshal. I'm taking command. I've brought two individuals with me. One is a blood mage. Both are critical to the operation and are not to be harmed. Zimmer, you handle the paperwork."

"Yes, ma'am," said the man they'd heard earlier, who was standing right next to them. Now that she could see who Nadja was talking to, Lola realized she recognized him as well. It was the fireball mage who'd scorched her car, the one the Rider had taken out.

The man didn't look any worse for wear, and he didn't seem to recognize Lola behind her new helmet, but his face was very grim as he leaned over to whisper next to the Grand Marshal's helmet. "We have a situation," he informed her in a hushed voice, tilting his head toward something at the lobby's far end. "It's worse than we feared."

When the Grand Marshal didn't respond, Lola got up on her tiptoes to peek over the Paladin's armored shoulder. She'd only seen the lobby of Hero's Tower once before, when Simon had carried her through inside Buster's cat crate. It looked more or less as she remembered: a big open room designed to impress with gleaming bronze fixtures, soaring arched ceilings, and black marble everything. The glass doors the Rider had broken when Orlando threw him were long since repaired, and the Paladins hadn't had enough time to wreck anything else. It mostly just looked like a big fancy lobby of the sort you'd find in any rich Skyways building, including the crowd of obvious civilians Lola could now see huddled in front of the elevators.

"Who are they?" she whispered, struggling to see around the armored people in front of her. "Victor's fans?"

People were always hanging around Victor's buildings, hoping for a glimpse of the Hero. It made sense that some of them would have run inside when the Paladins rolled up. She could even believe they'd use their bodies as human shields since the Hero worshipers who made it all the way to the DFZ tended to fall on the craziest end of the spectrum. When she glanced at Simon, though, the mage was shaking his head.

"Those are thralls."

That couldn't be right. There had to be nearly a hundred people crammed into the elevator part of the lobby. In all the years she'd worked for him, Lola had never seen Victor make more than thirty thralls at a time, and he *never* used them as guards. The same control that made them unflinchingly loyal also left them dumb, slow, and unobservant. They were *terrible* soldiers, and Victor hated anything that was bad at its job. They also didn't have a prayer against the Paladins. But while Lola was starting to get excited that they might actually have caught Victor off guard at last, Grand Marshal Nadja looked furious.

"Bastard knows what he's doing," she spat, raising the radio to her lips again. "All forces hold fire. Those people are thralls, innocent victims of blood magic. This is now a hostage situation."

"They're not hostages," Simon said as she lowered her radio. "Thralls only get that way because they submitted to Victor utterly. They chose this."

"Doesn't matter," Nadja replied, clipping the radio to her spellworked belt. "Our charter strictly forbids attacking noncombatants. If we give them so much as a papercut, this operation is over."

"It might be over already," her battlemage, Zimmer, replied. "Thralldom removes any sense of self-preservation. They'll throw themselves on our swords if we get too close. Even if we go in barehanded, it'll be a challenge *not* to hurt them."

"Can't you just knock them out or something?" Lola asked.

"They're already knocked out," Simon explained before the Paladins could. "Becoming a thrall takes a person down to their base functions. Their brains are switched off already, which means the only way to stop them is to make it so they can't move."

"Which risks injury," the battlemage said, looking ready to throw up from agreeing with a blood mage. "I could stun them, but even my mildest electrocution spell carries a fairly significant chance of cardiac arrest. If we kill one by accident—"

"We're not letting him put us in that position," Nadja said, turning to Lola. "Time to earn your keep."

Lola didn't like her tone, but getting them around Victor's defenses was the whole reason she was here, so she let it go with a sigh and turned around to see what she had to work with.

A nightmare was the answer. Now that the Grand Marshal had indicated Lola was the next step in the plan, all the Paladins were staring at her with an intensity that made her want to vanish into her armor. Working in front of crowds had never been her strong suit, but this was ridiculous. The whole lobby was filled with closed-minded, judgmental Paladins who were in a hurry. Lola couldn't have invented a worse environment for making anything out of gossamer, let alone something as challenging as a low road. She was scrambling to think up a story crazy enough to give her something to work with when Simon came to her rescue.

"I know a way past them."

Everyone turned to look at him, including Lola. To his credit, Simon didn't flinch. He just raised his chin, staring down the Paladins like he did this every day.

"I worked in this tower as Victor's apprentice before I turned on him. He has a private staircase so that his inner circle can move through the building without being noticed by the crowds or caught on camera. Follow me, I'll take you to it."

The moment he finished, he turned and started striding back toward the parking deck. The Paladins followed him immediately. A second later, Lola did as well, weaving through the armored crowd until she was walking right at Simon's elbow.

"I didn't know he had something like that," she whispered, speaking through the gossamer that formed their armor so no one else would hear.

"He doesn't," Simon whispered back as they tromped down the steps that connected the lobby to the garage. "I'm sure he's got some kind of escape hatch, but it'd be an elevator, not a stair. Can you imagine Victor climbing a hundred floors on foot?"

Lola couldn't. "He didn't even like walking up the stairs to get to his own mansion," she said, grinning at Simon through her face shield. "You made it up! I didn't know you could do that."

He rolled his eyes behind the faceplate she'd made for him. "Just because I'm not as good at coming up with these things as you are doesn't mean I'm incapable. I just hope it sounded plausible enough."

"You did a great job, Mr. Wizard," Lola assured him, looking around the cop-filled parking deck until she spotted an electrical closet. "There." She tilted her chin at the target she'd chosen. "Take them over there and pretend the door's got some kind of complicated security system. This isn't my barrow, so I'm going to need more time than usual."

Simon nodded and stepped ahead, leading the Paladins confidently to the closet Lola had indicated. He pulled out his phone when he got close, waving his hand above the screen as if he were entering a complicated code into an AR interface that only he could see. While Simon put on his show, Lola pressed her hand against the metal door to see what she had to work with.

Not much seemed to be the answer. Like most things within sight of Hero's Tower, the closet door had a hardness that had nothing to do with being made of metal. It pushed back as soon as she touched it, clenching like a fist.

Lola pressed down harder with a scowl. Whatever Victor had done to get the DFZ on his side, he'd certainly been thorough. As a changeling who was immune to pretty much everything, Lola normally only noticed magic when it was directed straight at her, but even she could feel the city clamping herself down tight, leaving Lola without so much as a hairline crack to squeeze her gossamer between.

That was going to be a problem. Actual fairies like Tristan and Morgan might not have to worry about the native magic of this plane, but Lola had been born human. The same magic that made the DFZ also ran through her gossamer. That didn't matter for spinning illusions or manipulating creations like her barrow, but even if she closed all her other low roads, tunneling through Victor's tower while the DFZ pushed back would be nigh impossible. The city spirit was just too strong.

The only way around would be for Lola to open a low road back to her own barrow and then make another road from there that led to Victor's penthouse. That wouldn't have been too bad usually, but Nadja hadn't even been able to handle Lola's living room. The idea of almost a hundred judgy Paladins tromping through her barrow was enough to make Lola start melting in anticipation. She was scrambling to think of a safe way to move them all through—an empty room, maybe, or a pitch-black hallway—when the clenched fist of magic she'd been pushing against suddenly fell slack.

Lola jumped. Simon must have been watching her, because he jumped too. This made all the Paladins glare, but other than grabbing their riot-armor costumes before the closed-minded zealots melted it right off them, Lola was too busy tapping her fingers against the door to care. She wasn't sure what or why, but something had just changed. The hard magic of the city's resistance was falling away, almost like it was letting her through.

That wasn't a good thing. Lola couldn't say how she knew, but something about the new opening felt reluctant, as if the spirit were being forced out of the way. Lola had no idea what that meant, but she couldn't afford to miss her chance. The moment the gap appeared, she flooded it with her magic, shoving her gossamer all the way to the top of the building.

When Simon finally opened the door a second later, there was a white-lit stairwell on the other side going straight up. Lola stared at it in apprehension. That was her magic, but she'd never made anything like this before. It reminded her of the spiral staircase Alberich had conjured to take her and Valente to the bottom of the Gameskeeper's arena.

That wasn't a comfortable connection to make, but Lola couldn't afford to dwell on old fears right now. The Grand Marshal was already charging forward, forcing Lola and Simon to flatten themselves against the door to keep from getting crushed.

"Alpha team, with me!" Nadja yelled as she charged up the stairs. "The rest of you, keep an eye on the thralls and stand by to reinforce."

Half the Paladins saluted and stepped back while the other half, including Zimmer the battlemage, charged up the stairs after the Grand Marshal. Simon went in last, followed by Lola, but not before she grabbed the junior Paladin who'd positioned himself as door guard.

"Do me a favor," she pleaded, giving him her best damsel-in-distress look. "The Black Rider turned against Victor as well. He's on our side, and he's a powerhouse, so if he shows up, tell him we went this way, okay?"

"The Black Rider?" the young man repeated in horror. "Absolutely not! I can't possibly—"

"He's going to come through whether you let him or not," Lola said practically. "But he's not going to hurt anyone except Victor. Every one of us hates the blood mage's guts, so make sure the Rider gets to the fight when he shows up, okay?"

The Paladin was still stammering his reply when Lola turned and bolted, taking the brightly lit stairs two at a time. She worked her magic as she ran, reinforcing the tendril of gossamer she'd shoved up Victor's tower until the staircase felt every bit as solid as the real building she'd cut through to make it.

She gave it fire extinguishers and doors on every landing. Very, very locked doors to keep the Paladins from accidentally opening one and blowing the whole operation. She gave it painted railings that made your hands smell like metal after you touched them and water stains in the corners. She gave it spiderwebs, she gave it dust, she even made it a hundred floors tall just in case someone was counting.

She knew she was going to regret that last one when her legs began to burn, but Lola absolutely could not afford to drop the ball here. She still wasn't sure what had convinced the DFZ to let her through, but this stairwell was her contribution to the attack. She was going to get these Paladins to Victor, and then she'd throw them magic-swords first straight into his smug face.

Just thinking about it gave her the manic energy she needed to get up the stairs, covering her ears against the deafening clatter of the Paladin's boots as the whole deadly force raced to the top of Victor's tower.

Chapter 8

Twenty minutes later, Lola was having serious regrets about her life choices.

Magically, everything was great. Her stairwell was rock-solid, and none of the Paladins had even nudged her with their disbelief. But while the armored soldiers were tireless stair-climbing machines, Lola had never done this much exercise in her life. Even knowing her muscles were technically no more real than anything else she made didn't keep her from feeling very believably like she was going to have a heart attack.

"You… just had… to pick… stairs," she gasped at Simon, leaning all her weight against the painted metal railing.

Simon shook his head in reply, too out of breath for a comeback.

Fortunately, they were almost there. Looking up the empty shaft in the center of the stairwell, Lola could finally see the ceiling just two flights above them. Grand Marshal Nadja was already standing on the final landing, waiting impatiently for the rest of her team.

When they all finally arrived, the Grand Marshal motioned for everyone to be still, holding up two fingers. Not being a Paladin, Lola didn't know what that meant, but it seemed to be the signal to take a break, because all the soldiers immediately bent over, sucking in huge, silent breaths of air through their mouths.

Lola wasn't nearly so dignified. She collapsed on the stairs in a panting heap. Simon flopped down right next to her, his whole body heaving as he struggled to catch his breath.

"How are they not dead?" Lola whispered when she could speak again, glaring at the Paladins, who were already back up and huddled in a knot on the landing just below the final door. "We just ran up a skyscraper, and they did it in *armor*. No one's cardio is that good."

Simon was still panting too hard to answer, which Lola suddenly found very odd. Thanks to Victor's insistence that blood mages learn to control every aspect of their bodies, Simon normally never showed physical weakness. She was about to ask if he was hurt when she remembered who they were with. Even if he was doing it to keep up with them, Lola was sure the Paladins would take any blood magic as an excuse to attack. A little panting was a small price to pay for not getting smited or whatever it was they did, but it did take Simon an uncomfortably long time to get himself together enough to answer.

"Paladins have… a lot of… tricks we don't," he wheezed, putting his head between his knees. "That's why we're… going through all this trouble."

Lola rubbed his still-heaving back and looked up at the breaching formation the Paladins were forming in front of the stairwell's final door. Unlike the locked fakes below, that one was the real deal. Lola had hooked her staircase straight into the door of the small room where she'd found Victor sleeping last time. All the Paladins had to do was kick it open, and they'd be deep inside Victor's penthouse, exactly as planned. It had *all* gone exactly as planned, which ironically made Lola more terrified than ever.

"It can't be this easy."

"What part of this was easy?" Simon asked, his breathing finally sounding closer to normal as he pushed back to his feet. "You kidnapped the head of the Paladins and got us all inside the most secure part of the Hero's fortress." He pointed at the wall of armor standing on the stairs above them. "There are fifty elite blood mage killers about to surprise attack Victor from behind. Even I don't know how he's going to survive this one, and I know Victor."

"So do I," Lola said, clutching her shaking hands. "That's why I'm scared. He'd never just let us—"

"He's not 'just letting' us do anything," Simon said sharply. "We did this, because this time, it's going to work." His voice softened as he reached down to squeeze her shoulder. "I know how you feel, but we can't let him get to us. Trust the plan, Tinkerbell."

Lola knew she should. She knew better than anyone the damage her disbelief could do, but the feeling of impending doom still weighed on her like a cement suit. Maybe it was because everything was moving so quickly, or because Valente *still* hadn't replied to any of her messages, or because some deep part of her just couldn't bring itself to believe that Victor could actually be defeated. Whatever the reason, the sound of the Paladins kicking down the door reminded her of the crack a tree made when it began to fall.

They poured into Victor's penthouse like a metal tide. Not even in her wildest dreams had Lola imagined they'd catch Victor sleeping, so she'd put the staircase door on the hallway side of his bedroom. This meant the Paladins came out in the area that used to be full of Victor's household thralls. Now, though, Lola didn't see a soul.

She told herself that made sense. Since the Paladins' ethics didn't allow them to attack thralls, Victor had probably sent his whole stock down to jam the lobby the moment he realized he was under attack. She would have expected him to keep a few back to use as his personal shields, but there was no one here.

Even the mailroom was empty, and not just of thralls. The whole place had been cleaned out, including the damage Dee had done when Lola had sent her to be a distraction. Now, instead of tables covered in letters from the Hero's faithful, the room was filled with one giant casting circle carved deep into the floor with Victor's meticulous handwriting all over it.

Simon went for the circle at once. Battlemage Zimmer joined him a second later while the rest of the Paladins fanned out through the penthouse kicking down doors and tearing open closets. They must not have found anything, because less than three minutes later, the whole attack team was back in the mailroom, staring at Simon with weapons drawn as he traced Victor's precisely written red symbols with his fingers.

"What do they do?" Battlemage Zimmer demanded, sounding very angry that he had to ask that question. "I never could make heads or tails of Conrath's spellwork."

"Not many can," Simon said, his voice distracted as his eyes flicked over the blood-colored markings. "He invented his own system decades ago with the goal of being obtuse, but this circle's not one of his usuals. He's got Thaumaturgical functions mixed in with his normal stuff, along with a whole bunch of Myronic Labyrinth methodology."

"What does that mean?" the Grand Marshal asked impatiently.

Simon ignored her, walking around the circle as he tried to read the spellwork from every angle. Then, as fast as he'd started, he skidded to a stop.

"It's a spirit-binding circle," he said, eyes going wide. "A *huge* one."

"Then we destroy it," the Grand Marshal ordered, nodding at Zimmer, who immediately sheathed his sword and pulled his gloves off to get his bare hands on the spellwork.

"The blood mage is not here," she continued, turning to give Lola and Simon a dirty look, as if that was their fault. "He probably sent down his thralls and fled to a panic room as soon as he realized he was under attack. I've already ordered our team on the ground to start searching the parking deck for hidden exits. The rest of us will split into pairs and start searching the tower floor by floor. Zimmer, you're in charge of breaking that spell. I've never heard of a circle that could bind a Mortal Spirit, but I've learned not to put anything past Conrath."

"It would certainly explain how he got the DFZ so wholly on his side," the battlemage agreed grimly. "But breaking this circle is above my abilities. There's enough magic flowing through here to blow the entire city sky-high. We need to call the Merlin Council, see if they can fly the Archmage in to—"

He stopped, grabbing the Paladin next to him for balance as the floor gave an enormous lurch. Lola stumbled as well, falling into Simon, who was struggling to stay upright as the entire building pitched like a ship going over a wave.

"What the hell was that?" Nadja demanded, turning to the Paladins who were standing near the windows. "What's going on out there?"

"I—I'm not sure, Grand Marshal," stuttered one of the soldiers. "But it looks like the building is—is—"

"Is what?"

"It's *moving.*"

Nadja screwed up her face. "What do you mean it's—"

The answer became evident before she could finish. The spellwork Zimmer had just been fretting over flashed like red phosphorus as the whole building twisted. The floor tilted sideways next, sending the armored soldiers careening toward the big glass windows, which were now looking straight down at the street below. The Paladins would have crashed right through, but Lola got there first, sending a silver mesh of safety netting through the glass to reinforce it. She got a kick for her trouble as the falling soldiers landed safely on the windows they'd been certain they were about to fall through. But no one questioned life-saving miracles for long, and the pressure faded a few seconds later as the Paladins scrambled back to their feet.

"*What is going on?*" Nadja bellowed above them, hanging from her glowing sword, which she'd stabbed into the floor to stop her fall.

"I don't know!" Simon yelled back.

"I do," Lola said, looking down at the rooftops she now had a bird's-eye view of thanks to the suddenly horizontal windows. "It's the DFZ."

There was nothing else it could be. The Living City was the only power that could move buildings like this. Even if the spirit-binding circle hadn't been pulsing like an angry wound, Lola could feel her. The same tense magic that had opened just enough to let her gossamer through earlier was now closing around them like a fist, and as it clenched, the building buckled.

Walls started cracking and collapsing. Lola's stairwell went next, the gossamer tunnel crushed flat as the city who'd permitted their entry withdrew her consent, cutting off their exit. Remembering the reluctance she'd felt earlier, Lola had a feeling that'd been the plan all along, but she didn't know what she was going to do. The walls were already buckling, pushing down on the windows under their feet until even Lola's metal grid couldn't stop them from cracking.

"I don't suppose you can make a door out of here," Simon said grimly as he shuffled his feet away from the spreading destruction.

Before Lola could even shake her head, Grand Marshal Nadja dropped down beside them, landing on a steel bar between the windows. She grabbed Simon and tossed him into the arms of the Paladins who'd already moved to the not-glass part of the wall. She tossed Lola next, flinging her one-handed while her other hand grabbed the radio off her belt.

"Helicopter teams!" Nadja yelled into the receiver. "Fly as close as you can to the building's north side and throw out your ropes. We're going to break the windows and try for a midair grab."

"That's impossible!" shouted one of the other Paladins.

"Better than being dropped," Nadja replied, reclipping her radio as she lifted her heavy boot to kick out the cracking window. "As soon as the choppers are in position, we jump on my mark. Everyone be ready to—"

An explosion drowned out the rest of her orders. A dozen floors below, one of the helicopters the Grand Marshal had been yelling at had crashed into the shorter skyscraper right next to Hero's Tower. The helicopter behind it was also flying out of control, its rotors tangled in a steel power cable that had shot like an arrow from one of the rooftops below. Yet another helicopter—which hadn't even begun its approach toward Hero's Tower—was taken out by a billboard that launched itself off its steel supports, sending the chopper careening into the streets several blocks away.

"*What is going on down there?*" Nadja roared into her radio.

"Victor's forcing the DFZ to attack!" Lola cried, softening her body to slip out of the hands of the Paladin who'd caught her. "You have to tell your people to fly away!"

"If they fly away, we're dead," Nadja snarled, clutching her radio like a talisman. "Someone else get in here! We're Paladins, dammit! I am *not* losing our entire order to a blood mage's stupid trick!"

"I wouldn't say it's stupid."

Lola's gossamer ran cold. The echoey words seemed to come from everywhere and nowhere, but no matter how distorted it was, she'd never not know that voice. Sure enough, the ground stopped shaking a second later. For a terrifying heartbeat, everything was still, and then the building began to open like a flower.

The blast of wind that shot through when the cracking glass finally gave way nearly took Lola off her feet. She saved herself at the last second by clinging to a metal window frame, which was curving outward as the floors and walls peeled away like petals. When the building finally stopped moving, they were kneeling on an open-air platform where Victor's penthouse used to be. The edges were still forming as Lola watched, the steel plates and rebar spreading out from the center like surging roots, almost as if the city were building a suspended stage. And sitting on the golden throne at the center of this new grandstand, his hateful face set in the smuggest smile Lola had ever seen, was Victor.

"Hello, Grand Marshal."

Nadja bared her teeth. "*Conrath.*"

The word was pure fury, but it still wasn't enough to match Lola's anger as Victor turned his smirking Hero's face toward her.

"Hello, my monster," he said without a trace of surprise, though his eyebrows did rise a little when he spotted Simon struggling to his feet beside her. "And look who you've brought with you. You're looking spry for a dead man, apprentice, but I should have known you'd survive. After all, you did learn from the best."

"*Shut up,*" Simon snarled, clenching his fists. "For once in your miserable life, just shut your goddamn—"

His voice cut off as wires shot out of the ground. All over the platform the DFZ had just made out of the top floor of her tallest building, copper wiring was tearing itself out of what was left of the drywall to wrap around Simon's throat. Still more wires grabbed his limbs and body, forcing him to his knees as Victor chuckled.

"That's more like it," he said as Simon struggled against his restraints with a string of very un-Simon-like profanity. "Failures such as you don't deserve to speak in my—"

He stopped speaking when a fireball the size of a charter bus flew past his head. It would have engulfed him if the platform hadn't been so quick, sliding Victor's throne out of the way seconds before the flames consumed him.

"We're not here to listen to the trash that falls out of a blood mage's mouth," Grand Marshal Nadja said as her battlemage lowered his smoking hand. "Come down off that golden cake stand, Victor Conrath, or we'll slaughter you on top of it like the animal you are."

"There's no need to be insulting," Victor said, getting more comfortable on the throne the DFZ had made for him. "I have no interest in fighting you."

"That's not your choice to make," Nadja said as her Paladins surrounded him. "You might have tricked the world into thinking you're a Hero, but a blood mage is always a blood mage, and all blood mages die by our hand."

"I am well acquainted with your murderous record," Victor said in a bored voice. Then he pointed at Simon. "So is he, which I'm sure is why you teamed up." His lips curled back into a smile. "Have you told him you're still going to kill him no matter how much he helps?"

"They didn't have to," Simon gasped from where the wires bound him to the ground. "I already handed myself over. A small price to pay for getting you cornered by the one group of people you still fear."

Victor chuckled. "I was wondering how they got the changeling on their side." He turned to Lola. "You shouldn't have let him drag you along. Surely, you've already realized that this effort is as doomed as all your others."

Lola set her jaw. "If we're so doomed, why are you hiding behind the DFZ?"

"Because I can," he said with a casual shrug. "What's the point of having a god on a leash if you don't use her to take care of all the little problems you can't be bothered to deal with yourself?"

Lola blinked. He was lying. She'd spent her whole life paying attention to Victor, and she could see that he was straining. Whatever he was doing to exert this much control over the DFZ must be taking a huge amount of effort, which meant Simon was right. Victor *did* fear the Paladins. They must actually be able to hurt him, or he wouldn't be working so hard to keep the DFZ between himself and them. Lola was wondering why he hadn't just dropped them all to their deaths already when Victor opened his hand and released a grapefruit-sized camera drone into the air.

Her jaw clenched as the little robot rose to hover just above Victor's shoulder. Of course. He hadn't trapped them up here just to gloat. He was doing what he *always* did. The Paladins were one of the few forces that could still kill the Hero because he was a blood mage, and killing blood mages was what they did. So long as the world believed that, they were his bane. But if he showed people that the Paladins couldn't hurt him, that invulnerability would become part of the Hero's legend, just like the rest of his immortality.

That was what the camera was for. That was why he hadn't dropped them all out of the windows. He *needed* the Paladins to attack so he could beat them and prove to the world that even the famous blood-mage killers couldn't kill him. Lola had no idea how he intended to do that, but given the rest of this ridiculous setup, she was certain they were playing right into his hands, which meant they had to *stop*.

"Don't fight him!" she cried, whirling back toward Nadja. "It's a trap! He's going to—"

But it was too late. The Paladins, who'd been moving into position the whole time Victor was talking, were already charging as one. Lola hadn't even seen the Grand Marshal give the order, or maybe she hadn't needed to. Maybe they'd trained so long for this, they all just knew when to go.

However it had started, Lola already knew how it would end. From the sad sound he made beside her, Simon did, too. This wasn't how it was supposed to happen, but neither of them could stop the Paladins as they leaped at Victor with their magic and glowing swords. This was what they'd come to do, what they'd pledged their lives to. Nothing could stop them now, and that was exactly what Victor was counting on.

The moment the Paladins attacked, a cloud of the same wires that had grabbed Simon shot out of the platform. Each one was too thin and small to break the Paladin's armor, but with so many wires shooting at once, a few were bound to find their way through the gaps into the flesh beneath. Since the wires were also too small to be picked up by the tiny camera hovering over Victor's shoulder, this meant—to everyone watching at home—it looked like the Paladins jumping at the Hero had been stopped in midair by an invisible force that just happened to coincide with Victor's outstretched hand.

If Lola hadn't hated him so much, she would have been floored by his brilliance. He'd literally black-wired the whole thing on live TV using the DFZ. The Paladins hadn't even gotten their spells off before the wires dug into their flesh, ripping them apart from the inside before dropping them to the ground at Victor's feet.

Their bodies landed with a bloody *crunch* Lola knew she'd never be able to forget. Most had died instantly when the wires entered their brains, but one seemed to have avoided the direct kill. Unsurprisingly, it was Nadja. At first, Lola thought that was because the old woman was just too stubborn to die. Then Victor got down off his throne, and Lola realized she was wrong. Nadja hadn't survived. The wires had stopped just before they'd penetrated her skull, because she was their leader, and Victor wasn't finished.

"Now you see the fate of all who face the Hero," he said, grabbing the hovering camera to make sure his audience had a good look at the Grand Marshal lying beaten on the ground. "The Paladins' noble hearts were in the right place, but like all zealots, they were blinded by their prejudice. They looked at me and saw only their own fear. Fear of humanity's magic, fear of our *greatness*. And so, like everyone who lives by fear, they fell. My only regret is that I could not save them."

"How can you say that with a straight face?" Lola yelled, shoving herself off the ground. "You murdered them!"

"Edit out that last part," Victor said, pressing a button on the hovering drone before sending the camera away.

Seething with fury, Lola hurled a lump of gossamer after it. The shimmering ball turned into a brick as it smashed the drone out of the sky, sending it plummeting back to the platform with a *thunk*.

"That was petty," Victor observed, frowning at the broken drone. "It was only a remote link. All of the footage gets fed straight to Jamie, and she's not even in the building."

"I don't care!" Lola yelled as she ran over to Nadja, who was rapidly bleeding out. "You're a *monster*!"

Victor chuckled. "Says the girl who smuggled the entire Paladin Order into my tower only to sit back and watch them die."

The truth of that stung, but Lola refused to let him needle her as she spun up a can of spray-on bandage and began applying it on all the parts of Nadja's skin that she could see.

"Let me do that," said Dee, who was suddenly right beside her. "You go help Simon."

"No," Lola said, refusing to give up. Refusing to let him *win.* "I've got this. You and Toothy go find—"

She stopped herself just before she said Valente's name. Given how they'd gotten here, Victor probably already knew the Rider was alive. On the small chance he didn't, though, Lola wasn't about to give it away.

Find Valente, she finished in her head, pushing the order through her gossamer instead. *Go!*

Dee's face crumpled into a worried ball. "But—"

"Just do it. I can handle him," Lola insisted, glaring at Victor, who was walking closer.

Her double clearly disagreed, but she did as she was told, vanishing as suddenly as she'd appeared.

"So you *did* make a copy of yourself," Victor said, sounding almost impressed. "I suspected something of that nature when you seemed to be in too many places at once, but I didn't realize you'd advanced so far."

"You never did think much of me," Lola said, keeping his attention on her as she covertly conjured a pair of wire cutters into Simon's hands. "That was your biggest mistake."

"I don't make mistakes," Victor said, placing his boot on top of the body of the dying Paladin she was still trying to save.

Lola rolled her eyes and started working around his foot. "I'm not listening to this," she told him. "And I'm not afraid of you anymore, so stop posturing. I may not be able to kill you, but you can't kill me either. That makes me the one element you can't control."

"Are you sure about that?" Victor asked right before something sharp and cold pressed down on the top of her head.

Lola froze. The object was directly above her, so she couldn't see it, but that didn't matter. She could feel the deadly burn of the blood magic bane along with something else. A metallic, overwhelming pressure the part of her that had been Alberich still remembered.

"You know this, don't you?" Victor said, turning his hand so she could see the gleaming blade of the Hero's golden sword resting on her scalp. "This is the weapon all the world believes killed the Wild Hunt and its Nightmare King. What makes you so certain it can't kill you?"

"Because if it was that easy, you'd have done it already," Lola said, as much for herself as for him as she resumed treating the Paladin so she could at least say she'd avoided leading one person to their death today.

"Is that really what you think?"

"Yes," Lola said as she emptied the last of her spray-on bandage can into the Paladin's helmet. "I'm patching up your enemy right in front of you. If killing me was an option, I'd be dead fifty times over."

That felt like solid logic to her, but for some reason Victor started grinning even wider.

"You poor, deluded child," he said, taking his sword off her head so he could crouch down to her level. "Your life has been in my hands from the day we met. It's true you've survived a few incidents I didn't think you should have, and I was in earnest when I ordered the Rider to kill you. I was under a lot of pressure at the time, and you'd made me very, *very* angry. It was certainly the most practical choice given how much trouble you've caused me, but even when I had you at my mercy inside my death, I could never actually bring myself to do it. Do you know why?"

"I don't care," Lola spat.

"I think you do," Victor whispered, leaning closer. "It's because I made you. Valente and Simon were useful tools, but you were my masterpiece. Do you know how difficult it was to forge a human-fairy hybrid that could actually survive to adulthood? How rare and unrepeatable and *genius* the matrix of circumstances I lined up for your creation?"

He reached out to touch her cheek. "You've been my monster your entire life, but you've never seen what you *are*. You are my greatest and most useful creation. Even when you thought you were fighting me, all your blind hatred did was show the world over and over that I couldn't be killed. I thought it'd take years to achieve true immortality, but you got me there in less than three months." He shook his head in wonder. "You are, truly, the best tool I've ever made."

"Stop lying," Lola snarled, shoving his hand away. "You don't get to cover up your failure by saying you *meant* to let me escape and ruin your plans all those times."

"What plans have you ruined?" he asked, waving his arm to encompass the bloody platform with its golden throne and the city he controlled stretching out to the horizon. "Look where we are! Even the Fenrir debacle played to my favor in the end. That's what happens when you're truly superior, but it's time to stop running, Lola."

She froze. Victor never called her by her name. Lola almost didn't recognize the sound on his lips, but when she looked up, his face was deadly serious.

"It's time to come back where you belong," he said. "The power of the Underground King blended with a human soul is too great to be left in the hands of a reckless child. You've always needed a master, and that master has always been me."

"You have got to be joking," Lola said when she could speak again. "I know you're the king of delusional egos, but even you can't *possibly* think I'd ever come back."

"I don't joke," Victor informed her calmly. "You will come back to me because there's nowhere else for you to go. Your barrow is in my city, and your kind is being hunted to extinction by my followers. Simon's bleeding to death from those wires as we speak, and it'll be centuries before Morgan comes crawling out of her hole. You have no more rescuers, my monster. Even your precious Black Rider can't save you this time."

Lola went still, and Victor's smile grew crueler. "Oh yes, I know he's alive, or at least he was. I suspected Simon was up to something when he ran out so eagerly to grab the Rider's body. My apprentice never could resist the urge to play doctor, but I knew it would come to nothing. Even if Simon did put Humpty Dumpty back together again, a knight cannot survive without his monarch. I thought it had already happened until I saw the news reports of him attacking the Paladins on the bridge. But he still fell in the end, so I suppose it makes no difference either way."

He finished with a sadistic curve of his lips, but Lola barely saw it. Her mind was back in that stupid 7-Eleven where she'd wrapped her magic over Valente's tepid, sickly-feeling gossamer. She remembered how he'd stopped taking off his helmet. How he'd said he was just going to check on the Paladins but hadn't answered any of her texts since. How Dee couldn't find him right now even though she was looking everywhere.

"There, there," Victor said, patting her on the head. "I know you're disappointed, but what else could you expect? Unlike your masterful creation, the Rider was always a hack job. I'm honestly surprised he lasted as long as he did, but I owe my slave some gratitude. Without his failure to become an urban legend, I never could have perfected the process and become the Hero, but that's how it always is with me. Even my failures come back around to lift me higher. Just look at yourself."

Lola looked at him with all the hate in her heart. "I will die before I *ever* go back to you."

"If that's how you feel, you should have let the Rider do it when I was still furious," Victor said, standing up with a huff. "Unfortunately for you, you wasted your chance. Now stop being stubborn and come. I might not be willing to kill my masterpiece, but I'm not afraid to be *very* rough."

He pointed at Simon as he finished. The last time Lola had risked a glance his direction, he'd been quietly cutting his way out of the wires with the snips she'd conjured for him. The moment Victor's finger landed on him, though, Simon screamed the way he used to when they were children. It was a horrible, inhuman sound from Lola's darkest memories. Then, as fast as it started, Simon's scream cut off like a switch, and he pitched forward, his body falling stiffly to the platform.

Lola was lunging to help him before he hit, but she'd barely made it an inch when Victor's hand swept back to grab her head. It was her turn to scream then, falling to her knees as Victor's fingers dug into her scalp like nails, pinning her in place.

"Don't make that face," he said as she writhed. "My apprentice is easy to kill, but he's very difficult to keep that way. It's the only part of his training he was actually good at, but even he can't cheat death forever."

His grip on Lola's head tightened until it was all she could feel. She tried to fight back, but Victor was holding her in the same inescapable way he used to when she was a child. Lola had always thought that was because he was stronger, but now she knew enough to understand. Victor wasn't holding her with his fingers. He was using his blood magic to pin her soul, trapping the part of her that was still human as he lowered his golden sword to her neck.

"You already know how this ends," he said as the gleaming blade began to burn through her gossamer. "Surrender quietly, and I'll leave your brother be. Keep pushing me, and you'll see very quickly just how much I've been holding back."

Lola writhed against his grasp, pushing on him with every new trick she'd learned. She even tried calling for Dee and Toothy, but they couldn't come to her. Victor's grip on her soul was a wall against movement. Lola couldn't even flee down her silver thread back to her body. Her magic might be everywhere, but everything that was *her* was trapped under Victor's thumb.

Exactly where it'd always been.

"*No!*" she roared, casting off even the semblance of humanity as she lunged forward, flying straight at him since she couldn't get away. Her claws were almost in his throat when he yanked her back, slamming her down with his blood magic and golden sword. The blood magic bane burned through her like a torch through sugar, but Lola didn't care. Victor might always win, but that didn't mean she had to lose. She was never going back to him. She'd die right here on this roof next to Simon before she *ever* called him master again.

The defiance must have shown on her face, because Victor shook his head with a sigh. "So be it," he said, yanking his golden sword out of her to ready it for the next swing. "Just remember, you brought this on yourself."

His sword crashed into her as he finished, splitting Lola from neck to knees in a rainbow of spewing gossamer. The next swing cut off even more, flinging her melting magic all the way back to the foot of his golden throne.

"Don't worry," he said as her pieces splashed across the ground. "I already said I won't kill you. I'm just whittling you down into a more manageable size. Once you're back to how you were, we'll see about rebuilding you."

He swung his sword like a woodsman's ax, moving so fast the bane didn't even have time to burn as he hacked her to bits. Dimly in the distance, she could feel her other selves beating against the wall he'd raised, but Lola frantically motioned for them to stay away. She wouldn't let Victor hurt them too. They were all she could save as he chopped and chopped and chopped. And then, just when Lola was sure the pain would never end, Victor's golden sword stopped.

Lola had no idea why. She'd lost anything resembling a head twenty hits ago. But as time ticked on and the next blow still didn't come, she managed to scoop enough of her face back together to see something that made her dead hopes leap.

Victor hadn't stopped swinging his golden sword. He'd *been* stopped, his blade caught in the grip of a black, leather-gloved hand.

Chapter 9

Valente woke up in the dark.

He wasn't sure he *had* woken up at first. For the first time since Victor had put the fairy's severed head on his shoulders, the dancing vision that came with it was gone. He wasn't sure if that was because his eyeballs had finally fallen out or if his entire head had given up the ghost, but it definitely felt like the end. He was wondering how long it would take before his thoughts rotted away as well when he heard the unmistakable sound of a boot landing right next to his head.

A gloved hand appeared next, as black as the void but somehow still perfectly visible, right down to the familiar notepad clutched between its leather-gloved fingers.

How long are you planning to lie there?

Valente sat up with a jolt, his own blood-stained gloves landing on the pavement he'd just realized was still beneath him. A second later, he saw that wasn't right. He *was* lying on a road, but not the highway bridge where he'd fought the Paladins. This was an ancient, cracked street from the DFZ Underground complete with potholes and an old Detroit municipal storm drain set into the curb.

He was still staring at it in confusion when a second gloved hand shot out and grabbed his shoulder. The padded-leather fingers clamped down with massive strength, yanking Valente straight up to his feet. He was reeling from the motion when the hand let him go, leaving him face-to-face with a terrifying figure wearing a black leather motorcycle suit and a black helmet so perfectly reflective, Valente could see every scratch on his own cracked visor. It was so bizarre but so familiar at the same time that the words popped out of Valente's mouth before he'd realized he could speak.

"Am I dead again?"

Not yet, the Black Rider wrote on the notepad in Valente's own hand. *We caught you just in time.*

"Who's we?"

The Black Rider pointed at the edge of the decaying street.

Valente followed the gesture, and then jumped back with a curse. The crumbling pavement they were standing on wasn't a road at all. It was an island, a tiny bit of land floating in a huge, empty black space, and below it lay the DFZ.

Not the DFZ he knew. This wasn't the city Fenrir had destroyed or even Victor's new monstrosity. This was a nightmare.

Looking down from the floating island, he saw the buildings from the bottom, as if he were standing far below the earth looking up at the city's foundations. Even from the strange perspective, though, Valente knew it was all wrong. Everything he could see—the sewers, the foundations, the pipes, the wiring, the roads—was twisting and tangling in on itself, as if the city were a giant knot being pulled tighter and tighter. As he watched everything squeeze, Valente realized he could see the point where the knot came together: an ever-shrinking ball of buildings and bridges drenched in a thick red liquid he'd know anywhere.

"That's Victor's blood," he said, turning back at the silent Rider standing beside him. "What's going on? What is this place?"

We're in the Gnarls, the Black Rider wrote. *The in-between space where the Living City's spirit meets her actual ground. And you already know what's going on.* His pencil dug into the paper, writing the words in vicious gouges. *Victor's using his control over the population to bind the DFZ to his will. If this keeps up, everything she was will be subsumed, and this will become the Hero's city, not hers.*

It was on the tip of Valente's tongue to say that wasn't possible. That one man couldn't *possibly* dominate a city of millions. What was left of his voice couldn't speak the words, though, because they weren't true. Valente had seen the birth of

Victor's Hero with his own eyes. There was nothing his old master couldn't do now.

Why do you think we saved you? the Rider wrote angrily, his shiny helmet leveled determinedly at Valente's cracked one. *Her magic might be clenched in his fist, but a city is never just one idea. The DFZ is many things to many people, too many for even Victor to control. You're one of those faces. The Black Rider is her urban legend, and your city needs your help.*

"I can't," Valente said. "I'm not actually the Black Rider. I can lean on his stories when conditions are right, but I was never able to make the jump to a true urban legend. Victor told me so himself."

The Rider tilted his visor. *And you believed him?*

"I do about this," Valente said angrily. "The Black Rider isn't some random ghost story that came to life. Victor made him up. He was using me to test his theory that a human soul could become a spirit if it got enough momentum, but I failed. His experiment didn't work."

He wouldn't have told you if it did, the Rider wrote. *He might even believe it himself, but although Victor started the story, no one controls a tale once it goes out into the world. The Black Rider belongs to the people who tell his legends. His power comes from every person who's ever looked over their shoulder in a dark alley, searching for his silent blue light.*

"If that's true, then I'll never be him," Valente said, clenching his bloody gloves. "The Black Rider is a monster and a murderer."

That's not *who he is,* the silent man wrote furiously. *It was Victor's Black Knight who killed those journalists. The Black Rider would never do something like that. Haven't you read your own stories?*

Before Valente could answer, the other man unzipped the pocket of his motorcycle jacket and pulled out a folded stack of crumpled papers. He thrust them forward like a knife, slapping the pages against Valente's ripped-up chest until he finally took them. Valente already knew what they were, but he was still surprised by how thick the stack was when he unfolded the papers to reveal a collection of Black Rider pamphlets, the ones Victor had bribed the tourist companies to hand out for free at convenience stores and information kiosks.

All the standards were there—the neat little booklets Victor had written to teach the city to fear his monster—but there were also pages Valente had never seen. Newer printouts in a different style written by amateurs looking to capitalize on the Black Rider's popularity. In those stories, the Rider wasn't just a ghost who attacked people in back alleys. He was an avenger, a silent shadow who hunted and punished those who'd gotten away with evil. The new tales were even wilder than Victor's originals. They were also far more numerous, making up fully two-thirds of the stack the Rider had handed him.

And those are just the ones that got printed, the Black Rider wrote when Valente had looked through them all. *The online stories are even more elaborate. That's how you got the ability to move through shadows. Victor didn't give you that. His Black Rider is just a headless ghost who rides around town searching for victims on his silent motorcycle. It was the people who believed your stories and made up their own that did the rest. In their version, you're a ghost who makes sure the guilty never get away with what they've done. You hunt down murderers and give bloody justice to the wronged. They took Victor's lazy ghost story and shaped you into the monster they needed you to be, because that's how legends work. They're not stories controlled by a single author. They're reflections of the society that tells them. Victor gave you to the people to build your power, but that power never belonged to him. That's why the DFZ sent me to find you.*

"Because I'm a killer?"

Because you're something Victor can no longer control, the Rider wrote, his fingers tight on his pencil. *Even when he killed you in front of the entire world, no one who believed in your stories thought you were really dead. If they did, I wouldn't be here.*

"So why are you talking to me?" Valente asked, looking the Rider up and down. "You seem to be doing fine on your own."

Because I'm not the actual Rider, the silent man wrote. *I might become him in time if the story keeps growing, but, as Victor discovered, it takes a lot of magic to make even a small spirit, and I'm not there yet. I didn't even have autonomy until the DFZ pulled me out and sent me to find help.*

"So you're the one who's been writing me all those creepy notes," Valente said, rubbing his numb arms. "I'd say it's good to know I'm not crazy, but I'm not sure if that's true, seeing as I'm talking to my own legend."

Believe me, I would have talked to someone else if I could have, the Rider wrote irritably. *Lola's far more accepting than you are. She would have helped me without all the questions, but you're the only one I can reach.*

"Because I'm the actual Rider," Valente finished.

The other man nodded, and Valente sighed. "If you pulled me in here because you need a body, I'm afraid you're out of luck." He pointed at his cracked helmet. "I'm done. Unlike Lola, I was made from a dead fairy, not a living changeling. She never needed Victor's pills, but I started falling apart the moment he let go. Victor always told me I was the inferior version, but I never knew how true that was until I saw her." His voice grew softer. "Even buried under Alberich's nightmares, she was always beautiful. I've never been anything but dead."

You are not dead, the Rider wrote, underlining the words for emphasis.

"My face says otherwise," Valente said, pulling off his helmet.

It was the first time he'd removed it since the problems started, but it was the only way to make this stupid ghost see. The sight must have been even worse than Valente expected, because the Black Rider took a step back, his helmet turning away from the ruin Valente had become.

"Now do you get it?" Valente asked, turning his blackened gossamer from side to side to give the spirit a good look. He pulled off his gloves next, showing the Rider how the fairy's black gossamer was peeling away from his human flesh, which was now little more than rotting meat and yellowed bones.

"This is what happened when you merge two corpses together," he said in a resigned voice, putting his gloves and helmet back on now that he'd made his point. "My life was sold to Victor long ago. I thought it was a small price to pay when I made the choice, but I was wrong. He made me a worse monster than you ever were."

Then help us stop him, the Rider wrote.

"Do you not understand what you just saw?" Valente snapped. "Victor bound my soul to a fairy head that's falling apart! Since he had to cut my real head off to do it, I'm not sure if this body was ever technically alive, but it's *definitely* dying now. So if you're looking for a hand to go inside your Rider puppet, you'll have to ask someone else, because I've got nothing left."

Valente felt that should have been obvious, but the Rider kept shaking his helmet.

It has to be you, he wrote firmly. *You're the grain of truth at the Rider's heart. Without you, I'm just a ghost story.*

"That's probably for the best considering what they were saying about us at the end," Valente muttered, looking down at his gloves, which still looked bloodstained even in the dark. "I'd rather be dead than go back to being that Rider."

Then don't be him, the Black Rider wrote as he stepped closer. *What Victor made you do after he became the Hero was awful, but it's a tiny fraction of who you are, a handful of tales among thousands. Just as some people didn't believe the Black Rider could be killed by the Hero, there are those who never stopped seeing you as a force for justice. If you go back out there and prove it, show the world that you're still alive and not the monster he named you, then it is Victor's legend that will weaken, not yours.*

He grabbed Valente's stained gloves with his clean ones and placed the notepad in his hands as he wrote. *You never failed to become an urban legend. The powers the whole world saw you use during the fight with Orlando prove that you are the real Black Rider. I don't know if Victor lied to you on purpose or if he actually believed you were a failure because you didn't become what he expected.* He tilted his shiny helmet. *Personally, I think he honestly believed you failed. Victor sees only himself when he looks at things, so when he looked at you and didn't see a monster, he thought you didn't make it. I bet it never even occurred to him that the Black Rider could become something good.*

Valente shook his head. "There is nothing good about the Black Rider."

There can be if you put it there, the man in the helmet wrote, pressing the notepad hard into Valente's palms. *Who do you think inspired people to change your stories? Victor's pamphlets describe the Black Rider as a mindless ghost who slaughters anyone stupid enough to be out alone at night. You could have easily become just another DFZ horror story, but you didn't, because you didn't kill just anyone. You went out of your way to target criminals and killers and avoided the innocent even when they would have been easy kills.*

"Of course I didn't murder innocent people," Valente said, insulted. "Victor ordered me to kill to get his legend started. I couldn't disobey him, but I wasn't just going to randomly slaughter anyone. I waited and watched until I found people that I wouldn't feel bad about killing, but that was for my benefit. I wasn't doing it to be a hero."

But that's still what you became, the Rider wrote, his mirrored helmet staring hard into Valente's own. *Everything good about the Rider started with you. When you drove past innocents without killing them, when you took the time to choose your targets, you changed the story. You made people believe in a better version of us, and then, when you defeated the Wild Hunt's champion in front of the entire world, you set it in stone. You killed the monster no one but the Hero was supposed to be able to touch using nothing but your hands and your motorcycle! Even when Victor killed you and lied about it right after, people aren't stupid. They know what they saw. That's why you can't be dead. Because the Black Rider people witnessed that night was stronger than any lie Victor could tell.*

"Then why am I falling apart?" Valente demanded, shoving the ghost's pad back at him. "I thought I had everything when Simon brought me back, but I didn't even get four days before I was right back to being dead! Worse than dead. I've spent the last three months watching myself *rot* and having to lie about it to the person I care about the most! The only reason I didn't end it all sooner was because I wanted to at least help Lola kill Victor first. If I'm so alive, why did I have to go through all that?"

Because we're not there yet, the Black Rider wrote in patient strokes. *I'm not big enough to become a spirit on my own, and you're not alive enough to stop dying. Together, though, we might be able to be both. That's why the DFZ sent me and why I brought you here.* He stopped writing to wave his pad at the yawning void around them before bending over the paper again. *We're in the place where the physical world meets the Sea of Magic. If you accept me here, accept the legend you made, the DFZ thinks we have a good chance of becoming the Black Rider for real.*

His hand began to shake, making the letters wobble. *You don't have to keep rotting. You can live, Valente, but only if you stop being what Victor made you and start being what you made yourself.*

"A spirit?" Valente asked in a low, trembling voice.

A legend, the Black Rider corrected. *Even together, we're not big enough to be our own god yet. We'll get there in time if we keep growing our story, but right now we're a facet of the city. The Living City, which is a lot better than you can say for your head.*

He took another step closer, his black boots moving silently on the cracked pavement until they were an inch from Valente's own.

The Black Rider hunts the wicked, he wrote, scrawling the words right under Valente's visor. *He avenges the abused. I know you weren't born in the DFZ, but you are her story, and she needs you. Victor's got the whole world thinking he's their Hero, but the Black Rider always knows the truth. If he comes back from the dead to hunt the Hero, everyone will know what Victor is, and what we are.*

He leaned forward, tapping his clean helmet against Valente's cracked one. *Help me become what I was born to be. Become the Black Rider and save your city. Save yourself, while there's still something left to salvage.*

The ghost was so close now that Valente could feel him, a silent pressure like the prickle on the back of your neck right before you turn around. He lowered his pad as he finished, his headless gaze staring into Valente's rotting one like he could force his way inside by sheer will before Valente stepped away.

"No."

Why not? the Black Rider wrote furiously. *Don't you want to kill Victor? Don't you want to live?*

"Of course I do," Valente said, "but not at that price. If all I cared about was killing Victor and saving my own skin, I would have let Lola make me a knight. She's a lot nicer to look at than you are, but I swore I wasn't doing this again."

Doing what?

"Selling my soul," Valente growled, taking yet another step back. "I've heard this pitch before, but I'm not the gullible idiot I was thirteen years ago. Even if I'm the one who shaped them, everyone knows urban legends are slaves to their stories, and I'll *never* be a slave again."

You wouldn't be a slave, the Rider wrote in incensed, angry jerks. *Did you understand nothing I just told you? You're the one who makes the story! Victor gave you that head to make you a weapon, a sword with no more say than an actual inanimate object, but the Black Rider is different. His legend is the product of the choices you made. That's the opposite of slavery!*

"But I'd still be bound to them."

The Rider made a frustrated gesture. *You say that like it's a bad thing! It's true that a spirit can never be anything other than what they are. The DFZ will always be a city. The Empty Wind will always shepherd the Forgotten Dead. The Black Rider will always hunt the wicked. But none of that matters if it's what you want to do! The fact that you and I are standing here having this conversation proves that you get a vote in this. We all do! Mortal Spirits might not be as free as the humans who create us, but the choices we do get count for a lot more. We get to decide how we are ourselves. That's why I came to you. You've been shaping who the Black Rider is from the very beginning, and you'll keep shaping your story every time you choose who to punish and who to save. That is not slavery. That is a higher calling, a divine purpose. That is what it means to be a god. Maybe you don't care about that, but I'm the Black Rider, too, and I'd much rather live as a legend of the DFZ than die as Victor's broken sword.*

Writing all of that took him eight pages. He tore them off and shoved them at Valente's chest when he finished. He still hadn't made a sound this whole time, but as he slammed the crumpled papers silently against Valente's rotting magic, it wasn't the Rider that Valente saw. It was Lola, the child version of her he'd found between the trucks back at Riverfest, beating her little fists against him just like this as she ordered him not to die until she saved him.

She'd done it, too. Simon had cast the actual magic that brought him back to life, but Lola was the reason Valente had survived long enough for Victor to kill him and break his oath. If he'd sacrificed himself to Orlando as he'd planned, he would have died a knight, Victor's slave to the end. It was because of her that he'd fought back long enough to be set free, because of her that any of this was happening, and she was *still* doing it. She and Simon were attacking Victor with the Paladins right now. If Valente could have wished for anything, it would have been to be there with her, standing at her side as they made the bastard pay. Now the Rider was offering him a chance to do just that, which meant he was telling the truth. The Black Rider *wouldn't* be a slave, because choosing to do what you wanted to do was the essence of freedom.

"Okay," Valente said with a deep breath. "I'll do it."

The Rider slumped in relief. *About time.*

"I'm not taking orders from the DFZ, though," Valente warned, crossing his arms stubbornly over his chest. "If I'm really the one who shapes the Rider, then he goes and does what *I* want. I don't care if I'm a part of her city or not. I'm never calling anyone master again."

She wouldn't let you if you tried, the Rider assured him. *It might shock you to learn this, but the Detroit Free Zone has strong opinions about slavery. She doesn't want vassals. She wants a free-thinking Black Rider she can trust to do his job well, starting with the Hero.*

"Don't worry," Valente said darkly. "If there's anyone who deserves to have the Black Rider appear behind him, it's Victor." His hands were already clenched in anticipation as he lifted his cracked visor. "I'm ready. How do we do this?"

We already are, the Black Rider wrote, looking at the void above them, which suddenly seemed much closer. *We're both already where we need to be. All we have to do now is merge.*

"Great," Valente said, holding out his arms. "Come on over, then, and let's get out of here."

Lola was probably worried sick, and now that he wasn't sacrificing himself to make it happen, Valente really didn't want to miss the Paladin attack on Victor. The old bastard had always been terrified of those zealots, and that was back when they'd hunted him in threes. The whole order working together was bound to be a force of nature. He couldn't wait to see Victor's face when he realized what they'd thrown at him, but when Valente wiggled his fingers at the Black Rider to hurry up, the ghost shook his head.

Not until you cut the dead weight.

Valente scowled. "What does that mean?"

The other man pointed at Valente's cracked visor. *You have to get rid of that.*

"My helmet?"

Your head.

"No way," Valente said, covering his face protectively with his gloved hands. "It might be nearly rotted, but my soul is still stapled to it. If it goes, *I* go."

Getting rid of it is the only way you don't *go*, the Black Rider wrote with an exasperated flick of his pencil. *Spirits are human magic. You and I have always been the same. The fairy is the part that doesn't belong. That's why it's causing you so many problems.*

"Not as big a problem as I'll have if I take it off."

It was impossible to tell through the helmet, but Valente would have sworn the Rider was glaring at him. *How can you be this dense? You're the* Black Rider. *If there's anyone who can get by without a head, it's you.*

When Valente still kept his head on, the ghost hunched his shoulders. *There's no other way. You're just going to have to trust me.*

Valente drummed his fingers nervously against his helmet. It was so stupid. He'd always hated the fairy's head. He'd thought he'd be glad to be rid of the thing, but now that he'd decided not to die, the thought of taking it off was terrifying. He could actually feel the presence he thought of as himself clinging to the rot behind his face. If he threw his head away, how would not lose that too?

He went back and forth for a solid minute before he realized he was being stupid. Whether he went through with this or not, it was only a matter of time before the rot made the decision for him. At least with the Rider, he'd get to see Lola again. Thinking about it like that made the choice easy, so, before he could lose his nerve, Valente yanked the fairy's cursed head off his shoulders and threw it, helmet and all, as hard as he could into the void.

The head broke apart as it left his fingers. He'd known he was nearly at the end, but even Valente wasn't prepared for how quickly it crumbled. He couldn't even watch because his eyes were falling apart with it, the world breaking into bits as his glowing gaze turned to dust.

He didn't even have time to be afraid before the rest of him followed suit. As soon as his head was gone, the magic keeping his human body alive collapsed. For a horrible moment, Valente was falling back into the darkness Simon had yanked him out of. But then, just before he dissolved into the same nothingness as his head, a strong hand grabbed the place where his shoulders had been as someone shoved a helmet onto the empty space at the top of Valente's neck.

As soon as the helmet made contact, everything changed. His body didn't stop falling, but it was no longer falling apart. It was falling into something new, something bigger.

The numbness of his rotting gossamer vanished, ripped away and replaced by the chill of wet pavement and blowing wind. His vision came back next, but not the dancing fairy perception or even the physical sight of his glowing eyes. When Valente looked around now, he saw himself from several angles at once, almost as if his perception was bigger than his physical shape. A few moments later, he realized there was no "almost" about it. He *was* greater than his body, greater than himself. A force built by multitudes.

Because that's exactly what you are.

The voice roared through his head like a passing truck, making Valente jump. He'd never heard anything like it in his life, yet it was also deeply familiar, a mother's voice.

That's because you were born here, the DFZ said, her disembodied words tense with pain. *You're a part of me as I am part of you, but you have to hurry. There isn't much time left.*

What do I need to do? Valente wrote on the pad that was in his hands now. His motorcycle suit, too, was clean and black again. There was no more blood, no more tatters. Even his helmet was as shiny as a pool of spilled ink, because he was the Black Rider for real now, and the Black Rider didn't bleed.

Stop him, the city begged. *Before it's too late!*

She didn't have to say who. She didn't even have to tell him where. This must have been what the Rider meant when he'd talked about a higher calling, because the moment Valente turned his mind in that direction, Victor's sins filled his new awareness like a stormfront, a mountain range of wrongs that demanded to be put right. That was the Black Rider's purpose—Valente's purpose now—and as soon as he felt it, he took off like a shot, driving his silent motorcycle out of the twisting magic of the Gnarls into the real city above.

The ground opened for him as he drove, the dirt and cement and pipes throwing themselves out of his way as the city made him a path. Now that he was part of her, Valente could feel the DFZ's frustration that she couldn't help him more, but the Rider didn't need help. He just needed her to let him through, opening a road all the way to the top of Hero's Tower. He made it to the roof with seconds to spare, shooting out of the ugly platform the DFZ had been forced to build, his gloved hand already extended to catch the Hero's sword.

The look Victor gave him then was something Valente would treasure for the rest of however long urban legends lived. Thanks to the new heightened senses he shared with his city, he was able to watch from multiple angles as his old master's face twisted from smug superiority to blank shock to red-cheeked, eye-bulging rage as the Black Rider wrenched the Hero's golden sword out of his grip.

The blade didn't even burn now that Valente was no longer made of gossamer. It actually felt quite comfortable in his hand, the flat settling against his palm like an old friend. A sense of deep rightness came with it, as did satisfaction and an alien anger that wasn't his own.

Valente had no idea what that meant, but when he turned to fling the Hero's sword off the side of the building, the golden blade stuck fast to his fingers. He was about to rip his glove off to get rid of it when Victor leaped at him.

"*No!*" his old master roared, his red face gone bloodless white as he tried to wrestle the sword out of Valente's hand. "Not to you! *Never to you!*"

He was digging his fingers into the Rider's gloves to pry the sword loose when Valente kicked him. He'd only been aiming to knock him away, but the moment his boot made contact, Victor went flying. He would have gone straight off the building if the DFZ hadn't caught him at the last second, snagging his body with her wires like a jellyfish. Victor slapped her tendrils off his body immediately and stomped back across the platform with his blue eyes full of hate.

"How?" he demanded, his normally calm voice cracking with frantic malice. "How did you do that? How are you *alive?* I cut your head in half! Even if you did manage to put yourself back together, I cast you off. The knighthood oaths that kept you alive are broken, so *how—*"

There was more, a whole unhinged rant of sputtering rage, but Valente didn't have to listen to him anymore, so he didn't. He didn't attack him again, either. Not because Victor deserved leniency, but because fighting him now would have also meant fighting his city, and the Black Rider had no interest in that. Victor was clearly spoiling for a brawl, too, which made Valente even less inclined. As Lola always said, they weren't giving Victor another damn thing, so Valente turned his back on him, leaving the Hero raging impotently as the Black Rider stuck his stolen sword into his belt and hurried over to Lola.

He hadn't seen her this small in a long, long time. What was left of her gossamer was no bigger than a child, but her eyes were full of wonder when she pulled herself back together enough to look at him.

"Valente?" she whispered, reaching a still-forming hand toward his helmet. "You're alive?"

As always, his name on her lips sent a shiver through him. He hid it by scooping her into his arms, and then he went for Simon.

The mage looked even worse than Lola. Valente wasn't sure what had happened to him, but the perfect stillness of his body didn't seem good. He was bound to the rooftop with a tangle of copper wires, but a cutter that felt like Lola lay next to his limp hands. Valente was about to use it to finish cutting Simon's body free when the prison of wires fell apart like cobwebs.

Valente felt the DFZ's smugness ripple through him before Victor stomped her back down. The blood mage shot across the platform next, moving on a wave of twisting metal to loom over his old knight.

"How did you do it?"

Valente turned away. The headless Black Rider had no mouth to reply, but even if he could have, he owed this man nothing. No answers, no explanations, no satisfaction of any sort. Just silence as Valente gently placed Simon next to Lola in his arms. One of the Paladins was still alive, so he grabbed her as well, happy to take anything from Victor as the old man seethed, staring at the silent reflection of his own rage in the Rider's mirrored visor.

"This means nothing, you know," he snarled, clenching his empty fists and not looking at his stolen sword so pointedly, he might as well have been staring. "I don't know how you survived, but you came back too late. The world just saw me defeat my last true enemy. Nothing can stop me now."

He lifted his chin as he finished, but the Rider just gave him a long, silent stare before walking back to his motorcycle, which was still waiting patiently where he'd jumped off it to grab Lola. The moment he settled back onto the seat with the people he'd rescued in his arms, the bike sank into the floor, its ghostly blue light turning Victor's enraged face a hideous shade of purple as the Black Rider vanished from view.

Chapter 10

Lola was pretty sure she was in shock.

She remembered very clearly Valente appearing from nowhere and stealing Victor's sword. She remembered him scooping up her and Simon and even Nadja while Victor screamed and did nothing. Everything was right there in her head like a miracle, but she didn't feel relieved or happy or anything at all.

Even when Valente's bike popped them out into an alley on the other side of town next to her barrow's most reliable door, she couldn't seem to do anything but lean against him like a dead log. She was trying to move her numb hands enough to at least open the magic and get them inside when her double burst into the alley.

"Lola!"

She wasn't alone. Toothy was right behind her, stretching the doorway like a rubber band with her claws to make room for Valente to wheel his entire motorcycle into the living room. Dee ran ahead to move the furniture, shoving the chairs against the wall as Valente carried everyone inside like some kind of magical rescue wagon.

Her other selves grabbed Simon first, placing him on the stretcher from the emergency triage clinic Lola and Simon had built together in what was supposed to be the formal dining room. They transferred the Paladin next. Then, when both stretchers were on the ground, Toothy looked at Lola with a keening sound.

Her creature never had learned to talk like Dee, but Lola still understood. Simon couldn't doctor himself while he was unconscious. They needed help, and this was her kingdom. Lola didn't know anything about real medicine, but they'd left reality behind the moment they'd stepped through the door. The part of her that had come from Alberich knew that anything she wanted was possible here. So, since she was too numb right now to feel the crippling impostor syndrome and terror that normally accompanied such thoughts, Lola decided to give it a go.

Heal them.

The house rumbled at the force of her command. Barrows were as tricky as the fairies that created them, and a big part of Lola still considered this Alberich's domain. She'd never trusted the magic enough to give it such an open-ended order, but the impossible had already happened once today, so Lola let go of her control, opening herself up to the magic she normally treated like a caged tiger.

Do it. I don't care how.

The thought left her head like a trumpet call. It was a good thing she was already in shock, because otherwise the similarity to Alberich's voice would have sent her into a panic. In her sorry current state, Lola could only watch passively from her seat on the Rider's silent bike as the floor of her living room opened like a mouth to disgorge a flood of low creatures.

She'd never dreamed there'd be so many. The trolls and monsters she was used to, but the little mice were a complete surprise. Even more shocking was how familiar they seemed to be with Simon. They called him by his name in their little squeaky voices as they wiggled under his stretcher and hoisted him up, carrying him and the Paladin into the hospital room on a conveyor made from their furry backs.

Lola was still trying to wrap her brain around that when a new, much bigger creature pulled itself out of the floor. It was such a strange sight that it took Lola several seconds to realize she was looking at a mole. A four-foot-tall star-nosed mole wearing a doctor's white coat and round glasses over its beady, nearsighted eyes.

"Majesty," the mole said, giving her a low but hasty bow. "We obey. Where patients?"

Lola pointed a shaky finger at the door Dee was holding open for the mice. The mole bowed again and hurried over, barking curt orders at Lola's double to get the hospital beds ready.

Toothy was also pressed into service as dozens of mice crawled up her fur and started shouting directions to the medical vault, which was apparently located seven floors down. Lola hadn't realized they had a medical vault, though given how barrows worked, it was entirely possible they hadn't until she'd needed one. Any other time, Lola would have been extremely curious to see it, but now that the shock was finally ebbing, her body was shaking wildly. She could barely control her arms enough to wave at Toothy to go ahead.

Her creature obeyed at once, ducking her huge, mouse-covered head and shuffling down the staircase that used to lead to the garage but now went somewhere else entirely. The door closed on its own as soon as Toothy went through, leaving Lola and the Rider alone on his silent, still-running motorcycle in the middle of her living room.

They stayed like that for a solid minute while Lola tried and failed to get a hold of herself. When it was clear the violent shaking wasn't going to stop, Valente vanished his bike and helped her to the couch. As soon as she was down, he moved his sword—Victor's golden sword, which was still stuck through his black leather belt—out of the way and sat down next to her. He pulled a small memo pad out of his pocket next and wrote something on the first page, which he then showed to her.

I didn't know you could do all that.

"I didn't either," Lola said through her chattering teeth. "It was more of a hope than a plan, but fairy barrows are famous for being whatever you want, so I just sort of…"

Her voice trailed off, and she turned on the cushions to look hard into the Rider's shiny—and no longer cracked—helmet.

"What happened to you?" she whispered, voice shaking harder than ever. "How did you drive through the building like that, or steal Victor's sword? I should have known he was lying when he said you were dead. Victor always lies, but why are you using the pad again? And why do you still not feel cold?"

The questions poured out faster with every word, but it was the last one that hit Lola hardest. Between all the shocks, she hadn't noticed until he sat down next to her that the chill of Valente's midwinter magic was completely gone. It'd been fading for a while, but this was different. The man sitting next to her didn't feel anything like the Valente she knew. He didn't even feel like gossamer. His magic was something totally different: a yawning chasm of power that made her feel like she was standing on the edge of a cliff.

"Who are you?" she demanded, jerking away. "Where's Valente?"

The man in the motorcycle helmet hesitated for a long time over the page before he wrote, *I am him.*

"Liar," Lola snapped. "I know what Valente's magic feels like."

That magic is gone, he wrote quickly. *But I'm still here.*

"Prove it."

The afternoon before Victor came back, I went to the corner store and bought the hot dogs you used to lure Buster into his crate.

Lola bit her lip. She supposed it was possible an imposter could know that, but that was Valente's handwriting. He had the same hesitant way of moving, too, like he was trying his hardest not to scare her. It was the same way he'd moved the first time they'd done this back in his apartment, and Lola let out a long sigh.

"It *is* you," she said softly, reaching up to touch his visor only to stop an inch short of the mirrored surface. "What happened?"

The Rider tapped his nubbin of pencil against the page as he struggled to find the words. *I died,* he wrote eventually.

Lola gaped at him. "You *died?*"

It happened a long time ago, he wrote in a rush. *To combine my soul with the fairy's, Victor had to cut off my head. That's when my human life ended, and I became his Black Knight. The fairy was also dead when Victor stitched us together. The only reason we didn't both pass on that night was because of the oaths.*

"The knighthood oaths can do that?"

Valente nodded. *Anything gossamer is capable of will be done at the monarch's command. That's how Victor was able to put a fairy head on a human body. You know better than anyone that a fairy can't die so long as its head is intact, but Victor destroyed that one utterly. He obliterated its head, and then he tried to put it back together using blood magic. I think he was trying to make a full fairy that he controlled the same way he did you, but he couldn't get the pieces to stay together. Real gossamer was too slippery, and the head kept falling apart. He was about to throw it away when I volunteered.*

Lola froze. "You volunteered?"

She hadn't meant to sound so accusatory, but the Rider kept writing like he didn't dare stop.

I'd just watched Victor kill the monster that destroyed my life. I would have done anything for him in that moment, which was how I ended up becoming his knight. I let him chop off my head and put the fairy one in its place, and then I used the fairy's voice to swear eternal loyalty. Once I was his, Victor was able to bind my human soul into the fairy's head, but nothing could bring it back to life. The oaths kept it from decaying so long as I served Victor, but once he was no longer my master, it stopped.

"What do you mean 'it stopped'?" Lola asked with growing panic. "I knew your gossamer was getting warmer, but you were still using it. Still walking around like normal, so I thought—"

She stopped when Valente's pencil moved to a new line. It hovered there for a long moment. Then, as if he'd come to a decision, Valente flipped to an entirely new page and started again.

I haven't been honest with you, he wrote. *I didn't realize what was happening myself at first. I thought I was fine since I could still use my gossamer after Simon put me back together, but I've always been two corpses. Without the oaths ordering me to stay alive, I began to rot.*

Lola's stomach clenched in horror. "Rot?"

Valente nodded. *That's why my gossamer was getting warmer.*

"Why didn't you tell me?" she cried. "I wouldn't have sent you into all those dangerous situations if I'd known you were having trouble! I would have helped you, found a way to—"

That's why I didn't tell you, he wrote quickly. *If you knew what was happening, you would have offered to make me your knight.*

"Of course I would have!"

Valente shook his head. *That's why I couldn't do it. I know you would've done it with the best intentions, but no matter how good the master, I could not make myself a slave again.*

"That's still no reason to hide it!" Lola yelled. "We could have found another way!"

I didn't want to distract you from killing Victor, he wrote. *And I was ready to die.*

"How can you say that?"

Because it's true, he wrote, his mirrored visor reflecting the words like a still pool. *I was the idiot who asked Victor to make him a slave. I knew I'd have to pay for all the blood on my hands eventually. I thought if I could just survive long enough to help you kill Victor, that'd be enough to let me die in peace.*

She scowled at him. "And it never occurred to you that some people might not want you to die?"

It did, he wrote slowly. *And for that I'm sorry. It was easier to push you away than to face what I was losing. I also didn't want you to make me your knight out of pity.*

"I've never pitied you!" Lola cried, desperate to make him understand. "Did you not hear what I said in the convenience store? You're important to me! I'd have been glad to have you as my knight whether it saved your life or not. I'd also have respected your wishes if you said you didn't want it, but I wouldn't have just given up. I'd never leave you to die!"

I know, Valente wrote, tilting his visor up to look at her face even though his hand continued to write on the pad propped against his knee.

You have no idea how much what you said that day between the trucks meant to me. I'd thought everything was over, but then Dee told me you'd gone into Victor's dreams to find my head. You put yourself back in that monster's mouth for my sake, and it made me feel like a coward. That was when I knew I couldn't give up. You're the reason I was able to beat Orlando and why I came back when Simon saved my head. Death was right there. I could have easily fallen into it, but you made me want to live. I'm here because you believed I could be.

He paused to squeeze her hand before writing four more words at the bottom of the page.

I love you, Lola.

"Wait," she said, leaning over the pad to make sure she was reading what she thought she was reading. "Do you mean in a gratitude sort of way, or—"

I mean it in every sort of way, he assured her, flipping to a new page. *You're the only person ever who's learned what I was and didn't hate me. You're beautiful and kind and brave and powerful. I don't see how anyone could know you and not love you. That's why I did this. I didn't come back so I could kill Victor. I came back for you.*

Lola fell back on the sofa, stunned. Her mind was still too shaken to process everything that had just happened, which was probably why the next thing out of her mouth was, "So does this mean you *do* want to go out for dinner with me?"

I want to do anything that lets me be with you, he wrote firmly.

She covered her face with a sob. Valente jumped when she did, which was a perfectly reasonable thing to do. Anyone would be alarmed when their confession was met with tears, but Lola couldn't help it. It was just too much. She'd thought it was over on that rooftop. Now her life had completely flipped around yet again, and as happy as she knew she should be, Lola couldn't keep up. She had to touch him, had to look him in his glowing eyes and be sure that this was really what he wanted. When she reached out to remove his helmet, though, Valente caught her hand.

There's more.

"What else do I need to know?" she asked as a smile finally broke through her stupid tears. "You're not dead and you love me. I'm good."

You might not feel that way in a minute, he warned, his body falling back into a nervous stoop as he wrote each word carefully. *Like I said, my head was rotting. Deciding I wanted to live didn't change that, so I made a bargain.*

"What kind of bargain?" Lola asked, going rigid. "Did Victor…?"

That question was too absurd to finish. She'd seen the rage on Victor's face. He hadn't known this was coming any more than she had. He *definitely* wouldn't have made any bargains that let Valente steal his sword and kick him off his building, but the blood mage was the only force Lola knew of that could've performed a miracle as big as the one sitting in front of her. Now that she was getting used to it, she was starting to realize just how big Valente's new magic was. Way, *way* bigger than his icy gossamer, so where…

The DFZ, he wrote, glancing up between each word to check her reaction. *The Black Rider is an urban legend of her city. She used that connection to reach out to me.*

"And?"

And I accepted, he wrote, his gloved fingers moving nervously on the pencil. *I threw away my fairy head and my gossamer and everything else that Victor had done to me and became the Black Rider for real.*

Lola's eyes were huge by the time he finished. "*That's* why your magic feels so crazy!" she cried, reaching out to grab his sleeve, which still felt like it had an arm inside but also like the edge of something infinite. "That's why you were able to kick Victor around even with his crazy new powers. You're a spirit!"

Technically, I'm only part of a spirit, he scribbled quickly. *The best way I can think of to describe it is that I'm a subsidiary of the DFZ, but since she's the city of freedom, she doesn't control anything I do, which means Victor doesn't either.*

"You're still crazy strong," Lola insisted, her stuttering mind finally spinning back up to speed as she stared excitedly at the magical golden weapon still that was still gleaming his hip. "Is that how you were able to steal his sword?"

I don't know how that happened, the Black Rider confessed. *I only grabbed his sword to make him stop, but it stuck to my glove and wouldn't let go. It was honestly more annoying than anything, but I was happy to get it away from Victor.*

"Any day Victor loses is a good day," Lola agreed, tapping her fingers rapidly on her legs, which had returned to their normal size now that she was back in the rich magic of her barrow. "But if you're a spirit, what's your domain? I used to read the Black Rider's legends back before I knew you. It was all standard American Headless Horseman ghost story stuff, so I wasn't too surprised when you told me Victor made it up. He always did like to let tropes do his heavy lifting, but that's just how you started. What are you now?"

Whatever people need me to be, he wrote, shoulders squaring with pride. *Victor started the story, but he couldn't keep it. As soon as people saw me on the streets, they started making up their own legends, much better ones. In those tales, the Black Rider isn't a mindless killer. He's terrifying, yes, but only to those who deserve it. He rides down the wicked and makes the villainous pay for their crimes. He brings justice.*

"I get it," Lola said with a nod. "You're DFZ Batman."

She saw Valente's shoulders move in silent laughter. *Not quite,* he wrote. *I don't have a mansion or all those wonderful toys, but the Rider is all about making people pay for their wrongs. That's why I was able to hit Victor so hard, even though the Hero's story is bigger than mine. He's what I was made to fight.*

Lola nodded at the perfect sense that made. Then her eyes locked back onto the sword that still gleamed like sunlight at Valente's side. "I bet that's why."

What's why?

"That's why you were able to take the Hero's sword," she said in a rush, getting increasingly excited as everything started to come together. "Victor's been working his ass off to teach people he's the Hero. The only reason his sword's a sword and not a lump of gossamer is because he's taught the whole world to believe it's the Hero's blade. But, as you just told me, he doesn't control the story! He's just riding on its back like a tick, so when you came in and did something that was *actually* heroic, his sword jumped ship, because it was never actually Victor's sword at all. It's the Hero's, and the only hero on that roof was you."

Valente tilted his visor skeptically. *I don't know if swords think that way.*

"They do when they're made of gossamer," she insisted, grinning from ear to ear as she pointed at the naked blade stabbing into her couch cushions. "That thing's literally made of belief. Victor started the story of a glorious Hero's Blade that slays any monster when he used it to beat up Fenrir, which means he's got no one to blame but himself for losing it. Unlike the rest of the world, that sword sees him when the cameras are off. I'm not surprised at all that it dumped him at the first opportunity. Now we just have to figure out how we're going to use it to win."

Beating him is the other reason I came back, the Rider wrote, nodding. *Do you still think we can do it?*

"More than ever," Lola said, rubbing her hands together. "I might not have felt that way five minutes ago, but then I found out you're the actual Black Rider who just jacked the Hero's sword. You saw Victor's face when you took it. He was *terrified*. That's not the face of a man who actually believes he's invincible. He must still have a weakness! And I think I know how we're going to hit it."

His helmet made it impossible to tell, but Lola swore Valente was smiling. *You have a plan, don't you?*

"I know I've said that a lot," she admitted, putting up her hands. "But if Victor could be taken down in one swing, we wouldn't be in this situation. The fact that you were able to steal his sword proves he can still be hit, though. All that's left is to figure out how."

Lola hopped up from the couch and began pacing the living room in smaller and smaller circles. She'd felt so defeated when the building had opened and shown her how badly they'd been played. In hindsight, though, she should have known it was coming the moment Simon told her the Paladins were their last chance. For all that he'd turned out totally different from his master, Simon had still been raised to be Victor's copy. They knew and feared the same things, so if Simon thought the Paladins were a surefire win, Victor must have too. That was why he'd been so ready for them. Even now, they were still playing by Victor's ruleset, which was why nothing was working. If they actually wanted to win, they needed to hit him with something he *didn't* know how to prepare for. Something totally unexpected.

It was the same conclusion Lola had come to three months ago. The difference now was that she finally understood the scale. She'd assumed they just had to kill him, but she hadn't been thinking nearly big enough. What she thought of as Victor was just a fraction, a sliver of the Hero's true power.

To beat something that huge, they needed to fight at the same level. The Rider had already shown what was possible when Victor was caught off guard. He'd lost his sword for good on that roof, and if they could take that from him, they could take more. Her head was spinning with all the possibilities when the Rider's pad appeared in front of her.

What are you going to do?

"I don't know yet," Lola confessed. "But if today taught me anything, it's that we're never going to beat Victor with normal tactics. If we want to win, we have to go bigger than he can. We need to hit him with something *so* powerful and *so* crazy that even the Hero gets blown away. You being a spirit is a good start, but we still need more, so I'm going to call in some backup."

Valente was still writing his reply when Lola turned on her heel and marched into the kitchen. He caught up just as she was opening the back door. When she looked for his pad, though, Valente slid it back into his pocket and motioned for her to lead the way. She did so with a determined nod, striding out into her low road garden to start tearing down the sliding door that led to the 7-Eleven.

She tore out all the others as well, including the door in the garage she'd used to capture the Paladin. It hurt to give up her exits, but whatever Victor had done to move the DFZ like a puppet must still have been in effect, because she could feel the city hunting for her like a tiger. Victor would find her doors as soon as she used them, so Lola threw everything away and started over, spinning her shining gossamer into a new path that, hopefully, Victor would never see coming.

Chapter 11

Ten minutes later, Lola and Valente were standing on top of a parking deck in Windsor, Canada.

She'd wanted to go farther. Technically, the DFZ's domain ended at the river, but it was hard to feel safe when Lola could still see the city looming only half a mile away. Even Frank's old house would have been better, but for all her fantastic new powers, Lola was still a fairy. She'd needed someplace where no one would question a randomly appearing door, and for all that it was closer than she liked, the parking deck was very convenient.

"Okay," she said, rattling the handle on the graffiti-covered maintenance door she'd set into the outside of the deck's elevator shaft to make sure her new low road was secure. "I think that's got it. Whip up your bike and let's get rolling."

The Rider shook his mirrored head and pulled out his pad again. *I think you should drive.*

"Why?" Lola asked. "We're trying not to get spotted, and you're the one with the crazy city-warping motorcycle."

The Rider shook his head again. *Victor's got the DFZ looking for me. Not sure if he made the city tell him or if he guessed, but he knows exactly what I am now, and he's ordered the DFZ to bring me to him.*

"And I'm guessing she can't disobey," Lola finished, turning to sigh at the city, which was still seething like a kicked-over anthill. She'd been counting on the Black Rider to get them safely through. Without his powers, sneaking through a city where the roads themselves could rat you out sounded like a lost cause. She was about to say as much when the Rider held out his pad again.

She can't directly disobey, the words said. *But the DFZ is part of me now just like I'm part of her, which means she understands that just because Victor gives you an order doesn't mean you can't find a way around it.*

"You always were the master of the technicality," Lola agreed, tapping her chin.

Valente nodded. *He's commanded her to bring him the Black Rider, but she's still a spirit made by humans, and tricking humans is a fairy's bread and butter. If we went in there looking like someone else—*

"She can't be expected to see through fairy gossamer," Lola finished.

The Rider nodded rapidly, and her face split into a grin. "You'd think Victor would've learned not to leave loopholes like that by now."

He's gotten very impatient.

Victor had always been impatient. It was just coming out more now that he was feeling pushed.

We'll still have to be careful, the Rider warned. *The Black Rider is part of the DFZ. She can't not know where I am. I'm sure that's what Victor was counting on when he gave the order, but the Detroit Free Zone doesn't take well to dictators. She's ignoring me so hard she's basically stuck her head in her own sewers, but you'll still have to lay it on thick. Even with her eyes shut tight, there's only so much the DFZ can avoid seeing, and Victor's leaning on her hard right now.*

"Then we'll just have to go harder," Lola said as she started covering them both in a shellack of gossamer so dense, it took up the whole parking space they were standing in. "But how do you know all of this? Does the DFZ live in your head now or something?"

Not all the time, he wrote. *But we're made from the same magic now, so I can't exactly keep her out.*

Lola scowled at the illusion she was shaping. She knew she was being ridiculous, but seeing Valente accept the DFZ so readily after saying he'd rather die than become her knight stung.

"So, is she like your god now?" Lola asked, struggling to keep the jealousy out of her voice. "I know you just said she didn't control you, but you're made from her magic, so I don't see how…"

She trailed off as the Rider began writing frantically. *It's not just that she doesn't control me,* his notebook read when he held it up again. *She* can't. *The DFZ is the city of freedom. Restricting choice in any way goes against the base principle of her nature. Even her priests get to decide how they worship her. That's why I agreed to become the Black Rider. We might share the same magic, but the only authority I serve is my own.*

As she read the words, Lola realized she should have known. She'd met the DFZ herself, after all. Neither of them had been at their best at the time, but Lola would've had to be deaf, dumb, and blind not to see how fiercely the city valued independence. The DFZ had even volunteered to get eaten by Fenrir again rather than accept Victor's rule. Remembering that made Lola feel better about the situation, but she still slathered the gossamer on extra thick before stepping back to examine her work.

Instead of an urban legend and a fairy standing next to a magic motorcycle, they now looked like two old workmen with their street sweeper. The truck was an absolute monster with a giant rattling vacuum tube and crusty old spinning bristles, the sort that always made a huge racket cleaning the streets at three a.m. She'd even covered it in a fine patina of classic DFZ Undercity grime, the greenish-black kind that was so sticky, people actually scraped it up to use as free glue.

She'd added the same grime to her own costume, too, piling it so thick into the wrinkles of her old-man face that he looked like an ink drawing come to life. To hide Valente's helmet, she'd covered him in a municipal hazmat suit, the kind with the wards sewn right into the waterproof fabric that cleaning crews used when they had to go *deep.*

It wasn't a setup you saw in the Hero's new, sterile DFZ, but despite Victor's best efforts, some original residents had moved back in and brought their stuff with them. The truck would stick out instantly if they tried to go into the new suburban-style neighborhoods Victor was forcing the city to build for his faithful, but Lola wasn't worried about getting spotted by Victor's mortal security guards. She was trying to slide past the city herself, and the DFZ saw trucks like this all the time.

Just to be extra sure, Lola added a shrine to the DFZ on the dashboard as she and Valente climbed into the cab. It took a bit more doing to get the sweeper truck out of the parking deck without breaking the illusion, but they managed in the end, only scraping the roof a little as they turned the huge truck onto the road that would take them to the New Ambassador Bridge.

The highway connecting the DFZ to Canada was much more fortified now than it had been when Lola was driving back from Frank's apartment. Just like at the southern border with the US, there were military checkpoints, cameras, passport inspections—all the stuff that usually melted Lola's gossamer into goo.

Fortunately, most of the security was aimed at vehicles coming *out* of the DFZ. Getting in was far less hassle, especially if you said you were going to one of the Hero's rallies. All Lola had to do was buy a ticket to the Hero's next miracle demonstration— which was already back on its regular schedule at the hastily rebuilt Hero's Hall—and the guard waved them through without a second glance.

"Guess even a Paladin raid can't stop the Hero's publicity machine," Lola said as their huge cleaning truck trundled across the bridge and into the city proper. "He must really need the worship."

And the money, the Rider wrote in big shaky letters since the illusionary hazmat suit's rubber gloves hindered his ability to hold his pencil. *Victor was burning through his fortune when I was working for him at the end, and I can't imagine he's slowed down. Even when people think you're divine, it takes a ton of cash to run a media empire.*

"Trade has slowed down, too, now that the famously free DFZ's been taken over by a religious dictator. It's all over the news that the US has been sanctioning the hell out of him." Lola smiled. "Good to know he can't escape *all* the consequences of his actions."

I just wish it was only him, the Rider wrote, nodding at the empty streets.

She didn't have to ask what he meant. Not having to worry about human scrutiny was nice, but Lola still hated seeing the lively, crazy DFZ so quiet. A few people walked around here and there, mostly diehard fans wearing the Hero's merchandise, but nearly all the stores were closed, leaving the new, orderly streets Victor bragged about every time he was on TV looking like an abandoned mall.

It was almost as depressing as the lack of dragons. Leave it to Victor to turn the world's most magical city into a sad, stale dystopia. Even their street sweeper, once a common sight all over the Underground, looked like a relic of another age. Fortunately, there was practically no one around to see them, enabling Lola to drive mostly disbelief-free all the way into the heart of what had once been the DFZ's most exclusive neighborhood.

The last time Lola had visited Morgan's barrow, it had been under Alva's control. That was no longer the case since Morgan, Lamb, and Tristan had used the Wild Hunt's attack to go on a head-taking spree. But while the barrow was back under original management, it was still in the same location.

Lola didn't know if that was because a royal barrow was too big to move or if Morgan hadn't cared where it was so long as it was hers. She was just happy it was easy to find. Despite Lakeside itself getting crushed during Fenrir's rampage, the door to the queen's barrow was still right where Lola remembered: under the wreckage of its white mansion. Tristan was even sitting on what was left of the front steps, tapping his white-sheathed sword against his shoulder as he watched Lola's truck roll noisily down the cracked driveway.

"I'm sorry," he said as Lola and Valente climbed out of the cab. "We're not in the market for cleaning services at this time. As you can see, we don't exactly have much street left to sweep, so kindly move along."

"Very funny," Lola said, ditching the street sweeper costume for her usual dark-haired body. The Rider was still being hunted, so she left Valente's disguise in place, but she felt better glaring at Tristan with her own eyes since he was clearly not going to be cooperative. "We need to see the queen."

"I'm afraid she's still indisposed," Tristan replied as he rose to his feet. He was even dressed like a doorman in a white uniform suit, but his normally cheerful eyes were hard as blue glass.

"You kicked the hornet's nest hard this afternoon, Lola-bear," he said, planting his sheathed sword on the ground in front of him. "What did I warn you about that?"

"At least we were doing something," Lola argued. "And we did have some success."

"That's not what it looked like to me," Tristan said, flicking his eyes to the reconstructed peak of Hero's Tower, which, as the new city's tallest building, was visible even from here. "The whole world witnessed the Paladins' defeat. Even the US is stepping down talk of an invasion now that Victor's proved even the blood-mage exterminators can't touch him."

Lola snorted. "I never thought you'd fall for his media game. A lot more happened up there than was shown on TV. The Paladins did get wiped out—that part is true—but it was hardly a win for Victor, since we got this."

She pointed at the Rider as she finished, and Valente dutifully fished the Hero's golden sword out of his bulky costume. At first, Tristan didn't seem to realize what he was looking at. Then his eyes grew huge as he took a step back.

"Is that...?"

"It's the real thing," Lola promised, flashing him a triumphant grin. "Turns out, it's a bad idea to give your Hero a symbolic sword when you don't intend on actually acting heroic. Victor might have the world fooled, but like every other spirit, his powers are tied to the story that gave him life. That includes his sword, which apparently decided Victor wasn't up to snuff for its service."

"So I see," Tristan said, drawing his own sword. "What I don't understand is who is *that*."

He pointed his naked blade at Valente's yellow hazmat suit, and Lola blinked. "Since when are you fooled by gossamer? That's the Black Rider."

Tristan clicked his tongue at her. "Lola-cat, just because you're capable of lying doesn't mean that you should."

"I'm not lying!"

"Then you're the one being deceived," he said, narrowing his eyes at the man behind her. "He might no longer be Victor's knight, but I know what the Rider's magic feels like, and that is definitely *not* him."

"Oh," Lola said, finally realizing the problem. "Yeah, that's the other thing that changed today, but we can't show you out here. The DFZ's not our friend right now. Let's get inside the barrow and I'll tell you everything."

"Absolutely not," Tristan said, keeping his sword raised. "You I was possibly willing to fudge, but I am *not* allowing a stranger wielding Victor's *fairy-killing sword* into my queen's abode."

Lola couldn't believe this. "Do you really think I'd come here with someone who would hurt her? I'm the one who *saved* her! Your queen's head would still be a figment of Victor's sick imagination if I hadn't pulled her out of her flower box. You owe me!"

She'd meant that in a general sort of way, but Tristan flinched, and Lola's face broke into a smile.

"You owe me," she said again, crossing her arms over her chest in triumph. "I saved your queen. You said *thank you.*"

"Don't do this," the knight warned.

"Oh, I'm doing it," Lola said, pulling herself straight. "We are way past the point where I can afford to leave cards on the table. I'm calling in your debt. Take us both to Morgan. *Now.*"

For a long moment, she didn't think he'd do it. She'd never seen the knight look this angry, but while Lola hated pushing him like this, they'd just gotten practically the entire Paladin order killed on that roof. Simon had nearly died. She'd nearly died. Valente *had* died. Now was not the time for pulling punches. If they didn't want to live in Victor's world forever, they needed all hands on deck. That definitely included Morgan's, so Lola dug her heels in deep, glaring at Tristan until, at last, the fairy slumped.

"I can't promise she'll talk to you," he grumbled, sheathing his sword. "But I can take you to where she is on the condition that your companion behaves." He turned his glare on Valente, who still hadn't gotten out of his hazmat suit. "There is no debt in the world more important than the safety of my queen. If you so much as twitch toward that blade, I'll kill you where you stand."

The Rider nodded rapidly under his costume, but Lola just rolled her eyes. "You're going to feel real dumb in a second," she warned as she tromped past Tristan up the broken stairs. "Let's just get inside. I don't know how much longer the city can keep not looking at us."

If Tristan found that comment odd, he didn't show it. He just stalked up the stairs into the collapsed mansion toward the white door that lay flat on the rubble-strewn floor. Lola was wondering if they needed to set it back upright when Tristan crouched down and grabbed the knob, opening the door straight into the ground.

"After you," he said, gesturing at the hole he'd just made.

Lola bit her lip as she glanced over the edge. Making her own doors and low roads had given her a greater appreciation for Tristan's skill, but it seriously looked like he'd just opened a portal straight into an endless blue sky. Going through it felt awfully like stepping off a cliff, but she was the one who'd just demanded his blind trust, so Lola did the same, jumping through the door with both feet straight into the yawning blue abyss.

And landed in a flower field.

She stumbled, looking around in confusion. There'd been no transition, no feeling of falling, but the dazzling blue sky she'd jumped into not a second ago was now above her head, and all around beneath it stretched an endless field of flowers. The same endless field of flowers that she, Valente, and Tristan had walked into the first time they'd come here.

"Huh," she said, craning her neck back to stare at the sky she hadn't fallen out of. "I thought it'd look different."

"Why should it?" Tristan asked as he popped into existence right next to her. "This has always been the queen's barrow. Alva was just a squatter pretending at power that was never hers. She couldn't actually change anything."

Clearly. This was just the entryway, but so far, everything looked *exactly* the same as Lola's last trip, including the wilting flowers. She would've thought those would perk up at least now that their true queen had returned, but Tristan must not have been kidding about Morgan being indisposed, because the barrow looked untouched.

"What's Morgan doing down here?" Lola asked as the still-costumed Valente finally appeared.

"Sleeping," Tristan informed her.

"Oh," Lola said, wrinkling her nose. "Why didn't you just tell us that before? You've been going on for weeks about how your 'queen is indisposed.' I thought she was off on some secret fairy business."

"Sleeping *is* secret fairy business," the knight said testily. "A sleeping monarch is a vulnerable monarch. Why do you think I didn't want to let you in? And speaking of." He whirled back to the Rider, who was looking highly out of place standing in the bucolic meadow with his filthy hazmat suit. "I'm not taking you another step until you strip your magic off that *thing* and tell me in *excessive* detail exactly what manner of horror you've convinced me to allow into my lady's home."

Lola sighed. She'd been hoping to avoid removing Valente's costume. They still had to get back home when this was over, and it was a lot harder to craft something so elaborate inside of someone else's barrow. It also shouldn't have made a difference. As a real fairy, Tristan could see through any illusion she put up. But he was clearly not going to let this go, so Lola bit the bullet and drew her glamour back, leaving the helmeted Black Rider standing under the sunshine with the Hero's golden sword shining on his hip.

"That's not exactly better," Tristan said, tilting his head as he squinted at the Rider. "Now he just looks like Victor's executioner. If he wasn't so clearly made of something other than gossamer, I'd cut off his head."

You already tried that, Valente wrote on his pad. *But I'm not Victor's anything anymore. My fairy head is gone. I'm the Black Rider for real now.*

Tristan didn't seem to know what to make of that, so Lola filled him in.

"He's a spirit."

Valente's helmet whipped toward her, and Lola sighed. "Okay, technically, he's an urban legend who's part of the DFZ, but functionally, it's the same thing."

Tristan looked even less happy. "So he's like Victor?"

Valente shook his head firmly and began writing furiously on his pad. *I'm nothing like Victor. His Hero sits on a throne of lies that serves no one but himself. I'm an actual urban legend with a purpose.*

"I don't see how being a murdering ghost is supposed to be a mark in your favor," Tristan said, leaning on his sheathed sword. "The Black Rider is hardly a cheery figure, *and* he was created by Victor, who also controls the DFZ." He shook his head. "Not making a good case, Lola-kitten. I think I preferred it when you were running around with Victor's apprentice."

"Simon's his ex-apprentice," Lola corrected. "And you need to stop being so closed-minded. Yes, Victor made the Rider. He also made me. That just gives us both more reason to hate his guts."

"But it doesn't mean he's not playing you," Tristan warned, glaring at the Rider. "He's done it before."

"So did you," Lola said, crossing her arms over her chest. "And I *still* saved your queen."

"Point taken." The knight sighed. "I'll take you to Morgan as promised, *but,*"—he stabbed his finger at Valente—"that golden letter opener stays down. If I see you doing anything remotely suspicious, I'll cut you into confetti before you can move. And don't think being a spirit will save you. I am a sworn knight in his queen's barrow. The only one stronger than me in this place is Morgan herself, so watch it."

"For the *last time*, we're not going to do anything," Lola groaned, but Tristan refused to move until Valente nodded and lifted his hands far away from the golden sword.

"Don't you think you're being a little overprotective?" she grumbled as they finally started walking across the field toward the stone steps she remembered from last time. "I thought fairy monarchs were unkillable in their barrows."

"Normally, yes," Tristan said. "But what sort of knight would I be if I didn't threaten to murder her enemies?"

He said this with his usual cheer, but the flippancy rang hollow in Lola's ears, and sure enough, Tristan wasn't finished.

"This is a delicate time," he told her quietly, nodding at the silent, empty forest they were suddenly walking through. "A fairy is never more vulnerable than when she is sleeping, but the battle to reclaim her barrow took more out of her than we anticipated, and there were other factors to consider."

Lola scowled. "What other factors?"

"Replenishment," the knight said cryptically. "There are some duties that can't be done while awake. If the queen does not sleep, she cannot regrow her court."

Lola scowled. "Regrow her court?"

Tristan waved his hand at the woods. Lola followed the motion curiously, and then she jumped back with a shriek.

The dark forest that had seemed so empty wasn't actually empty at all. Its floor was carpeted with leafy, flourishing plants. They almost looked like cabbages, and nestled in the center of each was a head.

"What are those?" Lola cried.

"Alva's traitors," Tristan informed her casually, motioning at her to keep up as he continued down the stairs. "They ran wild under the false queen, but my great Morgan has cut the weeds back to their roots. Soon they will be reborn as children of the true court, hopefully with more sense this time."

"I don't understand," Lola said, sticking to the middle of the path and as far from the creepy head-filled woods as possible. "I thought fairies came from low creatures eating each other until one gets big enough for independent thought."

"That's how we start," Tristan said. "But even low creatures have to come from somewhere." He tapped the ground under their feet with his pointed shoe. "All of us, even me, sprang from the roots of the court. That's why loyalty to our monarch is so important. Their barrows are our cradle, the soil we sprout from. Without them, we are nothing."

Lola made a face. "You mean you *grew* out of Morgan? Like a budding fungus?"

"I don't approve of the comparison," Tristan said sourly. "But yes, more or less." He smiled up at the golden leaves of the canopy above them. "I prefer to think of us as aspen trees. Every aspen in a grove springs from the same mother root. Even if the individual trees die, the grove can continue for thousands of years despite fires, avalanches, and drought. We start as tiny seedlings, low creatures with barely a thought in our heads. We compete with and eat each other, eventually becoming greater monsters, and from thence into true fairies. Once a millennium or so, one of us might even get big enough to break away and start producing buds of our own. That's now how new fairy monarchs and courts come into being, but great or small, every gossamer creature can trace its roots back to their own monarch. Even you sprang from Alberich, whose roots run deeper than the mountains."

He pointed at the rows of fairy heads that still surrounded the path on both sides. "These traitors are being reminded what it means to be loyal to the land of their birth. They're like onion tops right now, but give them a decade or so, and our queen will have them back to rights."

Lola nodded silently, unsure what to say. No one had actually explained the fairy life cycle to her before. It was a lot more alien than she'd expected, but fairies *had* come from outside this plane of existence. Victor hadn't been wrong when he'd called them parasites either. That was an accurate description for a race that burrowed into other worlds specifically to feed off the local population's dreams.

Lola had long accepted the less glamorous aspects of her fairy half. She just wished Morgan's methods weren't so close to an actual alien queen's as they walked past row after row of sleeping cabbage heads. It was almost a relief when Tristan finally led them into the large clearing where Alva had enthralled the Rider the last time the three of them were here. A clearing that was now entirely taken over by a giant flowering tree.

"What is *that?*" Lola whispered, her eyes going huge.

"Beautiful" was the only word she could think of. Even knowing what the clearing had looked like before, the tree fit so perfectly, Lola could no longer imagine it not being here. Its bark had the same pale smoothness as the aspen trees Tristan had just been talking about, but its trunk was the size of a redwood, spreading its branches so high into the air that Lola couldn't even see the tree's crown.

The leaves on the branches she could see were the same pale green as Morgan's eyes, and the small flowers that hid under them were golden like her hair. Down at the bottom, the huge tree was anchored to the ground by roots the size of cars, and the stream that had once divided the clearing in half now flowed in a circle around the tree's base, soaking it in an endless stream of radiant, clear water.

Between the flowers, the leaves, and the stream, the whole forest was filled with the clean, cool scent of early spring. Even for Lola, who could spin any wonder she wanted, it was a magical sight. She could feel the tree's power, its immense *age* like pressure in the air. Other than the gently burbling creek, no sound disturbed the peace, not even wind. She didn't need Tristan to tell her that something ancient and powerful was sleeping here, but despite being led straight to where she'd asked, Lola didn't see Morgan anywhere.

"Um," she said, speaking as low as she could to avoid breaking the reverent silence, "where's the queen?"

"You're staring at her," Tristan replied.

When Lola gave him a sideways look, Tristan rolled his
eyes and got down on his knees, bending over until his forehead
brushed the roots that filled the clearing.

"My queen," he said in a rich, ringing voice that filled the
clearing, "the killer of your husband has come to pay you a visit."

Now it was Lola's turn to roll her eyes. But while she didn't
appreciate Tristan's editorializing, it seemed to work. The
moment he mentioned Alberich's death, the whole tree began to
quiver. The ground shook next, groaning and creaking with a
deep, echoing sound that eventually formed itself into words.

"I hope this is important."

"I leave that to your judgment," Tristan said, shooting Lola
a *you-asked-for-this* look as he backed away.

Lola swallowed and stepped forward, taking Tristan's place
in front of the giant tree. Coming to Morgan had seemed like the
obvious thing to do. Now that she was here, though, Lola felt very
small and uncertain. She was still trying to come up with a good
open when the giant tree began to shrink.

It happened so quickly, Lola was afraid the tree would
collapse on top of them, but it didn't fall. It just folded in on itself,
the thousands of branches cascading back into the trunk, which
was itself sinking into the ground. Roots rolled up like streamers,
folding into the pale bark that was rapidly becoming pale flesh.
This took quite a long time because of how much tree there was,
but all the individual changes happened so fast that Lola swore it
was no time at all before the giant tree was gone and Morgan
herself stood naked on the bank of the stream that ran though the
center of the now-empty clearing.

"This had better be an emergency," the queen grumbled,
summoning a flowing white robe with a snap of her fingers.
"Getting out is easy, but do you have any idea how long it takes me
to relax into that shape?"

"I wouldn't know," Lola said, still awed. "I've never tried turning into a tree."

"I didn't 'turn into' anything," the queen said irritably, holding out her hand to receive the espresso Tristan had just summoned for her out of empty air. "The tree *is* me, or at least closer to the truth than this." She nodded down at her human-appearing body. "Unfortunately, it's not very mobile, and having leaves in my ears makes it difficult to listen, so here we are. Fill me in, knight."

Tristan dutifully began to whisper in his queen's ear as she summoned herself a cabana chair. Lola couldn't hear what he was saying from the other side of the clearing, but Morgan's golden eyebrows rose several times. By the time the knight stepped into his usual position behind her, the queen was looking at both Lola and Valente with new appreciation.

"How did you manage to get in so much trouble so quickly?" she asked, pausing for a sip of her coffee. "I was only asleep for a month."

"A month feels like a year when you're dealing with Victor," Lola said, clenching her fists. Here went nothing. "I've come to ask for your help."

Morgan's red lips curled behind the rim of her small white cup. "That's a dangerous word for a fairy. What do you offer in exchange?"

"Revenge on Victor and the end of the blood magic bane."

Morgan choked on her espresso. "That's quite the promise," she said when she'd recovered. "But I've heard words like these from you before. Weren't you the one who said we were going to kill Victor three months ago?"

"I've been *trying*," Lola said with a glare. "You're the one who gave up and went to sleep."

"It's called a strategic retreat," the queen replied flatly. "The Hero was too strong. Nothing we were doing was working, so I went to sleep in the hopes of restoring myself and my court to our full power."

"But that could take years!"

"Ten at the very least," Morgan agreed. "But what's a decade to the likes of us? You're a king now. You have to stop thinking like a mortal."

"It doesn't matter how long I live if I have to do it under Victor," Lola said sourly. Then she smiled. "But we don't need to wait for you to power up anymore."

When the queen arched a curious eyebrow, Lola turned and pointed at Valente, who was still hovering at the edge of the clearing, no doubt remembering what had happened the last time he'd faced a fairy queen in this place.

"The Black Rider came within an inch of beating Victor today," Lola said proudly. "I think he could have finished the job if he hadn't had to worry about saving the rest of us. *And* he stole Victor's golden sword."

She turned back to Tristan. "I know it looked like the Paladin raid was an utter defeat, but that's just what Victor wanted the world to see. The fight *I* witnessed was actually a draw. He had to become a spirit to do it, but the Black Rider proved that Victor *can* still be hurt if we hit him in the right way."

The knight crossed his arms over his chest. "Bold words from someone who had to sneak over here dressed as garbage men."

We were street cleaners, Valente wrote on his pad.

"We didn't want to tip our hand early," Lola said, ignoring the jab. "But I've failed to kill Victor enough times now to know when we're getting close. He looked genuinely terrified up there, especially after he lost his sword."

"So what?" the queen asked. "He's a man clinging to power by the will of the mob. Anything that makes him look weak is cause for concern. That doesn't mean he's actually in danger."

Lola shook her head. "This was different. I've spent my whole life watching Victor. If he was scared enough to let it show on his face, he must have truly been panicking. He also relied entirely on the DFZ to take down the Paladins. He didn't so much as take a swing at them himself, which means Simon was right. He *was* afraid of them. Why else would the supposedly unbeatable Hero sit back on his throne and let the city do his dirty work?"

"Maybe that's how it was this morning," Tristan said darkly. "But I watched his broadcast from beginning to end. This whole thing was a setup to show the world that even the famous blood-mage killing Paladins can't touch him."

"But before he did that, it *was* a weakness," Lola insisted. "And where there's one, there's more."

"Only if we have the means to exploit them," Morgan said, setting down her empty coffee. "I want to kill him as badly as you do, but he's just too strong."

"Then we hit him with something stronger! Victor's play has always been that the Hero is invincible, but there's one enemy he was never able to beat. One fight that he never won."

Morgan leaned forward. "Which is?"

"Me," Lola said, pressing a hand to her chest. "To defeat Victor, we need to bring back Fenrir."

The queen fell back into her chair. "And here I thought you had a *real* plan."

"It is a real plan! You're the one who told me I was the most powerful thing in the world back then. The DFZ said basically the same thing when she was in my death, and it's not as if Fenrir's gone. I've still got his corpse at the bottom of my barrow. All we have to do is get him back on his feet."

"Which is impossible," the queen pointed out. "You should know better than anyone how incredibly unique the circumstances that allowed Fenrir to rise were. It's not something we can just snap our fingers and recreate."

"We don't have to recreate it," Lola said confidently. "We just need to get Fenrir in front of people. Everyone in the world remembers what he did. Victor made sure of that, but we can use his plots against him! If we show people that Fenrir is back, their belief in the monster will take care of the rest."

"And turn you into something even worse than the Hero," Morgan told her darkly. "Have you forgotten what happened last time?"

"I'm not the same person I was back then," Lola said, raising her chin. "I know what I'm doing now, and I'm not afraid of him anymore. I can control it."

"And if you're wrong, you could become the monster that ends the world." The queen shook her head. "I like power as much as anyone, but this is too risky. Even if you do figure out how to get the wolf back on his feet, you'll be dealing with the belief of *billions*. If so much as a fraction of those people don't buy into Fenrir's resurrection, the backlash of their disbelief will smash you out of existence."

"Not if I'm big enough," Lola said, flashing Morgan a grin. "Any kick can be weathered with enough gossamer. Victor taught me that, and he had only one fairy monarch on his side. We're two. If we combine our powers, we can take anything."

Morgan snorted. "I think you're grossly overestimating our strength. Maybe we could have managed such a feat before the Hero's rise to power, but those aren't the times we live in anymore. That fool Alberich and his Wild Hunt gave Victor all the opportunity he needed to teach the world his bane. Everyone believes fairies are weak to blood magic now, which means Victor can break anything we build with a flick of his fingers."

When Lola opened her mouth to argue, the queen raised her hand. "I know you desire this greatly. Normally, I love that, but it's just not going to work. Even if our version of Fenrir could survive the world's kick of disbelief, the magic will crumble at the first touch of blood magic. Think it through far enough, and this plan actually plays to Victor's favor. Can you imagine how strong he'd become if the world saw him destroy Fenrir with his magic?"

"That would be true," Lola admitted, "*if* he destroyed it."

The queen gave her a quelling look, but Lola pushed on. "Blood magic has no effect on gossamer normally. The only reason Victor's magic works on us is because he's tricked people into believing it does, but that strength is also its weakness. If he hits us with blood magic and it *doesn't work*, everyone will stop believing, and the bane will be broken."

"And how do you propose we do that?" Morgan demanded. "Have you felt the bane? It's not something we can just shrug off."

"Anything can be overcome with enough power," Lola insisted. "That's how Victor keeps doing the impossible, and it's how we're going to do it too. If his bane burns our magic, then we just need to gather *so* much gossamer that we can instantly replace anything he destroys. That way, no matter how much he breaks us, his attacks will still *look* ineffective to everyone watching. Once his audience starts to lose faith, every hit will get weaker and weaker, which means we only need to survive the full-strength bane once to win!"

Morgan scowled, tapping her knife-sharp nails against the arm of her cabana chair in a rapid staccato. "It's not actually a bad idea," she admitted eventually. "Risky, expensive, practically impossible, but with enough power, it could work."

"It *will* work," Lola said confidently. "But it is going to take a *lot* of magic, which is why I need you. You and Alberich were the greatest fairy monarchs left in this world, and I've still got his barrow. I know you're not at full strength yet, but if we combine our remaining gossamer, I believe we'll be able to survive enough of Victor's attacks to crack his illusion of invincibility and finally bring him down."

"That's where we disagree," the queen said with a sigh. "You might think you know what power is now that you've inherited Alberich's, but trust me when I say there's not enough gossamer left in our courts to survive what you're suggesting. Luckily, however, there is enough gossamer left in the *world*."

Lola frowned. "What does that mean?"

"It means we'll need more than just the two of us," Morgan said, rising from her chair. "Alberich and I were the biggest, but that doesn't mean ours were the only fairy courts left on this plane. I worked with the smaller kingdoms once before to get the power I needed to seal the Nightmare King in his barrow. If we can convince them to commit their gossamer again, we might just have enough to pull this off."

"I completely forgot about the other courts," Lola said excitedly. "Do you really think they'd help us?"

"Normally, I'd say not on your life," Morgan admitted. "Fairies are a cutthroat bunch. We only cooperate when our very survival is at stake, and even then, it's not a sure thing. You wouldn't believe the bribery I had to lay down last time, and that was when Alberich's excessive hunting was pushing us to the brink of extinction. Victor's bane is a subtler, more insidious danger. That makes it a tougher sell, but I think we might still be able to threaten their collective self-interest enough to make them agree."

"Sounds great," Lola said. "How do we do it?"

"Carefully," the queen said, tapping her finger against her lips. "We'll need to pander to their egos, so I propose we start by calling a Court of All Seasons."

"A what?"

"A formal gathering of all the fairy monarchs on this plane," Tristan explained. "We used to have them all the time."

"Everyone loves a party," Morgan agreed. "But the magical drought and the rise of human disbelief made it dangerous to gather everyone in one place. We haven't called an All Court since Alberich's imprisonment."

"Fitting that he should be why it happens again," Tristan said with a scowl. "His arrogance was the only reason Victor was able to make his blood magic bane in the first place. I can't see anyone turning down the chance to be rid of it."

"But we'll still have to approach them in the right way," Morgan said, thinking furiously. "I'm sure everyone's gone deep to ground by now. If we're going to lure them out enough to listen, we'll need the pull of at least two full monarchs."

"No problem there," Lola said. "You and I are already in."

Morgan shook her head. "I meet the qualifications. But while no one can argue Alberich isn't dead, you still haven't risen to take his place."

"What are you talking about?" Lola asked. "I ate his gross head, and I live in his barrow. The whole reason you got so mad at me was because I stole his power from you. Doesn't that imply that I have it?"

"You do indeed command the Underground," Morgan conceded, her green eyes sharp. "But where is your crown? Where are your armies, your court? Where is the power that forces others to acknowledge you as king?"

Lola bit her lip. "I—"

"Save your breath," the queen ordered, looking her up and down. "Anyone who looks at you will know you're no monarch. Not as Alberich was. You have his magic, but you have not yet seized the strength that makes others listen, which means no one will."

"Then how do I get it?" Lola asked, frustrated. "What more do I have to do?"

Morgan shrugged. "How should I know? It's your kingdom, not mine. I've never been stupid enough to set foot in Alberich's barrow, so I don't know what you still need to do to fully claim it. But if this plan of yours is going to work, you need to put your court in order. None of the other monarchs will heed a word you say until you do."

"But that's ridiculous," Lola groaned. "Don't they want to survive?"

"We *are* surviving," Morgan said, waving a hand at her quiet barrow. "You forget how long fairies have been here. We'll survive Victor the same way we've survived every disaster: by burrowing down and waiting it out. That was my plan. You're the only one who's in a hurry."

"Excuse me if I don't want to endure Victor for centuries," Lola muttered, rubbing her hands over her face.

She desperately regretted breaking that ugly crown of teeth now. If she'd just bucked up and accepted the troll's gift, this conversation would have gone very differently. Even if she had taken it, though, Lola had the feeling the sort of power Morgan was talking about wasn't as simple as putting something on your head. She'd seen firsthand how an actual monarch worked today, and while Lola still didn't fully understand Morgan's tree, it was obvious that her own relationship with the Underground Kingdom was nowhere close. She still couldn't make the trip back from her body without having to climb a hundred floors, and she hadn't even known she *had* low creatures until her desperation to save Simon had summoned them.

No wonder Morgan didn't see her as a king. Even Lola didn't see herself that way. Had specifically avoided it, in fact, because who in their right mind would want to rule over Alberich's nightmare factory?

Just thinking about it made her shudder, but she hated the idea of giving up even more. Victor might have a lot of enemies, but none of them seemed willing to do anything to stop him. Even Morgan planned to go back to sleep if Lola didn't push, which meant there was nothing for it.

"All right," Lola said, pulling herself straight again. "You go ahead and contact the other courts. I'll get my crown."

"Excellent," the queen said. "Just make sure you're quick about it. I'm certain the others are as eager to be rid of the bane as we are, so if this is going to come together, it'll likely do so all at once. Issuing the invitations in both our names will increase our chances of success, but nothing I say can keep it together if you show up as you are."

"I'll be ready," Lola said confidently, happy that being half human meant she could lie, because she didn't feel confident at all.

"I'll take care of the arrangements," Morgan promised, summoning a sleek AR smartphone with a twist of her wrist. "You just focus on bringing the Underground Kingdom to heel."

"And try not to kill too many trolls while you're at it," Tristan added. "Alberich had more monsters than all of us combined. If you show up to the Court of All Seasons with even a few of those, the others will fall at your feet."

Lola didn't even want to think about the horrors that were Alberich's trolls, but she nodded, walking stiffly out of the Queen of Desire's barrow with the Black Rider hot on her heels.

Chapter 12

Simon had to put his soul back together piece by piece.

If he hadn't been exactly who he was, it would have been impossible. Victor's attack had blown straight through the layers of his mind, shattering his death like a dropped Christmas ornament.

Anyone else would have died in that moment. For Simon, though, death had always been familiar territory, and not just because of the comas. Back when he was training, Victor had killed him on a regular basis. Simon would never *ever* thank him for that, but he could admit it was a useful skill as he picked his shattered fragments out of the dust and put himself back together.

When he'd finally collected enough pieces to open his eyes, he was covered in mice.

As usual, they paid no attention to him. They were too busy cleaning the blood off his bandaged chest with tiny scrub brushes. Simon was hoping those weren't the same tiny brushes they used on his floor when he realized there was someone standing beside his bed.

"How feeling?"

He jumped a foot off the plastic mattress.

A four-foot-tall star-nosed mole in a white lab coat was standing just down from his elbow. It lifted its paw when Simon stilled, reaching out delicately to shine a penlight into the mage's blinking eyes.

"Any pain?"

Simon shook his head, not trusting his voice to speak. That must have been good enough for the mole, because it nodded and shuffled away, leaving Simon blinking at the emergency clinic he'd helped Lola design in her house's formal dining room.

The large, sunny room was filled with more low creatures than he'd ever seen. Whole legions of them were scrubbing blood off the sterile floor with their tiny mops. Yet more mice in little nurse outfits were holding a tray for the mole doctor, who was examining vials of glowing liquid while writing notes on its clipboard with a tiny fountain pen that fit perfectly into its curving claws.

"Charming."

The condescending word rolled over Simon like dirty water, and his eyes flicked over to see Victor's ghost sitting on the windowsill.

The sight made him go still. The other blood mage hadn't been able to manifest like that since Simon had bricked him up. Clearly, Victor's attack had done even more damage than he'd realized. He was about to start the long process of boxing the monster back in when Victor slid off the ledge.

"You probably think you're clever," his old master drawled as he strolled over to Simon's bed, stepping on the mice whenever possible even though his ghostly feet passed right through them. "But all you really are is desperate. There's no other explanation for why you'd keep coming back from the dead over and over when you know it won't change anything."

Simon closed his blue eyes.

"How many times does this make now?" Victor asked. "A dozen? Two dozen? You'd think a brilliant planner like yourself wouldn't need to be so skilled at failure recovery, but I'm starting to think that's your only real talent. You certainly aren't good at anything else. Every foolproof plan you've thought up to beat me has ended the exact same way. If you weren't so adept at coming back from fatal mistakes, I would have had to find a new apprentice ages ago."

Simon put his hands over his ears.

"You know *that* won't work," Victor said with a laugh, his voice so loud in Simon's head that he might as well have been standing inside it. "No matter how hard you try to pretend, the truth is always with you. The only reason you're alive right now is because I taught you blood magic. The only strength you have is the gift *I* gave—"

"*Shut up!*" Simon yelled, digging his hands into his skull as he curled over into a ball on the hospital bed. "Just stop talking for once in your *life!*"

Victor's ghost tsked. "There you go again. You know the man who loses his temper loses the argument, but I suppose you can't help it. Losing is an integral part of who you are. That's why you're so good at coming back from the—"

Simon slammed his mind shut. He hit his own magic in the process, giving himself an instant splitting headache, but it was worth it for the moment of silence. He was trying to breathe through the pain when a new voice spoke from across the room.

"You are haunted."

Simon's blue eyes shot back open to see the Paladin's Grand Marshal lying on the second emergency bed on the opposite side of the room. Her dented armor was piled on the floor beside her, and every bit of her body that he could see was wrapped in red-stained gauze. That was to be expected given what they'd just gone through, but Simon didn't understand why she was lashed to the hospital bed by hundreds of tiny ropes the size of twine.

"What happened to you?"

The Paladin's dark eyes hardened through the gaps in her bandages. "I regained consciousness to discover my body was covered in vermin. Naturally, I reacted poorly, and this is the result."

For all the horrors in his head, Simon couldn't help himself.

"*It's not funny!*" the Paladin snarled as he doubled over with muffled laughter. "We're being operated on by fairy monsters!"

"Not fairy, sadly," the mole doctor said as it handed its chart to the waiting crowd of nurse mice. "Not that big yet."

Nadja snorted and scooted as far away as she could inside the hundreds of little restraints tying her down, but Simon pushed himself up.

"Thank you for saving us," he told the mole sincerely. "The Grand Marshal doesn't know it yet, but we're both very grateful for your help."

The mole waved his words away like a bad smell. "King say 'heal,' so we heal. To disobey king is death."

"Not anymore," Simon promised. "I'm sure Alberich was a tyrant, but Lola isn't like that. She'd never—"

"King is always death," the doctor said, its beady eyes gleaming as if this were the world's greatest truth. "But you alive, so no death today."

It made a gesture with its claws. The mice obeyed at once, packing up their little mops and scurrying away so fast, Simon didn't even see where they scurried to. It looked like they'd vanished into thin air. The doctor vanished as well while his head was turned, leaving Simon suddenly alone with the tied-down Paladin.

"This place is a nightmare," she muttered, biting at the ropes that tied her to the bed.

"That's no way to talk about the people who saved you," Simon scolded, sliding off his own table to help her.

The Paladin looked appalled. "It was a mole the size of an eight-year-old with a giant fleshy nose covered in little fingers!"

"I've seen weirder," Simon told her as he started unpicking the tiny knots in the ropes that held her down. "Just be grateful you're alive."

Grand Marshal Nadja fell quiet, staring at the ceiling while Simon patiently untied her.

"Are we the only ones who made it?"

"Absolutely," said the ghost Victor, who'd reappeared on Simon's left. "His brilliant plan got your entire order killed. It was the highlight of my year."

"I think so," Simon said, stubbornly pretending that Victor didn't exist as he removed the last of the strings. "I'm sorry. This wasn't what I intended to happen."

"I don't need a blood mage's apology," the Paladin said, but there was no malice in her voice. "Every person on that raid was ready to give their lives defending humanity, and that's exactly what they did. The soldiers of my order died good, brave deaths. Normally, I could ask for nothing more, but we're not finished yet. The mission isn't over. The enemy is still alive."

Simon's hands tightened on the wad of tiny, balled-up ropes. "I'm starting to think he can't be killed."

"Never say that," the Grand Marshal ordered, her face pinched with effort as she pushed herself into a sitting position. "Never give your enemy that power."

"It's an objectively true statement at this point," Simon argued, putting his back to the ghost of his master, whom he knew was smirking behind him. "I've tried to kill Victor Conrath so many times now that I've lost track, but he *never* dies."

"Neither do you," the Paladin said, looking straight into the blue eyes Victor had left in Simon's head. "I was down pretty hard, but I still saw what he did to you on that platform. He shattered your soul. You should be a corpse, yet here you stand, and from the looks of your magic, this isn't the first time."

"I'm good at coming back," Simon said bitterly. "But that's clearly not enough."

"It's enough to keep trying, which is all you need," Nadja said, lifting her chin to look down at him even though the bed put their heads at the same level. "Nothing is over until you're dead, and even then, the gods negotiate. Victor Conrath especially has earned their hate. He enslaved the DFZ, one of their own."

"Then why aren't they acting?" Simon demanded. "If they're so angry, why aren't they helping us?"

Nadja's bandaged face pulled into a scowl. "I asked the Merlin Council the exact same question. Their Archmage wants to fight, but she and the death god she's sold her soul to cannot fight the beloved Hero by themselves, and the others refuse to help. They are afraid. They see themselves in the defeated DFZ, and it makes them cowardly." Her bloody stitched lip curled into a sneer. "No one fears being powerless more than a god."

"Then we can't win," Simon said, walking back to his own bed to flop over in defeat. "Your Paladins were my last hope, and Victor wiped the floor with you. If even the spirits won't fight him, there's nothing left."

"*We* are left," Nadja said fiercely, clenching her broken fists as best she could around the splints. "No war can end so long as someone is still fighting."

"You sound like Lola," Simon muttered, rubbing his hands over his face.

"They're both delusional," Victor's ghost agreed.

"I speak from experience," the Paladin insisted. "This is not the first time my order has been wiped out, nor will it be the last. But no matter how many times we are destroyed, we always come back. We can never *not* come back, because we are the sword of truth. Even if all memory of us was wiped from this world, so long as there are people who know that blood magic is wrong, we will *always* rise again."

"That doesn't mean you'll win," Simon said tiredly. "How do you know you're not just volunteering to die?"

Victor's ghost nodded as if this were just good sense, but the Paladin gave him a haughty look.

"Because no evil stands forever," she said with the fervor of a true believer. "Conrath sneers into his cameras and preaches that blood magic is humanity's true power, but if that were actually true, we'd all be blood mages, and we're not. Every soul on this planet instinctively loathes power like his. We hate it so much that even non-mages will fight back, which is why using blood magic against another human stains the soul. It's a wound inflicted by the victim, a scar. That stain is proof that using blood magic goes against humanity's most basic nature. We instinctually reject it the same way we do murder, incest, and injustice, which is why Conrath's plans will ultimately never succeed. Even if we must wear him down like rain wears down a mountain, every blood mage will eventually fall. It is inevitable."

Simon looked at the white floor Lola's low creatures had scrubbed clean. "You don't know how much I'd like to believe that."

"It doesn't matter whether you believe or not," the Paladin insisted. "It is the truth. But just because it is certain that Victor Conrath will be defeated someday doesn't mean we're free to stop trying now. My fallen comrades still cry out for his death, and we will see them satisfied."

Simon's head shot up. "We?"

The Grand Marshal shrugged. "You want him dead, too, don't you?"

"Yeah, but..." he trailed off as he looked down at his stained soul. "I'm a blood mage. I'm what you hate."

"That doesn't mean you can't be a weapon," the Grand Marshal said, turning to look at him head-on. "Do not mistake my words for leniency. I still intend to kill you when this is over, but after what I witnessed on that platform, I would have to be truly blind not to see how much you hate him. That's not enough to excuse your crimes, but great need always makes for strange bedfellows, and I'm not exactly in a position to turn down an ally as strong as you."

Simon couldn't believe his ears. "You think I'm strong?"

"I told you she was delusional," Victor's ghost quipped before Simon shut him out.

"You pulled yourself back from death," the Paladin said, looking at him as if this should be obvious. "What he did should have killed you twice over, but you're back on your feet just a few hours later. That's nothing short of miraculous, but I'd expect nothing less from the mage Victor Conrath chose to be his apprentice."

"At least she knows enough to give credit where credit is due," Victor said, suddenly appearing right in front of Simon's face. "But don't fall for her flattery. She's using you. She doesn't care if you live or die. She just needs a new idiot now that I've killed all her tin soldiers."

"So what?" Simon snarled, waving his hand through Victor's smirking face. "I don't care whether I live or die, either, so long as I get to take you down with me."

The ghost gave him an unimpressed look, but Simon had already turned back to the Grand Marshal, who was watching him with far more compassion than he'd expected.

"He's haunting you, isn't he?"

Simon sighed. "How did you know?"

"I can see him," she said, her eyes roving over Simon's face. "His blood is hanging over you like smog." She flicked her gaze back to his. "Would you like to learn how to kick him out?"

"You can do that?" Simon asked desperately.

"Of course." She lifted her bandaged face to give him a superior look. "Our entire methodology was built specifically to counter blood magic. You think Conrath invented mastery of the self? That's been part of human magic since the earliest records."

Simon had never thought about it that way, but... "Doesn't that mean you're also doing blood magic?"

"Only if you use the knowledge to shove your will into someone else's head," the Paladin said, reaching down to grab her battered armor. "But what you do inside your own soul is your business, and since blood magic is all about controlling other people, a core tenet of Paladin magic is the defense against such invasions." She glanced back up at him. "I'm guessing Conrath never taught you how to defend yourself."

"Of course I did," Victor's ghost said haughtily, but Simon shook his head.

"He taught me to guard my mind but never against him. He went in there all the time when I was younger, specifically to build himself a back door."

"Then we must unbuild it," Nadja said as she started strapping her armor back on over her bandages. "I will teach you to make that formidable resilience of yours into a fortress as well as a lifeline. Once you learn how to defend like a Paladin, Conrath won't be able to touch you."

"Says the woman who couldn't even land a hit on me," the ghost sneered, but Simon wasn't listening to him. He'd seen what had happened on that platform, how Victor had used the DFZ to defeat the Paladins instead of blood magic. He had no reason to do that unless he'd known his own power would be ineffective, which meant the Grand Marshal was right.

"Teach me," Simon demanded, leaping off the bed. "You can do whatever you want to me after, but until Victor is dead—"

"We fight," she finished, her face growing grave. "But know that I can only teach you defense. We kill blood mages with swords, but even I can't train up someone as scrawny as you in the time we've got."

"That's all right," Simon said. "Victor already taught me more than I ever wanted to know about attacking. I've even got a live target to practice on."

Victor's ghost gave him a murderous look. "What do you mean by that?"

The Paladin also looked angry. "I will never condone the use of blood magic in any fashion," she said as she donned her helmet. "But one goes to war with the army one has. I will pay for my sins by defeating you after Victor Conrath is dead, but until that moment, we are soldiers of the same side."

"The enemy of my enemy is my friend," Simon agreed with a smile. "How soon can we start?"

"Right now," the Paladin said, tucking the armored plate that wouldn't fit over her splinted leg under her arm. "I don't need my body to teach you mental defense, but we will need a place to practice. Building your soul into a fortress requires tearing everything else down first. We'll need to be somewhere you feel safe or it won't work."

"We can't do it here," Simon told her. "There's nowhere I feel safer, but I can't keep someone like you inside Lola's barrow."

She looked mortally offended. "What do you mean 'someone like me'?"

"You antagonize her low creatures," Simon explained. "And you're bad for her magic. I might not be able to feel gossamer, but even I can tell you're pushing her limits."

He pointed at the edge of her hospital bed where the metal was starting to droop like melted wax.

"If we can't stay here, then we should go to one of our safe houses," the Paladin said, her face growing bitter. "There should be plenty to choose from now that Victor has destroyed my entire order."

Simon nodded. "Sounds good to me. Where is it?"

"The closest one is in Toledo," she answered, "but the US military is using it currently, so I think we should go to our old training facility in Columbus. There will be no one to disturb us there."

"You mean no one to catch you training a blood mage."

"I am not ashamed to do what must be done," the Paladin said. "But it will be more efficient not to constantly be interrupted with different versions of the same question."

Simon couldn't argue with that, though he was far less sure about how they were going to get there. Despite the Grand Marshal's conviction, he had zero confidence the rest of the world would let her just take him into a Paladin facility, decommissioned or otherwise. He also didn't want to risk the real Victor finding out what he was doing before he was ready. They needed a quiet escape, something no one would catch. Fortunately, Simon had a pretty good idea how to get it.

Motioning for the Paladin to stay put, he walked over to the clinic door and stuck his head out into the living room. "Dee?" he called. "Are you here?"

His voice echoed through the empty house. Then, like the sun rising over the horizon, Lola's doppelganger burst around the corner from the kitchen.

"Heya, Simon!" she called cheerfully. "I'm so happy you're okay! You just missed Lola Prime. She went to pitch Tristan on her next Victor-murder plan. I'm sure she'll be back soon, but did you know you've got a Paladin right behind you?"

"I know," Simon said, smiling despite himself. He should have known Lola would already be getting back on the horse. It made him feel even better about his own decision as he put a hand on the copy's shoulder.

"I need you to make a door for me."

"Whoa," Dee said, backing up. "Make? As in open a new low road?"

When Simon nodded, she shook her head wildly. "I reeeeeeally don't think that's a good idea. Lola's the monarch around here. I'm just a copy."

"Who can do everything she can and has her best interests at heart," Simon said confidently. "I also know you've done it at least once before. Remember when you secretly went to New York to get her that special cookie sandwich from the bakery she saw on the internet and got obsessed with?"

Dee gasped as if he'd just revealed her darkest secret. "That was a dessert *emergency!*"

"This is an emergency, too. I need to get to Columbus, Ohio."

The doppelganger looked confused. "Don't most people consider getting *out* of Columbus an emergency?"

"I'm serious, Dee," Simon said. "We need to get to Columbus without anyone knowing, not even Lola."

Now she looked angry. "Why not Lola?"

Because the moment Lola learned Simon had left with a Paladin, she'd come running to save him. It was what he loved most about her but also what he couldn't allow. He didn't need to invade her mind to know that Nadja would conduct this training with zero concern for his safety. But while Simon was absolutely ready to stake his life on defeating Victor, Lola wasn't willing to let anyone but herself take that risk, which meant she couldn't know.

"You know how much she wants to keep us safe," he said, looking hard into Dee's eyes, which were so much like Lola's it hurt. "But safe isn't cutting it. If we want to win, we'll all have to take bigger risks. Lola's been doing that for months; now it's my turn. I know this is the right thing, Dee, but I can't do it without your help. You have to send me somewhere I can practice safely, and you can't tell Lola where that is."

The copy bit her lip. "She won't like it."

"Then you can blame me," Simon offered. "It was my idea, not yours. I'm going to go no matter what, but if you help me, you can at least make sure that I get there safely."

"Lola *does* want you to be safe," Dee said, gnawing on her lip. "Okay, I'll do it, but you need to understand that I probably won't be able to keep your secret for long. The rest of this place doesn't get it yet, but Lola's always been my monarch. If she asks me, I'll have to tell her."

"Then we'll have to do it before she realizes I'm gone," Simon said with a grin.

As always, Dee grinned back blindingly and waved for him to follow her into the kitchen. Simon assumed she was leading them to the yard, where the low road doors were, but the doppelganger didn't even glance at the back door. Instead, she walked over to the kitchen sink and yanked open a drawer beside it.

"Here," she said, handing Simon a dish towel.

"What's this for?" he asked.

"Her," Dee said, pointing at Nadja, who was glaring at everything through the glass shield of her still-bloody helmet. "Her disbelief is punching this place like whoa. She needs to cover her eyes and chill out, or the only place I'll be sending you is back to bed."

Simon didn't see that happening, but Nadja must have been more ready to get out of here than he realized, because she snatched the towel out of Dee's hand and placed it over her helmet before he could say a word.

"Let's just get this over with," the Paladin muttered, crossing her arms over her chest. "I hate this place."

"It hates you, too!" Dee informed her happily, crooking her finger at Simon as she led them into the pantry.

"This is where I keep my doors," she whispered conspiratorially. "Don't tell Lola, but her barrow isn't actually good at making food. She thinks all the cookies and stuff I bring out are gossamer like Tristan's banquet table, but I've actually been buying them from a Kroger's down in Atlanta."

Simon stared at her in disbelief. "You've been faking her fake food?"

"I didn't want her to feel bad," Dee said, twisting her fingers just like Lola did when she got caught. "She has enough insecurities about her barrow as it is. I thought if the food was good, it'd give her more confidence."

Simon smiled. "That's very sweet of you."

"Really?" Dee looked shocked. "I thought it was terrible, which is why I hid it, though I'm not sure how she hasn't figured it out yet. You'd think the fact that her 'magical' pantry was producing Twinkies and stuff would tip her off, but she's never even asked a question."

Simon had to laugh at that. "Lola would *absolutely* believe that her barrow produces junk food. It's always been her favorite."

"Aww, that cute little trash panda," Dee said, laughing as she opened what Simon thought was a built-in cupboard but turned out to be a crawl space. "I can get you to Cincinnati. Will that be okay?"

Simon was about to ask if she could possibly do anything closer when the blindfolded Grand Marshal shoved her way forward.

"Cincinnati will be fine," she declared. "Just get us out of this madhouse."

"Awesome!" Dee said, pulling off the dish towel and shoving the Paladin into the crawl space. "In you go!"

She shoved Simon in next, with much more strength than he'd expected. For a moment, he tumbled through the cabinet like Alice falling down the rabbit hole. Then his feet hit the ground with a sudden stop and a burst of cold, and he looked up in surprise to see he was standing inside the stocking area of a supermarket freezer.

"I'll leave the door open for you," Dee said, hopping down through the hatch in the ceiling—the other side of the low road—to give Simon a hug that was so much like Lola's, he teared up a little. "Come back to us fast, Mr. Wizard! You're our family."

"I'll be back before you know it," he promised, hugging her back as hard as he dared. "And then we'll win."

Dee didn't seem to care about that. She just squeezed him one more time and clambered back up into the low road. She waved one last time when she got to the top and closed the cabinet, leaving the door open a crack so he'd be able to climb back through.

"That was an experience I never want to have again," Nadja said, shoving a shelf of microwave pizzas out of her way as she opened the glass freezer door into the supermarket aisle beyond. "Come on. We have a hundred miles to cover, and I still need to get us a car."

Since she was a terrifying armored woman covered in bloody bandages, Simon didn't see how that was going to happen without someone finding out. But he was the one who'd asked for this, so he shut his mouth, paying no attention to ghost-Victor's constant eye-rolling as he followed the Paladin out of the frozen food section, apologizing profusely to the terrified customers she left in her wake.

Chapter 13

Lola opened a low road back to her barrow the moment she was out of Morgan's. She didn't even wait to find to a proper door. She just picked the first dark nook she saw between two pieces of wreckage and shoved her way through the DFZ's raging magic.

She was certain the city felt it, but by the time the spirit's enormous—and highly unmotivated—attention made it over, Lola was already marching into her living room. Valente stayed right on her heels, writing furiously the whole way.

You don't have to do this, his pad read when he shoved it at her. *Morgan's pushing you to be like Alberich for her own benefit.*

"That doesn't mean it's not also for mine," Lola said, rolling the rug off the manhole cover that led down to the levels she didn't control. "I've been putting this off since I got this place, and you heard what they said. The only way to get the other courts to go along with the plan is if I'm king."

But it's ridiculous, he wrote as he crouched beside her. *I saw your gossamer before I threw away my head. You've already got tons, even more than Morgan has right now.* His gloved fingers tightened on the pencil. *I think the queen's the one who needs you. She's so weak right now that the others won't listen to her unless you're there.*

"You might be right," Lola said with a sigh. "But it doesn't matter. As we just spent the last three months proving, I can't beat Victor as I am."

That doesn't mean you have to risk yourself!

"You did," she said, staring at her face's reflection in his visor. "You threw away your head and your humanity to become the Black Rider. Why do you think I'm not willing to do the same?"

That's different, he wrote frantically. *Killing the Hero is the Rider's duty, and I was dying anyway, but you're free. You shouldn't have to—*

"It's not about should," Lola said, staring hard at the iron manhole cover set into her living room's cozy wooden floor. "I can't keep living like this, Valente. I can't keep watching Victor hurt everyone, and I can't keep pretending I'm in control when I'm not. I'm the one who made the decision to eat Alberich's head. This is my barrow. I don't know if I can become its real king, since I'm not even a real fairy, but I owe it to the creatures who live here to try. It's not their fault Alberich made them monsters. He made me one, too. We all grew out of the same twisted root, but that just means I need to do this even more."

I understand that, Valente wrote, his hand slowing down as his glossy visor tilted toward the manhole cover. *But I've spent the last three months with my head on all the time. I've seen what's waiting down there, the things even Alberich thought it was better to bury. You're bigger than you were before, but you're still not bigger than he was. I just don't see—*

"You don't have to see," Lola said, putting her hand on his to stop his writing. "Because I'm not going down there to beat them. I don't want to be a conqueror or a Nightmare King. Even if I was willing to try, I could never be what Alberich was, so I'm going to go to them as myself and see what happens. Who knows? Maybe they're also tired of being monsters."

The Rider shook his silent head. *I don't think trolls get tired.*

"Nothing to it but to do it," Lola said, grabbing the heavy cover only to pause. "Um, you might want to wait outside for this. You're no longer made of squishy gossamer, and I can't guarantee things won't get weird down there."

The Rider shook his helmet firmly. *I'm coming with you.*

"No way," she said. "This is something I have to do myself." *But not alone.*

"I'm never alone," Lola said, smiling over her shoulder at Toothy, who was already hovering in the doorway to the kitchen.

Dee popped out behind her a second later, looking weirdly guilty, which would have made Lola suspicious if her copy hadn't been so adorably innocent. Even if she had done something worthy of those shifty eyes, Lola didn't care. All she cared about was that they were here, rushing to her side without her having to say a word.

Valente looked just as ready. He was already pressing his pencil against the paper again when Lola stood up.

"I appreciate the support," she said solemnly. "But you chose to become a spirit rather than my knight. I respect and accept that decision, but now you'll have to do the same for me. I need you to believe that I've got this, Valente."

He stared up at her for a long moment. Then, as if he'd come to a decision, he rose swiftly to his feet. *I do believe,* he wrote. *And to prove it, I'm staying right here until you get back.*

"I don't think that's a good idea," Lola said nervously, wringing her fingers as he strode toward the couch. "I'm about to meddle in seriously foundational stuff. If I mess this up, the whole barrow could collapse. The door to Windsor's still open. The DFZ can't feel you out there, so why don't you…"

Her voice trailed off as Valente sat down on her sofa with a stubborn *thump.*

You told me to believe in you, he wrote as he pushed his back into the squishy cushions. *This is how I prove it. If I can't go with you, I'll wait right here until you get back, but I am never leaving you to fight alone ever again.*

The thought of him being in the building while she kicked the supports still made her panicky, but no amount of fear could keep the smile off Lola's face.

"Thank you," she said, walking over to drop a kiss on his shiny visor.

He pulled her into a hug the second she got close, pressing her against his body, which no longer felt cold. Just like the night they'd spent together, he felt warm and alive under her fingers, leaving her giddy as she forced herself to break away.

"Don't move," she told him, grinning like an idiot as she walked backwards toward her other selves. "I'll be right back."

The Black Rider nodded and settled in to wait, making himself comfortable on the cushions as Lola grabbed Toothy and Dee and pulled them into the kitchen.

"You know what we have to do?"

It was a rhetorical question. Toothy and Dee always seemed to know what she was thinking even before Lola did, but it was still a relief when they both nodded.

"We'll need to get Simon and the Paladin out before we do anything," she said, opening the fridge to grab a slice out of the rectangular grocery-store sheet cake taking up the entire middle shelf. "I'm trusting Valente to handle himself since spirits are pretty unkillable, but Simon and what's-her-name are one-hundred-percent human. Also injured. That's not a good combo for barrow shenanigans, which means we need to make sure they're moved to a minimum safe distance."

"Oh, don't worry about that," Dee said cheerfully, looking enormously and inexplicably relieved. "They're already gone!"

Lola choked on the icing-rose-covered corner slice she'd just shoved into her mouth. "*Gone?*" she repeated when she could breathe around all the sugar. "Where? *How?* Last time I saw them, they were going into surgery. I was only at Morgan's for an hour!"

"Your low creatures do good work," Dee said, suddenly staring at the floor as she twisted her fingers. "They both got better super quick. Miraculous recovery! And then, um…"

"Stop," Lola said before this got any worse. "Where are they really?"

Dee looked even more determinedly at the kitchen tile, making Lola smile.

"It's okay, Dee," she said, setting down the part of the cake slice she hadn't choked on to give her double her full attention. "Just tell me what happened. I promise I won't get mad."

"I told him it wouldn't work," Dee muttered, taking a deep breath as she looked Lola in the face. "I let Simon out of the barrow to go train with the Paladin."

"You *what?*"

"You said you wouldn't get mad!" Dee cried with a betrayed look.

"I didn't think you'd send Simon to his death!" Lola yelled back.

Dee stomped her foot. "He insisted on going, and he told me not to tell you because he knew you'd act like this! He trusts you to know what you're doing. Why can't you trust him?"

Now it was Lola's turn to stare at the floor. Dee's words were especially pointed given what she'd just said to Valente, but it was so *hard* not to run after Simon and snatch him back. He was her family, the rock who'd protected her from Victor whenever he could, and that horrible woman wanted to murder him. She knew he wouldn't have gone with the Paladin without reason, but Simon's normally excellent logic suffered a critical malfunction whenever it came to their old master. Lola wouldn't have been surprised to hear he'd offered himself up as a human sacrifice to whatever god still had the guts to take the Hero on.

"Did you use the Windsor door, at least?" she asked nervously, praying that her double had had the sense not to send Simon and the Paladin into Victor's DFZ, but Dee shook her head.

"I sent them to Cincinnati."

Lola blinked at her in confusion. "I don't have a door to Cincinnati."

"I know," her double said, looking at the floor again. "I used mine."

"Yours?" Lola repeated, too flabbergasted to be upset. "*You* made a door? By yourself?"

Dee nodded, ducking her head lower. "And since we're doing confessions, I should also mention that all the food in the fridge and the pantry didn't come from your barrow. I've been making doors into the backs of grocery stores so I could stock things without telling you. I didn't mean to mislead you! It's just that I know your barrow's a big source of stress for you, and I wanted you to have food you liked to eat, so I sort of kind of... lied."

She finished with a nervous expression, but Lola could only stare. In hindsight, she couldn't say why she was so shocked. Dee was a copy of her, so it made sense that she could do everything Lola could, like lying and making doors. She was apparently even better at that last one than the original, but Lola was too shocked by the first to pay proper attention. Dee was normally open to a fault. The idea that she'd been lying for *months* over junk food felt impossible. Lola was still trying to wrap her brain around it when Dee's shoulders slumped.

"I'm sorry," she whispered forlornly. "I didn't mean to let you down. I was just trying to help and—"

"You didn't let me down," Lola said. "You've *never* let me down."

The simple truth of that made her smile wide as she wrapped her arms around her mirror image. "From the moment I made you, everything you've ever done has been to help me. How could I possibly be mad?"

Dee hugged Lola back so tight, their gossamer stuck together. "I'll always help you," she whispered into Lola's shoulder. "You're my queen."

Lola went still. She hadn't thought about it until this moment, but she'd made Dee *before* she'd eaten Alberich. Made a gossamer creation who thought and talked and loved for herself. Toothy was the same, as became evident when the shaggy creature tromped over and added her huge body to the hug.

Lola spread her arms wider to encompass them both, squeezing her eyes shut. She'd always thought of her girls as fragments of herself, just more sophisticated versions of her cars and costumes, but that wasn't true. They were their own people who made their own decisions, and they'd *always* decided to help. Even when she was afraid of them, even when she yelled, they'd never left. They'd protected her and fought for her and never, ever, *ever* let her give up.

"Lola?" Dee said, her voice alarmed. "Are you crying?"

"Yeah," Lola whispered, hugging her tighter. "Sorry, I know it's not exactly royal behavior. It's just… I finally realized that I *do* have a sister. Sister*s*."

She flashed a teary grin up at Toothy's flat face, and Dee snorted. "*Duh*, you're just figuring this out now?"

"I'm not as good as other fairies at seeing through my own illusions," Lola told her with a sniff as she finally pulled away. "But you realize what this means, right?"

Dee tilted her head. "What what means?"

Lola scrubbed the tears off her face with a grin. "You're fairies."

"Pshaw," her double said, rolling her eyes. "We can't be fairies."

"Dee," Lola said, giving her a flat look. "You made a low road."

"It's not that special," Dee said sheepishly. "You make them all the time."

"Yeah, after I ate a king's *head*," Lola reminded her. "I couldn't make one at all before Alberich, and I still can't make one to somewhere I haven't been, but you're in here popping off roads to Cincinnati without me even noticing." Her face split into a grin. "Don't you see what that makes us?"

"No, but I'd really appreciate it if you stopped asking questions," Dee said nervously. "I don't do well with interrogations."

"It means we're a *court*!" Lola cried, grabbing Dee's shoulder in one hand and Toothy's paw in the other.

She even had a pretty good idea of how it had happened. As Tristan had told her in Morgan's barrow, normal fairies were born when one low creature ate enough other low creatures to gain sentience, but none of them had ever been normal fairies. Dee and Toothy had come from Lola, who'd always been half human, and, as Simon was constantly saying, humans *moved magic*. Specifically into things they cared about, and there was nothing Lola cared about more than her family, which definitely included the two in front of her.

"This is going to be great," she promised, hugging them again. "All this time, I've been thinking I'm a weaker version of Alberich, but I'm nothing like him at all. *We're* nothing like him! We're something totally new, which means I don't have to go down there as a king. We're going down as a *court*, and we're going to give it the full-court press."

"We were never going to let you go down by yourself anyway," Dee told her confidently. "Lolas stick together!"

They did stick together. Agreeing with Victor went against her nature, but the old bastard had been right about one thing: Lola *was* a masterpiece, except she wasn't his. Her masterpiece was the three of them standing in front of the open fridge. Three impossible fairies who'd survived despite everything, and if they could do that, Lola believed—absolutely, truly, to-her-toes believed—they could do *anything*.

"Come on," she said, grabbing her sisters' hands. "We've got a monarchy to restore."

The others didn't even question. They just ran after her into the living room, Dee whipping back to close the fridge while Toothy flipped the manhole cover open. Valente was still sitting on the couch like he'd grown there, so Lola blew him one last kiss before she hopped down the hole, falling like a rocket into the dark with her girls right behind her.

Chapter 14

Lola had never tried going down in her barrow before. She normally just raced up, climbing as fast as she could toward everything she actually cared about, like Valente and Simon and the real world they were fighting to save from Victor. So long as the parts of the barrow she didn't control weren't bothering the parts she did, Lola had seen no reason to poke it. Even the troll who'd busted into her bedroom had been shoved to the edge of her mind.

That felt crazy in hindsight. Who ignored a monster trying to give them a crown? The only thing Lola could say for herself was that she'd been preoccupied. Dealing with Victor had always sucked up every available brain cell, especially since she'd considered him much more of a threat. The worst a troll could do was eat her. Victor ruined everything that made life worth living.

It pissed Lola off how much of her thoughts he still took up. Even the reason she'd agreed to try this was to get the power she needed to kill him, which she now knew wasn't right at all. If she pulled this off, Lola would be the Underground King for the rest of her life, which she was starting to realize might be a very, *very* long time.

That wasn't the sort of responsibility you took on to gain a strategic advantage, but Lola wasn't doing this to beat Victor anymore. She was becoming king for *them*, for herself and Dee and Toothy and all the others that had sprung from Alberich. She'd won this kingdom fair and square, and for the first time since she'd shoved Alberich's head down her throat, Lola believed she could handle it. This place wasn't a gossamer windfall she could use to beat Victor. It was hers—her kingdom, her land, her home for her family—and as she rocketed down through caverns she and her sisters used to crawl through, Lola felt it. Finally felt the connection that tied her to everything.

The feeling was still solidifying when her feet landed on firm stone. There'd been no crash, no snap to mark the end of their momentum. She was simply *there*, standing inside a tight spiral staircase on a step worn hollow by centuries of feet. As ever, Dee and Toothy were right behind her, looking around in confusion at the suddenly tight space.

"Huh," Dee said, running her finger across the wetness seeping down the stone walls. "Never been here before."

The spiral stair was *very* different from the caverns, lava pools, and troll pits they normally tromped through. Good different or bad different was yet to be determined, but Lola hadn't come this far down just to turn around and go back up. Wherever they were, it was new, so she put her hand on the cold, wet walls and motioned for the others to follow her.

Walking down took much longer than falling. The spiraling stair went on forever, making Lola dizzy as she turned in a tight corkscrew past endless walls that all looked the same. There were no torches, no doors, no lights of any kind. Lola wasn't even sure how she was seeing until she remembered Toothy's eyes. Her creature had always been nearsighted and colorblind, but even when they were little, Lola had been able to see in the dark just fine. That made sense for creations of the Underground King, so Lola plowed ahead, racing down the worn steps faster and faster until, at last, she spotted a light in the distance.

It was the most beautiful glow she'd ever seen. That could have been because she'd been walking in the dark for what felt like hours, but Lola swore she'd never seen anything as lovely as the rich, golden light shining like a promise below. It was so lively and pretty, she thought it was sunlight at first, but as the three of them came around the corkscrew's final bend, she saw that it was gold.

An entire cavern *filled* with gold.

The sight made her stagger. The staircase let out into a cave the size of an aircraft hangar, and every inch of it was covered in gold. There was red gold, white gold, butter-yellow gold, and rose gold. There were golden coins, golden statues, golden bricks, and golden chandeliers filled with glowing golden candles that hung from the golden ceiling on golden chains as thick as Lola's leg. There were golden lanterns, golden filigree, cloth-of-gold curtains hanging from golden rods. So, so, *so* much gold that Lola almost missed the biggest piece of all: a great golden boulder the size of a small house sitting like a monolith at the cavern's end.

It was the only piece of gold in the whole place that hadn't been worked in some way. Even the golden walls were hammered and polished, but the boulder still looked like exactly what it was: a giant lump of metal. Its surface was rough and asymmetrical except for the middle, where the gold had been smoothed out into a long, tear-shaped groove, almost like a tide hole.

Or like something huge had sat on it.

A shiver ran through Lola's gossamer. That giant boulder wasn't some natural formation. It was a throne, a great golden seat worn down through untold ages by something even bigger than Toothy, and gathered around its base like crows around a carcass were the monsters.

Even with all the dazzling gold blinding her eyes, Lola couldn't believe she hadn't noticed them sooner. The giant throne was surrounded by trolls, including the one that had broken into her bedroom, though it was hardly the biggest. Some of the creatures in here were so tall, their multi-horned heads brushed the cave's cathedral-like ceiling. Others were as long as freight trains and covered in telephone-pole-sized black spines, like giant porcupine snakes. Smaller monsters hid in the bigger ones' shadows, their hides and fur and scales a sharp contrast to the dazzling gold that surrounded them. They were all silent, but every one of them—at least the ones that had appendages recognizable as heads—was looking at Lola.

She gulped in reply. The massive cavern was clearly meant to hold far more than just the pack in front of her. Lola wasn't sure if that was because the Wild Hunt was missing due to Victor slaughtering them all or if this place had always been designed to make its audience feel small, but at least she knew where she was. Even if there hadn't been a giant golden chair positioned like an idol at the far end, the echo of Alberich that still rattled in her head remembered this place with great fondness. This was his throne room, war room, and treasury all in one. The cold, hard, glittering heart of the Underground Kingdom.

"Wow," Dee whispered from where she was hiding behind Toothy. "Do you think it looked this gaudy when the old king lived here?"

"It was worse," Lola assured her, trying not to look at the memories of the "games" Alberich used to play in this place. He and his horrible hunt used to paint this place black with the trolls' blood and then release the survivors out into the world to terrify humanity. Some of the creatures in front of her still bore the scars of that old cruelty. Alberich's memory cackled at the sight, but all Lola felt was a deep, deep kinship as she started forward, her gossamer sneakers slapping against the golden floor like punches as she marched toward the giant, empty throne.

The crowd of monsters parted when she got close, lowering their heads with an obedience that made Lola's jaw clench. Bile burned in her throat as she climbed up the rise to the golden boulder. The ancient seat was far too big for her in her current shape, but Lola had no interest in sitting on thrones. She scrambled up the boulder's front instead, prying her fingers into the gold's pitted surface until she was standing inside the gigantic hollow worn by Alberich's true form.

Toothy hopped up behind her, using her massive claws like picks to nimbly scale the boulder's surface. Dee had a bit more trouble with her stubbornly human fingers, but she made it up with Lola's help. When they were all standing in Alberich's seat like a united front, Lola stepped up to the edge of the hollow and raised her head to address the crowd.

More monsters had come in while they'd been climbing. Lola hadn't heard them enter, but the crowd of monsters she faced now was easily twice as large as it had been when she'd come in. It still wasn't close to filling up the cavern, but it was by far the biggest audience she'd ever been in front of. That plus the beady eyes and countless fangs should have made for an intimidating scene, but the rush going through Lola wasn't fear.

It was sympathy. These were monsters just like she'd been, tools made by Alberich to use as he saw fit, but that was over now. The Nightmare King was dead, and if Lola accomplished nothing else in this place, she was determined to let them know.

"Subjects of the Underground Kingdom," she said, her voice ringing through the golden cavern like a gong. "I'm Lola Daniels, a human changeling made by Alberich with the help of the blood mage Victor Conrath. Like you, he made me to serve, but my court"—she glanced over her shoulder at a grinning Toothy and a very smug-looking Dee—"and I rose up against him. Together, we defeated the Nightmare King, and I have eaten his head. That makes me your ruler now, and as my first official act, I'd like to apologize for taking so long to come down here. You deserved better than to be ignored, but I'm here now, and I'm ready to do whatever you need me to do as your monarch."

A heavy silence followed, making Lola shift from foot to foot. She'd thought that was a pretty good opening. It was certainly what she would've wanted to hear from her new king, but the crowd was staring at her like she was speaking nonsense.

She was about to clarify that this meant they were free when an irritated voice spoke up.

"We shouldn't have to tell you that."

"Sorry?" Lola said, crouching on the edge of the giant seat. She had to squint through all the glaring gold, but eventually she spotted a familiar white-coated figure. It was the star-nosed mole who'd come out to doctor Simon and the Paladin when Lola had asked the barrow for help. It looked comically tiny next to all the giants, but the bigger monsters deferred to the doctor as if the mole were a figure of great respect. One even lowered its black paw so the mole doctor and the other low creatures—who still looked like mice carrying scrub brushes—could climb on, lifting them high into the air until they were even with Lola.

"Thank you for your help earlier," she said as politely as possible. "I'm sorry for not asking before, but what is your—"

"No name," the mole interrupted, sticking its star nose into the air as if the very idea were insulting. "And no thank. Kings do not thank."

"I do," Lola said determinedly. "I'm not like Alberich, and you saved someone very dear to me. Of course, I'm going to thank you."

"King does not thank," the doctor insisted as all the mice nodded their little heads. "King does not make speeches either. King does only one thing: provide."

"Provide what?" Lola asked, suddenly feeling very out of her depth.

"Everything," the mole said, counting off on its curving claws. "King provides home. King provides purpose. King provides food. King provides order. King provides death."

"Death?" Lola repeated, waving her hands in horror. "No, no, no! That's not—"

She snapped her mouth shut when the bigger monsters growled, and the mole stomped its clawed foot.

"Death is most important!" it cried. "Without death, we cannot grow. Cannot turn into true fairies and leave this place. How you king and not know that?"

The crowd rumbled in agreement, and Lola's stomach began to shrink. "I meant no offense," she said, which only seemed to make the monsters even angrier. "I didn't grow up in a fairy kingdom, so I don't know what I'm supposed to do."

"Nothing to know," the mole assured her. "It very simple. King provides. Barrow obeys."

A great noise of approval followed those words. All over the cavern, monsters were beating their claws against the golden floor while the low creatures clapped their little paws. The mole looked extremely pleased by this reaction, puffing out its chest beneath its white coat as it looked at Lola again.

"You good king so far," it assured her. "Give much food."

Lola's jaw dropped. "What food?"

The mole didn't seem to understand the question, which was a serious problem, because Lola had no idea what it was talking about. So far as she knew, she'd never provided anything to her barrow, food or otherwise. It didn't seem possible that she *could* provide, since, unlike Alberich or Morgan or even Tristan, Lola was a dream giver, not a dream eater. This whole time, she'd assumed her barrow was still running off the leftovers from Alberich's ride of terror, but she didn't think the mole would lie. It probably *couldn't* lie, since, unlike her, Alberich's monsters were one hundred percent gossamer, but then where—

Her whirling thoughts stopped when a hand grabbed her elbow, and Lola was jerked back from the edge by Dee, who was bouncing excitedly on the balls of her feet. "You *are* feeding them!"

"Feeding them what?" Lola whispered frantically. "I don't know how to feed a barrow! You just confessed I haven't even been feeding myself."

"That's just it," her double said excitedly, waving at the crowd of monsters. "You eat *food*, not gossamer. Your magic has always been carb powered, and you've been putting away cookies like it's your personal responsibility to keep the sugar industry in business."

"I haven't been *that* bad," Lola muttered. "I'm a stress eater, and seeing Victor come back from the dead all those times was really stressful, but I don't see what that has to do with this."

"It has everything to do with this!" Dee cried, bouncing faster than ever. "Don't you get it? Alberich's magic was never supporting this place. He burned it all up fighting Victor, which was why he had to go for his head, but you got it first. You've been the only monarch around for three months, which means everything we've been through and seen and done with the magic here has come from *you*."

"That's ridiculous," Lola said, waving her arm at the giant golden cavern. "I think I'd notice if I was supporting something this huge."

"And I absolutely think you *wouldn't*," Dee argued, holding her ground. "Your fear of Victor supported this entire place plus Alberich and his Wild Hunt for *twenty years* without you noticing. Why should that stop now that you're king?"

She threw her arms in the air as she finished, but Lola could only stare, dumbstruck. It sounded so obvious when Dee put it like that, but until this moment, it had never occurred to Lola that she'd done this before. Which was *stupid* because Alberich had flat-out told her that her dreams were his food.

If she'd been able to feed him, Orlando, and all his other fairies back when she was just a changeling, then of course she'd be able to support his empty house now. In hindsight, the signs were all there. Not only was Dee right about her appetite, she'd also been having crazy dreams ever since she'd started sleeping in her barrow. She'd even compared them to the ones she used to feed to

218

Tristan, which made total sense because that was exactly what was happening. Her barrow was eating her dreams!

Lola's heart began to pound as the ramifications of that sank in. She was a fairy who *made her own food*. Even Morgan had to go hunting for desire to keep herself in shape, but all Lola had to do was go to sleep. She still needed to bring energy into the system, but processed carbs were way easier to come by than human emotions. Given her diet, that meant the creatures in front of her were *literal* sugarplum fairies, which would have been hilarious if it hadn't been so powerful.

The more Lola thought about that, the more excited she got. All this time, she'd been afraid of her barrow because she'd thought of it as Alberich's, but that couldn't be further from the truth. The Nightmare King had bragged about powering his kingdom using fear he'd stolen down her silver thread, which meant this wasn't *his* kingdom at all. All of this had been built off of *her* magic. That made it Lola's through and through, and the moment she accepted that, the crown appeared in her hands.

Not Alberich's nightmare ring of teeth. This was a crown of pure light as golden as the throne she stood on. It reminded Lola of what Valente had said the night they'd slept together, when he'd told her she looked like sunlight seen from far away. This crown was exactly that: a gleaming promise of something better, a flash of hope gleaming in the dark.

"See now?" the mole doctor told her smugly. "You good king, give much food, but food alone is not enough. King must also give purpose."

"What purpose would you like?" Lola asked, balancing the glowing crown on her fingers like a flower.

"Don't shove decision off on us," the mole scolded. "This your kingdom. Your job to decide. Old king said be monsters, so we monsters. Now you must pick." It crossed its stubby clawed arms over its chest. "King leads. Barrow follows. That is way until one of us gets strong enough to eat *your* head."

The mole smiled as it finished, revealing a wall of sharp yellow rodent teeth. Lola flashed hers right back, showing it the knifelike fangs that had eaten Alberich. The gesture wasn't a threat from either side. It was merely an acknowledgement of how things had always been with fairies. With the crown in her hands, Lola could feel the weight of all the kings who'd come before her: an unbroken circle of new life rising, ruling, and eventually being devoured by the next generation. She was part of that cycle too now, but Lola was determined to make the most of her time. Until someone took it from her, this was her kingdom, and she was going to make sure it was one she wanted to live in.

That was the only thought in Lola's mind as she placed the crown on her head. The light swelled as it touched her, growing brighter and brighter until everything was lost in a glare of gold. When it faded, she was alone. The throne room, the mole, the mice, the monsters, even Toothy and Dee were nowhere to be seen. It was just Lola standing in an empty cave, and not even a large one. This cave was barely bigger than her old bedroom. A good, comfortable, manageable size, because this wasn't a cave at all.

It was a new beginning.

Everything left over from Alberich's rule had been wiped out the moment she'd put on her crown. Not destroyed—nothing here was ever destroyed—but though the Underground Kingdom had existed long before her and would exist long after, it was not gossamer's nature to be static. It wasn't human nature either. The porthole to the Sea of Magic was still in the ceiling when Lola looked up, proving that this wasn't just a barrow. It was her death as well. A perfect home for both her halves, ephemeral and ever-changing just like she was, and now it was Lola's turn to build it into something new.

She did so with a grin, sweeping her hands across the emptiness to create a glorious sky full of glittering buildings. She added deep canyons as well, an entire subterranean world of tunnels, alleys, and shops that ran beneath the skyscrapers like a neon maze. That might have seemed like a strange choice, but this was still the Underground Kingdom, and for Lola, Underground had always meant the DFZ.

Not the hideous empty city it had become under Victor. Lola recreated the DFZ as she remembered it from the day Victor had first allowed her to move out of the mansion. She'd been through the city many times before, but nothing had ever matched the feeling of driving away from Victor in a car of her own making. She'd still been a monster with pills in her pocket, but that afternoon, driving through the city alone for the very first time, she'd had her first tantalizing taste of freedom. It was still one of her happiest memories and the reason her barrow upstairs looked the way it did. Lola saw no reason to change that, so she focused instead on making it bigger.

She added more buildings than the original DFZ had ever had. Built roads and tunnels and so many overpasses that every monster in her barrow could have their own bridge if they wanted. She brought them back next, tucking each creature into her creation like seeds into the ground. She even gave them their own little pockets of gossamer to use however they liked, because that was what her Underground was about: freedom, potential, the start of something better.

It was what she'd fought Victor for in the first place. Getting free, saving the people she cared about, living her own life without a boot on her neck: these things were her purpose, so Lola gave them to her subjects now, showering them with gossamer and setting them loose in her new world.

The king's gifts weren't just for the barrow's subjects. Dee and Toothy got their share as well, though Dee was the first to go crazy with it. The moment Lola handed her the reins, she'd used her new gossamer to turn her corner of the city into an insane version of Lola's old townhouse filled with fancy clothes, giant cakes, and stuffed animals the size of cars.

That was same sort of stuff Lola used to spin when she was younger, but that made sense from someone who'd been born as her copy. Toothy, on the other hand, had always been her own monster, and her creations proved it. Lola's creature used her gossamer to make a little A-frame house on the new city's outskirts. The building barely looked bigger than a shed from the outside, but once you stepped through the door, everything was sunny and pleasant and scaled to fit Toothy's size. She had a giant bed, a giant couch, a giant bookcase filled with giant books, and giant mugs for her giant tea. The setup reminded Lola of the rainy cabin in the dream she'd given to Tristan, right down to the bone-deep peace, but that only made it feel even more right. Her brave monster deserved some quiet after everything they'd been through, so Lola left her to it.

She left them *all* to it. She'd handed out gossamer to every creature in Alberich's throne room, and every single one of them had set right about making a place of their own. As they burrowed and dug and changed her city to suit their own needs, Lola was filled with an immense sense of rightness.

Only one thing was missing from her happiness now, so Lola went off to find a nook of her own. When she found a building with just the right bird's-eye view of the Underground glittering like a neon reef, she whipped up a new version of the penthouse apartment she'd been living in for the last three months. A smaller, cozier edition with a door that connected back to her house on the ground, which was still right where she'd left it.

She could have just walked over, but it was much more fun to bring what she wanted to her, snapping her fingers before she opened the new door to reveal Valente standing in the hallway.

He jerked when he saw her, turning his helmet from side to side as if he were very confused. *What just happened?* he wrote when he got his pad out. *I was waiting for you in the living room when everything started shaking. I stood up to see what was happening, and then...*

The writing trailed off as he struggled to find words to describe the indescribable, but Lola just smiled.

"I moved you," she said, grabbing his hand. "Come on! I want to show you what I've made."

Valente nodded and let her pull him inside. When Lola tried to steer him toward the giant windows overlooking her new city, though, his mirrored visor kept swiveling back to the glowing crown on her head.

You really did it, he wrote when she finally let him go. *I can't see like I used to, but I don't need the fairy's eyes to know you're a real queen now.*

"King, actually," Lola corrected. "Alberich wasn't called 'the Underground King' because he hated sunlight. The title was passed to him just as it's now been passed to me." She reached up to touch the glowing circle floating above her dark hair. "We both ate our kings to claim an ancient magic, but while Alberich took the name literally, I decided to go with my own interpretation."

She waved her hand at the dense urban landscape outside, and the Rider tilted his helmet.

I guess the DFZ does count as the Underground.

"I certainly like it more than living in a cave," Lola said with a grin. Then her face grew serious. "It was also a useful model. As my subjects informed me, a king is expected to provide purpose, so I went with the place where just being alive *is* the purpose. I wanted them to do what *they* wanted to do and be whatever *they* wanted to be. I don't know if that's the purpose they had in mind, but I also gave them gossamer, so I think they'll be okay. And if they're not, I'm sure I'll hear about it. Freedom to live is also freedom to complain."

I think it's beautiful, Valente wrote.

"It is beautiful," Lola agreed, smiling at her teeming city. "It also makes a good reminder of what's waiting for us when we finally kick Victor's butt." Her face fell again. "Assuming the city can come back from what he's done."

She'll rebuild, the Rider wrote in firm, confident strokes. *She always rebuilds. It's what the DFZ does.*

Lola arched an eyebrow. "Is that your opinion, or do you speak for her now?"

Bit of both, he wrote with a shrug. *She's not feeding me lines or anything, but it feels right.*

"She is the city of second chances," Lola agreed, leaning her head on the Rider's shoulder.

He jerked in surprise at the contact. Then, moving very, very slowly to give her every chance to change her mind, he wrapped his arm around her waist.

Lola responded by leaning her whole body into him, using her new control to scoot Buster, who'd been frantically nosing around her new apartment, over to Dee's place. As always when it came to stuff like this, her double already knew what Lola was thinking, and she gave her monarch a huge mental thumbs-up as she grabbed the cat and locked the doors, sealing Lola and Valente in.

"So," Lola said casually, running her hand over the soft leather of his sleeve. "You told me something earlier that was very important. I don't think I responded properly at the time, so if it's all right with you, I'd like to try again."

It was impossible to write without letting her go, so the Rider just nodded.

Lola nodded back, focusing on his leather jacket, since that felt more like him than the empty helmet. "You said you loved me," she whispered softly. "Did you mean it?"

The Rider nodded again, and Lola let out a happy breath.

"Would it be okay if I put some gossamer on you?"

His helmet tilted in confusion at that, but he spread his arms in welcome.

Lola flashed him a grin in reply and stepped back, reaching out with her magic. She could really feel the king's power now. Covering other people in gossamer was normally not a big deal so long as they accepted it, but what she was attempting was no mere disguise. Likewise, the Black Rider was no mere human, or even a human-fairy hybrid. He was a legend, a soul made up of humanity's collective beliefs.

That was the sort of thing fairy magic normally couldn't touch, but Lola was a monarch in her barrow. The only rules that applied here were her own. She still went slowly so he'd have time to refuse if she stepped too far, but Valente's faith in her must have been absolute, because Lola didn't feel a twinge of disbelief when she slid her magic under his helmet, covering him in the beautiful memory that was still one of her happiest dreams.

"Okay," she said when she was finished, "take off your helmet."

The Black Rider did as she asked, lifting his shaking gloves to his mirrored helmet, which no longer came off like an empty shell. It slid instead, the padding catching on tanned skin and silky hair as the headless spirit removed his helmet to reveal the man beneath. The handsome, smiling, dark-haired man Lola had seen in their shared dream what felt like a lifetime ago.

He did kick her with disbelief then. The Rider's black helmet dropped to the floor as Valente's hands shot up to his cheeks. He ripped his gloves off next and looked at his hands, which were no longer broken or scarred. None of him was, because this wasn't the body Victor had beheaded. It was the happy, carefree man who'd kissed her on the beach, and as he stared at his reflection in Lola's window, Valente's eyes—not the fairy's glowing blue but warm and brown and human—filled with tears.

"It's me," he said in his own, human voice through his human mouth filled with human teeth, not the fairy's fangs. "It's not him. I can see my own face without being enthralled! I'm—"

"You're you," Lola said, reaching up to touch his hair, which was thick and soft and carelessly shaggy above his ears. "This is how I saw you in the dream. The person I think you would have been if none of this had happened."

She kissed him on the cheek as she finished. It was just a little peck, but he jumped as if she'd dumped a bucket of water over his head. He whirled around next, his bare hands coming up to cup her face before sliding farther to tangle in her hair as he bent down to press his forehead against hers.

"Thank you," he whispered in a shaking voice. "Thank you. *Thank you.*"

"It was the least I could do," Lola said, cheeks heating. "I want you to be happy, too. I want to be happy *with* you. To have fun and be free in a world where we're not having to die all the time, because I..."

Her voice trailed off. She might not have the fairy's inability to lie, but that didn't mean she could throw words around carelessly. She had to be absolutely certain, say exactly what she meant. Fortunately, what Lola felt was very simple. The simplest, most human thing in the world.

"I love you."

She felt Valente's whole body expand as he breathed her words in. Then he pressed his lips to hers, telling her in English and Spanish how much he loved her. How he'd always loved her, and how he'd never let her go.

Lola was too busy to say anything back. She threw herself into him, kissing him with everything she had as he scooped her off her feet. She was so happy that she could barely keep her dancing magic together enough to spin up the bed she'd forgotten to add to her new apartment. The gossamer hadn't even finished solidifying before they fell on top of it, tumbling onto the too-soft mattress in a breathy, kissing tangle.

It was nothing like their first time. That had been a desperate thing, a sliver of happiness snatched in the terror of Victor's shadow, which wasn't to say it hadn't been good. Lola had treasured every second, and not just because sleeping with the Rider had been a thumb in Victor's eye. She'd liked Valente even back then. If anything, Victor had poisoned the moment. This time was much better, because Victor wasn't here.

Lola didn't even think about him as Valente stripped her clothes off. She had significantly more trouble getting him naked, fumbling and cursing with the endless zippers that held his new motorcycle suit together. She was about to spin herself a pair of scissors when Valente stopped kissing her long enough to strip out of his own clothes, dumping them and the Hero's golden sword on the floor before diving back into bed. He was kissing her all over when Lola put her hands on his shoulders.

"What?" he asked, alarmed.

"Nothing," she said with a huge smile. "Just having a look at you."

He was absolutely worth the viewing. She could feel her own gossamer humming under her fingers if she concentrated, but it was getting fainter by the second as Valente accepted the new body as his own. That wasn't the reason she'd chosen it, but it was looking more and more like giving Valente the shape he already thought of as his had been a stroke of genius. Not only did it remind Lola of the happy kiss on the beach, Valente seemed to have latched onto this new form far more readily than he'd accepted his real, scarred one back in the hotel.

Not that Lola blamed him. She hadn't minded his scars, but Valente had clearly hated them, and why shouldn't he? Each one had been a reminder of what he'd suffered.

Lola couldn't change his past, but here in this place, she could give him back what he'd lost. The move was also practical since kissing a man with no head would have been a severe logistical challenge, but the result was so, *so* much better than even her best intentions. With every kiss she pressed against his skin, she could feel Valente's belief reinforcing the gossamer until it no longer felt like her magic at all. It was just him. Just him and her in a hidden room high above the city where nothing bad could touch them.

Lola went a little wild then. She hadn't realized until now how cornered she'd always felt, how desperate. There wasn't a time in her life Lola could remember when she hadn't been on a clock, but here in her barrow, even time was hers to control. She could stretch the hours as long as she wanted, turn one night into a hundred years. That was the power of a true fairy monarch, and now it was hers.

She was still rolling in the feeling when Valente's mouth moved lower, knocking all the royal thoughts out of her mind. What was left was a panting, happy mess as Lola let the world go, leaving her new kingdom to fend for itself as she grabbed Valente's shoulders, pulling him with her into a place where nothing mattered but them.

Chapter 15

"So how long will this last?"

"Hmm?" Lola replied sleepily.

"This," Valente clarified, waving at his warm, naked body, which she was currently snoozing on top of. "It feels so real, but I know it's just gossamer."

"There's no 'just' about gossamer," Lola reminded him, getting more comfortable. "This whole place is gossamer. *I'm* made of gossamer. So to answer your question, you'll last as long as I do."

She looked up through her tangled hair, expecting him to be happy, but Valente's handsome, human face was set in a worried frown.

"I can't be this way outside," he said grimly. "Being the Black Rider has… restrictions."

"Like not having a head?" Lola guessed, pushing herself up. "Okay, then, you can leave it here."

His brown eyes widened in surprise. "We can do that?"

Lola flashed him a superior smile. "This is *my* Underground Kingdom. We can do whatever we like, and it's not as if putting you together again will be hard." Her smile grew wicked. "I've got a *really* good idea what all of you looks like now, so if I have to whip up a new body every time you come to visit, I don't think I'll have a problem."

He chuckled and pulled her back down to him. Lola went gladly, pressing her ear to his chest to enjoy the rumble of his laugh. His human voice wasn't as deep or smooth as the fairy's, but Lola liked it far better. It was silly to say since she'd never actually heard him speak outside of a dream, but it sounded like him. At least, that was what Valente believed he sounded like, which was all that mattered for her magic.

"Come on," she said when they'd lounged in bed long enough. "I want to check on the others."

His dark eyebrows rose in surprise. "Others?"

Showing him would be easier than explaining, so Lola smiled and spun herself up a new outfit. She was a monarch now, so she went with a responsible-looking pantsuit in electric blue. She paired it with bright-yellow flats, because no force on earth could make her wear heels again, and a crisp white shirt that screamed, "My life is so together that I iron things before I wear them."

Not that that was true, of course. Lola had never ironed anything in her life. She usually avoided crisp clothing like the plague because it was so hard to keep gossamer looking sharp without making it look like plastic. But being a king came with many unexpected benefits, one of which was a level of control so precise it was excessive. She could have set every individual thread if she'd wanted to, but she settled for imagining the feeling of crisp, fine cotton.

Valente took much longer to get ready. To be fair, his outfit wasn't gossamer and had a lot more zippers. He was also in far less of a hurry, taking several breaks to touch her or kiss her or otherwise imply that they really didn't need to get out of bed yet. Lola was determined, though, and eventually he had everything back in place except his helmet, which he looked at for a long minute before finally sliding it over his head.

"You don't have to wear that in here," Lola offered. "You believe in that face now, so the gossamer should be rock solid. There are no humans to doubt you, either, so—"

"I can still doubt me," the Black Rider said, walking over to check his reflection in the giant windows. "You've given me a great gift, but this is what I am. I need to remember that, or I won't be able to do what I need to do."

Lola knew how difficult it was to get back in a role once you let it slide, so she didn't question him again. She just spun herself a bright-yellow raincoat to protect her suit and walked over to the apartment door, which no longer connected to her house's upstairs hallway. When Lola opened the doorway this time, it let out onto a catwalk over a massive space teeming with activity.

Below them lay a factory floor lit up with floodlights and swarming with low creatures, who no longer looked like little mice. That had been Alberich's image for them, a diminutive shell to remind them of their place. Lola didn't even want to think of them as "low creatures" anymore. They were citizens of her Underground now, and they looked like whatever they chose.

They'd snapped up the freedom with greedy fangs. The factory floor teemed with every sort of body imaginable. There were big humans, little humans, and plenty that weren't human at all. Some were dogs and bears. Others looked like monsters or aliens from famous movie franchises. Some hadn't even picked a form yet. They were just blobs of raw gossamer rolling across the floor, leaving rainbow trails of slime behind them as they worked to patch up the giant corpse lying like a fallen battleship at the factory's center.

You really do have him.

Lola sighed when the Rider showed her the words written on his pad. The helmet she understood, but she'd hoped he'd keep the voice, if only for convenience's sake. Alas, it seemed she'd get to hear him only when they were alone. The rest of his time was dedicated to being the Black Rider, which was admittedly fitting for someone trying to be a legend.

How did you end up with Fenrir's corpse? he wrote as he leaned over the walkway's railing. *And what are all those things working on him?*

"They're not 'things,'" Lola said, insulted on their behalf. "Those are my subjects. As for Fenrir, where else would he be? I'm the ground Victor grew him out of."

The Rider nodded solemnly, scratching on his pad. *Do you really think you can get him back up? He looks a little worse for wear.*

"You should have seen him before," Lola said, gazing down at the workers shoving cotton stuffing into the wolf's paw like they were making a giant taxidermy. "He was practically roadkill. Trust me, this is *much* better, but I'd expect no less given how long they've been working on him."

The Rider turned his helmet toward her in confusion. *You just became King this afternoon.*

"Time moves differently in barrows," she reminded him smugly. "It can also move differently in different *parts* of the barrow." She nodded down at the busy factory floor. "You and I experienced it as one very, very long afternoon, but by their perception, they've been working on Fenrir for over two months. It's been quite the project, but it looks like we're almost done."

She grinned as she finished, but the Rider was standing so still, she could almost feel the dumbstruck expression on his hidden face.

You're better at this than Alberich was, he wrote at last.

"I think of it more as I've got options he didn't," Lola said with a shrug. "Alberich was very good at the things he cared about, but being the Nightmare King forced him into a narrow vision. My kingdom's all about freedom, which makes things a lot more flexible." Her face broke into a grin. "I'm also too new at this to know what I can't do yet. That gives me a definite beginner's advantage."

It seems to be working, he wrote. *How long until the wolf is up and ready?*

"Never if I don't get more gossamer," Lola said. "But that ball's in Morgan's court. I did my part and got my kingdom together. Now it's up to her to do the rest."

She whipped herself up a phone as she finished, a brand-new model with a purple case covered in unicorns. Serious-looking unicorns as befit a monarch, but she wasn't about to give up *all* her fun.

When she was happy with how it looked, she gave her new phone a shake to get time flowing again. Time in a barrow moved like cement. It could run very quickly or not at all, but you had to keep pushing it, and you couldn't go too far. It'd be all too easy to dig in down here for centuries while a single night passed outside, but while Lola didn't need to hunt like other fairies, she couldn't exist in a vacuum. Her stomach was already growling for dinner, which meant it was time to go back up.

Fortunately, it looked like she wasn't the only one who'd been making herself more time. Three messages from Morgan were waiting when her phone reconnected to the real world, all with increasingly urgent subject lines.

"Looks like the queen came through," Lola said happily, tapping her fingers over the screen. The answer came back immediately, followed by a pounding on her outside door.

"Here we go," Lola said, tucking her phone back into her pantsuit. "You ready for this?"

The Rider set his shoulders in a way that said *I'm always ready.* Lola got up on her toes to press one last kiss against his helmet before walking back down the catwalk to the door they'd come out of, which no longer connected to her bedroom. When Lola turned the knob this time, the door opened into a hotel suite.

An exquisitely *nice* hotel suite with its own indoor jacuzzi, private bar, and wraparound balcony showing off a sweeping view of Victor's ugly DFZ. It was all very luxe, but Lola was far more interested in the giant table set with a wedding reception's worth of food in silver chafing dishes that had been set up against the far wall.

"Ta-da!" Tristan said, coming out from behind the bar with a bottle of champagne in each hand. "Do I deliver, or do I deliver?"

"You deliver," Lola said as she raced toward the buffet table. "Please tell me this is—"

"It's real food," Morgan said from where she was keeping watch on the balcony. "Tristan had a feeling you would come out ravenous, and it seems he was right." She turned around to study Lola with her leaf-green eyes. "It seems you finally figured out what you are."

Lola paused loading her plate high with scalloped potatoes long enough to give the queen a shocked look. "You knew I could feed myself this whole time?"

"Not the *whole* time," Tristan said as he carried a glass of sparkling golden bubblies to his queen. "I used to think Victor was feeding you. Once you got off his pills, though, we figured out the truth fairly quickly."

"No one can make something from nothing," Morgan agreed. "And you were still obsessed with takeout despite no longer needing to pretend to be human. Seemed pretty obvious after that."

It *did* seem obvious when Morgan put it that way, but Lola was still annoyed. "If you knew I was making my own magic, why didn't you tell me? It would have been nice to have a heads-up."

Morgan snorted. "As if I'd tell someone how to be more powerful than myself. A fairy kingdom's size is directly proportionate to what its monarch can provide. I chose desire because humans never seem to run out of it, but even that pales next to the excess of cheap carbohydrates this world can produce." Her lovely face grew sour. "You could very well become the greatest of all of us, so excuse me if I wanted to give myself a head start before I put you on that racetrack."

"It was also better this way," Tristan said sagely, coming over to hand Lola her own glass of champagne. "You needed to learn what sort of monarch you'd be on your own, and look how marvelously it worked out!" He leaned sideways to flash a wicked grin at the figure standing behind her. "You even figured out how to dress the Black Rider."

Valente crossed his arms over his chest with a cold silence, and Lola took the chance to retrieve the gossamer she'd covered him in. She'd only meant to keep her promise not to interfere with his duties as the Rider and to stop Tristan from teasing him, but removing her magic turned out to be like pulling a curtain off a window. The moment her gossamer peeled back, the full force of the Black Rider swept through the hotel suite, filling the air with the smell of wet pavement and the intense feeling of someone standing right behind you.

"I can't believe I'm saying this," Tristan muttered as he poured a glass of sparkling wine for himself, "but I think I preferred you before."

"This is much worse," Morgan agreed, her green eyes boring into the Rider's helmet. "You have no place here, Legend of the DFZ. This is fairy business, so unless you're finally ready to become the Underground King's knight, I'd thank you to remove yourself."

"Come on," Lola said around the honey-butter dinner roll she'd just shoved into her mouth. "There's no need to be like that."

"There is every need," Morgan snapped, lifting her hand to show Lola three elegant envelopes stamped with golden wax. "All the invitations I sent out came back, which means we're about to enter a realm accessible only to monarchs and their most trusted courtiers. He had every shot at knighthood, and he chose to become a common ghost story. That's his terrible judgment, but he can't expect us to welcome him as if he were your actual sworn knight."

Lola swallowed her bread with a wince. Before she could say anything else, though, the Black Rider pulled out his pad.

It's fine, he wrote, turning the page so only Lola could see. *You don't need me for this. You've got your own court, and I know you'll make good decisions. I'll stay here and get things ready with the city.*

"*Can* the city get ready?" she whispered nervously. "She seems to be completely under Victor's control."

No one fully controls a city, the Rider wrote confidently. *We'll figure something out.*

Lola nodded and gave him a smile.

He nodded back, sliding the pad into the pocket of his jacket. Then he was gone, vanishing between one blink and the next.

"Must be nice to have a whole metropolis as your barrow," Morgan observed sourly as she stalked in from the balcony to loom over Lola. "Are you almost finished? Time means little to our kind, but it's still unwise to keep monarchs waiting."

Lola nodded and started shoving food into her mouth faster. While she crammed it in, Tristan walked over to the door Lola had left open in the hotel suite's wall.

"And there he is," the knight said, moving to the side so his queen could get a look at Fenrir. "I love what you've done with your low creatures, by the way. Very modern."

Morgan wasn't nearly as impressed. "You gave them all gossamer?" she shrieked. "Are you *trying* to breed rebellion?"

"I wanted them to be happy," Lola said between bites. "Gossamer was my favorite part of being a changeling."

The queen rolled her eyes. "You do know giving them gossamer accelerates their growth, right? All that creativity and freedom goes straight to their heads. You're going to end up with hundreds of brand-new fairies gunning for your crown if you don't watch out."

"That's fine with me," Lola said, washing her hotel food down with a huge gulp of champagne. "My city needs people, and you don't get rebellions if you don't treat your citizens like the enemy. We all suffered under Alberich, so I'm not following his playbook. I'll run my Underground my own way, thank you very much."

Morgan dropped the matter with a harrumph, but Lola already knew that wasn't because she agreed. Now that Lola had a crown on her own head, she could feel that hers was actually the bigger kingdom. Morgan knew it, too, which was why she'd deferred. That was a very different power dynamic than Lola was used to, and she wasn't sure if she liked it.

It felt crazy not to enjoy being king, but Lola had been at the bottom all her life. All of this new power was suddenly making her feel very out of place, especially since she still needed the queen's advice. She might have her own ideas about how to run her barrow, but Morgan was the one who actually knew what she was doing. If that advice was going to be any good, Lola needed her to feel comfortable speaking her mind, and there was a question she'd been meaning to ask.

"Queen Morgan?"

The Queen of Desire turned to give her a measuring look.

"I was wondering," Lola said, pausing to take a bite from a slice of hotel cheesecake to steady her nerves, "why did you marry Alberich?"

"Why do you want to know?" the queen asked, arching a sharp eyebrow.

"It just struck me as odd," Lola explained. "I assume it wasn't a love match—"

Morgan scoffed. "*Never.* Alberich didn't even know what that word meant."

Lola would have said Morgan didn't, either, but she wisely kept that to herself. "Then why did you do it?" she asked. "What did marriage get you that was worth putting up with the Nightmare King?"

"The same that's worth putting up with anything," she said simply. "Survival. As obnoxious as he could be, Alberich was strong. I was as well, which meant we were destined to destroy each other. I had no interest in a prolonged war with an enemy I wasn't sure I could defeat, so I made him a bargain. We would join our kingdoms, work together instead of against each other, and for a while it was quite effective. Our combined strength made us unstoppable. We devoured many courts and grew our barrows greater than any before us, but it wasn't entirely about conquest."

Her face grew wistful. "There was a time when I was genuinely fond of him. He was a true monster, and those are always attractive in their own way. I thought we'd divide this world between us, but expanding a kingdom also enlarges its faults, and Alberich fell head first into his. He'd always been reckless, but as he grew larger, he completely lost the ability to consider the long term. He became truly childish, a spoiled monster who refused to compromise any of his wants. So, for the good of my own court, I sealed him away."

"I'm surprised you didn't kill him," Lola said.

"So was I," Morgan said, looking down at her champagne glass with a bitter sigh. "I could have done it, but the price was so high. Even in defeat, the Underground Kingdom was still greater than my own. If I'd killed Alberich and eaten his head that day, I would have become him and lost who I was, and as great as my ambitions were, I wasn't willing to turn my subjects into monsters."

She cast a knowing glance at Tristan as she straightened her shoulders. "I was planning to let his head wither for a thousand years and give it another try, but then *you* happened."

Her eyes narrowed to angry slits. "I still intend to collect on that, by the way, so try not to get yourself killed by any of the traitors your reckless distribution of power will cause before I get my due."

"I'll do my best," Lola said, putting down her drink. "But I was thinking. You've been a monarch much longer than I have—"

"Ages," Morgan agreed.

"Exactly," Lola said. "Our courts are very different, but you've still got a ton of experience I'd be an idiot not to learn from, so I was hoping that maybe the Court of Desire and the Underground Kingdom could come to another arrangement."

"What sort of arrangement?" the queen asked, looking down on Lola with a sly smile. "Are you asking me to marry you?"

"Not marriage," Lola said quickly. "But I definitely like the idea of not being enemies. I know fairies are all about devouring each other, but I have zero interest in fighting you or your court. I could also really use your help beyond just this Victor thing. We've worked very well together so far, and now that I'm king, I'd like to formalize that. I know peace treaties aren't really a fairy thing, but it's obvious we're much stronger together than we are apart."

"I do love a good union," Morgan said. "Would I still get my recompense in this new treaty of yours?"

"You'd get it faster," Lola promised with an open smile. "I have no idea what I'm doing, so if you want my kingdom to expand to the point where I have something to give you in a reasonable amount of time, it's definitely in your best interest to help."

Morgan considered her a moment longer. Then she nodded. "Done."

Lola blinked. "Wait, that's it? Don't you want to write up a contract or—"

"A monarch needs no contract," the queen said haughtily. "Our rule is absolute, or at least mine is. I can't speak for whatever madness you've created, but I promise that the Court of Desire will honor the Underground Kingdom as our ally until you betray us."

"And I promise the Underground Kingdom will honor the Court of Desire as our ally until *you* betray us," Lola replied. "Which I hope will be never."

"Never is a very long time for fairies," Morgan said with a smile Lola didn't like at all. "But I find myself quite content with your offer for the moment, especially since it means I won't have to stay in the DFZ."

Lola stared at her in shock. "Why would you want to leave the DFZ?"

"Because it's horrible," the queen replied, glaring out the window. "Even before Victor's hideous renovations, it was an ugly, chaotic place full of ugly, chaotic people. I wouldn't even have come here if my territory in Los Angeles hadn't been ruined by the Hollywood earthquake. I'd only intended to bide my time in the DFZ until the rebuilding crews made my preferred hunting grounds hospitable again, but then I met Victor Conrath, and the rest you know."

She scowled over her shoulder at the city skyline. "I'm sure Alva would have moved back to LA in a heartbeat if she could, but she was never the true queen, so she couldn't move my barrow. Now that I have my head again, I fully intend to return to my beautiful lands filled with beautiful people, but I couldn't leave such a rich city open for just any fairy to move into. Your proposal solves my problem nicely, though, so I'm leaving this territory to you. Think of it as a gift to cement our new alliance."

That was a serious stretch considering Morgan was "giving" a destroyed city she didn't even like, but Lola loved that she'd get the DFZ to herself. "I accept it gladly," she said, reaching for another slice of cheesecake. "So does this mean we're good?"

"I certainly hope so," Morgan said, glancing at the elegant gold watch she hadn't been wearing a second ago. "As fond as I am of cementing new alliances that increase my own power, we're about to be more than fashionably late. If we weren't hosting, I wouldn't mind, but if we miss our own party, the other courts will be so insulted they'll never answer my letters again."

Lola nodded rapidly, shoving the rest of the cheesecake into her mouth as she scurried after Morgan, who was already striding toward the hotel suite's front door. Tristan fell into step beside his queen a second later, looking more like a dashing knight than ever in his pure-white dress uniform and ceremonial saber he'd clearly whipped up just for the occasion.

"Is there anyone from your court you'd like to bring?" he asked Lola as his queen grabbed the doorknob. "It's always good to go into these things with a show, especially if you're new."

Lola thought a moment, then she shook her head. She didn't need to make a show. She knew what she was capable of, so she just stuck her empty hands in her suit pockets and nodded for them to continue.

"Bold choice," the queen said, reaching out to adjust the glowing crown on Lola's head before doing the same to her own wreath of flowers. "I'm the host, so let me do the talking. Remember: we're all monarchs here. Pride will be prickly, so try not to give offense."

That was exactly the sort of advice Lola had entered this alliance to get, so she nodded again and pressed her lips tight. When Morgan was convinced they'd stay that way, she opened the door. Her magic moved at the same time, making Lola shiver as the queen's sweet, flower-scented gossamer covered hers like a hand. When it let her go, she, Morgan, and Tristan were standing on a barren rock in the middle of a windswept sea.

"Where is this?" Lola yelled over the crashing waves, putting up her hands to shield her face from the freezing spray. "I thought you were hosting a party!"

"No monarch is trusting enough to enter another's barrow even with the promise of hospitality," Morgan shouted back as she waved her arm at the choppy waves. "This is ancient neutral ground, too far from inhabited land to be claimed by any court. It's the closest thing we've got to a safe space."

It didn't look safe to Lola. The jut of rock was barely twenty feet across, and its surface was covered in knife-sharp barnacles and slippery green algae. It definitely wasn't the sort of place you expected to find a bunch of fairy rulers. Before Lola could say as much, Tristan took the lead, escorting his queen and Lola down a tiny ridge.

It looked like just another fold in the rock until Lola noticed the tiny steps someone had carved into the stone. Each one was barely more than a divot. Together, though, they formed a rudimentary stair that circled around the jutting rock into the hollow beneath.

Going below was even worse than being up top. The hollow they'd stepped into was protected from the waves, but it stank of rotten fish, and its walls were riddled with barnacles, proof that it was routinely underwater. Lola pulled out her phone to check the tide schedule to make sure they weren't in danger of being drowned, but there was no signal this far out. There were, however, other doors.

Even for someone as used to fairies as Lola, she still felt her own shock of disbelief when her eyes landed on the grid of doors covering the tide hollow's far wall. She saw two dozen at least, though all but three were in ruins. That was hardly surprising for wooden doors in a place this wet. Lola found it much more shocking that three were still intact.

Each one was different. The biggest looked like it had been carved from a single gigantic piece of live wood. The other two were closer to the sort of doors you'd see in a house, though still wildly different from each other. One was a two-part farmhouse door whimsically painted to resemble the night sky with beautiful blues, purples, and golden stars. The other was a slab of ornately carved oak reinforced with shiny, ornamented bronze.

All three were beautiful in their own ways but so, *so* strange, especially here. Lola was still gawking when Morgan nodded at Tristan, and the knight brought his sword down on the hollow's smooth, water-worn floor with a ringing *tak*. The noise was shockingly loud in the small space, loud enough to rattle the doors. One of the old rotten ones actually collapsed from the vibrations, but the good ones opened in unison as three figures stepped out.

They looked as unique as their doors and wildly different from Morgan or Tristan. Even so, there was no way Lola wouldn't have recognized them as fairies. The first one out came through the huge door, a gigantic man whose skin, clothes, and hair looked to be made of overlapping oak leaves. His every step shook the ground, but where he lifted his feet, seedlings sprang up in his wake. He acknowledged Morgan with a nod but ignored Lola completely, turning instead to greet the others.

From the starry-night door came a woman no bigger than Lola's thumb. She was surrounded by a swirl of billowing silks held aloft by a cloud of winged pixies no bigger than mayflies, and she was riding on a chariot drawn by mice. It took her much longer than the leafy giant to cover the same distance, but like him, she stopped to acknowledge Morgan before turning to glower at the third arrival, whose door was still swinging open.

At first, Lola thought this was just for dramatic effect. As the creaking ground on, though, she realized the delay was actually because the door was so enormously heavy. It took three gnarled goblins working together to push the wall of carved oak and bronze open wide enough for the third fairy—a bony old man with a beard as long as his entire body—to step out. He did so with great gusto, clicking his heels together as he danced out of what appeared to be a brightly lit workshop full of spinning wheels—the big, old-fashioned kind used to make thread—and dropped a dramatic bow in front of Morgan.

"My cunning Queen of Desire," he said in a rasping, mischievous voice. "How wonderful it was to receive an invitation from you again."

"Quite so," agreed the tiny lady from the star door, though her face made it clear she found the idea of agreeing with the bearded man on anything quite distasteful. "We'd begun to despair of ever seeing you again, Morgan."

"I am not so easily dispatched," Morgan replied with a haughty toss of her golden hair. "Welcome to you all, and thank you for responding so quickly."

"You said you had a way to get rid of the bane," the leaf-covered giant rumbled. "Speak it, if it exists, so I may return to my forest. This salt water does not agree with my leaves."

"I will speak it in due course," Morgan told him sharply, turning to gaze pointedly at the line of decaying, ruined doors that hadn't opened. "We may be a fraction of what we once were, but this is still a Court of All Seasons. Traditions must be obeyed, starting with the introduction of our newest member."

They all turned to look at Lola, who swallowed. "I am Lola Daniels," she said, looking at Morgan, who motioned for her to keep going. "King of the New Underground."

"What's new about it?" the tiny lady asked with a sniff. "You still smell like dirt."

"And you should not be so quick to dismiss a greater power," Morgan said coldly. "Alberich and his Hunt are dead, but his kingdom lives forever. You know this perfectly well, so hold your tongue."

That response seemed pretty sharp for someone who'd just warned Lola not to give offense. To her great surprise, though, the little woman just sighed.

"Welcome, then, King of the Underground," she said in a voice that was polite only in the most technical sense. "I am the Divine Mab, Queen of Visions."

Lola had barely started to duck her head when the little bearded man jumped forward to claim her attention.

"And I am He Who Shall Not be Named," he announced with a dramatic flourish. "King of Bargains and ruiner of kings! I am also an excellent tailor, should you find yourself in need of such services."

Lola was wondering what kind of fairy would need a tailor when Mab butted back in.

"Don't take any of *his* work," she warned. "He'll do the best job you've ever seen and then make you pay for it for all eternity. As for 'He Who Shall Not Be Named,' that's rubbish. Everyone already knows his name. It's Rumpelstiltskin."

"They only know because you kept blabbing it," the bearded fairy hissed. "Not everyone wants to be immortalized in the mortals' drunken stories! Some of us are trying to run legitimate operations."

"Legitimate scams, perhaps," Mab snapped before turning back to Lola. "Ignore him, new king. The one you need to convince is over there."

She pointed her sword, which was no bigger than a needle, at the giant made of leaves, and he bowed his head with a deep creak.

"I am the Green Man."

Lola nodded, waiting for the rest. That must have been all he was going to say, though, because as soon as he finished, Morgan retook control of the conversation.

"Welcome, monarchs, one and all," she said solemnly. "It is a true pleasure to be back among my own kind after so many years. There is much we'd be wise to discuss, but out of respect for the Green Man, I will stick to the most pressing."

She waved a hand at Lola, who straightened up at once.

"During her rise to power, the Underground King acquired a weapon capable of defeating the bane imposed on us by the blood mage Victor Conrath," Morgan continued. "The only reason we have not yet employed it is because its use requires more gossamer than our two courts can currently provide. I know these modern times have been difficult, but the situation will only get worse if the Hero is allowed to continue his campaign against us. To end his threat and secure a future for all our kingdoms, I propose we come together as we did when we sealed Alberich and crush this upstart before he can do any more damage."

"Of course *you'd* say that," Mab replied crossly. "The Blood Mage's tower is in the middle of your territory, and your husband was the one who enabled his rise. I'm sure this bane is wreaking havoc on your feeding, but my court has always operated on a smaller scale. The blood magic bane is still troublesome, but not as troublesome as attacking the cause would be."

"Especially since the man behind it is human," Rumpelstiltskin added with a stroke of his beard. "We've seen so many of these power-mad mortals. They all think they'll be the ones to bring the world to heel, but none of them has ever actually managed it. I don't see how this Conrath fellow will be any different. He'll be dead in a century anyway, so why should we risk our gossamer?"

"Because he's not going to just go away," Lola said, stepping boldly forward since, unlike fairy court politics, this was a subject she knew by heart. "I don't know what kind of humans you've dealt with before, but Victor is different. He's already made himself immortal, and he's got the power of mass media on his side. To keep that power, though, he needs an enemy, and we're the one he's chosen. If he's not stopped, he'll continue his campaign against us until every human thinks fairies are the bogeymen under their beds. He'll make the whole world hate us, and that hate will be our doom."

"The Underground King is right," Morgan said, stepping up to Lola's side. "Never forget that we are interlopers on this plane. Like all parasites, we survive only as long as the host tolerates our presence. That's why we sealed Alberich when his rampant hunting went too far. Now Victor is doing the same thing but with far more competence. He's teaching the world that fairies are the cause of all its problems, and once humanity decides we are a threat, even our barrows won't save us. The human ability to move magic will force our kingdoms right out of this plane, leaving us adrift in the void."

The others fell silent. So did Lola. She hadn't realized just how bad this could get until Morgan spelled it out, but the queen wasn't finished.

"We have lived in this world for a long, long time," she said in a dire voice. "So long that only one is left among us who remembers what life was like before we settled this plane." Morgan turned to the leafy giant. "You were there, Green Man. Tell us, what happens if the blood mage wins?"

The Green Man heaved a long, fluttery sigh. "It will not be the end," he said, his voice creaking like an old tree. "But that does not mean it will not be a loss. I am old enough to remember many worlds. We used to jump between them like fleas, gobbling up whatever we could before moving on. This is the only place we have ever stayed, because it is the only place rich enough to feed us. Even now, when all humans ask questions and disbelieve their own eyes, it is still a land of plenty. If we let the blood mage force us away from that, we will be the greatest failures of our race."

"Precisely," Morgan said, her eyes gleaming like knives as she turned them on the others. "Now is not the time to bury our heads and wait. I am ashamed to admit that Victor Conrath was once a favorite of my court. He understands how we work better than some of my own fairies, and everything he knows, he uses. He is the worst enemy we could possibly face, which is why we must do so together."

"But we *can't*," Mab said, clutching the reins of her mouse chariot. "You are still a great queen, Morgan, but the rest of our courts are in decline. We barely have enough gossamer to keep our own barrows fed, much less help you."

"Humans will always have desire," Rumpelstiltskin agreed. "But our food stores have been dwindling for centuries. It's not that we disagree with what you're saying. We just have nothing to give. Even I can't get blood from a stone."

"Then I'll help you," Lola said.

Morgan shot her a warning look, but Lola ignored it. She'd teamed up with the queen for her experience, but this whole thing had been Lola's idea, and unlike everyone else here, she still had something to give.

"I was human before I became the Underground King," she explained. "That means I can make my own food. If you'll agree to help me bring down Victor, I'll share it with you."

Her offer was met with stunned silence.

"How does a *human* become a fairy king?" Rumpelstiltskin demanded.

"It's a long story," Lola said. "But while I'm drowning in dreams, what I *don't* have is enough gossamer. That's why I'm offering to help you regrow yours. If I make the courts strong again, will you help me kill Victor?"

"If you make us strong again," the Green Man rumbled, "we will follow you anywhere."

"Agreed," Mab said, sheathing her little sword. "I am tired of being treated like a children's story. Give me the strength to drive men mad again, and my court is at your disposal."

"Mine as well," Rumpelstiltskin promised, rubbing his bony hands together in glee. "Just think of all the new bargains I can strike once I've got something better to offer than spinning services! No one even knows how to use a spinning wheel anymore."

"Then we have a deal?" Lola said.

The others nodded rapidly, but Morgan grabbed her arm in a viselike grip.

"You don't know what you're promising," she hissed in Lola's ear. "This isn't going to be like when you fed me up. These are full fairies supporting entire courts!"

"So am I," Lola said, giving the queen's hand a reassuring pat. "But I've got this."

Morgan's eyes narrowed. "Are you sure?"

"Very sure," Lola said, her lips curling into a cutting smile. "What's the point of being Victor's accidental masterpiece if I don't use that power to destroy him?"

The queen gave her a skeptical look, and then shook her head. "You can't change a king's mind," she declared as she let Lola go. "I just hope you know what you're doing. We fairies were always a greedy lot, but these three are the greediest by far. That's why they survived."

"I'm no different," Lola said proudly. "I also want it all. I want my city back. I want my family to be safe. I want Victor to die. I want everything that I can get, so if this is what it takes, I'll do it."

"Spoken like a true fairy," Morgan said, smiling at last. "When do we start?"

"Right now," Lola said, walking over to one of the broken doors that was still on its hinges. The others gasped when she touched it, but Lola ignored them, focusing on reaching out for her barrow. She didn't realize how far Morgan had taken them until she tried to bridge the distance with her own magic. Unfortunately, it turned out to be farther than her still-growing low-road-making ability could reach. She couldn't have gotten herself home right now, much less transported everyone else, so Lola shifted her focus to Dee instead.

Are you busy? I need a pick up.

The words had barely formed in her mind when the crumbling wooden door snapped back together. It swung open with a creak a second later to reveal Lola's own face grinning back at her.

"At your service, boss lady!" Dee said happily, looking over the others, who were all gaping in various states of shock. "Are these the old-timers?"

"Venerable guests," Lola corrected as she turned back around. "You are all welcomed to my kingdom under the full protection of hospitality. I know that's a stretch for some of you, but it'll be a lot easier to feed you dreams from my own bed, so come inside if you want to eat."

Not one of them looked happy with that offer. Even with the code of hospitality, entering another fairy's barrow meant placing yourself entirely in their power. As Morgan had said, though, these three were the greediest of fairies, the ones who'd never let fear stand in the way of their survival, and it didn't stop them now. It took several minutes and a lot of fidgeting, but eventually, every fairy, including Morgan, went through the door.

Lola's court welcomed them as soon as they were on the other side, her new citizens hurrying to fill the cheery, neon-lit street Dee's door had opened into with gossamer versions of all of Lola's favorite food trucks.

"I suppose that's your rendition of a banquet," Tristan said as he brought up the rear. "Are you sure you know what you're doing, Lola-cat?"

Lola snorted. "I didn't expect that question from you."

He held up his hands. "Don't get me wrong. I know how powerful your dreams are, but I was always a polite partaker. These others might not be so thoughtful."

"I can handle them," Lola said confidently. "I'm not the changeling I used to be."

"So I've noticed," he said, offering her his arm. "Shall we get this started then, your majesty?"

Lola took his arm and walked through the door, smiling warmly as her subjects, most of whom no longer looked like monsters in the slightest, rushed to welcome her home.

Chapter 16

Simon lay on his back, gasping up at the halogen gym lights he was learning to hate. His body was a mass of pain. His head was throbbing, his lungs burning. All he wanted to do was hide and rest, but he could already hear the uneven *clop* of the Grand Marshal's metal boots as she limped over, her head blocking the glaring greenish lights as her shadow fell over him like a pall.

"Again."

"I can't… do it again," Simon panted.

"You must," she told him sternly. "There are only two choices left to you now: do or fail. How long are you going to let him keep beating you?"

"It's not a matter of letting," he said, covering his face with his hands to get away from her, if only for a moment. "I can't do it. I can't beat him."

"Not with that attitude," the Paladin snapped. "Now get *up.*"

She grabbed his arm, yanking him off the gym floor into a sitting position.

"It's cute how she still thinks you can do this," Victor's voice whispered in his ear. "I would have given up on you ages ago."

Simon ignored him, focusing on his breathing as he forced himself back to his feet.

"Good," the Paladin said, limping back to her folding chair. "Again!"

Simon shook his swimming head. They'd been holed up in the abandoned Paladin facility in Columbus, Ohio, for three days now. In all that time, the Grand Marshal had allowed him to sleep only once. The rest of his hours had been spent repeating the same training over and over, which wouldn't have been a problem if it had been working.

"There's no point!" he yelled at her. "We just keep doing the same thing again and again, and it never works!"

"That's why we're repeating it," she said in the stern, patient voice he'd learned to fear even more than her anger. "If you have to take time to think about your defense, it will always fail. When you fall down, you don't think to your body, 'You must catch me now.' Your arms must move on their own even before the brain realizes the danger."

"I get that part," Simon said irritably. "My problem is with the defense itself. It's useless!"

"It is *not* useless," she hissed. "This is the method we have used to defeat blood magic for decades, *without* staining our souls. Blood mages are not inherently stronger than us. Their advantage lies in the fact that they always attack where most people are unprepared to defend. Even a child can push you down if he catches you by surprise, which is why we must never allow ourselves to be caught off guard. Our souls must be like iron, our minds like fortresses. No matter how strong a blood mage might seem, they are only ever one soul. Even Victor Conrath is but a single man, and a single man cannot push down a mountain."

She poked Simon in the chest with her sheathed sword. "Your job is to become that mountain. Close your mind. Harden your heart. Give him no entry. And while he is futilely beating on the locked door of your soul, your body shall move on its own to run him through. That is the Paladins' way."

Victor's ghost chuckled. "So, the secret of their order is being closed-minded? I could have told you that and saved us both a trip."

"I understand what you're saying," Simon said, focusing on the Grand Marshal. "And I see why it works. I've attacked plenty of people. I know the difference between breaking into a mind that doesn't understand it can be attacked and one that's locked, but you're not *listening*. Hardening my mind doesn't work when

Victor's already in it. What good is turning myself into a fortress if the enemy's locked inside with me?"

"Then you must force him out," she said stubbornly. "It's your mind, is it not?"

Victor cackled at that while Simon scrubbed his hands over his face. "If I was capable of kicking him out, don't you think I would have done it already?"

"You just need to try harder," the Paladin insisted, setting her sword back down. "He's there right now, isn't he?"

Simon's eyes flicked to Victor's ghost standing beside him, and the Paladin nodded. "Then you already have everything you need. Try again."

"Yes, Simon, try again," Victor taunted. "Beat yourself bloody against a superior opponent. That *always* works." He turned to smirk at the Paladin. "No wonder her whole order died."

Simon closed his eyes against his master's smug smile. This wasn't working. He'd asked Nadja to teach him because the Paladins were the only humans Victor feared, but this was all turning out to be useless. Their famously secret anti-blood-mage techniques were just a different take on the same lessons he'd been force-fed all his life: be stronger than the other guy. Keep punching. Be superior. And while Simon was sure that worked against normal blood mages who got their kicks by savaging people who had no idea what was going on, it didn't work on Victor.

"Nothing works on me," Victor's ghost assured him. "You know as well as I do that our craft is not without its weaknesses. Every system has flaws, which is why I take care to always be prepared and why no Paladin has ever been able to touch me. They think I'll keep banging on their closed minds like an idiot while they run me through with their archaic swords, but that's why I acquired the Black Rider, the Spirit of the DFZ, and everything else. A king doesn't need to watch his own back when he has soldiers to die for him. It's such a simple counter, yet these fools ran right into it, and you're the one who opened the door. You fell victim to the same flawed logic they did, and look where it got you." His blue eyes met Simon's as Victor heaved a long sigh. "It's just so disappointing. You had such promise as a child."

Simon clenched his teeth. He would not listen. This was how Victor undermined his walls. He played on Simon's insecurities, made him feel stupid and worthless, but Simon knew his game. He knew the weaknesses of blood magic as well as his master did, knew that even the great Victor couldn't enter another person's soul unless the victim opened the door.

That was the point of all his abuse. It wasn't just because Victor enjoyed being cruel. He couldn't get in unless he tore Simon down first, so Simon would make himself a wall, a mountain, a fortress, and everything else the Paladin said. He'd harden his heart, fill his death with stone, whatever it took to choke the bastard out. He'd fight with all he had, fall down as many times as it took until he was tough enough, strong enough, *enough* enough to—

"Don't lie to yourself, Simon," Victor said, his soft voice cutting through the mantras like a razor. "We both know you'll never be enough."

Simon shook his head. He would not listen. He would not succumb. He would become a fortress nothing could break. A wall strong enough to keep the monster out.

"You can't keep out what's already in."

Simon covered his ears with a grimace, but it didn't help. Victor's voice was inside him, a crack in his foundation. The harder he tried to push him out, the more everything fell apart.

Shame drove him back down to the floor. Victor's ghost cackled above him, but Simon was used to that. What hurt far more than he'd expected was the Paladin's long sigh.

"I'm not good enough," he said before she could. "I can't do it."

There was a long silence, and then he heard her chair scrape. The *thunk* of her boot came next as she hobbled over. He thought she was coming to yank him back up again, but no hard hand landed on his arm. Instead, Simon heard the soft clink of her armor hitting the gym's rubberized floor as she lowered herself down next to him.

"I'm starting to think I made a mistake," she told him quietly. "Not about you, but about how I should teach you."

"You taught me the same way you taught all the others," Simon said, hugging his knees. "It's not your fault I'm broken."

"I have taught hundreds how to be Paladins," she agreed solemnly. "But none of them started where you are. Most of our recruits come to us because a blood mage took someone from them. That's why I'm here."

Simon nodded sympathetically. "Who did you lose?"

"It doesn't matter," Grand Marshal Nadja said. "They're gone, and all I can do is keep fighting to make sure their tragedy never happens to anyone else. That's the only thing a Paladin can do. We can't keep people from becoming blood mages, can't heal the pain they cause. We can only be the wall that stops them, but that's not what you need to be."

"I don't know about that," Simon said, clenching his fists. "Someone needs to stop Victor."

"He will be stopped," she said with absolute conviction. "No one is invincible, but I'm sorry for pushing you so hard." She lowered her eyes. "I was angry and frustrated with my own failures, and I took it out on you. I tried to make you stronger because I felt weak, but you don't need those lessons. Your mind is already a powerful fortress. How else could Victor Conrath be so secure inside it?"

Simon's body tightened like a clamp. "Then what was all this for?" he whispered. "What have we been doing here if even the Paladins' methods can't stop him?"

"Effort is never wasted," she said. "You mastered the fortress defense faster than anyone I've ever taught, but that method was developed for fighting blood mages we'd never met before, not a villain who's already dug his way inside."

"I still should've been able to kick him out," Simon insisted. "Victor's the one who taught me that a blood mage is king of his own soul. Even if I can't beat him in an even fight, I should at least be able to kick him out of my own head, but I'm just not good enough."

"I think that speaks well of you," the Paladin replied. "Blood mages are powerful because they are cruel. I've fought more of them than I can count over the years, and every one was a selfish, callous monster completely lacking in natural human empathy. Some reveled in the suffering they caused. Others didn't even see their victims as people. They were each uniquely horrible, but not a single one was like you."

She reached out and slapped Simon on the back. "I'm glad you are no match for Conrath. If you were actually the monster he tried to make you into, we'd be dealing with two horrors instead of one, and our chances of victory would be that much lower."

Simon released the breath he hadn't realized he'd been holding. He'd never thought about it that way. To hear her say it, his inferiority to Victor sounded like a virtue, but it still didn't help.

"I'm glad you've found a moral spin to put on things," he muttered, digging the heels of his palms into his eye sockets. "But whether it makes me a better person or not, we still have to beat him, and I don't know how."

"What about the incident you mentioned yesterday?" she asked. "We were discussing how Conrath used your own mind to trap you in the coma, but you got out right before the battle with the Wild Hunt, didn't you?"

Simon hung his head in shame. "Not by myself. That was all Lola. If she hadn't come to rescue me, I'd still be stuck in there."

"Then perhaps that's your answer."

He shot her an incredulous look, but the Paladin set her jaw. "Do you know why Paladins always attack in groups of three or more? It's not because blood mages are three times stronger than us. It's because, even with all our training, mental fortitude, and physical strength, it only takes a single mistake to lose a fight. There's a million ways for things to go wrong, which is why no Paladin ever goes anywhere without at least two backups. Sometimes even that is not enough, as you saw the other day, but if blood mages were easy to beat, our order wouldn't exist."

She laid her hand on his arm, gently this time. "What I'm trying to tell you is there is no shame in needing help. Reinforcements are a critical part of any successful strategy, and you are by no means alone. You are surrounded by allies who wish the blood mage dead every bit as much as you do, so you don't have to worry about being stronger than Victor. He's the one who will fall in the end, because he's the only one in all of this who stands alone."

It was on the tip of Simon's tongue to tell her to save her sermons. If ganging up was all it took to win, why hadn't he and Lola done it yet? But the nasty words never left Simon's mouth, because while his bitterness was running away with his emotions, his mind was spinning like a top.

"Hold on a moment," he said, turning to look for Victor. As usual, the ghost hadn't strayed far. He was just a few feet away, leaning boredly on the gray cement wall of the gymnasium, but his lips curled into a cruel smile when he saw Simon looking for him.

"If you two are done with your daytime-movie moment, I'm happy to go again," the monster drawled. "These training sessions have been marvelously useful for me as well. I might just be a leftover bit of magic, but if you keep pouring this much attention and power into me, I'll get strong enough to take over your mind for real."

"Not likely," Simon said, reaching out with his magic to grab the shade.

It worked as well as all the other times he'd tried, which was to say not at all. He might not be the real Victor, but the ghost was just as impossible to control. He smacked Simon's hand away before it landed, vanishing from the wall to reappear right behind him.

"When will you stop wasting our time on lost causes?" the ghost taunted. "You've already tried to smother me, crush me, trap me, and cut me out. But while those tricks might have worked on your own patients, even the greatest surgeons can't operate on themselves, and you're far from the greatest."

Simon ignored him and grabbed again, chasing the ghost like he was trying to catch a fish.

"You can't be serious," the figment said between frantic dodges. "What are you even going to do if you catch me? Rip me out? Drive me off? Impossible. You know how deep my roots go because you planted them yourself. The only blood mage good enough to remove me now is the real Victor, and he'll never let you go."

"I'm not his to let do anything," Simon said as he grabbed the ghost at last. When he had a good grip on the old man's hateful magic, Simon pulled them both in the only direction he could: down into his soul.

The trip was surprisingly fast even for him. Victor had taught him to move freely in and out of his death, but it usually still took a good bit of work to sink all the way through his conscious mind. He must have been ready for it today, though, because Simon barely had to give himself the order before he and

Victor were standing face to face in the blood-tinged memory of Simon's old bedroom.

"Bravo," the ghost of Victor said with a slow clap of his hands. "You've managed to get all the way back to where you began. A truly spectacular waste of effort, since, unless you're here to die for real this time, I'm just going to pop back out the moment you leave."

"I know," Simon said, forcing himself to face him. "You always were stronger than me, though I can't understand now why I ever thought that was my fault. You were decades older than I was. Even if I'd loved blood magic as much as you do, I could never have matched your experience, which is fine, because I don't want to. I've never wanted to be you. I *hate* you."

"How very mature," Victor said in a bored voice. "Do you feel better now?"

"Not yet," Simon said, moving to the center of the small room that was also *his* center. "But I will. I realized something listening to the Paladin just now, something I don't think she meant to say. Every time you beat me, it always happened when I was alone."

"You weren't alone on the roof," Victor said haughtily. "You had the whole Paladin order with you that time, and I still shattered your mind. And while we're on the subject of spectacular failures, you know your little Paladin was speaking absolute nonsense just now about me standing alone. I have a whole army of followers who worship the ground I walk on. There are people selling their organs right now to buy tickets to my next miracle. My entire skyscraper is filled with fools who'd give their lives for mine in a heartbeat. I am hardly an isolated target."

"You're wrong," Simon said, holding his ground. "You are always alone. You might be surrounded by people, but they're not allies. They're thralls and slaves and suckers you've conned. Even the children you raised in your image can't stand you, because you are a *terrible* person."

Victor rolled his blue eyes. "If you're fishing for an apology, don't waste your breath. I told you exactly what you were to me when I took you in. You don't get to be mad now that I wasn't daddy dearest. You had a father, and you got him killed in that accident just like you killed your brother."

"I never expected anything good from you," Simon said, raising his chin. "I'm just letting you know that I've figured out your game. You had me thinking it was my fault that I kept losing, but I was always fighting alone against a stronger opponent who'd shaped my weaknesses to suit him since I was small. Of *course* I lost. It would have been a miracle if I hadn't, which is why Lola was right. If we're ever going to beat you, we have to stop letting you pick our battles, which means I have to stop fighting you by myself."

The ghost arched a dark eyebrow. "If that's your goal, you chose a poor battlefield. This is your death. The only people who can come down here are you and me. Even the stupid Paladin can't butt her way inside, since she's too good to get her hands dirty with *real* magic."

"I wouldn't bring her in even if she could come," Simon said. "She's being tolerant for now because you're that awful, but I know she'll turn on me the moment this is over. Even if she did have a change of heart, she's too straightforward to help me beat you, but I know who isn't. I've got someone you've never managed to beat no matter how hard you've tried."

The shade narrowed its eyes. "Who?"

Rather than answer, Simon raised his arm. He'd barely gotten his hand all the way up before someone else's shot down to grab it.

A grinning face followed, and then Lola dropped out of the ceiling just like she had the day she'd come to rescue him. Simon welcomed her with a grin of his own, but the ghost of Victor took a step back.

"How is she here?" he demanded, his blue eyes flashing back and forth between his two children. "It can't be through the dream again. We've only been down here a few minutes. She doesn't even know where you are!"

"She doesn't have to," Simon said, threading his fingers through Lola's. "This isn't the real Lola, but you can't think about someone as much as I've thought about her and not have a piece of them living inside you."

Victor stopped backing up with an indignant huff. "Your grand plan was to call in a figment of your unrequited love? How utterly pathetic."

"I'm no more of a figment than you," Lola said, pulling her body straight. Her real body, not the redheaded doll Simon had pined for during their teenage years. That really would have been pathetic, but he'd meant what he'd said to the Rider. What he felt for Lola had deepened into so much more than a crush. She was the only other person in the world who knew what it was like to live in Victor's shadow, and she and Simon had always been stronger together. That was how she'd been able to rescue him from Victor's coma, and it was why he'd brought her here now.

"A happy memory to fight a bad one," he told the scrap his master had left behind. "You've beaten me every time I've faced you, but you've never beaten her. I used to think that was because she was part fairy, but the truth is so much simpler. You defeated me because we were both using blood magic. Of course I always lost. You're the best blood mage in the world, and I'm so, *so* happy that I'm not your match. I'd rather die than become like you, but you still need to lose, so I'm going to do the one thing you never could."

"Fail?" Victor quipped.

A smile spread across Simon's face as he let go of Lola's hand and stepped back. "Give up control."

"You can't do that," his old master told him confidently. "This is *your* death."

"Exactly," Simon said as he took another step. "*My* death. That means I can do whatever I want, and right now, what I want most is to see you fall."

Victor still looked incredulous, but as always with the two of them, Lola understood immediately what Simon was doing. He didn't even have to explain how the magic worked. All he had to do was hold the walls of his death tight enough that Victor couldn't escape, leaving their former master nowhere to run as Lola reached out to grab Victor's shoulders.

"This is ridiculous," the blood mage snarled, bracing his polished shoes on the floor against her. "She's no blood mage. She's barely even human! She can't possibly—"

His tirade came to an abrupt halt as Simon's memory of Lola threw him to the floor. Victor's body vanished as he fell, wafting away like smoke to reveal the truth underneath. It was the painting. The floor-length portrait of Victor he'd forced Simon to hang in his death all those years ago.

Simon thought Victor had abandoned it after he'd walked away. The frame had always been empty every time he'd come in here looking for a way to shut the old man up. Now, though, he understood. Victor had never left. He'd always been here with his claws digging in until Lola ripped them out, tearing the giant painting off the wall of Simon's death and throwing it to the ground.

It landed face down on the red-stained stone. Simon could still hear Victor's muffled voice cursing them as Lola raised her foot. Then his curses became furious screams when she brought her sneaker down, stomping over and over until every part of Victor's painting—the canvas, the wooden backing, and the hideous gilt frame that anchored the red string that was still tied around Simon's throat—was smashed into pieces.

"Good work," Simon said when she finally stopped, ripping the last of Victor's thread off his neck like a piece of cobweb. "Thank you."

His happy memory of Lola beamed at him and vanished, leaving him alone in his death for the first time in decades. He was still a blood mage, so everything was still stained with red, but Victor was no longer there. His painting, his thread, his poison voice, they were all smashed to splinters, which meant—

"I'm free."

The words were barely louder than a whisper, but they filled his soul like a sunrise. The wreckage of the painting still lay all over the floor. Simon didn't know when he'd have the courage to pick it up, but that didn't matter right now. He could deal with it later, or never. He could do whatever he wanted, because he was free.

He shot out of his death with a whoop of pure joy, flying back into his body so fast, his feet left the floor. The Paladin jumped as well, stepping back with her sword ready in her hands as she scowled at his face.

"What happened to your eyes?"

Simon's hands shot up to his face. That told him nothing, of course, so he shoved them into his pockets next, digging through his jeans until he found the phone he'd kept turned off since he'd left the barrow. He didn't turn it on now, but he did use its black screen, tilting the reflective surface against the gym's harsh light until he saw his face staring back at him. His own face with his own brown eyes.

"We did it!" he cried, grinning at the Grand Marshal, who still hadn't lowered her sword. "We kicked him out!"

"We who?" she demanded nervously. "I didn't do anything."

Simon opened his mouth to explain before deciding it wasn't worth the bother. She didn't need to know what happened. He had more pressing matters, like turning on his phone and dialing the number he kept memorizing no matter how many times she changed it.

"Yello!" answered a cheerful voice he already knew wasn't Lola's but was happy to hear nonetheless.

"Hey, Dee," he said. "It's me."

"*Simon!*" she cried. "I'm so happy you're okay!" There was a pause, and then she said, "You *are* okay, right? 'Cause Lola will kill me if you're not."

"I'm fine," Simon assured her. "And I'm coming back. Can you open a door for me?"

"Sure! Send me a video."

That sounded a bit too easy, but Simon did as he was told, flipping on his camera and turning in a slow circle to give her a 360-degree shot of the Paladins' sparse training gym.

"Wow," Dee said when he sent it to her. "Where are you? PE class for sad people?"

"Something like that," Simon said, looking at Nadja, who clearly hated all of this. "Is that enough to—"

He was interrupted by the crack from the gymnasium's double doors, and then Dee burst in like a hurricane. She was carrying Buster in her arms for some reason, a situation the cat seemed *very* disgruntled about. Fortunately, Dee was even more gossamer-y than Lola. The angry cat's claws slid right through her like she was made of gelatin, though she did have to stop and get a better grip before the furry ball of fury ran off into the gym.

"Sorry about him," she said, clutching the yowling cat to her chest. "He keeps waking Lola up, so I had to put him in kitty jail. But look at you! You got your old eyes back!"

"I did," Simon said. "But what's Lola doing that she needs to be asleep for? Is she hurt?"

"Not at all," the doppelganger said, wrestling the cat back into submission. "She's just busy being a fairy All You Can Eat buffet. Tristan's all moody 'cause she was supposed to be *his* food, but he can't complain since she's serving as the soup kitchen for our entire army."

"We have an army now?"

That was news to him, but Dee's face lit up just like Lola's used to when she and Simon were kids.

"Ooooh, you are in for a *treat!*" she cried, spinning herself a third arm so she could grab Simon's hand without releasing her feline prisoner. "Technically, everything happened this afternoon, but Lola's been stretching time like taffy. She's pushing hard to get us all ready for action before Victor realizes what we're doing and thinks up a counter. They've probably gotten a full day of work done while we've been standing here!"

"Work done on what?" Simon asked as she dragged him toward the door.

"Something so big, even Victor won't be able to stop it," Dee promised. "Come on back with me, and we'll get you up to speed. Is the grumpy lady coming with us?"

Simon looked over his shoulder to find Nadja staring at them mistrustfully.

"I can put her to sleep if you want," Dee offered. "I can do that now! Lola gave me gossamer of my own, and it's *whoa* fun. I've been training my enthrallment like crazy. Wanna see?"

"I don't think that'll be necessary," Simon said, to Dee's great and grievous disappointment. "Grand Marshal Nadja?"

The Paladin's wary eyes flicked to his, and Simon stuck a thumb over his shoulder at the door Dee had come through. "You heard what she said. Want to come with us and give Victor some payback?"

The woman lowered her sword with a scowl. For a moment, Simon was certain she was going to say no, which might have been for the best. She'd already shown how intractable her mind could be when it came to gossamer, and Dee was a pretty strong dose for people who weren't used to fairies. But just as he was opening his mouth to say they'd manage without her, the Paladin sheathed her sword and hobbled over, dragging her still-broken leg behind her like a log all the way to the gym door Dee had opened into Lola's brightly lit—and very different-looking—living room.

Chapter 17

Four days.

Victor Conrath looked down on his quiet, orderly city from the window of his reconstructed penthouse, fist clenching over the empty spot where his golden sword should have been. It had been four days since he'd used the DFZ to defeat the only humans still capable of touching him and secured the Hero's invulnerability in the eyes of the world. Four days since he'd discovered his apprentice and his Black Rider were less deceased than he'd believed. Four days since they'd escaped.

For four full days now, he'd been braced for their attack. He'd filled his tower with fresh thralls taken from his faithful. The mindless dolts made terrible soldiers, but he knew none of his softhearted children would kill puppets who were incapable of controlling their actions. It was the same misplaced compassion that had brought down the Paladins, but there still should have been *something*. He'd been flogging the DFZ to scour herself for any sign of the enemy, but every time he summoned her for her hourly report, her hands came up empty. He knew they were still out there because he'd seen them escape, just as he knew they'd never give up the fight while any of them still drew breath. They had to be plotting something, so where were they?

"Master?"

Victor looked over his shoulder just in time to see Jamie flinch. She hid it immediately, but the reaction was still worrisome. Of all his servants, his secretary had been with him longest and knew him best. If his emotional state was unstable enough to make her grimace, then he was slipping beyond acceptable limits.

He pulled himself together at once, forcing down his frustrations as he turned to hear the report that, from the way his secretary's nails were digging into her tablet, wasn't going to do anything to improve his mood.

"How bad is it?"

"Not catastrophic," Jamie reported with forced cheer. "But we're definitely on the wrong end of the bell curve. Despite doubling the PR budget and keeping pro-Hero news running on every outlet we can bribe, response to the Paladin incident remains decidedly negative. This afternoon's polls are slightly better than yesterday's, but sixty-three percent of those surveyed still believe the Paladin raid on Hero's Tower was justified, and seventy-two percent rate your counterattack as unheroic. That's two points higher than this morning."

"What else was I supposed to do?" Victor snapped. "They attacked me in my own home!"

"And we've got experts arguing that exact point in fourteen languages on prime time shows all over the world," Jamie assured him. "But public opinion isn't budging. Maybe if it'd been more of a fight, the self-defense angle would be playing better, but you cut the entire order down before they could touch you."

"I showed the Hero's power."

"You looked like a bully," Jamie said curtly, clutching her tablet with shaking fingers. "I know that's not what you want to hear, but the numbers show we're losing control of the situation. The Paladins' popularity was never high, but it's proven much stickier than anticipated. Even after we exposed that the kidnapping of their leader was a lie, people still respect the Paladins for not compromising their values, and they're mad that you didn't at least try to talk to them."

"That's ridiculous," Victor spat. "You can't 'talk' to a lynch mob of zealots holding swords."

"Well, according to the polls, you still should have made the effort," Jamie told him, her voice getting that stubborn note it always took when she knew she had numbers to back her up.

It was highly infuriating, but the reason Victor had kept Jamie around for so long was because he trusted her to tell him the truth even when it wasn't what he wanted to hear. Kings who lost touch with reality were kings in decline, but this was still absurd. If Jamie's numbers were correct, then the same idiots who'd worshiped him for slaughtering the Wild Hunt without prejudice now wanted him to *talk* to the paramilitary vigilantes who'd broken into his home like he was the damned Peacemaker.

As frustrating as it was, though, this was nothing new. Blood magic's incredible power had always been tempered by the inconsistent irrationality of the human soul, and inflating it to the spirits' level had only made the situation worse. Humanity was even less reasonable about its heroes than it was about everything else, demanding sainthood and wrath in the same breath. It was a situation he'd been aware of and planned for during the run-up to Fenrir, but even Victor hadn't anticipated the public being *this* intractable.

"We could boost your numbers with more miracle shows," Jamie suggested. "Everybody loves a miracle."

"They love it too much," Victor said, pressing his armored hand against the empty spot left by his missing sword. "Performing miracles boosts me in the short term, but it teaches people that the Hero is at their service as opposed to the other way around. I have no interest in power if the price is being the public's slave. What we need is another attack. Something unambiguous that everyone can cheer for."

"I'm afraid our options are limited on that front," Jamie replied, flicking her finger through her tablet's AR field. "Our smear campaign against the Paladins is over for obvious reasons, but it never gained much traction, and our efforts against the dragons are going even worse. At least with the Paladins, we could work the hypocrisy angle, but there's pretty much nothing you can accuse a dragon of that they haven't already done. Take Bethesda the Heartstriker, for example. As Dragon Queen of the Americas, she and her children have been abusing the local population for centuries. She should be an easy target, and yet, for some reason, she's more popular than ever. Someone accused her of eating their baby last Christmas, and her only response was 'babies are the tenderest.'"

Victor chuckled at that, but Jamie's face remained grim. "I've run every scenario I can think of, but the Heartstrikers are not going to give us what we need. Your anti-dragon messaging never caught on like the anti-fairy stuff did. People just like them too much."

"They're still monsters."

"They're *popular* monsters," she insisted. "Bethesda might laugh about eating babies, but she's got a hardcore following, and the rest of her clan is even tougher. It doesn't matter how much negative PR we run. It's just not possible to come off as heroic when you're attacking the family of the dragon everyone in the world calls 'The Peacemaker.'"

"Then find me someone else," Victor growled. "There's dozens of clans out there that don't have the Peacemaker. Hire one of them to breathe fire on a refugee camp, and I'll be back above reproach in no time."

It seemed simple enough to Victor, but Jamie kept shaking her head.

"I don't know if there *is* anyone who'll fit that bill for us anymore, sir. I'm sure we can find someone to play the villain if we throw enough cash, but even when they're mad at you, polls consistently show that the majority of people believe you're undefeatable."

"Exactly," Victor snapped. "That's why we did all this."

"I know," she said, biting her perfect lip. "It's a huge success, and that's the problem. You rose to power as an underdog, but now that the world believes you're an unbeatable god, everyone you fight seems sympathetic by comparison. It doesn't matter what enemy we match you up against. People just don't like watching a strong man stomp down a weaker one."

"So they worship me for my strength and then hate me for using it." Victor shook his head. "How typically human."

"I don't know what to tell you, Master," Jamie said, tucking her tablet under her arm. "If only we could get the US to attack us, that'd be something—people always love sticking it to the man—but the president's changed his tune on invasion after watching the blowback from the Paladin raid. He's waiting for you to weaken."

"Then he's in for a long wait," Victor said, walking over to the folding table set up at the center of his office, where his new swords were waiting. They were all gaudy fakes made of actual metal, but they'd be good enough for television, and Victor had no intention of letting anyone get close enough to see they were props.

"This is merely a temporary setback," he announced, hefting each weapon until he found the one with the fewest defects. "One good victory is all I need to right the course. If the public sees me as too strong to fight an equal, we'll find someone universally hated to righteously stomp down. A rogue dragon attacking a children's hospital, a genocide spirit slaughtering a retirement center. Something like that."

"I'll see what I can put together," Jamie said nervously. "But I'm not—"

"Anything will do," Victor said, waving her away. "Just get it set up by tomorrow. We've let this Paladin nonsense dominate the news cycle long enough. We need a new story to shift the narrative back to—"

The building lurched under his feet, forcing him to close his mouth before he bit his tongue. He reached out to the DFZ the second it happened, but all he got was panic. When he squeezed her for the cause, the whole top of his building turned like a head, moving his window from the south to the west.

His eyes widened when he saw it. About half a mile away from Hero's Tower, directly over the spot where he'd ordered the DFZ to fill in the disgusting pit that had once been Rentfree, something was tearing its way out of the ground. No, he realized, not tearing. The city was fleeing before it, the orderly grid of roads he'd designed running away like panicked millipedes.

What are you doing? he hissed at his city.

It's not me! the DFZ cried, her voice breaking into rubble inside his head. *I don't know what it is! I'm just trying to get out of the way before—*

I didn't conquer you so you could get out of the way, he snapped. *You are the Hero's city! You will defend me until your last brick is broken.*

I can't! the city wailed, clawing her buildings out of the way. *I can't do this again!*

She spoke the truth. With his blood filling her vessel, Victor could feel exactly how fragile she'd become. Repairing Fenrir's damage had sapped all her reserve materials, and with such a shrunken population, she'd been unable to secure new ones. She was raising buildings out of concrete salvaged from the ruins of Old Detroit at this point. If whatever this was destroyed her again, she wouldn't be able to recover.

Victor didn't care about that. Servants existed to die for their masters. But while a human slave taken over by blood magic would have had no choice but to throw themselves onto the sword for his sake, the DFZ was still a spirit. Her population had fallen by seventy percent under the Hero's rule, but those buildings still had people in them. Her people, for the soul of a city *was* its people. Even with his blood crushing her like a fist, nothing Victor did could stop the DFZ from moving every inhabited structure out of the way, opening a path for whatever was coming up from below.

The city shook again as a giant paw burst out of the newly cleared dirt. Jamie screamed when she saw it and dove behind his desk. Victor was not so cowardly, but even he stepped back in surprise.

He recognized that paw, and he wasn't the only one. Through the magic that had lifted him to the Hero's lofty pedestal, Victor could feel the world drawing its collective breath. They *all* knew that gigantic black-furred foot digging its truck-sized claws out of the earth. The sight was burned into humanity's collective memory. He'd burned it there himself three months ago, but that didn't stop the shock as the great wolf Fenrir hauled its monstrous body out of the ground.

Victor's hand tightened on the grip of his pathetic fake sword. The wolf looked even bigger now than when he'd faced it at its height, so tall that its beastly red eyes were level with the top floor of his skyscraper. But... that was impossible. Growing Fenrir to that size the first time had been the labor of years. The movie wasn't even online anymore. He couldn't wipe the memory of the monster's rampage from humanity's shared trauma, but there still was no way it should have been this huge. It couldn't *possibly* be...

His racing thoughts stilled as his eyes found the wolf's giant feet again. Feet that should have been pressing craters into the ground from the monster's massive weight, yet were perched on the upturned dirt as lightly as a sparrow's.

Victor's lips curled into a smirk. Ah, there was the trick. This wasn't the rampaging spirit of destruction he and Alberich had unleashed. It was gossamer, a *fake.* A very impressive one given its size, but now that he'd seen through the ruse, Victor's fear transformed into a rush of joy.

That idiot changeling. Here he'd been despairing over his lack of suitable enemies, and she'd just delivered the greatest of all right to his doorstep. Victor had no idea where she'd gotten the gossamer to pull off such a stunt, but she couldn't have served him better if she'd still been hooked on his pills. Fenrir had been created for the Hero to slay. It was the one victory that still eluded him, the only blemish on his perfect record. It was also the only monster no one had defeated. The dragons, the DFZ, the spirits, they'd all fallen in the face of Fenrir's wrath. Even he had been helpless before it, which was why he'd had to go for the girl inside. But this wasn't *that* Fenrir. It was a paper tiger, a gossamer puppet, and he was the only one in the world who knew it.

Victor was certain of that last part. He could feel humanity's fear coursing through the Hero's vessel, giving him strength. The drones were already in the sky to catch every moment. A credit, no doubt, to the woman behind him.

"Good work on the cameras," he said, smiling over his shoulder at Jamie, who was just now peeking out from behind his desk. "They're part of your usual fleet, right? Give me the controls."

"I don't have the controls," his secretary said shakily, her perfect face gray with fear. "Those aren't ours."

"They have to be ours," Victor snapped. "Who else would have a fleet of drone cameras ready in our airspace?"

She shook her head wildly as she tapped frantically at her tablet. "I don't know, sir! But all our drones are still in their docks. Whoever's controlling those cameras, it's not us."

Victor's mouth pressed into a thin line before he forced himself to let it go. "It doesn't matter," he said calmly, sliding his fake golden sword into the sheath on his hip. "There's hundreds of agencies watching our city, but whoever's controlling those cameras can't change what they see, which means they still serve our purposes."

Jamie's ridiculous lavender eyes flicked back to the monster standing outside their window. "Are you sure about that? Not that I would ever question your judgment, but Fenrir suddenly appearing after months of silence into a cloud of cameras that were already waiting… I mean, it feels like a trap.”

“Of course it’s a trap, you idiot,” Victor snarled, pounding his finger against the window so hard the glass cracked. “That’s not the real Fenrir. It’s gossamer. This whole thing is obviously a fairy plot, but what Queen Morgan and my errant changeling fail to understand is that they’ve chosen the wrong weapon. That is *my* monster out there! I created Fenrir, which means there is no move they can make that does not serve *me*.”

His voice was quivering with glee by the time he finished. Victor couldn’t fathom the desperation that had led to such a terrible decision, but the first rule of war was to never interrupt the enemy when they were making a mistake. If the fairies wanted him to face off against Fenrir, Victor would welcome the beast with open arms, and then he would burn their gossamer to the ground with his bane.

Even the fact that they’d made it so huge worked to his advantage. At that size, every slash would look spectacular. He was already picturing the glory in his mind when Jamie’s manicured hand grabbed his ankle.

He looked down in disgust to see her kneeling at his feet. She winced at his disapproval, but she didn’t let go of his leg as she bowed her head to the carpet.

“I don’t mean to question you, Master,” she whimpered as her hand shook against his armored boot. “But I don’t like the way this feels. You are obviously superior in every way, but they wouldn’t have put in this much effort if they didn’t have a plan. We are at a delicate point. A defeat at this moment, even a minor one, could be—”

“Jamie.”

The woman froze with a squeak. She pressed herself even harder into the carpet next, but Victor didn’t allow it. He grabbed her with his magic, sliding easily into her small, familiar mind as he forced her to look at him.

"Surely you don't think that I could lose?"

"Of course not," she said, going limp in his hold. "You are Victor Conrath. You never lose."

"Precisely," he said, squeezing tighter. "So why are you suggesting that I might? Why is that even a thought in your mind?"

She squirmed like a caught fish in his grip, her eyes turning red as the blood vessels inside burst from the strain. "I—I—"

"I allow you great freedom because you have always served me well," he told her calmly. "But gossamer is powered by human belief. By even suggesting that I might lose, you give my enemy strength. That is disloyalty, and it will not be tolerated."

"I would never be disloyal!" she gasped. "I have always been faithful to you, Master! Please, I would *never*—"

"Then don't," he said, dropping her to the floor. "I'm going out to make the most of this moment. Get our cameras into the air and feed the footage directly to our loyalists at the networks. For creatures who can't lie, fairies are masters of the art. My victory tonight might be assured, but it could still be spun to the enemy's advantage if we do not take control of the narrative."

"Yes, Master," Jamie whispered. "It will be done."

Victor nodded and turned away, leaving her gasping on the carpet as he tapped his finger against the window once more.

The DFZ responded sluggishly, but she opened the glass before he had to stomp on her again, lifting and extending the roof of the building next to his to form a platform. Victor strode out onto it the moment the floor was secure, gesturing impatiently for the city to move him closer to the wolf, who'd now freed itself from the ground entirely. The camera drones were thick as gnats in the air above him, but this was Victor's show, so he let them look, turning his platform to be sure they got him at his most heroic angle. He was still working out the perfect words for the speech that would undoubtedly become his most famous yet when the wolf beat him to it.

"Victims of the Hero."

Victor froze on the platform. That was the same voice Fenrir had spoken with before: a deeper, huger version of Lola's. But unlike last time when she'd been speaking directly to him, the voice now was so loud that it rattled the windows of his skyscraper. As the sound reverberated, all the drones turned to focus on the wolf, flying around the Hero as if Victor were a mere obstacle. He was reaching out to snatch one when Fenrir spoke again.

"Victims of the Hero," she said in a voice that shook the ground, "listen to me! The blood mage Victor Conrath has been lying to you all. I am not a fairy monster created to destroy humanity. Victor Conrath made me himself to give his Hero a monster to slay."

Victor balled his hands into fists. Then he grabbed the collar of his armor where his microphone was built in. "Patch me through to the city's PA system," he ordered, glaring at the wolf. "I can't let her be the only one talking!"

"You've all heard Conrath bragging about the power of blood magic," Fenrir went on. "And he was not wrong. He used the Fenrir movie—a movie funded entirely by him—to teach you all to fear me, and then he used that fear to make me real."

"*Jamie!*" Victor hissed into his mic. "The loudspeakers, *now.*"

"They're not responding!" Jamie's panicked voice cried through the speaker that was also located in his collar so his ears would be free. "Every system we've got is reporting no signal!"

Victor clenched his jaw and turned his attention to the DFZ. *What happened to the speakers I told you to install?*

He squeezed as he spoke. Perhaps a little too hard, because the spirit couldn't even answer in words. All he got was a jumbled flood of images showing the loudspeaker towers he'd ordered her to put up at every intersection. The devices looked the same as the first time he'd inspected them a few weeks ago, but when Victor peered closer at the pictures the city was pouring into his head, he saw that every one of the wires connecting the speakers to the system Jamie controlled had been cut.

He ordered the city to repair the lines at once, even taking his eyes off Fenrir to make sure she did it properly. But while the DFZ did exactly as he asked, the wires never made it into position. Every time one snaked up to wrap its copper tendrils around the cut end, a fairy no bigger than his thumb appeared to slice through the connection with a sword made from the sharpened quill of a porcupine.

It was so unexpected, so utterly bizarre, Victor had to watch it happen three more times before he finally accepted what he was seeing. Once he'd acknowledged the truth, rage shot through him like lightning. He ordered the DFZ to show him all the speakers, flipping from image to image in his mind until he found the tiny figure perched on a rodent-drawn chariot that he was looking for.

He'd known it could only be her, but how? He'd tricked Lamb into giving him a lifetime's worth of information about all the fairy courts before deciding on Alberich's. He knew that Mab was a faded queen whose court was so weak, they could no longer appear before humans without getting snuffed. She shouldn't be able to leave her barrow, much less stand out here in the open half a world away. It should have been impossible, unless…

His eyes flicked back to the giant wolf with new fury. Of *course*. The fool girl must have fed them. He'd been careful to make sure she never understood the full potential of her dreams while she was his, but eating Alberich must have expanded her mind, because that was Lola's work if ever he'd seen it.

Victor tightened his jaw until it ached. Witnessing proof of Lola's expanded power—power *he'd* cultivated—would have been gratifying if she hadn't been wielding it against him. He tried ordering the DFZ to crush the saboteurs, but there were so many, and they were all so tiny, the city spirit was at a disadvantage. She simply couldn't catch them fast enough, and the longer she tried, the more time Fenrir got to speak unanswered.

That was enough to light a tiny spark of fear in Victor's chest before he crushed it. He was the greatest blood mage who'd ever lived, the man who'd done the impossible. A setback like this was trivial to one such as him, especially since Lola had already put herself in his hands. If she wanted to tell the world that Fenrir was blood magic, then blood magic was how he would treat her.

With that, Victor shoved the DFZ out of his mind and turned his full attention back to Fenrir, who was still talking.

"…created me so you would fear," she said, speaking slowly and solemnly to give the words weight. "He crushed your homes, used your terror and despair to build power for himself. He needed you to feel hopeless so that you would give all of your power to his Hero, but we are not his any longer. With the help of the DFZ, whom Victor Conrath also crushed under his heel, I have been reborn! I am free of his control, and now I am here to set all of you free as well."

It wasn't me! the DFZ cried. But even as she protested, Victor could feel hope rising through her magic.

It was the same everywhere. All over the world, people were reeling from Fenrir's claims. Victor could feel their confusion through the magic that gave him power, and while many rejected the words as lies from a monster's mouth, some— too many—began to doubt. The loss of their belief was a knife in his side, but the Hero had never been more than a costume he put on. The changeling's attack couldn't touch the man inside, but he could still hurt her.

"That's enough out of you."

He raised his hand as he spoke, seizing the wolf's snout in a fist of pure will. He had the DFZ move his platform closer at the same time, making sure all the cameras got a good look at what happened to foolish monsters who defied their masters. He'd have to slay her with the stupid fake sword to keep his mythology consistent, but there'd be time for that later. For now, Victor was content to watch as his blood magic bane seared her fur, flesh, and bone.

The flicker of pain in her giant eyes as his magic obliterated hers was deeply satisfying. Victor watched in triumph as cracks spread like lightning through her magic as the bane did its job. He was organizing what to say next, how exactly he would dismiss her claims while reconnecting her identity to the fairy menace the Hero existed to save humanity from. He had to get the spin exactly right, or even this lucky stroke risked turning into a disaster like the Paladins. But as he was finalizing the speech in his head, the cracks running through the wolf's muzzle began to reverse.

Victor stopped cold, staring in disbelief as the bane's damage—*his* damage—reversed itself. For a horrible moment, he thought the bane had stopped working, and then he realized the truth. His bane still hit as hard as ever. She was just replacing her gossamer faster than it could break. She was patching herself up, healing the damage as swiftly as he could deal it. Within seconds, the wolf's muzzle was right back to how it had been before he'd grabbed it, making it look as if he'd done nothing at all.

As if his magic wasn't working.

"*No!*" Victor roared, slamming his power into her. This could not be allowed. The Hero could not appear weak. He *could not lose.* Especially not to Fenrir, the monster he'd created specifically for this moment. He had to bring the changeling down *now*, before any more damage was done.

"You want to be blood magic?" he shouted, taking advantage of the broken speakers to scream directly at her as he slammed the fist of his will into her side. "*Be* blood magic! Be subject to me like you always were! It doesn't matter how many has-been fairies you dig up or how much gossamer you scrape together. You will never be stronger than me! You were born a monster, and you'll *die* a monster, just like you were always meant—"

He stopped short, magic wavering in his hand. He'd hit her so hard that even her excessive gossamer was having trouble keeping up with the damage, but something was off. Was it his imagination, or had his voice sounded louder just now? He was hoping it was just his anger when he heard a bit of reverb ringing through the speaker under his ear.

It wasn't until the DFZ nudged an image back into his head of a fleet of tiny elves standing smugly next to the reconnected speaker wires, though, that Victor realized the full extent of what had just happened.

"Anything else you'd like to say, blood mage?" the giant wolf rumbled, grinning up at Victor with Lola's defiance as the damage he'd just done melted away, smoothed out of existence by a seemingly bottomless well of gossamer. "Go ahead. The whole world's listening."

"I have nothing to say to fairy filth," he replied, recovering instantly, but still far too late. He could feel the damage he'd just done shaking the Hero's foundations, and not only with his words. The whole world had watched his bane fail to kill a fairy. People might not understand how blood magic actually worked, but they knew defeat when they saw it, and right now, they were all looking at him.

Victor clenched his fists against the backlash. Clearly, burning the wolf down was no longer an option. He needed another strategy, something she couldn't counter, so Victor lowered his hands and lifted his chin instead, wrapping himself in the magic of the Hero that still shone bright despite everything.

"I am the champion these people deserve," he proclaimed, letting his voice ring through the city now that she'd reconnected his PA system. "You sit there and spew lies, but we all saw what you did to this city the first time. We know what you are, monster, but I am Victor the Hero! Defender of humanity! And I will never allow you to hurt us again."

Magic swelled as he finished, filling him until he glowed, but the wolf didn't move.

"I'm not hurting people," Fenrir said, sitting calmly with its paws tucked under its tail like a good dog. "I have destroyed nothing today, and I never will again. That was the monster you made, blood mage, but I am no longer under your control."

"Enough of your lies!" Victor cried. "You claim to be my creation, but you're made of so much fairy gossamer that you can replace yourself as fast as my blood magic can burn you. How is that possible if I made you? Humans can't use fairy magic."

"I am gossamer because I was made by Alberich, your ally," the wolf replied calmly, bending down to show the cameras its restored nose. "And I wasn't healing your bane. It failed to work because the idea of blood magic hurting fairies is ridiculous. Blood magic was created specifically to hurt other *humans*, which is why the Paladins gave their lives to bring you down. They died as heroes facing down a stronger opponent for the good of all, and they worked with us to do it, because unlike blood mages, fairies have never been humanity's enemy. Our kind has lived in peace for millennia, so benign that the world didn't even realize we were real until you needed us to create your crisis. Alberich was a monster *we* imprisoned and *you* freed for your own power. How else could one of the oldest and most notorious blood mages of all time make himself a Hero?"

Victor couldn't believe what he was hearing. He'd always thought the changeling's ability to lie was a useful anomaly, but fairies being benign? It was beyond ridiculous. He was opening his mouth to tell the world exactly that when a new voice shot through the city.

"Fenrir speaks the truth."

He whirled in alarm, but there was nothing he could do. The new voice was speaking over his own PA system. He spotted the woman standing on the radio tower they used as their communications center a moment later. A flock of drone cameras surrounded her before Victor saw her face, but he already knew who it was. There was only one person who spoke with such undeserved superiority, and from the sound of her voice, she was already gloating.

"Victor Conrath has been wanted by our order for twenty years," Paladin Grand Master Nadja said over the city's speakers. "He is a serial murderer who has ruined countless lives. We have attempted to bring this information to the public many times over the last few months, but Conrath's media allies have blocked us at every turn. Even so, we attempted to do our duty and bring him to face justice in a raid on Hero's Tower four days ago, and you all saw how that ended."

Victor couldn't see her face through all the cameras, but it didn't matter. He could *feel* her eyes on him as the Grand Marshal delivered the final blow.

"He tried to paint it as a glorious victory, but what sort of 'hero' executes his critics on live television? My fallen comrades and I already know the answer, but you must decide for yourself. If Victor Conrath is truly your hero, then let him face the same justice as everyone else. Let him answer for his past crimes and show the world if he is truly the man he claims to be, or if this is just another of his cons, like the Fenrir movie *he* financed to teach the world to fear the monster *he* created."

"What are you doing?" Victor snarled into the mic on his collar. "Why is she still talking? That's our tower. Cut the damn feed!"

"I can't!" Jamie cried. "Nothing's responding!"

The DFZ was already pushing images into his head as to why that was, shoving the pictures of fairy saboteurs over his thoughts with malicious intensity before Victor slammed her away. *No.* He would not allow these *lesser beings* to do this to him! He was Victor Conrath, the man who'd made himself a god. If they sought to attack him with words, then he would strike back with action. He would crush this rebellion so utterly that no one would ever again dare to question his right to power, and it started with the girl. He was still loath to destroy such a unique creation, but she'd gone too far. Whatever happened from here was her own fault, and Victor was going to enjoy making her pay for it.

He didn't bother with words after that. Just raised his gold-plated sword high over his head so the cameras couldn't help but see who the Hero was here. Even if the weapon was fake, he was real. The world still believed he was unbeatable, which meant any sword could become the Hero's in his hands. He was already swinging to deliver the blow that would slice through the wolf's throat when something leaped off a neighboring building to land on Victor's platform. A shocked second later, he saw it was a motorcycle. A silent black motorcycle with a ghostly, blue-glowing light, ridden by a man dressed in all black, his face covered by a helmet as shiny as wet asphalt.

"*You,*" Victor snarled, narrowing his eyes. "You would be in on this, wouldn't you, traitor knight?"

The Black Rider said nothing. He just got off his silent motorcycle and planted his feet, turning to face Victor with a golden sword of his own gripped in his gloved hands.

The tremor that ran through Victor's magic then was the biggest yet. He'd thought the replica would be adequate so long as it was in his hands, but there must have been something about Alberich's original gossamer creation that mundane metal simply couldn't reproduce. Despite all the money he'd poured into it, his sword looked like a cheap fake next to the weapon that glittered like a sunrise in the Rider's undeserving hands.

"Yes," Fenrir's smug voice boomed over them. "That is the real Hero's Sword, and the one holding it is the real Black Rider. He was never a fairy monster like Victor Conrath claimed. He's an urban legend, a champion of the DFZ! Victor couldn't control him like he did the rest of the city, so he lied. You all *know* he lied, because you all saw Victor cut his head in half. If the Black Rider was really a fairy as the Hero claimed, he should be ash like Alberich, but he's not. He's alive, because anyone who's heard his stories knows that the Black Rider cannot die. He's a ghost, a specter who rides the streets and kills those whose evil deeds have gone unpunished."

"*Jamie*," Victor hissed into his mic as the Black Rider stepped into a fighting stance. "Get my speakers back *now*."

His secretary babbled something incoherent, but whatever pathetic excuse she had this time was drowned out by Lola's booming voice as the wolf continued.

"That's why he has the Hero's sword," she went on, the huge words rich with pride. "It jumped into his hands when he appeared to save Paladin Grand Marshal Nadja after Victor slaughtered her entire order in cold blood, because unlike the so-called Hero, the Black Rider uses his powers to help people. He is exactly what his stories say: a relentless spirit of righteous justice, and he will not stop until Victor Conrath has paid for his crimes."

Victor rolled his eyes at her dramatics, but he didn't bother yelling at Jamie again. Even if he could get a word through this farce, it was pointless given the obvious difference in their weapons. He was far more interested in having the DFZ bring her legend to heel, preferably under his. But when he grabbed her to do just that, her answer came back as careless as her street vendors when asked to present a health inspection certificate.

I can't.

"Why not?" he demanded through clenched teeth, keeping his eyes locked on the Rider's shining sword—Victor's sword, dammit—as they began to circle.

Because he's not actually mine, she explained with infuriating smugness. *He's part of my city, but his story has always been his own. I can't control him any more than I can change my weather, but do tell him hello for me.*

Victor responded by yanking on the blood he'd used to bind her. Her scream echoed through his head, but the Black Rider didn't even flinch, proving there must have been some truth to her words. Victor took a moment to consider what he was going to do about that before deciding it didn't matter.

As inconvenient as his appearance might be, the Black Rider was still just a local legend. He could never hope to match the Hero of all humanity. Victor didn't even have to kill him. He just had to get his sword back.

With that, Victor forced the changeling's circus out of his mind and focused on the enemy in front of him. She didn't know it yet, but Lola had just given him the perfect chance to show the world what happened to those who stood against its Hero. If Victor did his job well enough, this fiasco might actually end up working in his favor. Fear was also a form of worship, after all, and he was getting tired of putting on miracle shows for idiots.

Victor smiled as the new plan came together in his head. The changeling thought she could bring him down by attacking his heroics, but Jamie's polls already showed the world saw him as a bully. Why not lean into that? It would certainly be easier than trying to meet their ridiculous expectations, and much, *much* more satisfying. He'd always preferred being feared to being loved, and as he tossed his fake sword on the ground to face the Black Rider with his true power, the blood magic no one had ever mastered better than him, Victor Conrath felt very frightening indeed.

Chapter 18

Lola was holding things together by the skin of her teeth.

Making something this big had taken every scrap of her gossamer, and not just the malleable stuff she used to turn into cars. To resurrect Fenrir on a scale people would believe and still keep control of the magic, Lola had had to go all out, which meant the wolf wasn't actually a wolf anymore.

He was her barrow.

The new DFZ she'd built, the giant superscrapers and miles of bridges, the sprawling new Underground and the creatures of her court that lived inside it—she'd called the whole lot back together. Since her subjects were free, she'd worried it'd be hard to convince them to go along, but she'd underestimated her kingdom. Every speck of gossamer in her new Underground was part of her magic now, which meant they all knew what Victor had done. They'd come the moment she'd called, cramming themselves into Fenrir's corpse to form the monster that stood over the city now.

That was why she'd had to dig herself out of the ground. It wasn't just because the original Fenrir had appeared that way. She'd *literally* had to un-burrow her barrow, dragging her entire Underground Kingdom into the light, and it still almost wasn't enough.

Fear crashed over her in waves. Each one nearly ripped control of the wolf from her grasp as humanity warred with itself about whether or not to believe the story she'd so carefully prepared. Some agreed with the Hero that it was all a fairy trick, others couldn't get past the memory of the original Fenrir's destruction, and a huge chunk didn't know what to think about her at all. They just wanted her to go away and leave them in peace.

Their confusion tossed her like a ship on a stormy sea. It wasn't as bad as when the whole world had agreed that she was the apocalypse, but all the conflicting beliefs were still tearing her gossamer apart. If the other fairies hadn't been there to patch her up, Lola would have fallen apart a hundred times already, but they *were*. All the fairy courts had been fed their dreams as promised, and now each one was honoring their part of the bargain.

Queen Mab had taken the city, sending out her army of pixies to seize control of Victor's equipment, and not just the loudspeakers. She'd also shut down transportation, commanding her gremlins to sabotage every car, truck, and bus so that when the Hero's loyal followers tried to come to his aid, their vehicles drove them in the opposite direction. They attacked the infrastructure as well, knocking over cell towers, cutting power lines, breaking water mains, and generally making such a mess that even the DFZ couldn't keep up.

While the smaller creatures worked the outside, the bigger ones reinforced from within. The Green Man commanded his court from inside Lola's barrow, shoring up her battered sides with his walking trees. Lola didn't normally bother giving her creations bones, but the Green Man was a stickler for accurate anatomy. He'd filled her wolf with a skeleton of ironwood and strengthened her fur with granite.

With so much extra support, even the melting effect of disbelief hadn't been able to warp the wolf's shape. The only thing the Green Man's enchanted forest couldn't handle was the burn of the blood magic bane, but it didn't have to. That was Rumpelstiltskin's job.

True to his stories, the bearded fairy could spin like no one else. He and his gnomes had set up shop in the center of Fenrir's chest, filling his rib cage with an industrial-scale spinning-wheel facility. Every time Victor hit them with the bane, his gnomes set their wheels flying, weaving new gossamer over Lola's surface faster than the Hero could break it.

If the situation hadn't been so terrifying, it would have been amazing. Even Morgan said she'd never witnessed so many fairy courts working together so seamlessly. They'd taken Victor's sacrificial monster and made it into a marvel. It still wasn't quite enough to repair the wolf as fast as humanity was tearing it down, but the longer Fenrir stood against the disbelief and the bane, the more people accepted that this was really happening and Victor's magic couldn't stop it, and the weaker their waves became.

"It's actually working," Tristan said through the headset Lola had conjured to keep herself connected to all the interwoven parts of the plan. "I can see Fenrir firming up from here!"

"Don't sound so disbelieving," Lola scolded, locking Fenrir's head in position to make sure he looked regal for all the news helicopters that were coming in hot. "You'll ruin it."

"It would take millions of me to ruin what you've built, Lola-queen," Tristan told her confidently. "You've already weathered the hardest part. All you have to do now is stay together, and that wolf of yours will become as real as the ground he's sitting on."

Lola didn't want Fenrir to become real. Keeping her barrow exposed like this was terrifying, and the world didn't need another monster. That was why she'd concocted the part of the story about the DFZ summoning Fenrir, because summoned creatures could be sent *back*.

"I still don't understand why you're not just eating him," Tristan said. "Surely you're real enough by now to—"

"We've been through this," she said irritably. "Fenrir can't eat the Hero because that would turn him back into a monster, which might kick off the end of the world again. That's why I had to walk away last time, but we're not playing by his rules anymore." She lifted the wolf's head higher still. "This Fenrir is *not* on a rampage. He's a good doggo who's going to calmly watch while Victor is defeated by a *real* hero."

It'd taken a lot of pushing to get the others to agree to that part of the plan, but Lola had refused to accept anything else. She'd resurrected Fenrir because he was the only monster Victor hadn't beaten, but the whole point of doing this was to steal control of the story. If the wolf ate the Hero, they lost, and not just because it might tip Fenrir back over into "Ragnarök" mode. She *couldn't* be the one to kill Victor, because nothing she did as Fenrir would actually defeat him.

The world was full of stories where the hero cut his way out of the monster's belly. So long as people believed Victor could make a comeback, he would absolutely find a way to make it happen. She'd already spent the last three months proving he wasn't someone you could just kill. To truly defeat him, Victor had to be taken out in a way that everyone, even his most faithful followers, would accept as the end, which was why it had to be the Rider who dealt the final blow.

The Hero had to die in disgrace, cut down by his own sword. It was the only way she could think of to break the legend Victor had made for himself. But while the golden sword shining in Valente's hand was undeniably the real thing, Victor wasn't playing along.

Lola didn't know what he was doing, actually, and that terrified her more than anything. She'd set up this duel of heroes trusting that the truly heroic man would win, and not just because Valente had the Hero's Sword. Unlike Victor, the Black Rider knew how to fight. That should have made this a shoo-in, but Lola was starting to worry she'd misjudged the situation, because Victor had thrown his sword away and was going after the Rider with blood magic.

That shouldn't have been possible now that the Black Rider was a spirit, but Victor wasn't truly human either. They'd scuffed up his shiny image, but while people were definitely starting to question Victor's intentions, everyone in the world still believed that the Hero was unbeatable. He might not be able to dominate his knight anymore, but he could absolutely slam the Rider around, throwing him with nothing but his mind like the dark lord he'd always been.

He did just that as Lola watched, picking up Valente and hurling him off the platform. The Black Rider slammed into the road below like a cannon shell, cratering the pavement, but for all that that looked like the end, the Hero wasn't the only legend on the field. The Black Rider's story might not have been as big, but he'd been an underdog against Orlando, too, and everyone on Earth remembered how that fight had ended.

That belief plus the Hero's shining sword must have been some powerful stuff, because the dust from Valente's landing had barely cleared before the Black Rider was right back up on the platform, stepping out of Victor's shadow with his sword swinging for the old fascist's head like a golden guillotine.

He nearly managed to cut it off before Victor threw him again, tossing the Black Rider at Hero's Tower this time. Lola was surprised Victor would risk his own building like that, but then she saw the DFZ pulling the tower's protective steel plates together, getting ready to smash the Rider like a bug at her tyrant's command.

But as fast as they were, Valente was faster. He turned Victor's throw to his own advantage, straightening his long body out like a knife to slide into the shadows between the plates. He popped out a second later in the darkness behind his own motorcycle, vaulting over the bike to bring his golden sword down like an ax on Victor's shoulder before the blood mage tossed him away again.

On and on it went. The Black Rider never stopped attacking, and Victor never stopped throwing him. Every time

Lola thought Valente had him, the blood mage would just toss him off again. The Black Rider wasn't taking much damage thanks to his ability to move through shadows, but he had yet to land a single hit on Victor, and the longer the fight dragged on, the more Lola's hopes began to sink.

It wasn't working. She'd known Victor wouldn't be easy to kill given how many times she'd failed to do so, but she hadn't expected they wouldn't be able to hit him at *all*. This was supposed to be their big victory, the battle that proved they were in the right, but all they were proving so far was that Victor really was untouchable, which was the opposite of what they needed.

"We have to stop this," she said into her mic as Victor sent Valente flying through yet another building. "If Victor keeps not dying out there, there won't be a person left in the world who believes he can be defeated, and then we're *really* screwed."

"I told you you should have dressed me up as the Black Rider and let me do it," Tristan scolded. "I'm much better with a sword, and I'm *very* heroic."

"I'm sure," Lola said, trying not to roll her eyes. "But done is done. Phase one is a bust. Moving to phase two."

"Ready when you are," Tristan told her cheerfully before cutting off the call with a click.

Lola tore off her headset and climbed out of the VR theatre pod she'd whipped up for herself. It was a cheap trick, but treating Fenrir as a full-immersion entertainment experience rather than an actual world-ending wolf was much easier—and far less existentially terrifying—for her brain to accept. That was super important for Lola, since she was still half-human. She'd even made herself a cozy little VR parlor to make the illusion even more believable, though the giant furry monster siting patiently in the corner killed it a little.

"You're up, Toothy!" Lola said, tossing her the headset. "Victor didn't do us the courtesy of going down like a chump, so we're moving to phase two!"

Her creature nodded and slid the headset over her fur-covered ears with delicate claws. She was still wiggling her giant body into the VR pod when Lola ran out the door.

The quick exit was more for Toothy's sake than her own. Now that she'd given her furry half gossamer of her own, Toothy could transform the VR parlor into whatever served her mental model the second Lola was out of the picture. It was so convenient, Lola was kicking herself for not divvying up her gossamer sooner as she ran down the cement stairwell she'd imagined connecting the VR parlor to her apartment bedroom, which then connected back to her house.

Jogging through all the connected spaces was more work than her usual method of opening a door straight to wherever she wanted to go, but Lola had a lot going on in her barrow right now. She didn't want to complicate things further by moving rooms around, and it still didn't take that long. Not forty seconds after she'd handed control of Fenrir over to Toothy—who was far more experienced at being a gentle, patient monster than Lola was—she was all the way down in her low road garden, standing in front of the brand-new door that went straight to Victor's tower.

It was the same door she'd intended to make for Nadja before the Paladin had freaked out and forced them to go by boat, but Lola had made a few adjustments. Instead of opening straight into Victor's penthouse, Simon had helped her connect the door to the tower's lower levels, where Victor stashed his thralls. She changed her appearance the moment she grabbed the knob, ditching the combat flight suit she'd put on that morning to get herself pumped. The face she'd become so comfortable with changed next, followed by the rest of her body.

By the time she opened the door, she was no longer Lola. The person who stepped into the thrall room of Hero's Tower was a tall man with shining golden armor, perfect dark hair, and Victor's sneer plastered over his heroic face.

The empty-eyed crowd turned as one when she appeared. Lola had always found Victor's thralls creepy, but seeing hundreds of perfectly still people look at you in unison with the exact same vacant expression took the squick factor to a whole new level. The only reason she didn't flinch was because Victor wouldn't, and while thralls weren't the sharpest tacks in the box, they were highly attuned to their master.

Fortunately, Victor was a role Lola knew how to play whether she wanted to or not. You couldn't live with someone you were that terrified of and not learn their every expression and mannerism. She wasn't a blood mage, so she wasn't a hundred percent sure the illusion would be enough to fool his thralls. Simon thought it would work, though, so Lola put her trust in him as she strode into the room.

"Slaves."

The sound of Victor's voice in her throat almost made her sick. This was the first time she'd ever worn her abuser's face. She'd known it would be rough, but she'd thought she could push through... and then she'd spoken.

It wasn't just the sound. Victor's voice had always made her cringe, but hearing it speaking inside her own skull brought back an onslaught of horrifying memories. If she'd been doing this in front of anyone else, the terror on her face would have given the whole game away. But while thralls paid attention to nothing except their master, they were also completely non-judgmental. They didn't even blink when she froze in panic. They just stood there as silent as a petrified forest, waiting in absolute stillness while their "master" pulled himself back together.

"Listen, all of you," Lola said at last, speaking in a quick, clipped voice. Partially because that was how Victor talked when he was impatient but mostly because she wanted to get this over with as quickly as possible. "There's been a change of plans. You are to forget whatever orders I gave you before and walk through the door behind me into the garden. From there, you will be met by a reporter who will take you through another door, where you will do whatever he says. Obey him the same as you would obey me. Do I make myself clear?"

No one nodded. For a horrible moment, Lola thought she'd messed it up. Maybe her Victor hadn't been good enough after all, or maybe she'd simply been too shaken to give the orders like she meant them. She was working herself into a real panic until she remembered that Victor never asked his thralls questions like "Do I make myself clear?" He just told them what to do.

"Go through the door," she barked in Victor's voice. "*Now.*"

That worked. As soon as the order left her mouth, the whole room started rushing the door. She had to yell at them to form a line before they trampled one another, reminding her yet again how much she pitied thralls. Every one of these empty-eyed shells had been a person once with thoughts and feelings of their own. Maybe not the best judgment since they'd opened their hearts to Victor, but they still deserved better than this. Poor things were dumb as rocks.

"Over here!" called an unfamiliar voice behind her.

Lola glanced out the door she was directing the thralls through to see a man with a big curly beard and an even bigger belly standing in the middle of her low-road garden. He grabbed the flood of thralls as they came through, steering them toward another door that Lola hadn't made. One that opened into a white-painted hallway with a sky-blue carpet.

"I've got this lot," the man said, flashing her Tristan's smile. "Go see if there's more upstairs."

"More?" Lola raised Victor's dark eyebrow. "There's hundreds here already."

"My queen counted almost a thousand when she cased the tower as a bird this morning," the knight said, stroking his disguise's beard. "Not that it really makes a difference, since this should be more than enough for our purposes, but I thought you wanted to save everyone from Victor."

All Lola wanted was to take off this damn Victor costume, but Tristan was right. She was the one who'd pushed to evacuate the thralls. She knew she'd regret it if she stopped short, so Lola left Tristan shepherding the flood and walked over to the elevator to go look for the rest.

She found three more floors full. Victor must have been doing nothing but making thralls for the past four days. There were *way* more here now than there'd been during the Paladin raid. She had no idea what he planned to do with them all, but Lola was more than happy to hand them off to Tristan, opening a new door on each floor to avoid having to send the poor mind-controlled idiots through anything so complicated as a stairwell. She was still shooing out the last group when Lola heard someone gasp behind her.

Her gossamer sloshed like a dropped glass of water. She recognized that gasp. She recognized the sledgehammer of disbelief that followed, too, practically knocking her Victor to the ground as Lola turned to see Jamie standing in the elevator door.

Victor's assistant looked exactly as she always did. Even the new dark circles under her eyes and the haggard disarray of her normally perfect hair couldn't disguise the unnatural beauty her deal with Victor's devil had bought. She also clearly knew that the man she'd caught herding thralls wasn't Victor. Even if her actual master hadn't been fighting the Black Rider right outside the windows, Jamie had never tolerated Lola's disguises, and her stubborn refusal still hit as hard as a truck.

"Wait!" she cried as Lola turned to run, not that Lola had any intention of obeying. She was already sprinting past the thralls toward her low road. Unfortunately, Jamie's unnaturally long model legs were even faster. She dashed through the mob, pushing thralls and Lola out of the way to bar the door with her arms.

"Stop!" she ordered, looking Lola's Victor dead in the eye. "I know it's you, but this isn't what you think!"

"I don't know about that," Lola said, ditching her Victor costume so she could glare at Jamie with her own eyes. "You've never been much good at guessing what I'm thinking."

"I know you're fighting against him," Victor's secretary said in a shaky voice, "and I want in."

Lola scoffed. "You can't be serious. You were the first of all of us to know about Fenrir, and you *still* went along with it. You sold Simon out!"

"I had no choice," Jamie snapped. "I knew you couldn't beat him, and you *didn't*. I had to look out for myself!"

"So why are you changing your mind now?" Lola asked. "Don't tell me you've stopped believing in the Hero."

"I never believed in that rubbish," Jamie told her with a sniff. "I'm just doing the same job I've done for fifty years. Victor's the one who changed."

"Nothing changed," Lola said with absolute certainty. "He was always like this."

"Not to me," Jamie said. "I know you never liked him, but life under Victor can be great if you don't fight him. All I had to do was suck up and be good at my job, and he gave me everything I wanted. I was rich, young, beautiful, respected. Of course I sold you and Simon out to keep that. Why should I risk my good life for monsters who've always looked down on me?"

Lola couldn't believe what she was hearing. "You helped him abuse us!"

"I did what was best for *me!*" Jamie snarled back. "I'm not asking your forgiveness. You can think whatever you want about me, but I've got what you need to take down Victor for good, so I suggest you shake that chip off your shoulder and listen."

"Wait," Lola said, not quite believing what she'd just heard. "*You're* offering to sell Victor out?"

"Duh," Jamie said, waving her hand at the empty building as the last of the thralls shoved past her. "Look around. This place is going to hell in a handbasket. I have no intention of still being around when it falls, so here's my offer."

She reached into her designer handbag and pulled out a hard drive the size of Lola's palm.

"This is my burn file," Jamie explained, tapping her beautifully manicured nails against the drive's sleek surface. "Every illegal thing Victor's done that I could get evidence for is on here."

"Everything?" Lola repeated in an awed voice. "How long have you been building that?"

"Since I started working for him," Jamie said. "I've always known what Victor was. That's why he hired me and why we've worked together for fifty years without a hitch. I even paid people to bury backup copies in locations I didn't know about so I'd always have at least one left over when he took over my mind and tried to make me get rid of them."

Lola gaped at her. "You knew he was invading your mind and you *kept working* for him?"

"Life's all about weighing costs versus benefits," Jamie replied with a shrug. "I'd still be working for him if he hadn't let this Hero nonsense go to his head. We should have grabbed the money and bailed the moment the Paladin situation went south, but just because he's forgotten how to cut his losses doesn't mean I want to go down with him. I can tell when things are collapsing, so I'm going to give you this,"—she wiggled the hard drive at Lola— "and in return, you're going to put me in one of those magical fairy dream things so I can relax on a beach until this whole mess blows over. Once the Hero's dead and the coast is clear, I'll come out, write my tell-all book, and enjoy the good life sans Victor."

That definitely sounded like a Jamie plan, but Lola wasn't buying it. "What about your youth?" she asked suspiciously. "Isn't the whole reason you serve Victor because he keeps you eternally young and pretty?"

"Oh, I've thought about that," she said, opening her purse to show Lola the pile of orange prescription bottles. "Unlike your pills, which he only made when necessary because you were psycho, Victor trusted me enough to give me my dosage as a three-month supply. I've been requesting my refills one week early for the past thirty years and stashing the extras. I've saved up enough to keep my youth for another fifty years at least. Seventy if I'm frugal."

Lola gave her a flat look. "You've been planning this for a while, I see."

"Every job needs an exit strategy," Jamie replied as she zipped her purse back up. "I'm offering you Victor's reputation on a platter at a very reasonable rate, but if you want to keep being obstinate, I can always call our master and let him know you're stealing his thralls."

Lola didn't buy that, either. "Won't that ruin things for you as well?"

"My life's already ruined," Jamie said bitterly. "But that doesn't mean I can't still sink yours. I am absolutely ready to be petty as shit about this, so you might as well take the offer, 'cause things are absolutely going to get worse if you don't."

Lola clamped her jaw shut. She'd always hated the way Jamie talked to her, but as gratifying as it was to imagine leaving her to fall with Victor, the thought of him losing his last ally was even better. It didn't matter what was on that hard drive. Jamie ran Victor's empire. Even if they failed to kill him today, losing her would be a devastating blow.

Lola had fought Victor too many times to overlook a chance like that, so she held out her hand. Jamie handed over the hard drive with a smirk, motioning for Lola to lead the way. She did so only after telling the secretary to close her eyes, because even though Jamie had asked for a fairy dream, her mind was still as intractable as the Paladin's.

Closed minds and fairy gossamer did not mix. Lola was sturdier than she used to be, but too much was at stake for her to take any risks. She didn't let Victor's secretary into her garden until she'd conjured a blindfold and tied it around Jamie's entire face. Only when she was wrapped up like a mummy did Lola finally lead her through the door into her backyard, where a very scowly Tristan was herding the final clump of thralls into his own low road.

"*Please* tell me you did not just let Jamie join our team," he said when Lola got close. "That woman is a viper."

"Even rats deserve to jump from sinking ships," Lola replied, not caring if Jamie heard her. "And it's not as if she didn't pay her way."

She handed the hard drive to Tristan, who suddenly looked far less upset. "Is this her dirt file?"

"It is," said Jamie's muffled voice from behind the blindfold. "There's fifty years of evidence collected in there. Victor never made any huge mistakes like murdering someone on camera, but I've got enough financial crimes and tax evasion from when we lived in the US to put him away for life."

Lola shook her head with a grin. "It's always tax evasion."

"I've got him on kidnapping as well," Jamie volunteered. "Not all his thralls got that way voluntarily. Not to mention magical drug dealing, blackmail, and all the stuff he's done as the Hero."

She sounded very pleased with herself, but Tristan rolled his eyes. "We're not trying to build a court case," he said, shaking the hard drive at her. "This is a murder mission. Is there anything in here we can use to destroy his reputation as the Hero *right now?*"

"I don't know what else you're looking for," Jamie replied sourly. "But if you really want to burn him, I've got my entire media contacts list in my phone. We've been paying off reporters to bury Victor's bad news for years. One word from me—or you dressed as me—and all those buried stories turn into an avalanche."

"Now that we can use," Tristan said, tucking the hard drive into his pocket to free his hand, which he wrapped around Jamie's arm. "If you don't mind, Lola-lamb, I'll take it from here. My queen is already doing miracles with the thralls in her barrow, but with the added help of Victor's right-hand snake, I think we can really put it over the top."

"Do whatever you want," Lola said as Jamie squawked in protest. "Just be careful. She kicks like a mule."

"I know how to handle a closed mind," Tristan assured her, picking up Jamie and tucking her under his arm as if she weighed nothing. "You get back to Fenrir, and keep an eye on the news." His eyes flashed inside the unfamiliar bearded face he'd plastered over his own. "The Hero is about to have a *very* bad day."

Sweeter words had never been spoken. Lola waved Tristan off with a grin and shut the door on the now-empty Hero's Tower. When everything was sealed, she ran back through her house, through her apartment, and up the stairs *again* until she was back inside Fenrir's VR parlor, which was no longer a parlor, or even inside.

Toothy had clearly taken a very different approach to becoming Fenrir. Where Lola had chosen to think of the wolf as a virtual experience—i.e., something that couldn't kill her—Toothy had gone full vision quest, replacing the VR parlor with a rainy pine forest that smelled of moss and loam. Toothy herself was sitting on her haunches in the middle of a clearing with a wolf pelt over her head. Dee was standing right beside her in a hot-pink hiking outfit, looking very worried.

"Thank goodness you're back!" she cried as Lola came through the door, which was now inside a tree hollow. "Things are getting bad down there."

"Let me see," Lola said, holding out her hand.

Toothy dutifully handed over the wolf pelt. Lola didn't even bother asking questions. She just threw the skin over her head, ignoring the smell of wet fur and woodsmoke as she focused on becoming Fenrir.

The shift came on as fast as it had the first time. She'd barely gotten the pelt centered on her head before she was back behind Fenrir's eyes, looking down at a fight that was no longer evenly matched.

As deeply as she hated him, Lola had to admire Victor's persistence. He'd fought all-out this whole time, going after Valente with a single-minded vindictiveness that was wearing down even the vengeful spirit of the Black Rider. Valente wasn't wounded or bleeding—headless ghosts didn't do those sorts of things—but his speed had slowed considerably. He looked like he was moving underwater while Victor wasn't even winded.

"It's been getting worse and worse," Dee said, her disembodied voice floating from somewhere behind Fenrir's satellite-dish-sized ear. "The Rider's actually hitting the buildings now. I don't know how much more he can take. Do you think we should step in and help?"

Lola shook the wolf's head. "If we do that, this was all for nothing." She stuck her hand back outside the wolf pelt. "Can I have my headset, please?"

She felt the cool slide of Toothy's claws as the creature gently placed the headset in Lola's palm. Lola put it on at once, pushing the wolf pelt up to make room as she slid the padded cups over her ears.

"Morgan," she said as soon as the mic was in the general vicinity of her face. "Are you ready yet?"

"Considering you *just* sent my knight back to me, that would be impossible," the fairy queen informed her, but her voice was smug. "Fortunately for all of us, you're not the only monarch who knows how to take time off its tracks. You just sent the thralls over a few minutes ago by your reckoning, but I've had them for hours by my count, and I've done some excellent work, if I do say so myself. All we need now is for Victor's secretary to call her contacts, which unfortunately can't be done outside the flow of time. Give us ten more minutes."

Lola wasn't sure they had ten more minutes. Morgan was already working at miraculous speeds, though, so she said nothing.

"Keep an eye on the news," the queen suggested. "You'll know when it happens."

"Thanks," Lola said, but the fairy had already hung up.

She sighed and leaned forward, careful not to move Fenrir's head in any way that might be seen as aggressive as she looked down the wolf's long snout at the battle below.

Technically, everything was still going according to plan. Thanks to Fenrir's sudden reappearance, the air was so full of news helicopters and drone cameras there was a legitimate risk of a midair collision. They couldn't have gotten a bigger stage for the Hero's defeat if they'd announced the fight in advance, but while the Black Rider defeating him alone had always been a long shot, Lola hadn't expected Victor—crabby, stuffy, never-moved-faster-than-a-leisurely-stroll Victor—to put up this stiff of a fight. Even without his magical golden sword, he was dueling like he'd been training for this battle all his life, slamming the Rider with fistfuls of magic that would have killed a normal human.

He broke the platform the DFZ had made for him as Lola watched, dropping both combatants hundreds of feet toward the street below. Valente handled the fall no problem, sliding through the shadows to come out directly below Victor with his sword already up to skewer him. If Victor had been any other man, or even the man he used to be, that would have been the end. But despite everything they'd done, he was still the Hero, and heroes didn't fall onto stakes. He bashed the Rider away at the last second, catching his own body like a puppet on strings before setting himself neatly on the ground. He was on the Rider again as soon as his footing was secure, sending out a spear of raw, red-tinted magic that bashed Valente's helmet right off his head, revealing the horror beneath.

Just like the first time, the sight of the Rider's headless body hit Lola like a punch. Fortunately, the loss of his helmet didn't slow Valente down at all. He just summoned his motorcycle from the ground and threw it at Victor, crashing the wheel straight into the old man's hateful face.

It was a smart move. Unlike the Black Rider, who was at least human-shaped and thus within the bounds of disbelief, the motorcycle was obviously not a person, which meant blood magic couldn't touch it.

Unfortunately, Victor was also good at normal magic. He whipped up a new spell on the fly, grabbing the motorcycle's spinning wheel a second before it ripped off his nose and flinging it into the cloud of camera drones hovering behind them. The resulting explosion sent shrapnel flying in all directions, giving Victor cover for a punch of magic that sent the headless Rider flying straight at Fenrir's chest.

Lola scrambled to catch him, but the Rider was even faster. He straightened his headless body like a diver's and shot straight into the shadows beneath Fenrir's paw. For one long second, the battlefield was silent, and then the Rider shot out of the shadow of his own discarded helmet, landing it right back on his shoulders as he threw his golden sword like a spear at Victor's unguarded back.

Even Victor's blood magic was no match for that. The glowing blade shot straight through him, leaving a gaping hole in his torso and raising Lola's hopes to the sky. Surely, *surely* that had to be enough. Surely no one could survive that!

She shouldn't have gotten her hopes up. She'd killed Victor enough times now to know it wasn't that easy, and sure enough, the hole began to close before her eyes. By the time Victor pushed back up to his feet, the wound was gone as if it had never been, leaving the Hero's chest whole and unmarred beneath his sundered armor as he turned to punt the Rider into a truck.

Valente hit the cab hard, cratering the metal before he slid into the shadows beneath it. He popped up behind Victor a few seconds later to grab his thrown sword off the ground for another strike, but he was moving so slowly now that Victor was able to step out of the way. Valente might have become an unkillable ghost, but the Black Rider's story had always been smaller than Victor's, and the difference was showing hard. Victor didn't even look tired as he reached out to grab Valente's sword, planting his foot on the bigger man's chest for leverage as he tried to yank the weapon from his exhausted opponent's hands.

Lola was watching Valente struggle to hold on when Dee started rapidly thwacking her arm. Before she could ask what was up, her double shoved something under the wolf pelt. It was a smartphone, a lit-up one playing a full-screen video of a live news feed featuring the prettiest reporter Lola had ever seen.

It was obviously Morgan. No one else could look so beautiful while reporting from a war zone. But while Lola normally would have called that a terrible choice, the jaw-dropping loveliness played a critical role in this particular case. Unnatural sex appeal was the only thing shocking enough to tear people's attention away from the Hero's fight with the Black Rider to listen to her report.

"...outside with a breaking story," she cut in, her voice ringing in the perfect imitation of an excited reporter with a big scoop. "While the Hero continues his fight against the Black Rider, hundreds of people have poured out of Hero's Tower. They report that the Hero, Victor Conrath, used his blood magic to wipe their minds and keep them as slaves against their will. To verify these claims, we have footage taken from Hero's Tower this morning confirming the Hero's shocking abuses."

The picture switched away from her to a black-and-white video that looked almost too much like a security camera feed. In it, Victor Conrath, dressed in his classic Hero's armor, was yelling at the first room of thralls Lola had freed, calling them slaves and all kinds of other nastiness. The numerous censorship beeps only made the footage even more damning, leaving people to imagine their own worst versions of what was coming out of his mouth.

To someone who knew him as well as Lola, it was an obvious fake. She could practically see Tristan playing Victor, and not nearly as well as she had. His victims were also clearly frauds. Actual thralls didn't cry when you yelled at them, but that didn't stop Lola's chest from clenching.

Even though it was a fake from start to finish, filmed inside Morgan's barrow using her gossamer just as Alberich had filmed the original Fenrir movie, this footage was still the closest anyone had come to exposing Victor's real face to the world. It was honestly better than the real thing, because Victor's abuse tended to be subtle and personal, good for breaking wills but not for generating outrage. In true Queen of Desire fashion, though, Morgan's show was as tawdry and sensational as any news channel could wish. She'd even added children and dogs to the crowd Victor was yelling at to really tug at the heartstrings.

It was everything Lola had asked her for and more, but the follow-up was even better. When the fake security footage was done, the camera cut back to Morgan's reporter, who was now interviewing one of the thralls—also Tristan—that had come out.

It was their baldest front yet. Lola wasn't sure how they were getting around the fairy restriction against lying, but theatre must have had different rules, because both fairies were pretending that Tristan really was a thrall who'd just snapped out of it, which was absolutely ridiculous. Anyone who understood Victor's magic knew that his thralls didn't just "wake up." It took days for the mind control to fade, and even then, there were flashbacks. Fortunately for their side, no one but Lola, Simon, Valente, and Jamie knew enough to call them out. Since none of them would say a word in Victor's defense, that made the story as good as true. Especially when Morgan brought on the Paladin Grand Marshal to back her up.

"Using thralls as hostages is a common blood mage tactic," Nadja reported, looking straight into the camera so her judgmental nature wouldn't melt Morgan's gossamer. "These are the people Victor Conrath used as human shields to prevent my order from entering his building. We would never put innocents in danger, so we were forced to take an alternate route, which is what allowed the blood mage to channel us into his trap."

"Is it heroic, do you think?" Morgan asked, thrusting her microphone at the Paladin's face. "Using human shields to defend yourself?"

"It is rank cowardice," the Paladin replied with absolute conviction. "But blood mages are always cowardly bullies. What else can you call someone who uses their magic to crush those who can't fight back? That he lost his golden sword to the Black Rider is just more proof that he is unworthy. He might have put on a good show during the Wild Hunt, but Victor Conrath is no hero, and now everybody knows it."

Lola held her breath. It was nothing that she hadn't said earlier, but seeing the evidence must have given it weight. She'd never been particularly attuned to human magic, but even Lola could feel something shifting around the roots of her barrow, something deep. It'd started the moment Morgan showed the fake footage of Tristan's fake Victor yelling at the fake thralls, but Nadja was the one who'd really gotten things moving, because she *wasn't* fake. Her words rang with the conviction of a true believer, giving gravity to the fairy's illusions that gossamer alone could never create, and thanks to Jamie's connections, it was everywhere.

As connected as she was to everything that was happening, Lola could actually feel the world's opinion changing as the story spread. People still believed the Hero was strong—there was no way to disbelieve it after everything he'd done—but they no longer believed he was using that strength for them. They felt used, tricked, made fools of, and that made Victor their mortal enemy.

His fight with the Rider only drove the point in deeper, because Victor wasn't even trying to look heroic anymore. With his ugly sneer as he tried to steal the golden sword from the Rider's obviously more deserving hands, he looked like exactly what Nadja had named him. He looked like a bully, and it was human nature to want a bully to lose.

What happened next felt like a sea change. Morgan must have felt it, too, because she immediately turned the cameras back to Victor, zooming in for a close-up as he lost his grip on Valente's sword. He stumbled forward next, clutching his chest like he was having a heart attack. That was when Lola knew it was real, because Victor had no news feed. He didn't even have Jamie feeding him information through his radio anymore. There was no way he could know the drama that was playing out on screens all over the world, but he must have felt it just like everybody else, because he suddenly went from wrestling Valente for his sword to falling to his knees.

He wasn't completely out—his bloody magic still glowed around him like a haze—but he couldn't even push himself up straight as the Rider pulled his sword back one last time, bracing one gloved hand on the pommel for extra force as he drove the golden blade into the Hero's heart.

Chapter 19

Valente squeezed his black gloves on the Hero's sword, pushing with all his weight until the blade was buried up to the hilt in Victor's chest. He braced his boots on the pavement next, ready to fight the wall of magic he already knew was coming to knock him off his feet, but no magic came. His old master just coughed and slumped forward, gritting his teeth against the rush of crimson blood that stood out like a cardinal against the pale whiteness of his face.

It was the worst Valente had ever seen him, but while he was the one holding the blade inside Victor's chest, he knew he hadn't caused this damage. He'd seen Lola kill this man seventeen times only for Victor to be right back up giving interviews barely an hour later, but this was different. This looked final, which meant Lola's plan must have worked.

"I suppose you think you've won."

The Black Rider couldn't reply to that. Even if Valente had had a head, though, he wouldn't have answered. Nothing good came out of Victor's mouth, and his blood was even worse. There was already a great deal of it spreading across the road beneath him, but when Valente stepped back to avoid it, Victor wrapped his hands around the sword in his chest, pinning the Rider in place.

"My life's work isn't something that can be stopped by a pack of spoiled children," he wheezed, his blue eyes shining with a terrible light as he clutched the golden blade deeper into his chest. "You think you've changed something today? This is nothing. A minor setback."

Again, Valente didn't reply. He just tilted his head toward the sky, trusting his reflective helmet to show Victor the swarm of cameras flying down to record his final moments.

"This is nothing," Victor said again, letting go of Valente's sword to wipe the blood from his chin. "I'm no mere mortal to be cut down. I'm the Hero, and heroes never die so long as someone believes they'll return. That's the power I've cultivated. That's why I put up with all those fawning idiots. So long as they believe in their Hero, nothing you do matters. I'll *always* come back."

Valente did have an answer to that one. As cold and silent as the ghost he'd become, he slid his sword out of Victor's chest and pushed him backward, sending the Hero sprawling into his own blood. The cameras were swarming everywhere now, so the Rider stepped away, moving out of the shot so the world could get a good, long, high-definition look at the truth. Victor was no hero. He was just a man. A selfish, abusive, callous old man who'd finally been defeated.

The attention did more damage than his sword ever could. As the cameras swarmed over him, Victor's body began to collapse. His too-red blood grew dark and cold on the ground, and his handsome Hero's face shrank until it was nothing but skin over a skull. Even his piercing blue eyes, the only part of the Hero that had always looked like Victor, grew cloudy and dull as his body crumpled against the bloody pavement.

"This… is nothing…" he wheezed, his voice so low that he sounded like he was talking to himself as he reached his bloody hand up toward the buzzing cameras. "The Hero always… wins. He always…comes out… on top. I just need to defeat… the monster, and… all will be… reborn."

Valente's reply to that was to raise his golden sword again, pulling his arm back for the sweep that would take off the old man's head, but Victor just chuckled.

"I wasn't talking… about you."

The bloody hand he'd lifted toward the cameras closed into a fist. Valente thought it was just a final impotent gesture, but then the Rider's enhanced vision saw something glittering between the mage's bloody fingers. Something long and thin and shining beautifully silver in the dusty light.

Cold dread clenched inside Valente's chest. He'd never been able to see Lola's thread before this moment, but he knew what he was looking at. He hadn't realized Victor could still touch it now that Lola was off his pills, but the old monster must still have had some hold on her, because his eyes flashed back to life as he yanked his fist down like a lever.

A roar echoed through the city as he did it. The sound was big enough to shake the ground, causing Valente to stumble into the cameras that still swarmed around them. Then the news drones began to flee as the towering wolf—who'd been patiently watching all this time—suddenly jerked its head down, its massive mouth opening like a fanged canyon to devour Victor and the Rider in one swift, gigantic bite.

<center>~~~</center>

Lola ripped the wolf pelt off her head with a slew of curses. She hadn't known Victor could still do that. Stupid, stupid, *stupid*! He'd always been able to yank her around by her thread. She'd thought that was over since she was so much bigger now, but he was bigger, too, and she was still made of the same gossamer. He'd yanked her wolf as easily as he used to manipulate her monster back at the hospital, and now they were in big trouble.

"*Lola!*" Tristan's voice yelled through her headset.

"I know! I know!" she yelled back. "I'm sorry! I'll be right there."

Tristan had more to say, but Lola had already dissolved the headset back into gossamer. She was about to do the same to the wolf pelt when she changed her mind.

"Here," she said, handing it to Toothy, who was hovering over her like a nervous hen. "I'm the only one the thread controls, so you're in charge of Operation Good Doggo from here out. No matter what happens to me, you keep Fenrir on the ground and away from any kind of monster-movie behavior. Got it?"

Toothy keened deep in her throat, but she took the pelt, draping it over her giant head as she curled her furry body into a ball.

Lola waited until she felt her barrow copy the motion, curling Fenrir into a sad little heap with its tail over its nose. She wasn't sure if that would be enough to stem the panic she could already feel rising around her magic like a tsunami, but there was nothing else she could do. If she went back into the wolf to try to talk people down, Victor might yank her again. Until she figured out how much control he still had, she needed to keep herself away from anything he could use against them. Luckily, there was no sweeter, gentler soul than her Toothy.

If anyone still had a shot at making the world believe this Fenrir wasn't a monster, it was her. Meanwhile, Lola would take care of matters on the inside. Starting with Victor, whose disgusting blood she could already taste in the wolf's throat.

"How does he *always* find a way to mess things up?" she snarled as she ran through the forest Toothy had conjured to grab the door in the tree. "Why won't he just *die?*"

This launched her into a string of new curses as she ran into the stairwell. When Dee tried to follow, though, Lola grabbed her shoulder. "You stay here, too."

Her double bit her lip. "But—"

"You and Toothy are the only members of my court who were made directly from my gossamer," Lola said in a rush. "Since my barrow *is* Fenrir right now, that makes you and Toothy the only ones other than me who can control him. If we let the fear take over, we'll be right back in the world-ending, Ragnarök-wolf scenario Victor set up last time. That *cannot happen,* so I need you to stay here and help Toothy."

"I will," Dee promised, but her face was so scared. "Just watch out for him, Lola. Wounded animals are the most dangerous."

Lola didn't need her double to tell her that. She'd been the monster backed into the corner with its teeth bared plenty of times. She knew *exactly* how dangerous Victor was right now, but unlike every other time her former master had flipped the tables on her, she wasn't facing him alone.

Case in point, Tristan was already running up the stairwell to meet her. The knight was back in his usual handsome body and taking the cement steps two at a time with his longsword gleaming in his hands.

"What are you doing here?" Lola cried, struggling not to show how happy she was to see him. "You're supposed to be on media duty with Morgan!"

"And miss the blood mage's final defeat?" He scoffed, tossing his sword to his left hand so he could help Lola hop down with his right. "Never! My queen has already taken the liberty of cornering Victor in your… stomach? Gullet? Whatever. He's surrounded, and he's *not* escaping this time."

Lola tried her best to believe that. "What about the news coverage?" she asked as they raced down the stairs ahead of him. "Victor just made Fenrir eat him on live TV. That's precisely what we were trying hardest to avoid. If we don't get a counternarrative going immediately—"

"Already done," the knight assured her. "I left Jamie running the whole show in my barrow."

Lola almost fell down the stairs. "You left *Jamie* in charge?"

"I could ask for no one better," Tristan said as he helped her back up. "Her survival's tied to ours now, and you can always trust a parasite to make it out alive. I also might have hedged our bets with a bit of enthrallment. Leveraging vanity is one of my court's specialties, and that girl has a very high opinion of herself."

Lola hoped he was right about that. But Tristan was an old hand at this stuff, and she didn't have attention to waste on Jamie right now. Her focus had to be on the man she could already feel standing at the center of her gossamer. The one who tasted like blood.

They would be the last to reach him at this rate. Since this whole wolf was her gossamer, Lola could feel the net that was closing around Victor, and it wasn't just Morgan. All the magic in her barrow that didn't belong to her was rushing that direction. Valente was the closest since he'd been swallowed with Victor, but there were plenty of others.

Sure enough, when Lola and Tristan finally burst through the door that connected her barrow-wolf's head to its stomach, the giant spinning facility she'd built for Rumpelstiltskin's gnomes was gone. The room itself was still there, but all the spinning wheels had been shoved out of the way to make way for a wall of dense forest evenly divided between the Green Man's ancient trees and Morgan's spindly aspen. Above the woods was a net of Rumpelstiltskin's beautifully spun gold. It enclosed the entire area like a glittering spiderweb, providing footing for Mab's army, who stood ready in every gap.

Queen Mab herself was already at the front, perched on a war chariot made from a snake's skull and drawn by six Arctic voles, the most aggressive and vicious of all Earth's predators. The other monarchs stood beside her with Morgan herself taking point, looking down from her towering height on Victor, who was still bleeding on his back.

"Hello, Conrath."

The queen's voice filled the room like a cold draft. Tristan had already vanished from Lola's side to reappear behind Victor, his sword pressed against the mage's throat to cut off his head at his queen's command. This confused Lola because, last she'd felt, Valente had been standing there. By the time she'd realized he was missing, though, the Black Rider was already right behind her. He wrapped his arms around her shoulders at once, pressing her gently but firmly into his chest as he showed her his notepad.

Don't worry, it read, the words written in hard strokes. *If he grabs your thread again, I'll catch you before he can do anything.* The lines grew even bolder after that, the letters practically carved into the paper. *We've got him cornered. This is the end.*

Lola nodded weakly, barely daring to believe as she raised her eyes back to Morgan, who was looming over Victor like the victorious queen she was.

"That was a very stupid move," she purred, lifting her lovely white dress to plant her dainty bare foot on Victor's bloody chest. "If you'd stayed out there, you could have just died. What we have in mind for you is much worse."

"Is it?" Victor replied, making Lola twitch, even though his voice was weaker than she'd ever heard it. "That's your problem, Morgan. You always assume you know what I'm thinking, but you're never right. You still haven't realized that you can't read me like you do other men because you're the Queen of Desire, and I have none of that. Desire is a wish, a fantasy. What I possess is conviction, and that's a whole different animal."

"Bold words from a man drowning in his own blood," Morgan said, pressing her foot down on his wound until he choked. "But what you think doesn't matter anymore. You're beaten, done for. The only reason you're not dead already is because you've stuffed yourself so full of power, but you're bleeding that out as well. Even now, your secretary is airing your dirtiest laundry for all the world to see, showing everyone that their Hero is nothing but a fraud."

She leaned closer, her lovely lips splitting to reveal a wall of razor-sharp teeth. "There is no coming back from this, Conrath.

The only thing you have left to look forward to is death, and I won't be giving that to you for a long, long time. I spent twenty years in that box thinking about what I was going to do to you when I got free. As you'll soon see, confinement made me *very* imaginative. I've planned enough to keep you suffering for centuries. How's that for conviction?"

"Quite poor," Victor said, making Lola frown. Maybe it was just her paranoia, but she swore Victor's voice sounded steadier. His bloody taste seeping through her magic was stronger as well, though that could have been from all the actual bleeding. Still, even the hint that he might not be as defeated as he appeared was enough to make her shiver. She was actually getting scared before she forced herself to stop.

No. She wasn't doing this anymore. *Couldn't* do it. No matter what it looked like right now, this was her barrow. She was the one who made things real here, so if she believed Victor was getting better, it might actually happen. She should be telling herself that he was hopelessly defeated or, better yet, already dead. Anything was better than fear, because fear had always been his power. She should just walk away right now and leave him to Morgan. But when Lola started extracting herself from the Rider's arms to do just that, a voice whispered in her ear.

Not yet.

She froze. Valente froze, too, looking down at his feet as the whole barrow started pounding like a drum.

Did you really think you'd won?

Lola clapped her hands over her ears, squeezing her eyes shut. No. No, no, *no*, he couldn't be doing this! He was lying on his back in a pool of his own blood with the fairy queen's foot on his chest. How could they not have won? He couldn't even move.

You know it doesn't work like that, Victor whispered, the sound sliding right into her despite the hands over her ears. That was when Lola realized it wasn't a sound at all. It was her thread.

Victor's words were vibrating through the silver thread that was still tied around her wrist.

It's the one thing you never let go of, he taunted. *That's why you can't win. You know that better than anyone. Don't you, my monster?*

"No!" Lola screamed, doubling over. "Get out of my head!"

"Why do you think I came in here?" the Victor on the floor croaked, raising his bloody fist where he still clutched her silver thread.

No one escapes me, Lola.

He pulled as he finished. Lola pulled back, but even now, even here, something about Victor sent her right back to being that crying child on her knees. Even in the heart of her barrow, surrounded by monarchs and legends, all it took was his voice in her ear to make her feel one inch tall again, pulling with her tiny strength as he yanked her back to him.

Not Lola herself. She was still in the Rider's arms. Victor was pulling on the other side of her string, the one connected to the wrist of her human body, which she'd moved to a secret, cement-walled bedroom at the top of Fenrir's left haunch for safe-keeping.

Not that it mattered. Victor yanked her out so fast that even Tristan couldn't beat him. By the time the knight's sword cut into his flesh, Victor's bloody hand was already wrapped around Lola's human neck. Even from way back here, she could feel his cold, clammy fingers digging into her throat. Feel the strength he'd been hiding as Tristan's sword sliced his head off his shoulders.

Too late. Victor's wrist had already moved, snapping Lola's human neck like a twig. The crunching *crack* of her own vertebrae was the last thing Lola heard before her barrow slipped from her grasp, and she plunged into the dark.

~~~
~~~

Lola was no stranger to death. She'd made this fall several times, but never so fast, and never so hard. She plummeted like a meteor, falling down, down, down through the darkness. But then, just when she was sure she was about to splat against her death's stone ground, the blackness she'd been hurtling through exploded in a burst of blinding crimson.

She stopped falling with a jolt, rubbing her eyes in an attempt to get the red out, but it wouldn't go. No matter how much she blinked, this wasn't the bottom of her barrow or even the black, featureless, strip-mined pit Fenrir's creation had left in her death. This enormous space was red. Solid, dripping, bloody crimson everywhere she looked.

"Welcome back."

Lola whirled around, hands coming up to defend herself even though she already knew it was pointless. Sure enough, Victor was standing right behind her. Not the bloody dying man who'd just broken her neck or the glorious Hero or even the monster from her childhood. This was the real Victor: the skeletal, shriveled truth that hid behind his illusions, which should have been visible only in *his* death.

"How did you get in here?" Lola demanded, backing away. "What did you do?"

Victor arched an ancient wispy eyebrow at her. "I should think that would be obvious. We both died in the same moment, and since I'm a blood mage and you're not, I took you with me."

Lola swallowed against her throat, which still hurt from the break. "We're in *your* death?"

"As you can see," he said, waving his hand up at the yawning redness, but Lola *didn't* see. This wasn't his giant red room with its weird furniture and endless pictures. This was nothing, a big red emptiness. She was about to call him out on his lie when Victor spoke again.

"Before you jump to any conclusions, this is only temporary. I'm in the midst of a renovation, but I'll have everything back to rights soon enough."

"Yeah, right," Lola said, refusing to buy that bullshit. "It probably looks this way because you're actually dead this time."

"That's partially correct," he said with an amused expression she didn't like at all. "I did die. Inside of *you*."

What was left of Lola ran cold as his smile grew wider.

"Finally getting it, are we?" He pointed up at the redness over their heads, which seemed to be slowly expanding despite the lack of edges. "I didn't make Fenrir eat me because I wanted to turn him back into a world-destroying monster. I made you eat me because doing so got me inside your barrow, which, thanks to the incredibly genius way you were constructed, is also your death. Once I was inside, I ended both our lives at the same time, creating confusion, which has always played to my advantage."

"No," Lola said, refusing to believe it. "*Get out of my death!*"

"It's our death now," he replied, lifting his arm.

Lola stepped back, fighting not to be sick. Wrapped around his wrist was her silver thread. Not a copy, not a fake. She could feel him on the other end just like she used to feel her own body, but she couldn't feel herself at all anymore. When she reached out now, all she felt was Victor.

She *was* sick then. She doubled over, heaving as hard as she could, but nothing came out. Nothing could come out, because nothing was inside. She was dead. Really, *really* dead this time, and Victor was still here. She still hadn't gotten away.

"Don't look so upset," he said as she fell to her knees. "It's not as if this is a new development. I've always been part of you."

"No," Lola growled, clawing her fingers against the insultingly red floor. "I bled you out. I got free!"

"Ah, but that's the lovely thing about blood," he replied with a smirk. "It *stains.* Even when you scrub it away, you're never truly rid of it. How else do you think I was still able to yank your string?"

Lola bent lower.

"I'll admit it is harder now," he continued. "Pulling your thread these days is like trying to control a rampaging water buffalo with a strand of hair. You could have broken my hold easily if you'd known what was happening, which is why I took care never to use it until just the right moment. But when I did, it *worked*."

He waved his hand grandly at the endless dome of red above them. "With this one move, all that was yours is now mine. By merging our souls together, I've gone from dying under Morgan's heel to future fairy king, *and* I'll still be a blood mage, which means becoming the Hero again isn't off the table." He took a deep, satisfied breath. "Am I not a genius?"

"You're a *monster*," Lola snarled, baring her sharp teeth. "And you're not going to rule anything. Even if you did infest me like a parasite, we're both still dead."

"We are," he agreed with a cruel smile. "But *you've* got people trying to save you. I'm sure my lovesick apprentice is using his magic on your corpse right now. He always was good at fixing broken things, so a simple snapped neck should be nothing, but what he doesn't know is that *you* won't be the one coming back. By the time he realizes his mistake, it'll be too late."

"So what?" Lola said. "He'll just kill you again."

"He won't be able to," Victor replied. "I'm sure he'll try, but I'll be stronger, because I'll have your barrow."

Lola set her jaw. "It won't accept you."

"It won't have a choice," Victor said, his sunken eyes shining in triumph. "Merging a human soul with fairy gossamer was the greatest idea I've ever had, but it has a critical weakness. Because your human soul and your fairy magic are one and the same, anyone who enters your barrow also enters your death.

That's a horrific vulnerability, as evidenced by what I just did. I had to raise Simon from a child to get access to his death, but you just let anyone in!"

He crouched down to grin in her face. "That's why I never tried to copy your success on myself. A mage of my caliber can't afford such a gross liability, but at this point, I'll take it. I must admit I rather like the idea of a physical world I control as surely as I do my own soul."

"It's not your kingdom yet," Lola said with a flash of her teeth. "I'm still here."

"Not for long," he assured her, rising back to his feet. "Our deaths are finishing their merger as we speak, but whereas you only mastered your kingdom a few days ago, I've been the absolute ruler of mine for decades. It won't even be a fight. The only reason I'm allowing your continued existence is because you're the one Simon will be looking for. Once he starts dragging you back to your physical body, I'll destroy what's left of your soul, put mine in its place, and be off to the races. I can already feel him reaching for you now, actually, so I suppose this is goodbye."

He reached down to give her one last pat on the head. "Farewell, my monster. It was a good try, but you really should have thought better before you challenged your master."

Lola jerked away from his touch, but there was a smirk on her face when she looked at him again.

"Don't worry. I did."

The smile slipped off Victor's thin, cracked lips. Then he leaped away from her with a curse, bringing his hands up to defend himself as Simon stepped out of the redness behind Lola.

"*You,*" he snarled, his sunken blue eyes locking on Simon's back-to-brown ones. "You should be pulling her out! What are you doing in here?"

"Waiting for you," Simon replied in a voice as haughty as Victor's. "You think I spent all those years as your apprentice not paying attention? I *knew* you'd try something like this as soon as you were cornered, so I was lying in wait with Lola's physical body."

He turned to offer his hand to Lola. "Sorry it took me so long. I thought he'd be coming *to* your body. I didn't expect him to yank it out of the room."

"You still made it," Lola said, grabbing his hand to haul herself to her feet. "That's what counts. Now, let's finish this."

"Finish me with what?" Victor demanded, glaring at Simon. "His arrival changes nothing. I'm still a blood mage inside my own death. That makes me a god. Simon wasn't even a good apprentice."

"And I'm grateful for that," Simon said, giving his old master a hateful look. "I've *never* wanted to be like you. I'm proud to be the inferior blood mage, but there's a factor here that you haven't considered." He lifted the hand Lola was still holding. "It's two against one."

Victor scoffed. "You could be two hundred and it wouldn't make a difference. You'd still be too weak to beat me."

"Think so?" Simon asked, squeezing Lola's hand. "Shall we put it to the test?"

Victor had no witty comebacks that time. He just lashed out, grabbing Simon with the same gigantic red hands he'd used to crush Lola the last time she was in his death.

The attack was even bigger than she remembered, but where her monster had been helpless, Simon wasn't. He caught the hands well before they crashed into Lola, pushing back with his own magic. Victor's was still greater, but while he was getting pushed back, Simon didn't fold. He held the line, buying Lola time to run in the other direction.

She might not be a blood mage like them, but Lola *was* a monarch, and this was *her* kingdom. She was done letting Victor shove her around, so while Simon held him back, Lola threw her magic in the opposite direction, plunging her hands through her gossamer—because that's what this place was: *her* soul, *her* magic—to grab whatever leaped into her fingers first.

It turned out to be a leather glove. The moment she reached through the red haze Victor had painted over her soul, a hard, strong hand grabbed back, and then Valente was suddenly at her side. The Black Rider's magic came with him: a cold, windy, brutal power that scoured the giant red hands away.

Victor crushed them right back down. For all that he was a chronic liar, he'd never been wrong about his power. He *was* strong, he *was* absolute, but he was also facing three opponents now with no physical body to act as his anchor. As soon as the Rider joined the fight, Simon went from holding the line to slowly pushing back, buying Lola the space she needed to pry her magic open and let the rest of her pour in.

There was a lot. Victor wasn't the only one who'd gotten an upgrade. Now that she'd accepted her role as king, Lola's soul was home to hundreds, and every one of them answered her call to war. They poured through the hole she'd opened, overwhelming Victor's ugly crimson in a tide of fangs and fur and angry gnashing teeth.

He tried to beat them away with his blood magic, but the bane was broken. Lola wasn't sure if Fenrir's healing had done the trick or if people had stopped believing in blood magic when they'd abandoned the Hero, but without the bane to give it teeth, the magic that had burned the Wild Hunt out of the sky didn't even ding Lola's subjects as they ripped into the man who'd tried to steal their kingdom. There was so much gossamer flying, Lola didn't feel Dee arrive until her double stepped right in front of her with Lola's glowing crown in her hands.

"Here," she said, placing the ring of sunshine on Lola's head. "You're going to need this."

"Why?" Lola asked nervously.

The fairy flashed her a wicked grin. "Because it's about to get really dark in here."

Lola was still giving her a funny look when the red nothingness above them cracked.

It was just a hairline fracture at first. Once it got started, though, the crack spread like lightning, forking and splitting until the entire dome looked like the inside of a broken egg. Even Victor stopped fighting to watch it, shoving Lola's subjects away from him as he stared in horror at the broken sky. For one heartbeat, everything was silent, and then the red dome of Victor's death broke into a thousand pieces as a giant hand shoved its way inside.

Lola screamed when she saw it, but not in fear. She knew that hand with its overlapping layers of municipal plastic and bent metal signs. It was the DFZ, and she was *pissed*.

BLOOD MAGE!

All the color left Victor's wrinkled face. Then he snatched back the magic he'd been using to keep Valente and Simon at bay and whipped all of it at the giant hand. He caught the fingers just before they crushed him, but his power must have been truly nearing its limit, because that was all he could do.

YOU SHOULDN'T HAVE TAKEN YOUR EYES OFF ME, the city roared as the Sea of Magic's chaos began pouring through the broken ceiling like a waterfall. *YOU TRIED TO CONTROL TOO MUCH, AND NOW YOU CONTROL NOTHING.*

"I control everything!" Victor yelled, falling to his knees as he struggled to keep her giant hand from crushing him. "I conquered you once. I can do it again! I will *never* die, do you hear me? Never—"

You already have.

Lola shivered as the new voice passed over her like a freezing wind. That was not the DFZ, but it was definitely a spirit. A huge one, and he was not alone.

Now that the DFZ had broken through, the magic pouring into Lola and Victor's shared death was taking shapes. Some were human, some were not. Some were lovely, some were hideous. All of them were strong, though, and all of them were furious, turning on Victor with a wrath that almost made Lola feel sorry for him.

"No!" he shouted, wrapping what remained of his power around him. "I'm a spirit, too! The Hero, beloved by all! You can't take me!"

Not so beloved anymore.

Lola shuddered. It was the cold voice again, the one that felt like someone was walking on her grave. A body formed out of the swirling magic as it spoke, the power condensing into the shadowy image of a tall soldier wearing a gladiator's helmet with nothing but darkness inside.

"Wait, I know him!" Dee cried. Far too excitedly, in Lola's opinion. "That's the Empty Wind, Spirit of the Forgotten Dead! He's a big one."

"Big" was grossly inadequate. Now that the Empty Wind had shown himself, every other spirit in the room looked minuscule by comparison. His helmeted soldier might have stood no taller than the Rider, but his presence filled the broken dome with the infinite weight of oblivion.

"Stay back!" Victor shrieked. "You're a spirit, a slave to your purpose, and I'm still remembered. That means you can't touch me!"

Not yet, the Empty Wind rumbled.

"Not ever," Victor snarled. "I'm the Hero! Even if they hate me, my memory will live on! You'll never get me, Merlin's dog!"

I'm her cat, actually, the spirit replied with a smile Lola felt like an ice cube down her back. *But you're right. I will not be taking you into my fold, because your soul will not survive long enough to be forgotten.*

For the first time in her life, Lola saw real fear flicker across Victor's face. "What does that mean?"

It means you have finally gone too far, the DFZ said as her giant fingers finally closed around him. *You mock the Empty Wind for honoring his purpose, but while he cannot crush a soul that is still remembered, I have no such limits. I'm the Detroit Free Zone, and I do whatever I want.*

We're just here to watch, the Empty Wind added, stepping back to give the city room.

"You can't," Victor said as the giant hand lifted him into the air. "You can't do this! You're a city, not a death god!"

A city with the world's highest murder rate, the spirit reminded him as she pulled him toward the broken ceiling.

Lola watched in confusion. She'd expected the DFZ to crush Victor like a bug, but the giant hand wasn't squeezing. It was taking him up, pulling Victor out of the cracked dome into the darkness beyond.

Lola's panic rose with him. No, no, no, the DFZ couldn't take him away! Victor had to *die.* Right here, right now. She'd already raised her head to shout at the spirit when the Black Rider's notepad appeared in front of her face.

It's all right!

She looked frantically over her shoulder, and then Valente pulled back his arm to write his explanation.

Trust your city, the words said. *She knows what she's doing.*

Lola supposed the Black Rider would know, but letting Victor go was still the hardest thing she'd ever made herself do. If Valente hadn't already been a spirit, she would have crushed every bone in his hand as she watched the DFZ lift Victor into the air like a prize in a crane game. The only thing that kept her even slightly calm was the fact that Victor looked terrified.

He screamed the whole way up, beating the plastic and twisted metal of the DFZ's hand with so much blood magic that

Lola could taste it even this far below. But while he was definitely still kicking, his power wasn't a fraction of what it had been every other time Lola had faced him. No one thing had been enough, but all of it together—all of *them* together—had finally broken the great Victor Conrath, leaving nothing but a shrill old man screaming for his life as the DFZ lifted him out of their broken death into the Sea of Magic.

The moment the swirling chaos hit him, Victor's screaming changed from fear to pain. Listening to it, Lola felt stupid for not realizing what was coming earlier. She'd been through the Sea of Magic enough times to know how bad those raging currents hurt if you weren't spirit-sized. The Hero probably could have weathered it, but Victor wasn't him anymore. He didn't make it two seconds before the roaring magic blasted him to nothing, leaving not even the scent of blood behind.

Chapter 20

Lola stood in the circle of light cast by her crown, staring at the emptiness where Victor had been as the lump in her throat got bigger and bigger.

She'd thought seeing Victor die—truly, absolutely, irrevocably, no-second-chances die—would feel more like a victory, but the reality was a complicated mess of emotions she didn't know how to process. Joy was in there, certainly, as were relief and giddiness. But the good feelings were nearly overshadowed by the rage. She was shaking with fury that this—*this*—was what it had taken to finally make him stop. Fear, too, at how close it had come to not working. One mistake at any step and…

Lola stopped herself with a hard shake. No. She wasn't giving Victor any more of her. He deserved nothing, not her worry, not her thoughts, not even her anger. She'd fought too long and too hard to give the old man another damn thing, so Lola pushed him out of her head to focus on what was actually important: all the people around her that she *did* care about.

They definitely needed her help. Now that He Whom She Would Not Waste Another Thought On was gone, the mashed-up mess he'd made of their deaths was rapidly falling apart. It wasn't just the cracked ceiling. The whole place was going, torn apart like a shipwreck by the Sea of Magic's whirling chaos. Even the ground was crumbling, leaving everyone who wasn't a spirit— Simon, Dee, all the subjects of her Underground Kingdom, and Lola herself—huddled in the light cast by Lola's crown, the only thing protecting them from the encroaching destruction.

Not for long. Human magic and fairy gossamer were a powerful combo, but neither did a thing against the Sea of Magic's currents. Withstanding that much pressure took spirit-scale power, but while Lola had reached that peak once the night when Fenrir had been the most feared thing on the planet, this was not the same situation. The only reason her crown was doing anything was because the Underground Kingdom was simply too big to fall in the short time since the DFZ had cracked their deaths open like an egg, but that didn't mean Lola could keep it up. The circle of light was already shrinking, forcing them closer and closer together. She was scrambling to find a way back to the real world when the roaring chaos suddenly faded, replaced by a wave of quiet.

Not silence. Lola could actually hear a lot of things—cars, clanks, people shouting—but they were muted and soothing. It reminded her of lying in her bedroom back in her old apartment. Very appropriately, it turned out, because when the huddled clump of survivors finally spread out enough for Lola to see, the DFZ was waiting for her, pushing back the dark with her protective streetlight just like she had the last time she'd rescued Lola from the Sea of Magic.

I knew you'd beat him! the city cheered, her orange eyes gleaming happily.

"I think that's my line," Lola replied, stepping to the front, since that felt like the kingly thing to do. "You did the actual beating."

Only because you got him off me, the spirit said, scrunching up her androgynous face. *The old bastard had me drowning in his blood. It was the grossest thing that's ever happened to me, and that's saying something considering the state of my sewers. I hated every second, but with his magic all over me like that, I couldn't do anything but what he said. When he went into Fenrir to get you, though, he had to take his boot off me.* She bared her teeth, which were as sharp as Lola's. *Fatal mistake.*

Lola laughed in delight. "I knew making all those enemies would come back to bite him!"

No one can hold a city forever, the DFZ said with a shake of her giant plastic fist, which still hung in the dark above them. Then she smiled at Lola. *But I would have been stuck under him a lot longer if not for you. I owe you a great debt, King Lola Daniels. How can I repay you?*

"Easy," Lola said. "Go back to how you were."

The city frowned. *That's it?*

"That's it," Lola assured her. "I don't want anything that comes from Victor, not even your gratitude. I just want to go home, and for that, I need my city back."

She'd expected the DFZ to be over the moon at getting off the hook so easily, but the spirit just tapped her thin finger against her chin. *Will you make me your home?*

That struck Lola as a strange question until she remembered she wasn't just a changeling anymore. She came with a whole fairy kingdom now, and the DFZ didn't exactly have the best relationship with her kind. But as she opened her mouth to assure the city that her rule would be nothing like Alberich's or even Alva's, the DFZ raised her hand. The real one sticking out of the sleeve of her shapeless vending-machine clothing.

You're already welcome, she said with a beaming smile. *Even without the Hero riling up his torch-and-pitchfork mobs, fairies won't be able to go back into hiding after this. But I've always been the city where people start over, and you're the Underground King! Seems like a perfect match.*

"Are you serious?" Lola blurted out. "I mean thank you, yes, absolutely, I'd love that, but… are you sure you want me? I'm not exactly a normal fairy."

That's why you'll fit right in, the DFZ said confidently. *I've never been a normal city, and while I do owe you a massive debt for saving my asphalt, I didn't make the offer for your sake.*

"Then why?"

The spirit's young face grew sour. *I haven't exactly had the smoothest start as a metropolis. People are starting to say I'm cursed, and you know better than anyone how rumors like that can become a real problem once enough people start believing. If I keep getting destroyed by monsters and magical disasters every ten years, no one will want to live in me! That's why I want you to make your kingdom inside my borders. I need more help, and I think Fenrir will make a great deterrent for the next time someone tries to treat me like Tokyo in a Godzilla movie.*

"Oooh! Oooh! Like a fairy version of the Peacemaker!" Dee cried as she grabbed Lola's arm. "Come on, your majesty, you gotta do it! This is our chance to get in with the cool people!"

"We're already the cool people," Lola said, but she was smiling too. Even though she'd been the one asking the question, she'd never wanted to leave the DFZ. Outside of the nightmare that was Victor's mansion, the city was the only place she'd ever lived. She'd even modeled her own kingdom in the DFZ's image, because when she heard the word "Underground," that was what she pictured: an endless maze of neon-lit streets under a canopy of bridges, just like the one she'd grown up with.

"I'm not sure if I'm in the same league as the Dragon of Detroit," she told the spirit. "But the DFZ has always been my home. I'd be happy to help defend it if you'll welcome us."

Lola waved at the crowd behind her as she spoke, because they were a group ticket now. Fortunately, the DFZ had always been an accepting city. She never turned anyone away. But while she smiled warmly at all of Lola's fairy creatures—and shot a big grin at the Black Rider, who tipped his helmet in salute—her glowing eyes narrowed when they landed on Simon.

"He comes, too," Lola said before the spirit could even open her mouth. "I don't blame you for banning blood magic forever after Victor, but Simon's stain isn't his fault. Victor caught him as a child just as he did to me." She grabbed Simon's hand so tight he jumped. "He's my brother. I'll never leave him behind."

She felt Simon turn to look at her as she finished, but Lola didn't dare take her eyes off the DFZ, who looked extremely displeased.

"He won't ever hurt anyone," Lola promised. "Simon grew up in the DFZ just like I did. His clinic was one of your buildings, so you know what he did there. He used his blood magic to help people!"

The spirit was still scowling, so Lola scowled back. This was absolutely non-negotiable. But before she could push any further, Simon spoke up.

"I understand your concerns," he said, stepping away from Lola to stand before the DFZ on his own. "This isn't a situation where 'hate the sin, not the sinner' applies. Blood magic is an invasive power that was created to abuse and control. It is the worst form of humanity's magic, but the fact that one use is enough to taint your soul forever means it's also our most tragic. There are lots of mages taken in by Victor's propaganda whose souls will be stained for the rest of their lives, and as deserved as your hate of blood magic is, that's too great a price for one bad decision."

He smiled at the DFZ. "You're famous for being the city of second chances. If these people want to redeem themselves, you're the only place they can go, so here's my idea. Don't accept me for Lola's sake. Take me as a citizen in my own right. Give me back my clinic, and I'll help those mages learn to live with their new magic safely. You don't have to make blood magic legal—it absolutely shouldn't be—but I know the DFZ would never reject someone who truly wanted to change."

I don't need you to tell me what I am, the DFZ muttered. Then she sighed. *But you make a good point. I still intend to move blood magic to the top of my "absolutely not" list, but I will offer amnesty to anyone with a stained soul who wishes to change.*

"And this means you don't have to keep your promise to let the Paladins arrest you," Lola whispered to Simon.

"That has nothing to do with this," he whispered back, but his eyes were gleaming. "Thank you, DFZ."

Don't thank me yet, she warned. *You're the one who just signed up to deal with the most toxic part of Victor's fallout. But know that I'll be watching you closely. If you or any of the mages you take in use blood magic to hurt my people, I'll drop a bus on your head.*

"I understand," Simon said, stepping back behind Lola before the city could change her mind.

Well, the DFZ said, rubbing her hands together. *If all that's settled, I'd like to get to work. My city has been in ruins, empty, and under a dictatorship for months. If I don't start patching myself up, I'll go from the Living City to the Living Pile of Rubble.*

"One more thing before you go," Lola said.

The DFZ shot her an impatient look, but Lola just smiled. "Would you mind taking us back to the real world with you? Victor jacked my thread, and while I was able to pull everyone in here, I don't actually know how to get us back out."

"You don't have your thread?" Simon said in alarm. "How? I healed your broken neck before I came in."

Lola shrugged. "I don't know. My powers didn't exactly come with an instruction manual."

"Her magic always has been very squishy," Dee agreed. "But don't worry. I can get us back. Check it!"

She lifted her arm like a trophy, showing everyone the glittering silver thread that was now tied around *her* wrist.

"*You've* got it?" Lola cried, grabbing Dee's arm in horror. "Wait, does this mean you're the real me now?"

"Don't worry about it," Dee said blithely. "We started as a changeling, remember? 'Change' is right there in the name! Here, I can give it back if you want."

"*No!*" Lola said, grabbing her double's hand before she could yank off their only lifeline. "I mean, let's do that after we get home."

Then get to it, the city told them impatiently. *I can't leave until you do or you'll all end up shredded like Victor, but I'm a busy city with a big to-do list, so if you wouldn't mind...*

She made a shooing gesture. Fortunately, Dee had gotten even better at moving through magic than Lola. Four seconds after the DFZ said scram, she'd whipped up a doorway complete with a glowing green exit sign right back to Lola's barrow, which—shockingly—was still shaped like a giant wolf.

"Toothy held it together," Dee explained at Lola's look of disbelief. "I told you we had this!"

"You did," Lola said, hugely impressed and immensely grateful. "You really, really did."

Dee beamed and bopped through the door. Everyone else had already gone through except for Lola and Valente. But when she motioned at him to go ahead so she could close the door behind them, the Rider shook his helmet.

He goes with me, the DFZ explained as the Black Rider walked to her side.

"Oh," Lola said, unaccountably hurt.

It's not like it was with Victor, the city assured her quickly. *He's not my servant or anything like that! He does live inside me, though, so I'm exercising my privilege as his landlord to ask for his help. Things are a horrid mess right now, and I need all hands on deck.*

That wasn't what Lola was worried about, but the DFZ's words made her feel better all the same. Especially when the Rider wrote on his pad and held it up, summoning his motorcycle so Lola could read the message by its ghostly blue light.

I'll be back as soon as I'm done.

"I'll be waiting," she said, walking through the door. "See you when you get home."

She waved at them one last time and grabbed the handle, closing Dee's surprisingly sturdy door on the swirling chaos the spirit of the Living City had been keeping at bay.

~~~

It took months to clean up everything Victor had broken. The city never did get back to normal, but that was only because there was no such thing as "normal" in the DFZ. She had Victor's grid of ugly fascist buildings torn down by nightfall her first day back, but it took several weeks before their replacements were ready and almost two months before the big landmarks like Merlin Tower and the Dragon Consulate were back where they belonged.

Not having such mundane things as plumbing and fleshly mortal citizens to worry about, Lola had her kingdom back in order much more quickly. Since Toothy had done such a good job as Fenrir, she didn't even make her creature put the wolf away. Instead, Lola made her a gigantic forest in the basement where she could be a sharp-toothed sweetheart or a wolf or whatever else she wanted. It was the least Lola could do to thank her fairy half for keeping their kingdom together while the rest of them were lost in the void beyond death, and it wasn't as if they didn't have the room.

Now that she'd mastered eating her own dreams, there seemed to be no limit on how big Lola could grow her barrow. To keep her new home safe—and because it just felt natural for an Underground Kingdom—she dug deep beneath the foundations of the DFZ's rebuilt skyscrapers. Then, because she was still a DFZ girl at heart, Lola spread her magic out like tentacles, connecting her Underground to the *actual* Underground in hundreds of places all over the city.

Since these were actual entrances, not low roads, normal people occasionally wandered in, but Lola saw that as a bonus. It made the DFZ feel even more magical, and all the new fairy tales about the mysterious Underground Below weren't bad either. Hearing them made her feel like a real part of the city instead of
~~~

just a squatter, and she definitely preferred being known as "that magical place with the best ramen shops that you can only find by getting lost" to Alberich's nightmare kingdom.

This was way more fun, and the food was *much* better. Not that Lola had ever eaten a nightmare, but there was no way they tasted as good as the Chocolate Sprinkle Explosion sundaes from the ice cream parlor Dee had built with her share of Lola's barrow. Her doppelganger had even set things up with the DFZ to make sure her shop never appeared on the same street twice, ensuring she always stayed at the forefront of maximum food-trend hype.

Lola stopped in whenever she had time, which admittedly wasn't often these days. Now that she'd officially joined Team DFZ, the city had wasted no time getting her together with the Merlins, the city priests, even the famous Peacemaker himself. She'd been super nervous about that last one, but the Dragon of Detroit turned out to be really nice. She hadn't known dragons came in nice, but he was a genuine joy to work with, and they had a *lot* of work.

The DFZ hadn't been kidding when she'd talked about all the disasters doing a number on her reputation. Even after she was completely rebuilt, her population was less than half what it had been before Fenrir's first appearance. As the local fairy monarch, Lola did her best to help rehabilitate the city's image by making sure visitors always had some kind of positive magical experience during their stay. Magical vegan restaurants staffed by giant talking rabbits, night markets that only appeared when you went around the wrong corner, unicorns standing under streetlights— she did it all. Usually by herself, because while her subjects were happy to help, most of them had been born under Alberich, and their idea of a "positive" magical experience could be a little... unpositive.

That was fine, though. Unlike the previous Underground King, Lola was a very hands-off monarch. She let her creatures travel and live and do whatever they pleased, which suited her role as the DFZ's fairy perfectly. It did mean she had to fish the occasional troll out of the sewers, but such inconveniences were a small price to pay for not having to micromanage an entire underground full of developing fairies. And when she *did* need a break, she had her very own urban legend on call for whenever she needed to go out for emergency pizza.

"I feel like such a celebrity," Lola said, snuggling into Valente's back as his silent motorcycle whisked them through the backstreets of the new Underground toward Marco's Under Midtown, a literal hole-in-the-wall joint built inside one of the DFZ's new subway platforms that was Lola's current favorite. "Everyone's taking pictures of you again."

"I don't like it," Valente grumbled through his mirrored helmet, which he wore religiously whenever they were outside her barrow, even though she'd put his head on him for their date. "Self-driving cars might be everywhere, but taking pictures in the street is still a safety hazard."

"Spoken like a true civil servant," Lola teased.

"They could be taking pictures of you, you know," he said, raising his voice over the rushing wind. "You're more famous than I am now."

"Yeah, but unlike you, no one knows what I look like. Depending who you ask, the Underground King is either an enlightened super-mage living in the sewers, a gold-plated alligator, or a dragon in disguise."

He chuckled. "Better get a handle on that before you actually turn into one of those things."

"I could do with being an alligator," Lola said as they stopped at an intersection. "I always did have big teeth."

"Please don't," Valente begged. "I like you just the way you are."

"I like it, too," she said, sliding up his back to press a kiss against his helmet before the light turned green.

Valente reached out with the powers the city had given him to flip it back to red, giving himself time to turn around on his bike and hug her properly. His gloved hands roved over her with the promise of better things to come when they were back in her barrow and his helmet wasn't in the way. *Much* better things.

"I don't think that's why the DFZ gave you control over her streetlights," Lola said in a happy daze when he finally let her go.

"But that's the best part about working for a city of freedom," he replied smugly as he got them moving again. "She gives me the power and trusts me to use it, just like how she trusts you."

Lola hugged herself tighter against his back. She did feel trusted. Trusted, loved, and safe in the city where she felt most at home. Soon she'd have pizza, cheap wine, and cannoli too. Not a bad ending for a sad little monster.

"Thank you."

"For what?" Valente asked.

"Just in general," Lola said, relaxing into the wall of his back as they raced through the neon city where there were no more masters, no more tragedies, and no one to call them monsters.

Thank you for reading!

Thank you for sticking with me to the end of Lola's story. I hope you enjoyed reading it as much as I enjoyed writing it!

If you enjoyed *To the Bloody End*, or any of my books, please consider leaving a review. Reviews, good or bad, are vital to every author's career, and I would be extremely grateful if you'd take a moment to write one for me.

So where are we going next? I've got something really good in the tank that I can't wait for you to see. It'll be coming out sooner than you think, so if you want to be the first to know, sign up for my **new release mailing list** over at rachelaaron.net. List members always get first dibs on anything I put out, and I only email when I've got something new coming out, so there's no spam. You also get access to exclusive, list-only bonus content like the Heartstrikers short story, *Mother of the Year.* Signing up is easy and free, so come on in and join the fun!

Again, thank you so, *so* much for being my reader. I'm so grateful you decided to spend this time with me and my stories. Seriously, there would be no books without you. Thank you from the bottom of my heart, and I'll see you in the next series!

Yours sincerely,
Rachel Aaron

Want More Books?

Lola is only the latest addition to the DFZ. I have plenty more titles of all sorts for you to enjoy! Keep paging forward to see my top picks for new readers or visit www.rachelaaron.net for the full list, and, as ever, thank you for reading!

Minimum Wage Magic

The DFZ, the metropolis formerly known as Detroit, is the world's most magical city with a population of nine million and zero public safety laws. That's a lot of mages, cybernetically enhanced chrome heads, and mythical beasties who die, get into debt, and otherwise fail to pay their rent. When they can't pay their bills, their stuff gets sold to the highest bidder to cover the tab.

That's when they call me. My name is Opal Yong-ae, and I'm a Cleaner: a freelance mage with an art history degree who's employed by the DFZ to sort through the mountains of magical junk people leave behind. It's not a pretty job, or a safe one-- there's a reason I wear bite-proof gloves--but when you're deep in debt in a lawless city where gods are real, dragons are traffic hazards, and buildings move around on their own, you don't get to be picky about where your money comes from. You just have to make it work, even when the only thing of value in your latest repossessed apartment is the dead body of the mage who used to live there.

"A catchy title, a plucky protagonist and a maximum effort by the author, honestly readers can't ask for more in the urban fantasy genre."- **Fantasy Book Critic**

"I love what Rachel Aaron has done with this novel to expand her stories within this unique world of her creation. I have developed a trust in her ability to write engaging stories of great characters which I feel most comfortable and eager to spend time with, and this book is no exception." - **TS Chan**

Nice Dragons Finish Last

As the smallest dragon in the Heartstriker clan, Julius survives by a simple code: stay quiet, don't cause trouble, and keep out of the way of bigger dragons. But this meek behavior doesn't cut it in a family of ambitious predators, and his mother, Bethesda the Heartstriker, has finally reached the end of her patience.

Now, sealed in human form and banished to the DFZ--a vertical metropolis built on the ruins of Old Detroit--Julius has one month to prove to his mother that he can be a ruthless dragon or lose his true shape forever. But in a city of modern mages and vengeful spirits where dragons are seen as monsters to be exterminated, he's going to need some serious help to survive this test.

He just hopes humans are more trustworthy than dragons.

"Super fun, fast paced, urban fantasy full of heart, and plenty of magic, charm and humor to spare, this self published gem was one of my favorite discoveries this year!" - **The Midnight Garden**

"A deliriously smart and funny beginning to a new urban fantasy series about dragons in the ruins of Detroit...inventive, uproariously clever, and completely un-put-down-able!" - **SF Signal**

The first and most popular DFZ series, complete at 5 books.

The Last Stand of Mary Good Crow

A gaslamp epic fantasy featuring a sprawling cast of colorful Western characters, crystal-mad bandits, ambitious necromancers, and cursed gunmen. Welcome to the Crystal Calamity!

The Montana Territory, 1876, and the discovery of magical crystal has sparked a rush that makes gold a thing of the past. The US Cavalry, the Sioux tribes, and the criminal underworld will stop at nothing to control the mines that produce the new miracle stone, but the beautiful crystals bring a darkness, a madness, and a horror that threatens to consume all who seek their power.

Mary Good Crow, a half-Lakota guide, can hear the crystal's song. She makes her living leading miners to fortune, but there's trouble brewing in the depths of the crystal caves that even she can't navigate. Bandits with crystal-augmented strength, ghosts that roam the living darkness, and madmen driven by the crystals' power to destroy all who seek their prize.

With Josephine Price, a mining heiress with secrets to hide, and Tyrel Reiner, a gunslinger haunted by a necromancer's legacy, Mary must navigate the dangerous world of the new Magical West. The beautiful song of the crystal has never led her false so far, but with war brewing on the plains and enemies in every shadow, embracing the power that's driven so many mad before her might just be Mary's only shot at survival.

What people are saying about Mary

"Possibly the best alternate historical fantasy that you will read."
*- **Fantasy Book Critic***

*"Brimming with imagination, wonderful characters and captivating magic." - **Novel Notions***

*"I very much enjoyed the twists and turns throughout this book and strongly recommend it. No one's allegiances are entirely set and the only genuinely good person in the story is Mary Good Crow. Even she has a dark side that she struggles to keep suppressed as a matter of sheer survival. I think fans of the Weird West and urban fantasy both will enjoy this novel." - **Grimdark Magazine***

Forever Fantasy Online

Forever Fantasy Online is the gritty, battle-filled tale of a raiding guild vs the world featuring rules-driven combat, incredible tanking, and the good side of guild drama!

In the real world, twenty-one-year-old library sciences student Tina is invisible and under-appreciated, but in the VR-game Forever Fantasy Online, she's Roxxy--fearsome warrior, respected leader, and main tank of a top-tier raiding guild.

In the real world, James is a college drop-out drowning in debt, but in FFO he's famous--an explorer who's collected every item, gotten every achievement, and done every quest.

Both Tina and James need the game more than they care to admit, but their favorite escape turns into a trap when FFO becomes a living world. Wounds are no longer virtual, stupid monsters become cunning, NPCs start acting like actual people, and death might be forever.

In the real world, everyone said being good at video games was a waste of time. Now, stranded and separated across thousands of miles of new, deadly terrain, Tina and James's skill at FFO is the only thing keeping them alive. It's going to take every bit of their expertise--and hoarded loot--to find each other and get back home, but as the stakes get higher and the damage adds up, being the best in the game may no longer be enough.

"Rachel Aaron and Travis Bach have written an amazing story and a realistic LitRPG." - **The Fantasy Inn**

"Forever Fantasy Online is definitely a book for the gamers among us." - **Fantasy Book Critic**

"Excellent characters, an engaging story and geek humour. What more can one ask for?" - **TS Chan**

About the Author

Rachel Aaron is the author of over twenty novels both self-published and through Orbit Books. When she's not holed up in her writing cave, Rachel lives a nerdy, bookish life in Colorado, with her perpetual-motion son, long-suffering husband, and far too many plants. To learn more about Rachel and read samples of all her books, visit rachelaaron.net!

Cover Illustration by Luisa Preissler
Cover Design by Rachel Aaron
Editing provided by Red Adept Editing

As always, this book would not have been nearly as good without my amazing beta readers.

Thank you so much Linda Hall, Julia, K Stoker, LJ Andrews, Sally Jenkins, Javier Rentas, Nancy Wise, Sarah Braun, Judith Smith, and Christina Vlinder.

Y'all are the BEST!